The Truth About Suzie

Find more work by Erica Rimlinger at
http://ericarimlinger.com.

The Truth About Suzie

A Novel

by

Erica Rimlinger

Copyright © 2014 by Erica Rimlinger. All rights reserved.

No part of this publication may be reproduced, distributed, or transmitted in any form or by any means, without the prior written permission of the author, except in the case of brief quotations embodied in critical reviews and certain other noncommercial uses permitted by copyright law. For permission requests, please use the contact form at:
http://ericarimlinger.com/contact.

This is a work of fiction. Names, characters, organizations, places, incidents, and events come from the author's imagination or are used fictitiously.

Published by Sylvia Jaye, LLC.
PO Box 27611, Towson, MD 21285
http://sylviajaye.com

Edited by Kim Ledgerwood.
Cover photo by Igor Balasanov licensed from iStockphoto.
Book and cover design by Smartfare Media.

ISBN 978-0-9908288-0-8 (trade paperback)
ISBN 978-0-9908288-1-5 (ebook)

For Kevin and Max

Chapter 1

May 21, 2011, 8:00 p.m.

TV Watch, May 21, 2011

Tonight, Dr. Dick checks in with his 2011 Therapy Family, the Londons—a local Montgomery County family from Pine Hill. Brad and Wendie London tell Dr. Dick they still struggle with Brad's 17-year-old "out-of-control" son, Peter. Dr. Dick's cameras capture Peter cutting school, hustling alcohol, and taking drugs during the school day.

To give Peter one of Dr. Dick's famous "reality checks," Dr. Dick takes Peter to Los Angeles to visit his aunt, Suzie, who's on her deathbed suffering from liver failure—the result of a lifetime of alcoholism and drug abuse. Will Peter's "reality check" change his ways? Tune in for this very powerful Dr. Dick, tonight on TLC at 8 p.m.

The square of newsprint was cut neatly from the Washington Post Montgomery County suburban edition and tucked under a 10-dollar bottle of Pinot Noir on the kitchen counter. A pink ribbon-shaped sticky note topped the newspaper cutout and read, "Cecily: This is Suzie London. I think she had a lot more going on than we realized. Check this out."

At 8:00 p.m., Cecily bounded down the stairs and scooped up the wine bottle, the usual gift her sister left to thank her for babysitting.

She was reading the wine's label when the sticky note caught her eye. What is Cait talking about now, she wondered, rolling her eyes just a little. Cecily peeled off the note to read the newsprint underneath. The words "deathbed," "liver failure," and "alcoholism" all rose up to meet her eyes like she had turned around to face an unexpected ocean wave. Without thinking, she clamped both hands over her mouth so quickly she forgot to set the newspaper and the wine bottle down beforehand.

Cecily watched, eyes blurring with tears, as the bottle fell toward the hardwood floor. In that fraction of a second, she made no move to catch the bottle. She thought of the babies upstairs. Cooper, sleeping, waking up crying to the noise of glass shattering. Eileigh running downstairs barefoot in her nightgown, glass everywhere. She thought of red wine splashing all over her socks, jeans, the construction paper artwork on the refrigerator. She thought of Suzie London, allegedly scheduled to die on TV (at this very moment), of red wine. Not cancer. Red wine. Cecily tried to instruct the adrenaline that held her motionless to move her arms and reach out, reach out and catch the bottle.

The bottle bounced once, twice, then rolled down the kitchen floor, intact.

Posted October 18, 2010 at 12:13 a.m.
Cecily Murphy

Well, it's official. I have breast cancer. I hope it's ready to get its ass kicked, because I'm ready to start kicking it.

Posted October 19, 2010 at 12:01 a.m.
Cecily Murphy

In trouble for posting about Voldemort, er, cancer. Mom thinks I should've called, invited you to coffee. You'd say: "Sure, what's up?" I'd say: "You'll see ..." all coy and evasive. You'd think: "Why is Cecily acting weird?" Then, after we sat down, I'd say the dreaded word: Voldemort! Er, cancer. Apparently this is how you tell people. But the way I see it, I saved you $4 at Starbucks and an hour of your life.

Sent: October 25, 2010 at 11:11 p.m.
From: Suzie London
To: Cecily Murphy

Everything is beautiful in Santa Monica. Cancer is horrific. Say goodbye to our hair. Nurses are way better than doctors. During radio, I have nothing to complain about. Peace be with you.

Sent: October 25, 2010 11:12 p.m.
From: Cecily Murphy
To: Suzie London

Do you have cancer too?

Sent: October 25, 2010 at 11:19 p.m.
From: Cecily Murphy
To: Caitlyn Murphy Doyle

I'm having the most surreal week of my life. *Alice in Wonderland*: down the rabbit hole. And then, I look around and, unbelievably, I *am* down the rabbit hole—with Suzie London, of all people.

Posted October 26, 2010 at 5:00 p.m.
Cecily Murphy

Pathology report came back quickly. Looks OK. Need an MRI in both breasts. Doctor confident there's just the one tumor & it's small. "You found this very early," he said. "If you were larger, you wouldn't have found that lump for 10 more years." Um, did he just insult my size? Grateful, in any case!

Posted October 26, 2010 at 5:26 p.m.
Cecily Murphy

Ha! Now Mom says I need to find another word for "breast," rather than continuing to post the word "breast" in my FaceBreast updates. Oops! Too much breast. It's breast cancer, people. If you can't abide by reading the word 'breast' occasionally, please feel free to hide me on your update bar.

Sent: October 26, 2010 at 5:38 p.m.
From: Lilian Schultz Kaufman
To: Cecily Murphy

Ceci! I'm trying to write this as I laugh, but go easy on your mom, OK? We're of a different generation! We didn't discuss these things publicly! We don't know how to use FaceBreast! :) I'd never hide you on my update bar, even if I knew how to do that. And you're very welcome for the cookies and the 'Stop the War on Our Racks' t-shirt. The t-shirt made me laugh and think of you in DC! Don't wear it in front of your mother! I'd love to come visit and give you "the overview" as you said. Don't know how much help I'll be, though. Everything was so different then ... 25+ years now? Even the chemo is different now. Heck, you probably won't even have chemo. I wish I'd kept my wigs—you remember my blue Mohawk wig I wore around the house? I burned them in the fireplace. I'm sure that will cause lung cancer someday. Ah, well. Eat broccoli and kale every day, Cecily. Every day! I love you, Aunt Lil

Posted October 28 2010 at 2:01 a.m.
Cecily Murphy

Whoa! Hot flashes! Not a myth! Otherwise doing fine on Tamoxifen (a drug that depletes my estrogen in preparation for the MRI next week.) I have the genetic test Thursday, the MRI Friday, then it's decision time re: surgery.

Sent: October 28, 2010 at 2:04 a.m.
From: Suzie London
To: Cecily Murphy

What are you doing up?

Sent: October 28, 2010 at 2:05 a.m.
From: Cecily Murphy
To: Suzie London

I don't sleep much these days. I just want the MRI over with. What are you doing up?

Sent: October 28, 2010 at 2:19 a.m.
From: Suzie London
To: Cecily Murphy

It's only 11 here in LA.

I understand how hard it is, the waiting. It sucks the technicians "aren't allowed" to tell you things. So then, you've waited for the test, then you have to wait to get the test results. I had to wait a week each time. I was just sitting there with that ultrasound thing up my hoo-ha for like 20 minutes and she kept typing notes. Type type type. When you ask her: What are you doing in there, searching for Tupac? She smugly says "I'm not allowed to tell you." Really. Because I usually expect a little more communication from people whose hands are in my vagina. At least buy me a drink. And then they're like: you'll hear back next week! They make me stabby. But you've got to be zen about it. And your head's on straight. You got this. Like Tom Petty always said: "The waiting is the hardest part." I'm proud of you for being strong. Look at you: a self-contained unit. You always were the rebel.

I'm still fighting. Just think: "We can do it!!!!" I guess babies are out unless I can afford to buy or rent one. Radiation and all. It's like cooking your ovaries in a microwave.

I was on Facebook having a pity party for myself, reading people's posts. Look at me I got into Dreamland and photo bombed Leo DiCaprio, look at me in a bikini! Look at me! I was so pissed off. Narcissists. But I use too. I narcissate on Facebook with the best of them. That's all it is. I was listening to Comfortably Numb, Pink Floyd, with the lyric: "Is there anybody in there ..." and it was right then, right at that moment I read your post. I freaked out. It's like fate took your hand and put it on top of mine. I can't explain it. But it felt like I was given an order: I would have to give this fighting thing a shot.

So fight, girl! Get your rest on because we have to fight. That was my sign, and this is our directive. We can do this together from coast to coast!!

**Sent: October 28, 2010 at 2:34 a.m.
From: Cecily Murphy
To: Heather White Kolakowski**

Please tell me what happened to Suzie London from our Pine Hill years? Where did she go when she left? And why does she think I'm "the rebel?" Is she confusing me with someone else? Are you Facebook friends with her? She was almost a year older than us, but she failed and joined our class in third grade. She had an older brother—Brad or Chaz—what was his name?

**Sent: October 28, 2010 at 6:15 a.m.
From: Heather White Kolakowski
To: Cecily Murphy**

Why are you freaking out about Suzie London at 2 a.m.? How are you feeling? Are you sleeping OK?

**Sent: October 28, 2010 at 8:17 a.m.
From: Cecily Murphy
To: Heather White Kolakowski**

She has cancer, like me! This has all the markings of a cancer cluster. We both grew up on Summer Hill Road, and we're both well under 40. There were those power lines. Remember the power lines? Coincidence?

Sent: October 28, 2010 at 9:22 a.m.
From: Heather White Kolakowski
To: Cecily Murphy

Hold up, Erin Brockovich. Breast cancer runs in your family. Your mom is BRCA positive. You might be BRCA positive, and this has nothing to do with Suzie London, who, yes, lived on Summer Hill Road for five or 10 (?) whole years before her crazy family was chased out with broomsticks. I'm not Facebook friends with her. I couldn't pick her out of a lineup. I am sorry to hear she has cancer though. That's sad. She's so young. Do you think you might be trying to grasp at other reasons now that you're getting ready to take the genetic test, and you might not be ready to deal with the results?

****

Cecily could deal with most everything, except for pity. Any attempt to patronize her was met, in her single-digit years, with defiance. And, when she was older, with a de-friending as easy as the click of a mouse. And she did not "love the devil," another charge leveled against her in first grade by one of her Pine Hill Elementary classmates, Graham Stollis. Graham insisted that Cecily's red hair was proof of this. Cecily countered the argument by insisting that Graham's front baby teeth needed to be loosened further with the help of her small, freckled fist. Both were sent to the office where the principal, Mr. Lovegood, dialed Cecily's home number while shaking his head at Cecily, who sat kicking the legs of her small wooden chair. She would be a pistol, he predicted correctly.

Suzie London spent her elementary school years living two doors down from Cecily on the grid-straight suburban streets of Pine Hill, Maryland, five miles northwest of the District of Columbia line. Suzie was a year ahead of Cecily in school, and—it seemed to

Cecily—about a dozen years ahead in worldly wisdom. Suzie London screamed and threw rocks at the boys who chased her on the blacktop playground. Cecily studied Suzie through her thick, bottle cap glasses while playing Chinese jump rope with her friends.

By the ages of eight and nine, the foundations of Suzie and Cecily's friendship—proximity and convenience—had eroded away like the sand in the Murphy's sandbox. Cecily tattled to her mother when Suzie wielded a steak knife to settle an argument that erupted during one of their many attempts to recreate Go-Go's videos in the backyard. Suzie insisted on playing Belinda, always. When Cecily protested this arrangement just once, Suzie produced the black-plastic-handled steak knife and gently pressed its dull, serrated edge to Cecily's arm to enforce the casting status quo. Cecily's mother had been forced to abandon her handmade pierogies to march Suzie London and her pilfered tableware home to a furious Mrs. London.

Cecily also told on Suzie after watching Suzie drag the Londons' garden hose across the lawn to the house of the elderly neighbor who lived between them, feed the hose gingerly, like a live snake, through Mrs. Douglas' living room window, and turn on the water. Upon hearing Cecily's excited, lisping tale, Dahlia Murphy grabbed her neighbor's key off the hook and pushed open Mrs. Douglas' front door to discover a small pond in her gold, scalloped carpet. Suzie denied responsibility, but Cecily's eyewitness report served to condemn and sentence Suzie to both imprisonment and community service: a month-long grounding and one summer of free yardwork for Mrs. Douglas. Whenever Cecily walked past Mrs. Douglas' house in the months that followed, Suzie would sneer, pick up her hedge clippers and, using them as a microphone, chant, "Ceci the baby, the big, fat BABY." It infuriated Cecily because it didn't even rhyme.

From that point forward, Cecily turned a stony eye away from Suzie or any of the Londons, whose older, high-school-aged brother was suspected of multiple neighborhood grievances including beer cans in the Wentworths' azaleas and a street sign on Cecily's block that perpetually went missing no matter how many times the county replaced it.

The London kids were volatile, Cecily knew from an early age. Cecily learned the word 'volatile' from her sister, Cait, who used the word to describe their mother's potential reaction when Cecily spilled Berry Cherry nail polish onto the canary yellow carpeting in her room. Cait told her, "You'd better clean that up before Mom sees it. You know how volatile she gets." Cecily asked, "What's volatile?" hoping it meant something akin to forgiving or understanding. Cait crossed her arms and looked down at her sister heavily from under caked black eyelashes. "Hot-headed," she said. "Unpredictable."

Cecily envied what she labeled Suzie London's volatility, a hard-to-define quality that manifested itself in Suzie's ability to boss Cecily around and know things Cecily considered unknowable. Cait and Suzie were both privy to information such as when to retire the red Fozzy Bear jumper and why everybody suddenly had a purple unicorn purse. Suzie had the knowledge the older kids had, and she roller skated in bright-green, OP corduroy shorts with confidence, never tripping, never scraping her knees, swaying her hips to the tune on her Walkman.

Cecily also envied Suzie's more material qualities: the cassette-tape-playing Walkman which had a feature called "auto-flip" that Cecily's didn't, Suzie's wide-set juniper eyes, black hair and wide, disarming smile. By second grade, Suzie was thoroughly unsuitable to play Barbies with, but suitable for observation and very subtle attempts at imitation. Cecily missed nothing that happened in Suzie's life from her vantage point across two flat, sunny lawns with skinny new sycamore trees planted with precise intervals between them.

On the last day of fourth grade, walking home in the puffy-sleeved white dress she wore to perform in the fifth-grade graduation ceremony, Cecily stopped scratching at the itchy crinoline long enough to listen in on her mother, who followed behind in a group of moms discussing Suzie London's latest (and last) Pine Hill antics: failing another grade, developing breasts, and spray painting the tips of her black hair red with a costume spray that was supposed to be temporary but hadn't come out.

The London family then moved away, presumably for these crimes and more.

Fifteen years later, Facebook suggested Suzie London among 200 or so former classmates as "friends" for Cecily. Swept up in her first week of using what she found to be an amazing new tool of open espionage, Cecily "friended" Suzie London and maybe 50 more people that day. Cecily snooped on some of their pages: she discovered Pam Coving had moved to Kentucky to become a racehorse breeder. How does one get into that profession? Cecily wondered. She noted Christine Collins married and divorced her high school sweetheart in quick succession, but not before giving birth to twin boys ... and all of this before age 20. Facebook answered the question: "Whatever happened to ..." while providing a safe cover.

A friend request, Cecily discovered, wasn't personal like a phone call or even an email. It wasn't even a request for friendship. In the beginning, in college, she simply collected people, trying to get her "friend" number up to a respectable level so someone didn't look at her newly created profile page and think she was a loser. (If pressed, she would vehemently deny this.) As she found more and more people from her past, though, she discovered she was glad to reconnect. This was the aspect of Facebook her college friends had sold to Cecily. (They had labeled her a "late adopter," but Cecily just considered herself shy.) Cecily's friends described the modern marvel of picking up old friendships where they left off, of ladling up ex-boyfriends out of the virtual stew, examining their lives, and raising eyebrows at their new girlfriends. Even after a few years, Cecily still loved looking through these near-strangers' pictures, though the album titles had changed from "Party Down at the Ocean!!!!" and "Lillith Fair" to "Josh and Ashley's Wedding" and "Hayley Emma Rosenberg 8/22/08." Everyone still looked exactly the same, except they were grown-up versions of themselves now. The men had thicker waists. The women posted fewer bikini shots and drunken extreme-closeups. They had spouses, jobs and lives. Some of them even had kids. Everybody was training for a half-marathon. Facebook faithfully, mechanically recounted their transformations. Its existence had rendered their upcoming 10th reunion virtually obsolete.

Cecily had snooped on Suzie London's page, of course, years ago when she'd found her on Facebook. Cecily had wondered if Suzie even accepted her friend request. But when she typed in Suzie London's name, Suzie's profile page popped right up. Cecily was in. Hmm, she thought. All their stupid fights as little girls—they're all just water under the bridge for Suzie, too. Suzie London's profile picture, however, showed only the back of her head, chin-length black hair swinging toward the camera in a blur, and behind her hair, the sun setting into the ocean. Their 12 mutual "friends" from their days at Pine Hill Elementary were listed in a long line down the side of her profile page, forming a thread of connection between the two of them as faint as a strand in a spider's web. Cecily clicked away from Suzie's page and, once again, forgot about her.

Sent: October 29, 2010 at 6:28 a.m.
From: Cecily Murphy
To: Jack Schwinn

Hey Jack! Great to hear from you. So many people have come out of the woodwork since I was diagnosed.

It's not all strange or mysterious. Nearly every woman in my family has fought this disease. I've been warned it was my genetic legacy since I was a kid ... since my Aunt Lil had it last, when I was two. I'm not surprised by its appearance and I'm not ashamed of appreciating my friends' and family's well wishes and support during this time. I'm not going to hide it or be all passive-aggressive and post weepy little emoticons in the hopes of provoking a "What's wrong?" (my biggest Facebook pet peeve!) Are you on Twitter? I'm the only one not on Twitter. Still the late adopter, or so you claim ...

But Facebook is great because I don't have to be on the phone all day, repeating the same information over and over. And I can deal with the people who aren't as helpful in my own time. I can just post the news; everyone knows who cares to know, and I'm done thinking about it for the day. Which I need, because believe me, I'm not brave. I only seem brave because 1) we tend to be BRCA+ in our family (BRCA 2: 6174delT mutation, if you remember that from Legenhausen's class), so that's how we Kaufman/Murphy women roll, and 2) we caught it early, so my prognosis is good.

Everybody translates this to "bravery," but it's more a solid belief in the progress of cancer treatment, self-delusion or social skills that have been stunted from technology overuse. Isn't that what's supposed to happen to our generation? Social incompetence?

Speaking of social incompetence, I scared the heck out of the counselor woman who visited me at my follow-up appointment yesterday. I guess her job is to temper the blow of the diagnosis. She raised her eyebrows at my chart, looked up at me and said, "You're so young. I'll bet you're wondering why this is all happening to you." I thought, er, wrong. Why is a ridiculous question. Because of things beyond my control: it's written in our DNA. Because of things within my control: environmental factors. Because of the interplay of these two factors. We don't know, we might never know, and if we did, what does it matter now? If we're going to waste precious time spitting into the wind with questions, why not pick a non-rhetorical question, something that would provide useful information to the universe?

But I didn't say any of this out loud to her. Instead, I said, "This isn't the time for self-indulgence. This is the time for planning." I didn't mean for it to be rude, but it was. She should have been offended, but she dug up her psych training and told me I was experiencing the "anger stage of loss." Psych 101 to the rescue! But at that point, I just felt like a jerk for saying the wrong thing, and wanted to get out of there so I could start researching oncologists. (I have a surgeon but not an oncologist.)

I'd forgotten you were moving to Baltimore. You're right up the street now! Yes, everything you've heard about DC people being workaholics is true. I got to work at 6 a.m., and I was not the first one here. It's kind of like Cornell, but instead of complaining about it, people brag about it. I'm only here this early to beat the crowds and expenses on the Metro. If I leave before 3 p.m., I can get home for half the price. That's pretty rare, though.

I stalled on the academic ladder for a few years. I was distracted by shiny objects: i.e., money. Government grants pay more than TA'ing, and the pay helps keep me in the style to which I've become accustomed … meaning, I can now make the car payment on a used Honda Civic, and Jane and I were able to move out of our Capitol Heights group house/tenement with six roommates into an apartment uptown, in Tenleytown. Stylin'! Don't know how long we'll keep it though. It's close to the Metro, and it's a nice neighborhood, but our next-door neighbor situation is interesting. The women who live there are nice enough (might be hookers), but there's a frequent visitor named Ralph who's kind of scary (might be their pimp.) Yeah. So.

I'm liking soil science and the Smithsonian. I get to manage a team of sprightly young grad students who do my evil bidding. Someday I might become a "Doctor of Dirt'" as you so charmingly put it. There's a great soil science program at UMD, and the scholarship money for women is ample. They are eager to get women into the field—it helps them get grants. I'm impressed you went into nanotech, mainly because that's the most creative way to avoid grad school

I've heard of. I do want to remind you, however, that electronic engineering is a slippery slope: remember the saying: "It takes two E's to spell geek?"

Yes, we definitely should go to an Orioles game sometime!

Best, C.

Sent: October 29, 2010 at 7:00 a.m.
From: Jack Schwinn
To: Cecily Murphy

Hey there! Thanks for writing back. It's great to hear your life is going well, with the exception of He-Who-Must-Not-Be-Named and the next-door neighbor situation: yikes! I think we're the only two people in our class who are not finishing up med school. And, of the two of us, you're the only one still looking at molds and fungi every day. I'm beginning to think all that talk of getting bribed with scholarships is just bluster. Admit it: you fell for the smell of iodine and the promise of flesh-eating bacteria. You're in it for the glamour.

It also sounds like you're taking the random blows of life in stride, and to me, that seems far more like bravery than self-delusion. How's Jane doing? What are you doing for Halloween? This time of year reminds me of fall in Ithaca and our first year at Cornell at the Sigma Chi party. I still tell that story. Can you believe that was almost 10 years ago? Feels like a whole lifetime. Anyway, Parsons, Chang, Bangladello and I are going out in Federal Hill. You and the girls should come up. We'll make a reunion of it.

Jack

Posted October 30, 2010 at 10:00 a.m.
Cecily Murphy

Hit snag when I decided to read Internet—against the doctor's explicit orders to avoid it. That was unwise: triggered first meltdown. Luckily, my friends must have been conducting meltdown drills in preparation for this because their intervention was flawless. 15-minute response time to my house with margaritas. Thank God for you people!

Sent: October 30, 2010 at 10:32 a.m.
From: Jack Schwinn
To: Cecily Murphy

Since your doctor has banned you from reading the Internet, I did some research myself, to spare you the trouble. I do not agree with his diagnosis at all. After 10 minutes of research online, I believe I have an extremely detailed understanding of your situation. Please have him call me, and I will discuss with him directly.

The most important issue is that, apparently, bed bugs are everywhere nowadays, and we should consider getting your medical facility checked. I can launch a pre-emptive whistle-blower call to the American Medical Association if you like. Also, there's a Nigerian fellow with a business proposition for me. He's willing to cut you in, but will probably need both of our account numbers. When I talk to your doctor about this, I'll see if he wants in too. It should be very lucrative, but we need to keep it quiet. This fellow is getting edgy and I don't want to lose the deal! Anyway, I hope that information from the Internet helps. :) Now you don't have to look.

Sent: October 30, 2010 at 11:02 a.m.
From: Cecily Murphy
To: Jack Schwinn

Jack, you're crazy! You're the only person I know who still talks to me the same way!

Sent: October 30, 2010 at 11:08 a.m.
From: Jack Schwinn
To: Cecily Murphy

The same way as what? You aren't getting a lot of stupid jokes thrown your way? I have more. #themesongtoJaws

Sent: October 30, 2010 at 11:16 a.m.
From: Cecily Murphy
To: Jack Schwinn

Your stupid jokes are appreciated, even if I reserve the right to roll my eyes at them. No, I've been getting a lot of pity, I guess, and fear of saying the wrong thing to me. Oh, and advice. You were joking, but you would not believe how many people have told me in all seriousness that they've Googled my diagnosis and now think my doctor should know about [fill in the blank with flaxseed oil, acupuncture, alkaline water, etc.]

Sent: October 30, 2010 at 11:22 a.m.
From: Jack Schwinn
To: Cecily Murphy

Chang will be disappointed. He had some seaweed/ginger root recipes he was planning to share with you. Come up to Baltimore tomorrow night!

Sent: October 30, 2010 at 7:00 p.m.
From: Suzie London
To: Cecily Murphy

Hey, Thelma, it's Louise. Don't read the Internet. Let's go hold up a bank! We just have to be quiet (act normal everyone). "If you don't give us the money, we'll sing a really bad song to you!" As the teller looks at us, shivering in fear, we'll pull out the big guns. "Everybody dance now!" Remember that? And we'll give you a REALLY bad haircut, the Princess Diana, 1989!

Hugs and love,

Your partner in crime,

Suz

**Sent: October 30, 2010 at 9:00 p.m.
From: Cecily Murphy
To: Suzie London**

Do you want to be Thelma or Louise? I remember you always wanted to be Belinda when we played Go-Go's, so I don't want to cramp your style!

When did your fight begin? How far along are you in your battle?

**Sent: October 30, 2010 at 9:32 p.m.
From: Suzie London
To: Cecily Murphy**

Whichever one got to sleep with young Brad Pitt. I have lots of wigs for our new career as bank robbers: hot pink, Charo, Dolly Parton. I'll give you first choice this time! I'll take the Charo wig, but only if I get to have a pineapple on top. Let's just sing Love Boat and go for a cruise. You totally want the Dolly Parton. That's your outfit.

Chapter 2

May 21, 2011, 11:58 p.m.

"You really didn't know?" Cait asked, regarding her sister over the top of her glass. Cait sprawled at the kitchen table, her feet now free of her sadistic black kitten heels, her Spanx straining against the forces of gravity to anchor any wayward flesh to her hip bones and rib cage. Tonight's soiree, Danny's co-worker's wedding, had been Cait's first attempt to wrangle her post-partum body into her pre-partum black summer cocktail dress, and although she had lost some of her baby weight already, her ribcage and chest still strained against its restrictive casing, squeezing her all night like a blueberry between two fingers.

Also contributing to Cait's discomfort was the third glass of champagne, which waltzed clumsily with the salmon in her stomach. Tired, tipsy and tightly bound, Cait couldn't tell if her sister was trying to make her feel guilty about leaving the newspaper clipping, or if Cecily really had spent the entire evening drinking wine and crying. The evidence—Cecily's red-rimmed eyes and blotched cheeks—suggested Cecily was telling the truth, but Cait refused to believe this mini-breakdown was the result of concern for their troubled childhood neighbor. Because that would be ridiculous.

"Come on, Cec. What about the crazy emails she sent you? About her interventions and her brother and AA? You didn't have an inkling? I wasn't shocked by this. I never would have guessed it would surprise you. I mean, I thought you'd find it depressing in a broad, sociological way, in the way that all those shows are like watching human trainwrecks."

Cecily had practiced her tone of voice in her head while waiting for Cait and Danny to get home. She knew Cait had clipped the newspaper article as an honest curiosity, a subject of random but interesting gossip, nothing more. When Cait offhandedly asked, "So, did you watch it?" while struggling to remove her tight-fitting, ill-advised heels, Cecily silently recited the first group of the Periodic Table to herself: Hydrogen, Lithium, Sodium, Potassium ... before answering aloud, "No."

"No. I did not find it depressing from an anthropological standpoint. And you don't have the right to assume how I'd react to my friend's death."

"Friend? You mean, *Facebook* friend?" Cait actively refrained from rolling her eyes (a habit Danny had pointed out to her lately).

"Yes, friend, as in Facebook friend. Like you have ... Gymboree friends. Or teacher friends. Or friends from college. You've heard of them: friends."

"Cecily. This is Suzie London. I thought you'd written her off months ago. Years ago, and then, months ago."

"You'd written her off months ago. My relationship with her has changed. A lot," Cecily paused, wondering if this statement were actually true. Quite possibly, Cecily had been duped, and now Suzie was an anecdote. Cecily pictured herself in Cait's vicious kitten heels with her hair grown back at last: gorgeous, long, wavy auburn hair, more beautiful in her memory/projection than it had ever been in real life. She pictured herself at a wedding, telling an acquaintance, "The strangest thing was, I had cancer at the same time as a childhood neighbor who lived two doors down from me. Except, then it turned out she didn't. She lied about the whole thing. Or maybe not ..." If their relationship had been anecdotal, it had just become a complicated anecdote.

Cait sat up, wiggled herself into a comfortable position, and said with more sarcasm than she intended, "Well, then, I apologize for not understanding the intricacies of your relationship with a girl who once used a purple magic marker to draw mustaches on all your stuffed animals. Truthfully, I don't think this is about Suzie, but about ..." Cait balked at the word "cancer." "Your fears," she continued. Then, in an effort to sound as conciliatory as she felt, added, "I shouldn't have reminded you of this whole ordeal this past year. I'm sorry. I honestly didn't even think about that aspect of it."

Cait chastised herself. How could she have been so dense? She couldn't mention death around her sister anymore. That topic was off limits. Even if it was kind of an unusual and salacious death, and it was someone they knew. She had never known a more apt recipe for gossip fodder, but it was insensitive to bring up dying.

"I'm sorry. Come here, Cec. I feel like an idiot," Cait circled the table and stooped down to hug her sister who sat slumped in her pajama pants, staring at her empty wine glass. Only a burgeoning headache kept Cecily's annoyance from hardening into anger. She reached up and caught Cait's arm with her own, half-hugging her back. Cait didn't get it, Cecily thought. Not only is she clueless to her offense, she will now awkwardly avoid the subject of death and treat me like her old doll collection, for display purposes only.

Then, to Cecily's surprise, Cait announced, "I kind of want to watch it."

"Oh, come on!" Cecily wriggled free of Cait's hug, crossing her arms and pressing her shoulders against the back of the chair, hard enough to feel the cross-hatched bamboo dig into her back. From this vantage point, she managed to convey her disgust, although it was difficult, with Cait standing over her like that.

"Well, I don't hope it's graphic or anything horrible, but yes, I'm curious. I DVR'd it."

Cait's husband Danny, who had been leafing through a magazine on the kitchen counter, finally sensed the drop in barometric pressure that warned of a simmering sister spat. He warily regarded the two redheaded sisters who had looked so much alike until last year. Cecily's wan appearance still jarred him. He was guilty of peppering Cecily with boisterous compliments, telling her she looked "so much better" every time he saw her. His encouragement was sincere enough, even if his words fell somewhat short of truth. In reality, Cecily's complexion still seemed gray next to his wife's. And while Cecily's short, post-chemo hair still possessed the striking Murphy auburn color, its new texture didn't seem to be working out too well. It reminded Danny of that horrible crimping-iron trend his sisters were into in the 80's. Cait also frequently complained that Cecily was way too skinny. He knew enough not to argue that Cecily looked fine. His wife was sensitive to weight comparisons with her sister after giving birth to Cooper.

Danny placed his water glass on the kitchen counter and stepped backwards to the kitchen's exit. He planned to escape unnoticed, look in on his sleeping children, then watch Sports Center in bed.

Cecily couldn't remember the next element on the Periodic Table; she couldn't remember which group she was reciting to keep her temper in check. Too loudly, Cecily spat at her sister, "Suzie London is dead. She was my friend. And I found out from the *TV Fucking Guide*. And it appears, from the information in the *TV Fucking Guide*, that she was lying to me—about some of it definitely, about all of it maybe. I don't know. And I don't know why. And you don't even understand … you don't even comprehend … why I'm upset. You think I'm sad about 'the cancer.' That's not it! That's not it!" Cecily was standing, yelling now, but she didn't care.

"And I can't believe, I *can not* believe you would watch Dr. *Dick*," Cecily continued. She jabbed her finger toward Cait's ribcage for effect. "He. Is. Sickening. And. Exploitative."

Cait once again resisted the urge to roll her eyes at her little sister's tantrum. Here comes the Finger of Doom, she thought. She walked around to the other side of the kitchen island to put some distance between them, in light of Cecily's tendency to get jabby when she yelled. Their father and brother had the same tendency. It was a family tradition of sorts. Cait tried a conciliatory tone. "Honey, I'm so sorry your friend died. I just don't think she was much of a friend." Cecily opened her mouth to speak, but Cait held up her finger to stop her. Realizing what she was doing, she quickly dropped it.

"I know it's not my place to tell you who's your friend or not, or to categorize your friends into good friends and bad friends. But just listen. Just listen. Don't you want answers? I want answers, and I wasn't even the one who was duped." She paused, avoiding Cecily's glare. "Possibly duped. I want to watch it, because I want to know the truth about this Suzie London person."

Cecily sat back down at the table and resumed glaring at her wine glass. "Of course I need answers. I need to figure out what happened and how she got involved with this crap. But watching a human being die on TV is not a plan. And I actually do have a plan. I'm starting with the brother. I'm finding the brother. I think." The truth was, the plan had started with Suzie. She had been sending increasingly frantic emails to Suzie all night, to no response. Something was up, but maybe Suzie wasn't dead. Maybe this was all some big misunderstanding.

Cecily rubbed her temples. Her headache seared through her sinuses, her face, her whole head. The wine didn't help, and neither did Cait.

"You really had no idea she was doing so badly?" Cait asked again, shaking her head as she marveled at this.

"None," Cecily answered. But she already knew that wasn't true. She had spent the evening rereading every one of her email exchanges with Suzie London. No answers materialized. Just one question: why? Why would someone go out of their way to seek out a cancer patient on Facebook, befriend them, then ... Suzie London had to have had cancer, Cecily thought. Why would someone lie about that? The stuff Suzie knew, only a cancer patient would know. And now Suzie's dead? That couldn't be. Nothing made sense.

The questions, frustrations and anger tumbled around in her head like towels in a dryer, but it was the guilt that weighted her head, her face, her temples. The guilt of not knowing where Suzie was, or if Suzie even still existed.

"God, do I need answers," Cecily stood up. She thought of Suzie London's last e-mail to her, two or three weeks ago, which had recommended another song. Suzie always recommended songs for Cecily. Cecily now had a playlist on her iPod called "Suzie," filled with Suzie's eclectic music recommendations and the contents of the many CDs Suzie had sent her during chemo.

"There's a song I want you to download," Suzie had written. "Go do it now. It's called *Say Goodnight Not Goodbye*. It's an old one. So pretty. I've been listening to it all night and crying. It's so beautiful. Go do it now. We'll listen to it together."

Cecily downloaded the song, logged back on to Facebook with Dorothy Squires' 1940's-era song playing, and emailed back, "It's so sad, Suzie. Beautiful, but so sad."

Suzie had written back, "Imagine me dancing, when you imagine me. I love you."

Cecily would never hear from her again.

Posted November 3, 2010 at 12:35 p.m.
Cecily Murphy

Is STAGE I, baby! Two tumors <1 centimeter. This fight will be a decisive routing: like watching the Redskins play the Falcons. I've named the tumors Peaches and Pansy. They are small, weak and ugly. And they're gonna regret choosing me.

Sent: November 3, 2010 at 12:42 p.m.
From: Jack Schwinn
To: Cecily Murphy

Peaches was the name of my childhood pet hamster. Turned out she was pregnant when we got her, and when she had the babies, she ate them. Peaches the Cannibal became a sensation among the 4th grade boys at my school. My brother was so jealous I had a cannibalistic pet. His rabbit, Attila the Bun, did nothing but bite him and try to escape. I charged people $1 to see Peaches. She paid for my first skateboard.

Sent: November 3, 2010 at 12:44 p.m.
From: Cecily Murphy
To: Jack Schwinn

LOL! You made that up! You're just mad about the Falcons jab.

Sent: November 3, 2010 at 12:46 p.m.
From: Jack Schwinn
To: Cecily Murphy

How about Centurian and Skinjob? As names for your tumors.

Sent: November 3, 2010 at 12:48 p.m.
From: Cecily Murphy
To: Jack Schwinn

Too nerdy! I don't watch Battlestar Galactica.

Sent: November 3, 2010 at 12:49 p.m.
From: Jack Schwinn
To: Cecily Murphy

Hmmm. Methinks you do or you wouldn't have caught the reference to Battlestar Galactica.

Sent: November 3, 2010 at 12:52 p.m.
From: Cecily Murphy
To: Jack Schwinn

Oh, frak it. Keep it on the down low. I don't need to broadcast the full extent of my nerdiness.

Posted November 3, 2010 at 1:03 p.m.
Cecily Murphy

Apparently my tumors' names are the names of some people's beloved pets. Sorry about that, but I have to say: Peaches seems an unlikely name for a 4th grade boy's hamster. Anyway, out of respect, I'll rename the tumors. Henceforth, my tumors are Hoda and Kathie Lee.

The Truth About Suzie

Sent: November 3, 2010 at 1:18 p.m.
From: Jack Schwinn
To: Cecily Murphy

The full extent of your nerdiness is my favorite thing about you.

Chapter 3

May 22, 2011, 12:30 a.m.

Cecily typically slept in her sister's guest bedroom on nights she babysat. Tonight, however, Cecily wanted to get into her car and drive, even if the commute back to her own house was just a ten-minute straight shot down the Rockville Pike into the city. She was halfway out the door with her duffle bag when Cait reminded Cecily of her promise to take Eileigh to a Children's Theatre performance of Cinderella the next morning.

Cecily had forgotten about this, and she allowed her duffel to slip off her shoulder in defeat. It was probably better she didn't drive anyway. She finished drinking the wine hours ago, and had probably long since metabolized her two glasses, but these days wine condensed into a persistent cloud in her brain that took nearly a whole day to dissipate.

Cait gave her sister another hug, apologized for their argument, and reminded her that—if Cecily woke up first—the Pop Tarts were in the cabinet over the microwave.

The bed was huge and soft and smelled of freshly washed sheets, but Cecily couldn't sleep and spent the night staring down the ceiling fan. She had been supplied over the past year with a selection of medications that was as extensive as it was useless, including several brands of sleeping pills. She could have fished any combination of them out of her large, black medication bag, but, knowing the futility of this effort, she didn't. Instead she laid still, listening to the distant whoosh of traffic on the Beltway, a quarter mile away. She usually enjoyed the silence of Cait's house when the kids were asleep, and the smells of new carpet, new hardwood floors, Johnson's baby shampoo and laundry detergent. Cecily could also detect a touch of Cait's hairspray on the second floor: Pantene Touchable Volume.

The smell made Cecily miss her hair: her previous hair, that is. The new growth was proving hard to love with its convoluted texture and its errant, weed-like clumps—thick here, thin there, curly here, straight there. Her friend Michele had affectionately dubbed it "Lucille Ball Vs. Audrey Hepburn Vs. Crimping Iron." No amount of hair product could give it coherence. No matter. She'd let go of the idea of controlling her hair the day her hair had let go of her. It was Suzie who had taught her how. Suzie, who now existed as a question mark.

Down the hall in the master bedroom, Cait tossed her shoes into the back of her closet and paused in front of her dresser to take off her earrings. She bared her teeth at the mirror to see if any of the vegetarian pesto linguine served at the wedding had ended up in her smile. She was clear, but she suspected that, although Danny wouldn't have noticed, Cecily would have told her. Behind her, Danny brushed his teeth with the TV remote in hand, scanning the channels on the flat screen that hung over his dresser. Cait met his eyes in the mirror and smiled. She loved going to weddings because they were the only occasions when Danny would dance. Danny smiled back, toothpaste creeping down his lip. Danny loved going to weddings because they put Cait in The Mood, no small feat with a baby in the house.

Cait's smile disappeared, and she turned around to frown at Danny.

"What's wrong?" Danny asked, alarmed that his window of opportunity could close before he finished brushing his teeth.

"Was I right to tell Cecily the truth about this Facebook 'friend' of hers? She would have found out somehow." She nodded, answering her own question. "What a con artist. Taking advantage of someone who has cancer. Unbelievable. If Suzie London wasn't dead, I'd be tempted to finish the job myself," she stated and slipped out of her black dress.

Sent: November 9, 2010 at 5:54 a.m.
From: Caitlyn Murphy Doyle
To: Cecily Murphy

I'm so sorry things went badly last night. We love you. Mom and Dad love you too, and Mom will calm down. I thought Dr. Schumaker did an excellent job talking her down off the ledge.

We were all shaken up when we got home, and Eileigh noticed and asked questions, so I told her about your cancer. I said, "She'll have surgery and be lazy on the couch. Like Daddy watching football. Ha! Instead of being Speedy Gonzalez, she'll be Slowpoke Rodriguez. But then she'll be right back to normal. Any questions?" Eileigh said, "Yes. Is she going to die?" I nearly choked! But I recovered quickly. "No," I told her. "Promise?" she asked. And I promised her. I don't lie to Eileigh. I know you're going to be OK. I love you.

Posted November 9, 2010 at 6:06 a.m.
Cecily Murphy

Meeting started badly with immediate biopsy of another newly found tumor: did not improve from there. Second tumor pathology is back. Tumors are both triple negative (not responsive to hormones). Aggressive. Mastectomy, chemo. No surprise with genetic test results … makes decisions more involved. Only good news of night: radiologist said I had the "most developed pectoral muscles" he'd ever seen. The gym membership pays off at last!

Posted November 11, 2010 at 3:21 a.m.
Cecily Murphy

Decision time. Mastectomy next Wednesday. One-month recovery followed by chemo January-July, then possible radiation. I thought I'd have more time, but I guess it's time to make the call.

Sent: November 11, 2010 at 3:39 a.m.
From: Suzie London
To: Cecily Murphy

What are you deciding? Lumpectomy / mastectomy / reconstruction? I don't know your situation but I read all your credentials on Facebook. Oh, and Cornell. Ooh la la. Impressive. So you are smart. I'm not smart right now. I just got suckered into buying something called Scurrilous? Sienna? Sierra Mist? Salvia? It comes in bong form and my doctor didn't prescribe it but, even though you're smart and I'm not: you've given me something, so I'm going to give you something.

Don't let anyone tell you it's just a boob. I believed that and wished I hadn't. It's a body part and it's YOURS. They pick apart your body like it's a yard sale: do we need this anymore? Nope. Hey that's my goddamn breast! F--- you! When you've had as much surgery as me, you start to get pissy and a little bit protective of your body parts. That person who commented that it's "just a breast," who is that? It's not. It's a part of you and it hurts to lose a part of you. Who has the right to divide your body parts into essential and non-essential categories? That's your call. Not the anesthesiologist's. He didn't even bother to move my tongue aside before jamming the tube down this time. Oh, don't let that bother you! That's just my tongue! I didn't need that! Letting the surgeons in is like inviting vampires into your house. I don't want you to be scared. I just want you to be informed. I just want you to know that everything is your choice. Everything. Do not smoke this shit. It makes you nauseous and your eyes see type double. Shit, girl, it does.

Sent: November 11, 2010 at 4:12 a.m.
From: Cecily Murphy
To: Suzie London

I don't know what to do. I've been up all night. I don't think I've ever been this pissed off.

Here's the deal: I've been living with the idea of a double mastectomy in my head my whole life, ever since my mom tested positive for BRCA and had her double mastectomy and hysterectomy. Her sister fought it, twice. Her mother fought it and lost (the year I was born). Since the moment I had breasts, I was told not to get too attached to them. I've been told not to panic about this. I was going to find out if I had the gene by taking the blood test, which I was going to do ... later. Maybe after I had kids, if I ever got married and had kids: not a huge priority right now. Well, my dad always said, "If you want to make God laugh, tell him your plans." So God laughed, and I got cancer first. But whatever. Like I said: everyone was prepared.

Or so I thought. Our meeting tonight (last night? Yes, it's morning already—crap!) was chaos. My mom was crying hysterically, my sister too. I felt like, OK, you've told me since I was five-years-old there was a good chance this could happen. We've prepared, and now, the minute the battle starts, everyone runs away screaming, and I'm sitting there holding a machine gun saying, "Are you kidding me?"

So I spent the whole night, get this: comforting my family. It was ridiculous. I have all these choices to make now, and they're totally worthless. Why didn't I just run the blood myself in my lab, you ask? Well, I wish I did. But actually, that wouldn't have worked, because all I can do with my equipment is reproduce Microcystis Aeruginosa (algae blooms).

So whatever. The cancer is in one breast. There are three tumors now. Doctor wants me to get the double mastectomy fast, before it moves into the lymph nodes, if it hasn't already. He doesn't want to stop to line up the reconstructive surgeon. He says that would "take time we don't have." He says I can do it later "if I even want it." Is he kidding?!

I don't know if I should get the hysterectomy now. I'm leaning against it, but only because the whole family would have a collective aneurysm if I did it now. My mom and sister were running around screaming, "It's genetic! It's genetic! We're doomed! But have a baby first!" Well, what if I don't want a baby because I don't want to pass my genes down? My sister got married and started having kids right away because of this. She hasn't been tested yet, much to my mother's chagrin. I still think it was selfish of her, without knowing whether or not she would be throwing a grenade (a genetic predisposition) at them.

I have got to either go to bed for an hour or just get ready for work. Can't believe I spent all night on Facebook!

Sent: November 11, 2010 at 4:36 a.m.
From: Suzie London
To: Cecily Murphy

I need the genetic predisposition for digesting the kebobs from the all-night kebob stand in front of Morty's. I know—I know—those kebabs are made of ground up people. Shh. Don't tell anyone. I've always known an evil bitch lives in my brain. Like the Great Spirit in the oak tree. Or the Great Pumpkin. But my body, too? Why does my body have to be such an asshole too? That's what I'd like to know.

Sent: November 11, 2010 at 6:12 a.m.
From: Cecily Murphy
To: Suzie London

OK, you're making me laugh, and I didn't think I was capable of that now! You may have even prevented the migraine sneaking up on me. Genetics was so exciting to me. There's this beautiful rhythm, rhyme, reason, equation for every living organism, from amoebas to galaxies. And now our DNA can talk to us. I was so prepared for this meeting last night, I can't even tell you.

I'm going to get a second opinion just to get someone else's fresh eyes on the situation. My mom's freaking out about that too. Dr. Schumaker is OUR doctor. We go to HIM.

Bottom line: ugh. But that salvia you're smoking (salvia is just an herb—it's sage, BTW) seems pretty appealing right now. I had a blistering headache from crying, and reading that you're out in California having a party with a hallucinogenic variety of sage, well, that made me laugh. Wow, that was a long e-mail. Thanks for listening. Didn't realize I had that much angst to dump!

**Sent: November 11, 2010 at 6:38 a.m.
From: Suzie London
To: Cecily Murphy**

You can too! Smoke salvia. Even if you don't live in California. I'll mail you some, but it sucks: the pot we have here is better. The mastectomy is a long recovery. They give you good drugs, so it's not the pain that makes it long. You can't lift your arms. You'll need someone to help you out of bed, to help you put a shirt on. There is no feeling like it: helplessness. You're lucky you have your mom. (Too shrieky is better than too drunk, trust me!) I had to stay with my brother and his wife. They're always nice on the surface, but they didn't want me there. They did it because it was their "Christian duty," but they're such hypocrites. Their kids hate them. They judge me for getting off on medical marijuana, but they get off on feeling superior to everyone. It's the same thing.

Get the reconstruction: it will be hard to see your body disassembled.

Get the reconstruction: it's the law. If they take you apart they have to put you back together: for free!!! I wish that law applied everywhere, to everyone. When a rare piece of universal justice falls out of the sky, don't question it! That kind of justice is rarely available.

Get the reconstruction: it will make the process longer, but it's worth it. And I say this as someone who hates surgery. I hate lying on the table and looking up at the masked men staring back at you like the naked piece of meat that you are. I hate counting backwards from 100 and knowing that before I hit 96 I'll wake up somewhere else, god knows where, in god-knows-what state. Sometimes I wake up happy, high on a perfect note of pain meds. Sometimes I wake up screaming, terrified, confused. Or like last time, swimming up for hours to reach the surface, hearing the nurse saying, "Wake up. You have to wake up," before floating back down and beginning the climb all over again.

There are always surprises. The bruise on the back of your arm. The reasoning behind the anesthesiologist's decision to jam the damn tube through your damn tongue, rather than simply moving your tongue, or the tube, aside. The parts that are gone, the parts that have appeared. The locations of the scars.

I'm done with surgery now. I wish I was as brave as you going in. You were always the rebel. Oh no! Now I have Billy Idol's song stuck in my head!

Dear Cancer, Cecily and I are going to have a party when you're gone. RuPaul will perform. Seriously. I know her. Him. We'll laugh at how weak you were, how unprepared, how little. We have great wigs.

Sent: November 11, 2010 at 7:31 a.m.
From: Cecily Murphy
To: Suzie London

Rock on, Thelma. Louise. Whoever slept with young Brad Pitt. I don't need salvia, but thanks. I need to know ... lots of things, really. But most important things first: how do you know RuPaul? And where are you now in your treatment, now that you're done with surgery?

And I'm sorry to hear about your mom. I had no idea. I'm sure that added a layer of difficulty to an already tough situation.

Yes, I'm having the reconstruction: I don't care if it's a pain for my surgeon's planning assistant. That was my cousin's wife Harriet who posted "it's just a boob," and really, she's just a boob. I agree with you 100 percent, and I haven't even been up on the chopping block yet. Reconstruction is so necessary it isn't even a choice for me. I was surprised to learn that about myself. I didn't think I cared that much about my Wanna-B breasts. All they've ever been to me are potential liabilities, now actualized.

Sent: November 11, 2010 at 7:35 a.m.
From: Cecily Murphy
To: Caitlyn Murphy Doyle

Sometimes she's so lucid. And other times she's wasted. She's funny, though. I just wish she'd answer more of my questions about her. Anyway, just rambling about Suzie London.

November 11, 2010 at 7:42 a.m.
From: Caitlyn Murphy Doyle
To: Cecily Murphy

Yeah, I know the feeling. I asked you a question about a certain Jack who's been commenting on all your Facebook posts and was rewarded with the sound of crickets.

How is Suzie doing? I friended her when you told me she had cancer like you. She accepted my friend request, but she doesn't post anything. Her pictures though: wow! Nice bikini body! Clearly she doesn't have kids! And did you see the picture of Seal?

Sent: November 11, 2010 at 8:39 a.m.
From: Cecily Murphy
To: Jack Schwinn

Things are moving along quickly, and I'm sorry I keep missing your call. I have my second opinion at Georgetown tomorrow and my mastectomy Wednesday at GW (if the second opinion is similar to first opinion, of course).

Everyone has asked me why I'm at GW instead of Georgetown. I'm with the breast surgeon who treated my mom and my Aunt Lil. Dr. Schumaker is like a member of the family, albeit a cranky one. He was one of the pioneers in genetic counseling and putting the advances in DNA testing to use in a clinical setting. Look up his work in *JCOP*. So I'm definitely going with him, but he wasn't happy about the second opinion. He's cocky. And I don't think he likes that I have a microbiology degree. "A little bit of knowledge can be a dangerous thing," he said. "This isn't phytology." So I corrected him: phycology. (A little snarky, I admit. But fun to be right, I'll also admit.)

But then he went over the report with me in detail, like a fellow scientist, even though my sister and mom were annoyed about being sidelined. Dr. Schumaker stood up for me too, saying that my questions and understanding came first because I was his patient. So my mom was already irritated/upset. Then, when we learned the BRCA test came back positive, that was it for her. Statistically, this was a 50/50 possibility, but it still makes decision-making more … complicated. From then on, Mom was a wreck. Dr. Schumaker spent 20 minutes just talking her down and then another 20 minutes trying to appease Cait and her Hardball-style questions, while Dad and I sat on the couches, drank tea and made faces at each other. Surreal.

I've been up all night. I just told my boss about the cancer, and I'm not in a wonderful mood. (Actually, telling him went well. Other than the awkward hug, I mean.)

Oh, I've attached my pathology report if you want to geek out with me. Check out the s-phase percentages. You can look up breast cancer treatment protocols online at NIH.gov, and plug in the results from the pathology report. There's a treatment plan calculator tool for breast cancer: it's wild. I think "triple negative" gets a bad rap because it doesn't respond to the new hormone therapies, but it does respond well to chemo—so in my case, it actually makes my prognosis better. It changed my survival odds for the better when I plugged it in to the NIH survival odds calculator this morning. (I found the calculator on my own. Wonder why Schumaker didn't show me? He thought I'd freak out like my mom, no doubt!)

They originally considered me Stage I because the first tumor was so small—then they found the makeup of the second tumor is the same, and there was another one they biopsied that might be a third. Shumaker thinks if it is, it will also be genetically identical, because it's so close to the other two. They theorize it's one big tumor split into small pieces. Schumaker said they'd probably re-adjust my official cancer stage after the mastectomy, once this was confirmed. I told him, OK, if you do change me from Stage I to Stage Something Worse, don't tell me. You can write it in my chart and I'll read about it later, once this is all behind me. I put a lot of emotional stock in being Stage I. I know it's stupid because staging isn't really the biggest issue: a tumor can be big or small, but what matters most is how good it is at spreading. But Stage I: it sounded so mild, like: "oh, I have a mild case of the flu." Or cancer. Maybe a mild case of cancer is like being a little bit pregnant, but my Stage I diagnosis was propping me up through this.

I'm thinking about launching a blog when I go into the hospital Wednesday. It'll be called "The Blind Smurfs Take Their Beating." Don't ask. Jane came up with that name, and it's a long story! -C.

Sent: November 11, 2010 at 10:01 a.m.
From: Jack Schwinn
To: Cecily Murphy

Hey there, C.

I'm so sorry to hear all of that! I know all of this must be a real kick in the gut and makes the future scarier. I know you can do this though, and your Baltimore-based cheer squad (Parsons, Chang, Bangladello) and I will be here to support you.

Definitely launch the blog. Chang and Bangladello are on Google Plus (Chang says he likes it because "nobody's there"), and they have to log into my Facebook account to get your updates. I'm afraid Chang will start posting hundreds of pictures of his cats, articles on how to be a hoarder, and his mother's seaweed recipes. One day, you'll see some seriously weird stuff on my page, and only you will know why.

I see what you mean with your pathology report. You're right. A high s-phase isn't terrible in your situation. As for your treatment plan, you're also right. That website's very easy and straightforward to use. Now anybody can treat breast cancer if they have WiFi! :) I'm not factoring in genetics. I wouldn't even bother trying to call on my vague (some would say "repressed") memories of Legenhausen's classes. I, too, veered off the pre-med track at Human Genetics, but in favor of nanotech, not algae. But I sincerely doubt your doctor is basing his recommendations on your mother's potential reaction, no matter how shrieky she may get. I'm sure he hears shrieks all the time: diagnosing people with cancer, that's an occupational hazard.

But, yes, get the second opinion. It'll make you feel more confident about your treatment plan. That's important going into this. You're feisty and stubborn as hell, and you need to use those qualities to let cancer know you are its overlord, its conqueror.

Remember when we had to get rid of the bat that got loose on the third floor of Brighton? And you handed me the tennis racket and said, "It's GO TIME, Jack!" I have never felt like a bigger pansy in my life than I did in your presence. When you backhanded that bat out the window, I thought to myself: she is a fearless force of nature. And we should play tennis sometime.

I like Jane's blog name suggestion, and I think I can guess how she came up with the name. If you translate this report into English Major/Jane-language, which I have to assume you did, you changed the word "cells" to "Smurfs." Am I close? According to this report, the Smurfs are "legally blind" but might be able to make out some shapes and objects. But they still can't operate heavy machinery, nor do they know when to duck at the proper time. They will, most assuredly, take their beating.

Please let me know if there's anything I can do to help: cook (seriously!), clean (not promising miracles), hold your hand and sing Grateful Dead songs to you in the hospital (for old time's sake), steal hospital socks for you (again, for nostalgia purposes ...) I can take time off work and I'm happy to.

Kick ass, take names,

Jack

Sent: November 11, 2010 at 10:19 a.m.
From: Cecily Murphy
To: Jack Schwinn

That's exactly right! About how I explained this all to Jane. Impressed you figured that out!

Sent: November 11, 2010 at 5:00 p.m.
From: Suzie London
To: Cecily Murphy

I've performed with RuPaul—most fun I ever had. Also performed/wrote songs for/worked with Nigel Baker, Satan's Ejaculation, Bloat, Baked Alaskans, bunch of bands you've never heard of. Come out here and I'll take you to some parties where your senses would go supernova.

Sent: November 11, 2010 at 5:22 p.m.
From: Cecily Murphy
To: Suzie London

You're a songwriter! I knew it! I read your poetry on your Facebook notes page and thought to myself: these are songs.

Sent: November 11, 2010 at 5:59 p.m.
From: Suzie London
To: Cecily Murphy

Songwriter, actress, singer, artist, set designer, stagehand, dog walker, singing telegram deliverer, primary muse. In other words: barely employed.

Download "Road Trip to Venus" by Circus Eclesiastica on iTunes. That's one of mine. That's the only self-plugging I'll do, that song. All the other ones I can take or leave. They're nothing like Jace's. I stopped writing songs when I read his. I thought, this guy is big time.

Posted November 15, 2010 at 9:49 a.m.
Cecily Murphy

Surgery FAQ:

What? Double mastectomy w/ reconstruction. Plus lymph node biopsy to see if the cancer has spread beyond my breast.
When? Tomorrow.
How long in hospital? 24 hours.
Recovery locale? I'll be tormenting my parents at their house in Columbia.
Do narcotic pain meds really turn you into reckless kleptomaniac? Yes & I have a purse full of hospital socks to prove it. Nail down my room!

Chapter 4

May 22, 2011, 10:00 a.m.

Eileigh was far more interested in the costumes and spectacle of Cinderella than the story, but Cecily felt obligated nonetheless to point out the plot points where Cinderella had been needlessly rescued instead of asserting herself. Eileigh had no idea what her aunt was talking about, but she listened intently and nodded at the right times. She loved dressing up and going to the theater with her aunt. If Aunt Cecily seemed less energetic or engaged than usual, well, that had been explained to Eileigh several times. It was a side effect of breast cancer. Breast cancer would do that to you.

Eileigh was proud to understand this, and explained authoritatively to her friends from school that Eileigh herself had once come down with a case of breast cancer, just like her Aunt Cecily. She got to stay home from preschool for a whole day while she recovered. Her friends had seemed appropriately impressed. Her mother, however, had choked on her Diet Coke.

Cecily used the two hours sitting in the dark to sort out her feelings and put together a better action plan. She wasn't looking forward to pursuing Brad London for answers, but she figured she could start there. Cecily simply didn't believe the scenario Dr. Dick had laid out: that Suzie London died of alcoholism and liver failure with her brother at her bedside. Suzie had a troubled relationship with her brother. There could be any number of explanations, Cecily figured. Suzie's brother could have been twisting the truth to get on a reality show. Suzie herself had explained how fake those shows were. Or, the show might not have featured the correct Brad, Suzie, Wendie and Peter London of Pine Hill, Maryland. Of all the possibilities Cecily vetted that morning, that one seemed the least likely—even to her hopeful mind.

Cecily wasn't convinced Suzie was dead, but as the hours passed, Suzie's silence allowed the specter of the possibility to whisper louder, more urgently. Suzie hadn't told Cecily she was dying. And, if she was dead, the betrayal could be as hard to bear as the loss. Cecily repeated the words to herself, to see if they rang true. "Suzie is dead," she told herself. "Suzie is dead."

No. It didn't ring true. She never said goodbye. And she didn't die of cancer, according to the TV. Did she ever even have cancer? Of course she did. "She had to," Cecily thought. "She had to."

But there was the very real possibility that Cecily didn't know Suzie at all and never did. There were just a few Facebook messages exchanged. Anyone could choose to present any incarnation of themselves they wanted on the Internet. Suzie herself had said as much. Suzie said it all the time.

Cecily told Jane earlier that morning on the phone, "Suzie got me through this past year. You can't say she doesn't exist anymore, and in fact, she never existed at all. I'm only here today because I was carried through on the support I had—thought I had. And now she's gone, I think, and what's worse—even the truth of my memory of her is gone."

Jane, as shocked as Cecily over the news, urged caution in contacting Brad. "Dr. Dick always has that unsavory element."

"Really?" Cecily had countered. "Unlike the Jerry Springer show hookers you hang out with next door?"

Cecily regretted saying it the moment it left her mouth, and said as much. Jane told her it was OK, and urged Cecily to get a nap soon. One of the few benefits of having cancer was your friends giving you more leeway when you said regrettable things to them.

Cait was even less enthusiastic about Cecily's intention of contacting Brad. Over pancakes and coffee, she lowered her fork and said, "God Lord, Cecily. Do you think a man who allows his family's problems to be filmed on television and exploits his sister's death will give you the answers you need? If she was lying, you may be able to find that out, but does it matter? It still doesn't change anything. Does it? Learn from this experience and move on. Stop getting embroiled with that crazy family."

Danny, on pancake duty at the stove, ignored the red warning light flashing in his head, and said, "Or maybe they weren't lies."

Cait tilted her head at him across the kitchen, meaningfully.

Danny backtracked. "Or maybe some things were lies and some weren't."

"Or maybe they were all lies. If they were, they were the sickest ones I've ever heard of. And it's best to just put all this behind us," Cait said.

"Us?" asked Danny.

"It's just not that simplistic," Cecily countered. She repeated what Jane had told her on the phone earlier, "The only thing worse than survivor's guilt is not knowing if you should have it or not."

Posted November 16, 2010 at 5:29 p.m.
Cecily Murphy

Surgery went well. Lymph nodes cancer-free. Need more socks. Groggy.

November 17, 2010 at 3:35 p.m.
Cecily Murphy

Yay! My big brother, Jimmy, is coming to visit me from Paris! Guess I'll have to lift the moratorium on calls/visitors today, since he's going to all that trouble. But no need to call/visit. I'm sleeping a lot & want for nothing. Round 1 was tough. But your support, well wishes, meals and caretaking helped so much. And made out with a purse full of stolen socks.

Sent: November 18, 2010 at 4:32 p.m.
From: Jane McCann
To: Cecily Murphy

Are you up for a visit? Michele's been clamoring to see your tissue expanders. I'm not entirely sure about that, I'm squeamish. :) Love you.

Sent: November 18, 2010 at 5:20 p.m.
From: Cecily Murphy
To: Jane McCann

Maybe tomorrow? Thanks! But you guys don't have to drive all the way out to Columbia. I'll be back home soon. But Dr. Schumaker was right about his recovery estimation: harder than I thought!

Posted November 20, 2010 at 9:12 a.m.
Cecily Murphy

"You're wussy," my surgeon says, re: my pain levels. That's Queen Wus to you and unashamed. It's 2010. We don't have to bite sticks anymore. God made Percocet, thank you, for just these occasions. Surgeon sighs. "Wash her hair," he tells my dad. "Women are so much happier when you wash their hair."

Posted November 21, 2010 at 12:14 p.m.
Cecily Murphy

Took a walk with Jimmy today. We hid my tubes/drains under giant sweater of Dad's and scuffled around the block twice. It was glorious: a stolen 20-minute break from my new job as Cancer Patient. Don't like new job, but can't afford to quit, so I'll have to sneak in the joy where I can.

Sent: November 21, 2010 at 2:10 p.m.
From: Suzie London
To: Cecily Murphy

You've been training for sneaking in the joy since the day I pulled you under the fence at Pine Hill Pool in 1st grade.

Remember that? When you didn't have your membership card and they wouldn't let you in without it? Who was that pool manager: Chaz? He was power mad. The power of the pool manager: bwahahaha! So we had to sneak around and we dug a hole!!!! We thought we were so subtle!!!!

Sent: November 21, 2010 at 2:29 p.m.
From: Cecily Murphy
To: Suzie London

I forgot about that! Suz, I'm going crazy here. You were so right about not being able to lift your arms. It's terrible. I have to ask my mom for everything, and she's so fretful. I feel like it breaks her heart fresh every time I ask for something. At least I thought to bring my laptop here. That's nice. I try to look at the positive. And I have so much support, I don't want to sound ungrateful. But here's something I'll never post on Facebook: today, I peeked under the bandages in the mirror and cried for an hour. I'm a scarred, disfigured mess. Franken-torso.

Sent: November 21, 2010 at 3:11 p.m.
From: Suzie London
To: Cecily Murphy

I know. They hate us and they're trying to kill us. I spent hours on the bathroom floor, crying. You're beautiful and you'll be whole again, sooner than you think. My friend Lisa is a photographer/cinematographer. She photographed me before I went under the knife, after, and then again one year after. I want you to see the "one year after" shots. The scars fade. I call the tube scars my bullet holes. I hardly notice them anymore.

Sent: November 21, 2010 at 3:13 p.m.
From: Cecily Murphy
To: Suzie London

Can I see them? Is that too personal?

Sent: November 21, 2010 at 3:34 p.m.
From: Suzie London
To: Cecily Murphy

I wouldn't have offered if it was. I just didn't want to send them unless you said yes. I only send *unsolicited* pictures of my tits if you're a director (Michael Bay, ahem). See attached. When I'm a famous actress/songwriter/wife of Brad Pitt, you can sell them to a tabloid. I don't care. I've been to all the topless beaches in southern California. I was self-conscious about the scars until I did these pictures with Lisa.

Sent: November 21, 2010 at 3:42 p.m.
From: Cecily Murphy
To: Suzie London

Thank you for this. Wow. You are beautiful.

Chapter 5

May 22, 2011, 12:35 p.m.

Cecily told her trainer, Jaclyn, she wanted to "pound on things" that day, so Jaclyn reserved the boxing room, and waited with her clipboard at the ready for Cecily's rushed arrival, five minutes late.

"Nice shoes," Jaclyn pointed to Cecily's brown, low-heeled slingbacks.

"Uh, thanks. Sorry I'm late! Give me two minutes," Cecily answered, digging through her gym bag for her gym clothes and cross-trainers as she dashed toward the women's locker room. Cecily believed lateness was a rudeness on par with texting during a children's theater performance (which she had just witnessed an hour ago).

Jaclyn didn't care. She got paid for the hour whether she was training Cecily or waiting for her to emerge from the locker room. She used the time to review Cecily's chart. It was thrilling to behold: Cecily's goals and objectives, neatly plotted out with benchmarks that showed steady progress. If only all my clients were this easy to motivate, she thought. A native of Montreal, Canada, Jaclyn found herself amazed at American attitudes toward movement. Before she had married her DC-resident husband, Jaclyn trained people for bodybuilding contests, triathlons and Olympic events. Here, where the suburbs of Washington, DC oozed out to blend with the suburbs of Baltimore to form one gelatinous stretch of tract housing 30 miles long, Jaclyn's planning talents seemed as useless as sidewalks had seemed to urban planners. She was now paid to nag people. And people paid, gladly, willingly, for the service of being treated like a naughty child.

Jaclyn spent the months of October through December sending out client emails touting her services as "the perfect holiday gift," but nevertheless thought personal training sessions were an odd gift for a father to give his chemotherapy-bound daughter. Jaclyn almost turned Cecily down, imploring the cancer patient on the phone to wait until her body recovered, but Cecily insisted. It didn't matter what fitness goals were met, Cecily argued, as long as *some* goals were met. Any goals. She needed to keep moving forward; it was the only way to keep a step ahead. Cecily didn't specify what she was attempting to outrun, but Jaclyn guessed easily enough. Depression. Inertia. The trappings of disease.

So Jaclyn consulted with Cecily's surgeon, a cantankerous man who told Jaclyn to make herself useful and put some meat on Cecily's bones, and Cecily's oncologist, a kind, quiet woman who seemed downright apologetic about her treatment regime. From that, Jaclyn put together a program that would keep Cecily mentally occupied with the activity of goal-setting, but more closely resembled a physical therapy regime than a fitness program for a client under 40. Jaclyn loved watching Cecily's strength, vigor and color return this month. The changes were subtle, slow, almost imperceptible to the eye, but apparent enough on the chart attached to Jaclyn's clipboard.

Jaclyn looked up when she heard Cecily re-enter the room. Cecily wore a furious look in her eye along with her pink boxing gloves. Jaclyn smiled to see Cecily—tiny, pale Cecily—looking so alive, so rushed with color.

"A great day to hit some bags, eh?" Jaclyn asked.

"Let's do it," Cecily answered.

The boxing gloves had been another Christmas/Hanukkah gift that year, these from Aunt Lil who had advised on the attached card, "Punch it out." How well Cecily's family knew her, or how much she resembled them, had seemed like a detail to Cecily in her busy daily life before cancer (or BC, as Suzie called it), something to mention on first dates. "I'm close with my family," she'd say, hoping to ferret out an enthusiastic "me too!" from her companion. But once surgery and chemotherapy had whittled her life down to its most basic elements (eating, sleeping, surviving physically and mentally), her family filled up all the cracks in the foundation, kept her standing. The fill was imperfect, rough, and uneven, but it held. Suzie never had that support. What Cait didn't understand, Cecily thought, was that Suzie's foundation, when exposed to the hurricane of cancer, simply crumbled. Before last night, Cecily believed Suzie didn't lack morals as much as she lacked mortar. Cecily hated being called a hero by the people who held her up, supported her. That's not a hero, that's a mascot, she thought. But to Cait it was black and white: Suzie was probably a liar and she died.

As Cecily threw turning roundhouse kicks, her assumptions about Suzie flipped over and over again like Cooper making seal-like progress across the kitchen floor. She kicked her way through Jaclyn's drills, circling the giant red Everlast bag again and again.

What did she know, for a fact, about Suzie's life? And sudden death? Only that Cecily was, and perhaps had always been, alone with her computer screen as a companion. Step, spin, WHAM. The tops of her shoelaces hit the bag harder than she thought she ever could. It was an irrational anger, maybe even a distraction to hold creeping grief at arm's length. But it was as real as the bruise that was developing on the top of her foot. Jaclyn raised her eyebrows.

Jaclyn thought to herself, look at Cecily go. Soon she could start training her prize client for a marathon, maybe a triathlon. *Local Trainer Helps Cancer Survivor Win Triathlon,* Jaclyn imagined the headline. Local athletes would seek out her counsel, and Jaclyn could drop her overweight, pre-diabetic, and terminally bored client roster in favor of serious athletes. Then her reputation would grow further, beyond the region. She could return to Canada triumphant, dragging Lionel, her husband, behind her as a prize. Whose job was more important now, Lionel? Jaclyn dreamed on as Cecily punched away.

Sent: November 21, 2010 at 4:58 p.m.
From: Cecily Murphy
To: Jack Schwinn

Thank you for the gorgeous flowers! I love them. They're the first thing I see when I wake up in the morning. And wake up again at 11 a.m. And wake up again at 1 p.m. :) Kidding, but I *am* napping like a 90-year-old lady, and it's pretty surreal. Thanks again!

Sent: November 21, 2010 at 5:09 p.m.
From: Suzie London
To: Cecily Murphy

BTW, you can see my original breasts on YouTube ... on the Jerry Springer show. To compare apples to peaches and all. My agent set up the Springer gig: me and Rothner and his friend Tiffany. The story line was two girls fighting over Rothner (you know my roommate, Rothner, is gay, right? We're talking massive suspension of disbelief here) and the whole show was hysterical: literally hysterical. Histrionics and hair pulling and me flashing my tits to show Rothner what he was missing. What did I say my name was? Oh, yeah: Tangerine Bletchley. Classic. And Rothner was Ray-Ray Davids. This was way back in the day, before cancer (BC) when I was going to focus on acting. My agent got me that show, a dog food commercial and a horror movie. It was actually the dog food commercial that changed my life. I started my celebrity dog-walking business after that. (Although the horror movie got me an IMDB page.)

Sent: November 21, 2010 at 5:15 p.m.
From: Cecily Murphy
To: Suzie London

Those Jerry Springer things are fake? I really don't watch those shows. I'll YouTube it. Not to see your original breasts, though! The reconstructed ones are lovely, and I'll have to trust you liked your original models as well. Which celebrities' dogs have you walked?!

Sent: November 21, 2010 at 5:17 p.m.
From: Suzie London
To: Cecily Murphy

OK, honey bunches of oats. All those shows are fake! All. Of. Them. Not dogs that belong to celebrities: the dogs themselves are celebrities. Working actors. I was just starting to figure out dogs were the only actors worth spending time with. I can't have dogs where I'm living now, so I have to get my dog time somehow.

Sent: November 21, 2010 at 5:32 p.m.
From: Jack Schwinn
To: Cecily Murphy

Are you up for visitors yet? I'm just up the road in Federal Hill—15 minutes away. You're probably not up for beer pong yet, but we can play Mexican Train or Scrabble.

Sent: November 21, 2010 at 5:35 p.m.
From: Cecily Murphy
To: Jane McCann and Michele Geraci

Hey! Jack wants to visit. Here's the deal. 1) I'm deformed, swollen and unbathed. 2) Seriously, I reek. 3) I'm not allowed to shower until 3-4 days from now. And 4) I refuse to ask anyone in my family to bathe me. 5) Well, OK, I could have Cait wash my hair, maybe. I haven't seen him in five years!

Sent: November 21, 2010 at 5:39 p.m.
From: Michele Geraci
To: Cecily Murphy and Jane McCann

So put him off a week. You're not deformed. You're on a convoluted road to having boobs like Scarlett Johansson. Remember? We talked about this. Eyes on the prize! The headlights at the end of the tunnel! Who is this guy again?

Sent: November 21, 2010 at 5:52 p.m.
From: Jane McCann
To: Michele Geraci and Cecily Murphy

I can come up and wash your dang hair. "Women are so much happier when you wash their hair." I was dying laughing when I read that. Your surgeon is over-the-top sexist!

Sent: November 21, 2010 at 5:55 p.m.
From: Cecily Murphy
To: Jane McCann and Michele Geraci

Actually, this is a bad idea. I still have tubes! Drains. Four of them, coming out my sides. (Sorry, Jane. Aren't you glad I didn't stay home and turn our house into a sterile recovery site for this?) I'm wiped out. Going to bed again.

Sent: November 21, 2010 at 5:57 p.m.
From: Michele Geraci
To: Cecily Murphy and Jane McCann

Wait, wait, now. Not necessarily a bad idea. Who is Jack?

Sent: November 21, 2010 at 6:00 p.m.
From: Jane McCann
To: Michele Geraci and Cecily Murphy

Refer her to Grateful Dead Appendicitis Incident (GDAI) of 2000.

Sent: November 21, 2010 at 6:02 p.m.
From: Michele Geraci
To: Cecily Murphy and Jane McCann

Oh no. It has an acronym? You're such nerds. Is it better than the Kenny Debacle (KD)? If there's medical gore in this, tone it down. I'm squeamish like Jane.

Sent: November 21, 2010 at 6:05 p.m.
From: Cecily Murphy
To: Jane McCann and Michele Geraci

Nap first. No, Percocet first. No. Eat first, then antibiotic, then Percocet, then empty drains, then I can nap. I swear, this is just like being at work: the schedule, the having to keep everything sterile. I'll tell you about GDAI tomorrow. G'night!

**Sent: November 21, 2010 at 6:17 p.m.
From: Cecily Murphy
To: Suzie London**

My armpit kills from the lymph node biopsy incision. Not my chest, although my chest aches all the time. But my armpit is far worse. It's just a terrible place for an incision. And I can't even reach to wash it. Not allowed to wash of course, but I took these alcohol swabs home from work. I've been using them around my bandages. I reek, my hair's greasy, and I can't get clean. And my arm isn't comfortable up or down or anywhere because of the armpit incision. Was it like that with you?

**Sent: November 21, 2010 at 6:58 p.m.
From: Suzie London
To: Cecily Murphy**

I felt the armpit incision for months. But it'll feel better by next week, and after that you can have the scar tissue lasered to break it up. Ask your doctor. I didn't do it. I was all doctored out by then and wanted to go home to LA. The chest area known as my first breasts: I lost all feeling there. Thank God. You'll be grateful for it too in the days and weeks to come. Don't lose sleep mourning that and don't look back. They'll start to feel like yours, eventually. It just takes time. Time is on your side. And drugs. The unnaturally preserved walking corpse of Keith Richards would never lie.

Chapter 6

May 22, 2011, 1:30 p.m.

Cecily's phone vibrated its way across the narrow wooden bench in the locker room and teetered on the edge just as she opened the shower curtain. She lunged for it, her dripping wet fingers circling it just before it succumbed to gravity. Then, embarrassed by her naked, restructured breasts in the empty locker room, she stepped back just as quickly into the shower. She toweled off the phone before toweling off the rest of her body, hoping the water hadn't seeped into its protective pink bulletproof-looking shell.

Three messages claimed responsibility for the phone's near miss with the locker room floor: two from high school friends she hadn't spoken with in years and one from Jack. Cecily correctly guessed her high school classmates were now buzzing with the news of Suzie London's nationally televised death. She skipped those messages after listening to the first three seconds of each: "Did you hear about ..." and "You are not going to ..." and listened to Jack's, which, to her surprise, also concerned Suzie. Not directly, however. Jack said he'd read something in the *Baltimore Sun* that morning and needed to speak with her. Jack sounded anxious, unhappy. Unlike Cait, Cecily noted to herself, whose Sharpie-on-newspaper method of news delivery was beginning to smack more and more of triumph the more she stewed it over.

"It is what it is," Cecily said aloud. She learned that phrase from watching *the Real Housewives of Beverly Hills*, a show the nurses followed religiously in the infusion center. Despite Cecily's defense against the show (a set of headphones and a playlist from Suzie), parts of it had seeped in to her consciousness as the meds dripped into her IV.

Cecily hopped out of the shower and dressed quickly, facing the wall to don her new 32C bra, whose large, unwieldy cups still surprised her, then slipped her t-shirt down over her head before letting the towel drop to the floor.

Cecily smeared some concealer under her eyes, then, realizing it was still several shades too dark, wiped it right off again. She performed this ritual, a litmus test, every day, hoping her skin would someday regain the healthier hue it had sported a year ago when she bought the concealer. This spring, shopping at Macy's with Jane, Cecily had asked the woman behind the cosmetics counter for the palest shade available, then hurried away after catching a glimpse of her blue-veined, translucent skin in the mirror. I'm so pale I'm actually disappearing, she thought.

Cecily dialed Jack's number as two older men with squash racquets held open the gym door for her. She nodded and smiled thanks, then noted how dismally muggy the air had become already in late spring. She and Jane had resolved to keep their air conditioner off until July; this seemed unlikely now. Jack picked up on the second ring.

"If it's Suzie London, I know about it," Cecily said, after their usual round of greetings, during which Cecily always introduced herself and Jack always answered, "I know." She realized her habit was old-fashioned, and reminded herself Jack had caller ID, just like everyone else in the Western world.

"I'm so sorry, Cecily," Jack said. "I'm sorry for your loss. I'm shocked."

Cecily opened the car door and dropped herself into the low seat of her Honda Civic. She sat, holding the phone to her ear, then asked, "Want to take a drive?"

Sent: November 22, 2010 at 11:15 a.m.
From: Cecily Murphy
To: Michele Geraci

I'm all propped up in bed and had my morning pills. Don't I sound like a nursing-home patient? My only plan for today is to manage my nausea (I hate Percocet but wow, do I need it) and re-watch Battlestar Galactica season 1 on YouTube. And feel guilty about avoiding my work emails. But persist in avoiding them anyway. After all, I am on "vacation." I was saving up all my flex-time to go backpacking through Italy or something (never been abroad), but maybe next year (if my medical bills aren't as bad as the legends say ...)

So, here's the story on Jack. He was in microbio with me at Cornell, but he was pre-med, and I was more interested in the ecological applications of micro. He was my lab partner junior year in Symbiotic Associations class. He made me laugh. Memorizing the characteristics of endosymbiotic bacteria could actually be fun with Jack. I realize that sounds unlikely. Well, even more unlikely: Jack developed a crush on me, asked me out, and I rejected him. Awkwardness ensued.

I didn't want to date Jack because I didn't want to date in my department. I was always the only woman in my microbio classes. The professors were all men, the TAs were all men, and my classmates were all men. I worked hard to be "one of the guys." Also, and this was less of a factor, I happened to have a real, live, actual boyfriend at the time. But it wasn't going well. (Something new, something different!) I had complained to Jack about the boyfriend several times, and Jack thought I didn't want to dump the boyfriend for him. That wasn't the issue, but I couldn't convince Jack of this. Anyway, it all came to a head at the Dead show, when my appendix went pyrotechnic.

This was junior year. I'm dating Michael, and he's a Deadhead and a fixer-upper, to say the least. Michael basks in the glow of my caretaking the same way his crop of marijuana plants flourishes under their 800-watt grow light. But let's be clear: it's my fault the relationship is doomed. Michael did not change from day 1 to day 100 of our relationship. I'm the one who wanted to change him. Anyway, there it is: an abstract on 20-year-olds in love: stupidity.

I didn't want to go to the Dead show in Syracuse. But Michael claimed I'd "understand everything" once I saw them in person, and to be with Michael was to make some sort of peace with a pantheon headed by Jerry Garcia.

We went in Mark Armbruster's van with five of Michael's friends. I was the only girlfriend attending—a point of contention for Michael's best friend, Phil. Phil pointedly ignored me during the ride, Ty doled out sheets of acid which I politely declined, and Michael smoked his dancing bear purple bong for the entire hour.

I wasn't much of a pot smoker, but I took a few hits off the bong because I thought it would help with the sharp, stabbing, abdominal pains I took for cramps.

I pretended to be fine, but I wasn't doing the best job of it, as I kept spontaneously doubling over and cussing, quietly. (Sometimes not so quietly.) Through the thickening haze of pot, Michael started to notice there was something wrong, and of course he offered more hits. Because he was nothing, if not hospitable. And a pothead. I pointed out to him that after 9,000 tokes I shouldn't be feeling any pain at all, and yet, the pain was getting worse.

Tyler asked me, "Want to lie down in the back?" And Phil rolled his eyes at me and sneered, "Got cramps?"

I truly, madly, deeply hated Phil. I hate it when "smart and rich" translates into "entitled and smarmy" in these frat boys. Cornell was filled with them. I mean, you can be smart and not be a douche; you can be rich and not be a douche. There's even a chance (albeit a smaller one) that you can be both and not be an entitled, superior douche. But Phil was the lord of the douches—the worst that Ithaca could spew onto its female population.

Anyway, Ty, who was in my biochem study group and a nice person, took my arm and half-led, half-carried me to the long backseat of the van, and arranged me into a lying down position while Michael and Phil argued in whispers. Phil hissed, "Why the f--- is she here, dude?" Michael tried to defend me, in his way. "Chill out, dude, I asked her to come." "Why?" Phil hissed.

I stopped listening, rolled over onto my side, and concentrated on taking deep breaths to calm myself. I've never been in labor, but I was there when my sister was, so I feel like I can say with reasonable confidence that it felt like I was giving birth to roughly 5,000 wasps.

We got to the show while I was sleeping/dozing/suffering quietly. The pain was getting worse, but it hadn't dawned on me yet that this was an emergency. By the time they finished tailgating and woke me up to go inside, I finally understood I was going to need medical attention. I told Michael, and he said, "OK, after the first set."

And then God spoke to me. He said, "Cecily, this is God speaking. You're dating a moron." And I told the voice in my head, "If I get out of this alive, I swear I'll never date a moron again. And I'll stop lying to my mom about wearing my mouth guard at night and getting my oil changed."

So Michael hoists me up to carry me, but I tell him no, I have to stay in a hunched over position. I'm secretly planning my escape to one of the medical tents around the stadium. Then Ty sees me, and God bless him, throws me headfirst over his shoulder to carry me inside. So, I'm kicking and screaming, and Ty drops me on my head in the gravel. At that point I think, wow, I'm going to die of God-knows-what, picking gravel out of my teeth in the parking lot of the Dead show. I honestly thought my end would be more dignified than this. At that point, I was guessing I'd perforated my intestine. Or had immaculately conceived a package of thumbtacks.

Anyway, somehow, with Ty apologizing and trying to carry me like a football under his arm, I manage to Quasimodo myself into the stadium, where I bolt into the nearest ladies room and collapse in a stall. I don't know how long I'm there, but I'm sweating through my clothes, and it feels like it takes me 40 minutes to find my phone in my purse. I dial 911.

Except I don't! I dial Jack's number!!! (Remember Jack? This is a story about Jack.) He's from Durham, North Carolina, and his area code is 919! So his number pops up and starts ringing. I think he's the 911 operator, so I tell him I need an ambulance, and he starts asking, "Where are you? What's going on?" Then I realize I'm on the phone with Jack, and I think, "Wow. This is rock bottom." So, I try to get off the phone with him, saying, "Oops, sorry, I meant to call 911," which of course only serves to alarm him more.

Meanwhile, this girl in a long, flowy skirt and long, flowy hair floats into the bathroom and calls, "Is there, like, a Cecily Murphy in here?" I squawk, "Yes! Over here!" She pushes open the stall door with one finger, looks down at me and says, "Man, your friends love you, man. They sent me in here to find you. They want you to come out of the bathroom." I say, "Uh, can you get help? I'm dying." She leaves the stall and comes back with a dripping wet, brown paper towel, which she proceeds to wipe all over my face. "Look, man. You're not dying, man. Just feel the cool water, man. Just feel the cool water." She's trying to talk me down from an acid trip! I'm going to die! On a bathroom floor in Syracuse! *This* is rock bottom!

Then Ty and Michael burst into the bathroom. Michael grabs my arms, and Ty grabs my feet, and they rush me out. The hippie chick follows us, carrying my purse. (She could have just robbed me, so whoever and wherever she is, I send thanks into the universe on her behalf, man.)

I yell at Michael to put me down, and because I'm crazed with pain, decide to use this opportunity to break up with him. I said something to the effect of, "After the first set?! You can shove your purple bong [redacted]!" But Michael, who's tripping on acid, simply stares at me. I don't even think he hears me. I tell Ty, "Get me to the medical tent, please!" He says, "No can do! Too many narcs there." So I ask, "Can you drive?" He nods. I say, "Drive me to a hospital."

He nods again, gets Armbruster's keys, then drags me out to the car. We must look like two zombies, one of which is howling. After he backs out, it occurs to me he's not divulging something. I say, "Wait, aren't you tripping?" And he says, "Only when I look in the rear view mirror."

I think, wow, *this* is rock bottom. I scream, "Stop the car!" when my phone rings. It's Jack, who's driving to Syracuse! He says he'll be there in 30 minutes, and I have to get to a medical tent and he'll meet me there. I tell Ty. Then I pass out.

I wake up several days (OK, hours) later in a hospital bed. My abdomen feels much better. In fact, I can't feel it at all. I'm so relieved I fall back asleep. But before I do, I look up and Jack is holding my hand. Then I wake up again and he's gone. The End.

Well, not the end. He was still my lab partner.

I thanked him profusely for helping me, but he just shook his head. I wanted to tell him, "Hey, I dumped Michael." But there would be no point. I was humiliated. Proven wrong. If things were awkward before, they were even worse after this.

And then, years later: Facebook. And, once again, I'm in a medical crisis and he is ... swooping in. And, once again, I'm finding the situation kind of embarrassing. I don't think he's hitting on me. I think we're just trying to hammer out a friendship. We had such a nice friendship, before the "feelings" mess. I'm happy to have it back, and can't believe we let it get screwed up so badly before. There. I've just made a resolve. I'm just happy to have the friendship back.

P.S. That hospital stay, the GDAI of 2000, was the first time I realized morphine makes me obsessed with stealing hospital socks. I don't know why. But it happened again this past week! I got five pairs in this haul, baby! Don't judge.

Sent: November 22, 2010 at 1:21 p.m.
From: Michele Geraci
To: Cecily Murphy

Wow. I had to wait for my lunch break, your email was so long. That is crazy. I was AT that Dead show! That was my senior year. I can't believe we met in massive DC but not in tiny Ithaca. I know we traveled in different circles, but it's still amazing. I knew Michael Baines! Not well ... he was cute, though. I also knew Mark Armbruster through Jane's sorority sister Lisa.

I'm trying to remember if I saw you in the ladies room! I saw a lot of crazy shit that day. I, too, was not a Dead fan but had friends who were, and I went to check it out. It's actually the reason I'll never be able to run for political office: too many pictures.

So. This Jack situation. I'll lay it out there. I'm getting vibes that you like him. Either because I'm psychic or because you spent three hours writing a story about him when you could have just answered me in five words: "I met him in college."

I read the comments on your Facebook posts. He posts on them every single day. So, my psychic powers tell me he might be interested in you as well. I agree, friendship is far easier and this isn't a great time to start a relationship, etc. BUT... just because it's not a great time now doesn't mean there won't be a great time in the future. And that future is nearer than it feels at this moment.

Keep your chin up, babe. I think that, with a little time, this whole Jack thing may have some potential.

BTW, I think it's Phil's fault your appendix burst. Like me, you have a severe allergic reaction to assholes.

Chapter 7

May 22, 2011, 2:15 p.m.

Cecily circled the block four times in Jack's Federal Hill neighborhood before abandoning the quest for a legal parking space. She pulled over, called Jack, and asked him to meet her outside his building.

In less than a minute, Jack emerged, squinting into the sun and pulling sunglasses out of the pocket of his plaid, button-down shirt. Those shirts were becoming trendy again, but Cecily knew Jack had his long before they'd come back in style. He'd become an inadvertent *fashionisto*, and she made a mental note to warn him about this. As he opened Cecily's passenger door, she became keenly aware of her car's week-long accumulation of trash, and quickly fired three coffee cups into the back seat over her shoulders.

Jack handed her an empty Starbucks cup he picked up off the seat. "Missed one," he said.

"I know. I need rehab."

"Wow."

"Jane is worse than I am. I'm actually down to two cups a day," Cecily said defensively.

"No, I mean, wow, your color, your face. You look so much more vibrant than you did even a week ago. You're getting healthy. You look—" Jack stopped and cleared his throat. "Where to?"

"Pine Hill."

****

Cecily and Jack stopped at a supermarket to pick up flowers, and Cecily took her time choosing them. Traditional white lilies seemed wrong for Suzie. Sunflowers seemed wrong for the occasion. Roses, too formal. Then, behind a giant display of spring-themed bouquets, Cecily noticed a plant called "Blazing Star." The long, purple flower stalks reminded Cecily of Beaker from the Muppets.

"Is that it?" Jack asked her.

"That's it," Cecily said, picking it up and inspecting it.

They took Route 29 to Pine Hill. Jack offered to drive, but Cecily told him she couldn't navigate. When she was young enough to live there, she just knew where to go by osmosis, not street names.

Cecily wanted to put flowers at Suzie's house, the house where Suzie grew up. This seemed important to do first. After, she could start the formidable task of trying to figure out what happened.

Functioning on one or two hours of sleep, Cecily understood she wasn't going to solve anything today. Today was a day to acknowledge Suzie, to visit the house where she grew up and to absorb its indisputable reality.

Cecily's car seemed to drive itself back to her first home, pulling up to a stop in front of the curb of her old brick house. She was annoyed to find the brick had been painted white in her absence. The once-skinny sycamore trees with their peeling bark now towered over the sidewalk on the narrow strip of meticulously edged grass between sidewalk and street.

"These sycamore trees were planted too close together 30 or 40 years ago. Now, they're blocking out each other's sun. They'll get powdery mildew if they don't prune them back. And who paints brick? When I grew up here, the house was red brick. It looks ridiculous white."

Jack nodded and patted Cecily's hand. "Painting brick is wrong," he agreed. He didn't have a strong opinion on this, but agreeing with Cecily seemed the better choice.

"Is this a weird thing to do?" Cecily stared ahead, not wanting to show Jack the tears in her eyes.

"Cecily," he said. "It's not weird. Come here." He unbuckled his seatbelt and leaned over to pull her into a hug. Cecily buried her face into his soft, pilled shirt. He smelled wonderful, like Downy fabric softener and coffee and cinnamon Tic Tacs. She smiled into his shirt, in spite of herself. Oh boy, am I screwed, she thought. She pulled back and looked up at him.

"You're just agreeing with me because I'm upset," Cecily wiped the edges of her eyes with her pinky, careful to not smudge her light mascara. Cecily used it to exaggerate the presence of the seven eyelashes that remained after chemo, but it never seemed to work.

"This is weird. But I don't know what else to do. She's in California. I'm in Maryland."

"It's not weird," Jack insisted. Cecily raised her (12) eyebrow hairs at him until he conceded. "It's a little weird but only because you don't know for sure who lives in this house now."

"I just have a feeling it's someone in her family. Their aunt took the house when they moved, but it stayed empty for a while. If it stayed in the London family, they'll know someone was thinking about them. If it's not ... well, I suppose I'll start divorce proceedings in that house. 'Hey, who's giving you flowers?!' 'Well, Rick, I didn't want to tell you this ...' This is probably insane, but I don't know what else to do."

"I don't think unexpected flowers ever hurt anyone. And you need to do it, so ...," Jack opened the car door. "Let's do it."

"First, I want you to see her," Cecily said. "I want to say a few things to her bedroom window before I put the flowers down. I want you to know who she is and what she looks like. Looked like."

Cecily pulled her laptop out of her gym bag and pulled up Facebook. She typed in Suzie's name. Suzie's profile picture popped up on her page. It was one of Cecily's favorites: Suzie smiling with her face up to the sun on the beach. Cecily wondered if Jace had taken it.

"She's beautiful, yes?" Cecily asked Jack, holding the laptop under his nose.

"Yes ..."

"But ..." Cecily prompted.

"She's got that look. Rough. Like she's had one hell of a life," Jack said. "Maybe it's the empty whiskey bottle in her hand."

"I know. I see it too. It's not the whiskey though. What is it?"

"Her face," They both answered in unison.

"Like life has been a battle," Cecily said.

"Like she's had a hangover for a year and a half," Jack observed.

Cecily abruptly snapped the laptop shut. "Let's just do this."

She walked around to the back of the car, and carefully lifted the top-heavy plant out of the seat where Eileigh had sat that morning. She leaned down and wiped the dirt off the seat. When she turned back around, she saw Brad London—an older, grown-up version of the Brad London she remembered—step out of the old metal storm door and onto the narrow top step of the entrance to his family's house.

This, she hadn't planned for.

Posted November 27, 2010 at 6:55 a.m.
Cecily Murphy

Is hearing a lot of, "Oh, I feel stupid talking about this stuff to you when you're dealing with all this." 1st, You, friend, are not obligated to talk about my cancer. It's boring & it makes my cancer feel special. 2nd, tell me about your stupid problems already! I know you want to bitch about them! I want to bitch about them with you! Permission to speak freely: granted.

November 28, 2010, 10:30 a.m.

In the kitchen of Dahlia and Jim Murphy's home, tucked into a wooded cul-de-sac in Columbia, two women stared down Jim Murphy as he held a forkful of pumpkin pie aloft in front of his open mouth. As the fork neared his mouth, the women glared harder.

The Truth About Suzie

"What?" he finally asked, surrendering and dropping the fork back onto his plate. "What is it?"

His daughter Cait spoke first, as always. "You got Cecily a gift certificate for a personal trainer for Christmas? Are you seriously out of your mind?"

Dahlia shook her head reprovingly and turned back to washing dishes at the sink.

"What? It's the perfect holiday gift," Jim argued. He couldn't believe the one year he started his Christmas shopping four weeks early, he was taking grief over the gift.

"She's going into CHEMO," Cait spat out over her crossed arms.

"That's what makes it perfect." Jim concluded his argument, and picked up his fork again.

Cait glared again, but Jim, believing he'd successfully defended his position, was not going to be diverted from his pie and continued eating.

As he ate, Cait nagged and berated and cajoled, throwing her hands up in exasperation and pointing her finger at him in aggravation. How Jim had survived the teenaged years with two daughters like this, he would never know.

When he finished his last bite of piecrust, he placed his fork on his plate, crossed his arms on the table, and looked at his daughter.

"Caitlyn," he cleared his throat. "Please believe I've thought this through. Are you familiar with your sister?" He held his hand up to his chin. "About yea tall, as beautiful as you and your mother, and as stubborn as you and your mother combined?"

Dahlia turned around from the sink again to help Cait glare at this.

Jim continued, "Cecily is self-disciplined, competitive, ferociously independent and thrives on goals. This is the best thing for her. She's about to have her feet swept out from under her, and this will give her something small to hang on to. She loves to measure progress. Does anyone else get these emails from her with the Excel spreadsheets? I know you do. You must."

Dahlia stopped glaring and leaned on the counter, still holding and now contemplating her kitchen sponge. "It's control," she said, nodding. "It's control over her body when she'll have none—when she has none."

Jim stood up and walked around the table to put his arm around his wife. Dahlia leaned her head gratefully into him until Jim handed her his dirty pie plate. She sighed.

Dahlia looked up, out the glass sliding doors that led to the backyard, and Jim followed her gaze. Jimmy, their eldest son, emerged from the bike trail that ran behind their house, holding something resembling a heavy, brown, furry pillowcase in his arms.

Dahlia asked: "Is Jimmy holding ... a cat?"

****

The doorbell rang, and upstairs in her room, Cecily didn't hear it.

At her insistence, Cecily's childhood bedroom stood relatively undisturbed for the past ten years. A dual purpose crept in, however, as Dahlia's sewing projects grew more ambitious and elaborate. One corner of Cecily's room was heaped with yards of fabric, which Dahlia had meant to sort for months. An old Singer sewing machine, which Dahlia sometimes preferred to her newer model, sat on Cecily's desk. The sewing machine reminded Cecily she was imposing on her parents' space, and as much as she refused to relinquish owners' rights to this room, her family's house was no longer really hers.

A poster of Michael Stipe, seeming to understand it was time to let go of the wall, peeled away slowly. Michael's eyebrows furrowed with the melancholy and earnestness of the nineties.

Cecily's furniture was her grandmother's old bedroom set, with a heavily burnished walnut four-poster bed and a dresser with two cabinets above the drawers that still smelled of the Strawberry

Cheesecake dolls Cecily stored in them as a child. Cecily loved the vanity the most—the creaky upholstered bench that faced the floor-length mirror. The mirror was so old it couldn't be cleaned anymore. Foggy spots and dark patches could be rubbed for hours with Windex and newspaper to no appreciable effect. Cecily used to believe the enduring foggy spot in the upper left-hand corner was shaped like her grandmother's profile. A pragmatist and lifelong devotee to the scientific method, she occasionally allowed herself a few small superstitions: a lucky penny in her pocket, a piece of her grandmother's spirit frozen in glass. She would touch the glass of the mirror and think of her grandmother, who had battled breast cancer for five years before succumbing the year Cecily was born.

Cecily sat at the bench, trying to brush out her long, stringy wet hair without lifting her arm too much. Her doctor threatened to send her to physical therapy if she didn't lift her arms more. She countered that if he'd stop stabbing her with the pointy objects, draining incision sites, and filling the tissue expanders, she'd feel more inclined to cooperate.

Although Cait was right downstairs, Cecily had rejected her offer to help brush Cecily's hair after washing it. Constantly needing help was wearisome, and Cait's inclination to help far outmeasured Cecily's inclination to accept help, causing friction along the well-worn groove of their dynamic. Cecily had almost felt guilty, and tired enough, to let Cait de-tangle the wet, scraggly pieces that stuck to her cheeks and forehead. Almost. Cecily lowered her bathrobed arms again to rest and stared forelornly in the mirror, once again feeling like she had been dropped into the body of an elderly woman. She was gearing up her next self-pep talk when her mother sailed in with a pile of fresh sheets from the dryer, and caught the look on Cecily's face in the mirror. Cecily's face transformed instantly. Smile! She ordered herself. Quickly! And not so fake!

"Thanks, Mom," she said, in what she hoped was a bright voice. But Dahlia had seen her daughter's countenance, and her eyes had instinctively filled with tears. She forced a smile back at her daughter.

"Your friend Jack is downstairs," she said.

"Oh," Cecily was alarmed. "He's early." She looked at the clock: 11:00 a.m. He wasn't early. She'd taken an hour to limp along this far in her morning routine. The clock in her room melded in her imagination to the timer posted on the damp, echoing wall at swim meets. As a child, she'd look up—her astigmatic, chlorine-rinsed eyes squinting to focus on the numbers, guessing her results with reasonable accuracy the second before she actually read them. She knew she was having a not-so-great day before the clock confirmed this. When she was younger, she'd had no problem processing her athletic strengths and weaknesses into "teachable moments," as her coach Mysti dubbed them. Pain, she had recently found, was the game changer. On days that her armpit stung and chest ached, she forgave herself and the world nothing. As much as she tried to remain conscious of this and resist the downward pull of the pain, she hadn't made much headway against it today.

"Thanks, Mom. Tell him I'll be down in a minute and apologize for my lateness. So rude," she added, shaking her head.

"I'm sure he understands, honey," Dahlia said. "It's not a contest, you know."

"What's not a contest?" Cecily countered, but she knew exactly what her mother had meant and was just arguing.

Dahlia pressed her lips together in a tight smile and nodded at Cecily. "Just get dressed," she added and closed the door behind her.

"Thanks, Mom," Cecily mouthed to the door. "Because I'd forget if you didn't tell me." Wow, she thought, I'm regressing into my teenaged self. I need to get out of here and get my head together. She felt a surge of relief that Jack had arrived just in time to oblige this need—although she had no idea where he was taking her. That was fine. Anywhere would suffice.

****

Jack clicked the car doors unlocked, then ran around to the passenger-side door to open it for Cecily.

"Thanks," she smirked at him. "I'm not an invalid." Her wet hair, partially covered by her knit Viking hat, threatened to form icicle spears in the subfreezing air.

"Sheesh, just trying to be a gentleman. Cut a Southern boy a break." Jack smiled as he said it, teasing her.

"You're going to patronize me and call it Southern charm?"

"Just try not to slip, Great Aunt Cecily," Jack replied in an exaggerated southern twang, holding her elbow and guiding her into the seat before shutting the door.

Cecily laughed as he ran around to the other side and lowered himself into the bucket seat of his old Toyota.

Recognition hit her. "This is the same car you had in college! Holy OCD, Jack, it's meticulously preserved! Look at this!" She ran a mittened hand across the dashboard. "Not a single speck of dust."

Jack reached his arm back behind her seat as he backed out of the driveway. "I had it detailed yesterday," he said.

"For my sake?" Cecily asked, and hoped he said yes.

"Well, you can't be exposed to germs in your condition. Seriously, Chang is usually my passenger and he's a pig. It's disgusting. You look fantastic, by the way."

Cecily wasn't expecting a compliment in that exchange and was awkward fielding them even when prepared. "Thanks. I don't," she said, looking out the window.

"Well I know you probably don't feel fantastic, but I wanted you to know it doesn't show," Jack explained.

"Where are we going, by the way?" Cecily asked, realizing she still wasn't aware of their plan.

"Well, first, I'm going to get you some coffee at this place close to here that had really great coffee reviews online—"

"Arabica?" Cecily interrupted.

"Yes! You said your dad's coffee-making skills were sub-par, so I thought we'd get you nice and properly caffeinated, and then—" he paused. "Well, this is probably a bad idea."

"What? No, I love your bad ideas! What?"

"I don't know. I just met your sister today and she was pretty adamant about not tiring you out," Jack said. "I don't want to start off by antagonizing your family."

Cecily rolled her eyes. "Poor, tired, frail Cecily," she lamented, positioning her hand melodramatically over her forehead. She really was tired, but she'd never let on to Jack. "They're overprotective. And crazy. Ignore them."

Jack smiled. "Well, it's a drive, but you were saying that with everything going on you felt like you missed fall, and how you loved going out to see the leaves—"

Cecily gasped. "We're going to Catoctin! Really?"

"Only if you're up for it. And most of the leaves are probably gone now, but I looked it up online and it still looks like a nice drive."

"Oh! There's the turn," Cecily pointed to a narrow drive that broke up a row of hedges. "Columbia's so weird. You can't see any business signs from the road. This Arabica is known as 'Arachica.' The other one, on Nottingham Way, is known as 'Arafreaka.' Better people watching."

"Would you rather go there?" Jack looked like he was going to reverse out of the parking spot he'd just found.

"No, no! That's OK, I was just ... talking," Cecily mentally slapped herself. Stop being awkward! "And I love the idea of going to Catoctin. That's probably an hour drive from here though. Maybe more. Are you sure you have the time?"

"We have all day," he said. "I do, I mean. If you want to go. You don't have to—"

"Yes," Cecily said. "I really want to." She did. A smile flickered to life. She felt lighter than she had all morning. Anticipation, she noted to herself. I haven't anticipated anything but doctor visits lately. She allowed herself to enjoy the feeling, tempered as it was by the weight in her chest.

They took their coffees to go. After a brief argument over who would pay, the teenaged barista/cashier suggested a card-off: the person who could toss their card directly into a small, wire cookie basket across the counter won. Cecily's aim was off, but Jack's card floated into the basket effortlessly, underhand with a flick of the wrist.

The cashier shook his head at Cecily. "Sorry. It wasn't even a contest," he said.

"Yeah, but he had all those years on the Frisbee Golf team."

"It's all in the wrist," Jack explained. "That was a putt. Don't say I never taught you anything new. Thank you, sir," he added to the cashier.

"One thing I'm learning is when you have," Cecily made the letter "c" with her hand, "people trip over themselves to buy everything for you. This could turn into a total racket for me."

"Yeah, lucky you. Free coffee and 40 grand in medical bills."

"Right? Well, I am lucky. I have health insurance and a family that's raring to help me out. Some people don't have either." Cecily thought about Suzie. "And I'm starting to do OK now. For working in nonprofit, it's not bad. I could never imagine being able to afford living without a roommate though, not in DC. You're lucky; you have your own place."

"Well, that's the tradeoff. Working for a defense contractor, I get a nice salary, but instead of going to work every day to save the Chesapeake Bay, I'm using my knowledge of microorganisms to build weapons."

"Weird that both our companies rely exclusively on government funding for survival. Life versus death. Their priorities couldn't be more clear. In our office, we have to fight tooth and nail for every penny to keep our water drinkable and safe, but the government simply can't pour enough money into your ... what are you making there? Flesh-eating robots?"

Jack nodded. "Yes. Well, mutant, flesh-eating robots. Oops, shouldn't have told you that."

"Now you have to kill me? You'd lose that match, Frisbee boy."

"I have no doubt that anyone who made the mistake of underestimating you would wake up in a pile of their own teeth."

"Don't forget it," Cecily nodded over her mocha. She let the steam from the tiny sip-hole in her cup warm her nose. "Thanks for the coffee," she said. "And for the adventure. I think I needed this."

"It's my pleasure," said Jack cordially, with enough formality in his voice for Cecily to suspect he was overcompensating. In spite of herself, she smiled.

Posted November 29, 2010 at 6:16 a.m.
Cecily Murphy

Had an amazing weekend. **Suzie London**, it was on par with getting pulled under the fence at Pine Hill pool ... sneaking in the joy.

Posted November 29, 2010 at 9:39 p.m.
Cecily Murphy

Surgeon appointment = hell. I asked, "Why do you have to open that drawer of sharp pointy things every time I come in?" "Squeamish?" he asked. I said, "Depends on where the pointy things are going today and how long they are staying there." He just nodded. Yep. It's a doozy. Today will be what I refer to as a Two Pill-er.

Posted December 2, 2010 at 8:30 a.m.
Cecily Murphy

Dr. Sharp Pointy Objects, wielding sharp thing: "How's Jimmy?"
Me: "He's driving my mom crazy. He found a cat in the yard, brought it inside, and decided my parents were going to spay and adopt it."
Dr. SPO, positioning sharp thing: "Why'd he do that?"
Me: "Why do men do anything?"
Dr. SPO: (stabs me)

Sent: December 2, 2010 at 8:34 a.m.
From: Jack Schwinn
To: Cecily Murphy

Just want you to know I've alerted the Hypocrisy Police to the sexist comment in your update today. In SA lab, nobody could even point out your gender without getting verbally lashed. Are you back in your apartment or still at your parents'? I was confused by your updates/emails this week.

Sent: December 2, 2010 at 8:52 a.m.
From: Cecily Murphy
To: Jack Schwinn

I've been home, to my house with Jane, but not really living there yet, at my parents' insistence. Two reasons: 1) Dr. Sharp Pointy Objects has a Columbia office, and it's easier to get there from my parents' than it is to get to GW from my house. And 2) they're overprotective. It's funny. They're from Baltimore and were raised to think DC is this hotbed of crime and mayhem, this rough place where "sick" people shouldn't be. Irony, right? People from the number one murder capital of the world are scared that I live in the number two murder capital of the world. Oh, and with another "defenseless" girl! With no dog! With no expensive security system! Now, granted, they're in the suburbs of Columbia now, so yes, their place is in a less rough neighborhood than mine, but what kills me is that I'm in a decent neighborhood! Well, except for the possible hookers next door. But aside from Fantasia and Charlene and their loud porch parties, I essentially live in the suburbs too. But in my suburbs, you can walk to the Metro, walk to Whole Foods, and walk to any restaurant you could ever want, including the best Mexican restaurant in DC, Guapo's, home of "surgical margaritas" (margaritas so strong you can perform surgery on yourself after two).

You should come down sometime and see my house. Plus, to save my reputation, I need a Scrabble rematch. I'm still shame spiraling after my performance last week. Your 50-

point "pain pill handicap" was too generous and still didn't save my pitiful score. That was the most fun I've had in weeks—since I've been diagnosed.

Sent: December 2, 2010 at 9:15 a.m.
From: Jack Schwinn
To: Cecily Murphy

I actually was writing to ask you about that. I wanted to know when we could get together again. This weekend, maybe?

Sent: December 2, 2010 at 9:16 a.m.
From: Cecily Murphy
To: Jack Schwinn

So ... not just to call me a sexist?

Sent: December 2, 2010 at 9:17 a.m.
From: Jack Schwinn
To: Cecily Murphy

Well, that. And to get a date on the calendar with a sexist.

Sent: December 2, 2010 at 6:00 p.m.
From: Suzie London
To: Cecily Murphy

The scaly she-dragon known as my oncologist slithered out of her lair, inspected my burned, radiated flesh, her red eyes glowing ever redder as they sucked the color out of my cheeks, her breath in rhythmic hisses, like a child's pool toy deflating. She smiled, flames licking her lips. "Chemo next." Two words. She snapped shut the 3-inch binder with my name down the spine: Lucky London. "Get your bloodwork." Then she swept out, her tail flicking once before the door slammed. Leaving me naked, burned, scarred and barren. Yes, I said BARREN, bitches. The nurse asked me: "Are you OK? Are you going to puke or something? You don't look well." And I said: "Bitch, I am one Aimee Mann song away from a complete nervous breakdown."

But I'll take my Dragon Lady any day over Dr. Sharp Pointy Objects over there on the East Coast. He sounds delightful.

**Sent: December 2, 2010 at 7:02 p.m.
From: Cecily Murphy
To: Suzie London**

Dragon Lady and Dr. Sharp Pointy Objects make quite a pair, don't they? So: choices. You're always telling me we have choices. I want you to go back in there demanding answers, or, failing that, at least some statistics. (They sure are good at handing out statistics when you ask for answers, aren't they?)

Why do they want to do chemo? Are they going after something specific or is this just a prescribed treatment protocol? A "just-in-case-we-didn't-get-everything" chemo, like my chemo is apparently going to be? Sit the dragon down, look her in her red eyes, and demand answers. I wish I were on the West Coast, so I could go with you.

**Sent: December 2, 2010 at 7:15 p.m.
From: Suzie London
To: Cecily Murphy**

No, I agree. I made my choices when I read about your cancer. I'm fighting. Now it's the choice's turn to make me. Goldschlager opens worlds in my painting. Then I look at the mess on the living room floor and think Rothner's gonna scream like the slutty teen in a horror movie. I want a career like Tori Spelling. Not the reality show, but the Lifetime Movies. What would your Lifetime Movie be called? Mine would be "Lady Sings the Blues (And Regrets Her Tattoos.)" Or "Not Without My Whiskey: The Suzie London Story." Or "London Calling: Uh Oh. Is She Calling for Bail $?"

Sent: December 2, 2010 at 7:30 p.m.
From: Cecily Murphy
To: Suzie London

Those are awesome! Mine would be: "Cecily Murphy: A Life Too Boring To Be Documented by Lifetime as She Did Not Murder Her Husband, Run A Prostitution Ring Out of Her Home, Or Battle Iranian Terrorists To Save Her Child."

Sent: December 2, 2010 at 7:35 p.m.
From: Suzie London
To: Cecily Murphy

No, no! Yours would be: "Battle Royale: Breast Cancer vs. Redheaded Fury." Sponsored by L'Oreal "don't try this at home" Home Hair Color. You know what? I've always envied your red hair. Do you know that in Hollywood, on your head shots, you're supposed to use the word auburn instead of red? I took a class.

Sent: December 2, 2010 at 7:40 p.m.
From: Cecily Murphy
To: Suzie London

A head shot class? Again, your life is far more Lifetime-worthy than mine. I like my movie title though! Again, why do you think they want chemo for you? Preventative or active? How long? When does it start?

Sent: December 2, 2010 at 7:43 p.m.
From: Suzie London
To: Cecily Murphy

Only the Dragon Lady knows … bwahaha! Not really. I just wasn't up for sitting down in her office today with my hands folded in my lap professionally discussing the destruction of my body organs as though discussing little Peter's behavior problems at boarding school. Nope. I fled. I'll ask questions tomorrow, digest today. Chemo is not good for digesting. I'll remind Rothner of that when he gets home. I'll say: yeah, there's a mess in the living room, but you won't have me to yell at anymore because I'm going to be parked toilet-side for many months to come. But I might not tell him any of that. He's the landlord, and I don't want to be shipped out again, so maybe I'll just shut up and try and wash the oil paint out of the curtains before he gets home.

**Sent: December 2, 2010 at 7:47 p.m.
From: Cecily Murphy
To: Suzie London**

OMG! Yeah, you'd better! My roommate's a bit of a slob herself, and although she's never gotten oil paint on the curtains, it drives me mad when she leaves her socks on various tables. I tell her: you know what else goes on tables? Food. Maybe now I'll just be glad she doesn't paint …

**Posted December 7, 2010 at 6:32 a.m.
Cecily Murphy**

My surgeon is awesome at returning emails. Freedom to work out has been granted! Going to gym to walk slowly on elliptical. Very excited. Loaded the mix CD **Suzie London** sent me onto my iPod. I love a mix tape. This one is especially excellent and random. It was a little risky to include a Smiths song on a mix called "Kickass" but I think the risk worked out.

**Posted December 10, 2010 at 3:07 p.m.
Cecily Murphy**

The Cancer Card: what's in your wallet? With Cancer Card, you earn points toward getting out of any obligation! Don't want to take cat to the vet? Swipe! Don't want to cook for Chrismakkuh dinner? Swipe! Forget deadlines, birthdays? Swipe! Prone to abuse, Cancer Card may be revoked by family/friends at any time. Might be getting close …

Sent: December 10, 2010 at 9:23 p.m.
From: Suzie London
To: Cecily Murphy

You haven't maxed out your Cancer Card till you've used it to 1) get a job interview with Drew Barrymore's production company or 2) meet Barry Manilow in Vegas. Now that was shameless. (Worth it.) Also, free drinks for years. I should have declared that sucker on my tax returns as my primary income in 2006. Like all magic, however, it's deceptive. Read the fine print. Mine is in semi-retirement. I learned some interesting lessons using it though. Don't cut it up just yet. It's your Get Out of Jail Free Card. Sometimes literally.

The real fun begins when you get your wigs. Not only do you get to be a new person every day, but you can freak out random strangers by ripping off your wig and cackling. I can do chemo again. I can do this. When we're done, we're going on a Richard Simmons cruise. Cruise to lose our baggage! I'll pick out our wigs: beehives and cat sunglasses. When we walk, we'll swish. Boys will look, but we'll shove them in the pool if they try to talk to us. I can do this.

Chapter 8

May 22, 2011, 3:00 p.m.

Cecily pivoted on her foot, and lowered her forehead into her hand as though shielding her eyes from the sun. "I did not want to run into Brad today," she whispered toward the sidewalk. "I'm too ... discombobulated. Plus, if he says it's real, it's real." Jack placed his hands on her shoulders lightly, then, meeting no resistance, let his arms drop around her side. They stood on the sidewalk hugging loosely, Cecily holding the plant awkwardly to the side when Brad recognized Cecily Murphy's telltale Murphy hair, perhaps because he saw it in the context of the habitat in which he once knew it.

"Cait Murphy?" his voice boomed out. A belly that made him look like he was shoplifting a bowling ball stuck out over his faded jeans and a gray beard covered half his face. Despite these changes, Brad's face, hidden as it was under whiskers and eyebrows, looked remarkably similar to his 20-years-younger self. Cecily's mind conjured an image of Brad chasing Jimmy and Cait, running through the backyard on a summer evening playing kick the can.

Cecily inhaled and turned back around to face him. Brad took two slow steps down the front walk. "Or ... Cecily Murphy," Brad called again, squinting.

"Hi," Cecily waved and gestured awkwardly with her plant. "Cecily, Cait and Jimmy's younger sister. I heard about your sister?" She posed it as a question.

Jack hooked his arm into Cecily's and led her toward the London house. Cecily scuffled along as though her legs hadn't quite thawed from a stint in a sub-zero freezer. Brad opened his arms to envelop Cecily in a full-contact hug that lasted several seconds longer than she anticipated. Yes, her presence had been interpreted as a condolence call, and thus, Suzie was actually dead. Cecily dropped the plant on Brad's foot, half by accident, half to make him release her from his massive torso.

"It's so good to see you," Brad said warmly. "Thanks for coming. Please, let me help you with this," he leaned down to pick up the plant, whose stems now lurched unhappily to the side. "I wish it was under better circumstances. I assume you saw our program last night."

"I read about it in the paper. I was shocked."

"We're sorry for your loss," Jack said, and Cecily was grateful for this interjection, as social graces were failing her.

"Please, come inside, sit down," Brad gestured for them to follow.

Cecily's "OK" was automatic, flat, and prompted a full-body shudder of shock. A desperate voice in her head whispered, "Run!" She gave Jack a worried side-eye, but Jack nodded at her. As they followed Brad up the short, stone path leading to the Londons' two-story, brick-box house, Cecily saw a pair of white roller skates lying in the grass. She stopped short. Not Suzie's, of course. She shook her head again, hard.

Cecily tried to bring to mind what it would feel like to revisit this, their childhood stomping ground, if she had not reconnected with Suzie in the past eight months. She probably wouldn't remember much, just note that their houses seemed smaller than she remembered. She'd probably think it was a sad story, in a "this-is-a-sad-comment-on-problems-in-our-society" way, the way she felt when she read about those mothers who went missing, and it turned out the husbands did it. (It was always the husbands.) She'd have probably watched it unfold on Dr. Dick last night, called a few childhood friends to say, "Hey, you aren't going to believe—" and shaken her head about the tragic, multi-generational waste of addiction.

The Truth About Suzie

What had happened here, in this house, while Cecily sat in the sandbox, daydreaming, humming, and digging for treasure? She looked up at Suzie's bedroom window, which still sported white eyelet curtains, blowing against the screen. The cicadas sang her welcome in the box hedges, which encircled the house unchecked, reaching around and halfway up the first floor windows.

Brad held the screen door open for Cecily and Jack, who squeezed past his belly into Suzie's childhood living room. Some of the furniture pieces remained: the bric-a-brac cabinet and the wooden, smooth-armed rocking chair. But the wallpaper and carpeting had been replaced with a light, ivy-colored paint and gleaming wood floors. Cecily smelled the sharp aroma of fresh flowers tempered with an undertone of wet dog.

Cecily could see into the dining room where the table was filled with flower arrangements and cards, all pastel in cream, white, yellow, pink and blue.

"Wendie!" Brad called. "We have visitors!" He motioned for Cecily and Jack to sit on a massive and impossibly fluffy-looking floral print couch.

"I'm Jack, by the way, sorry," Jack stuck out his hand, which Brad grabbed and pumped. Cecily murmured an apology for neglecting the introductions.

"Jack, I'm Brad London," he said. "Are you Cecily's fella?"

"Yes," Jack said, and his dimples appeared, though his mouth was closed and he appeared to be forcing himself not to smile in the face of the grieving. Cecily smirked. Her thighs sank three inches into the deep cushions of the couch, a sensation that brought to mind sitting on a marshmallow.

"Cecily, you're wearing your hair very short," Brad noted the obvious, circling around the question he wanted to ask. "Please forgive me for asking a personal question but—"

Too late, Cecily thought. "Yes," she blurted. "I'm growing it out from chemo. I never wear my wigs anymore. It's too hot out," Cecily said, thinking: and just like Suzie told me I would, I grew to hate the wigs with the fire of a thousand suns.

"I know Suzie had breast cancer too. That's how we reconnected, on Facebook."

"Ah," Brad said. "Facebook. Technology's amazing, isn't it? Growing up you think you're the only person in the world with problems, then you get on the Internet and you see everyone's got the same problems as you."

The back door opened, and a dog's paws scratched the floor frantically. A golden retriever burst through the dining room into the living room like a drooling, crotch-seeking missile. The dog buried his nose first in Jack's pants, then Cecily's, then finally settled into Brad's.

A woman's voice called out, "Hello?" Brad shoved the dog aside and answered, "Wendie! Our old neighbor is here. Cecily Murphy. Turns out she had breast cancer just like Suzie."

Just like Suzie. There it was. Cecily sat straight up, or rather tried to get enough leverage in the couch cushions to lean forward. Jack was sprawled back against the cushion, looking engulfed and uncomfortable. Just like Suzie, Cecily thought, eyes wide and hopeful.

Posted December 11, 2010 at 11:33 a.m.
Cecily Murphy

Called Dr. SPO about info I read on Internet this morning. Was told: "Stop reading Internet." Countered: "It's everywhere. With Elizabeth Edwards dying, there's no avoiding it." Survival rate of triple negative breast cancer is 75%. "Who are the 25% who die?" I ask. "Women who read the Internet," he said. "Look, if I knew the answer to that, I'd be polishing my Nobel Prize."

Sent: December 11, 2010 at 11:52 a.m.
From: Suzie London
To: Cecily Murphy

She wasn't triple negative like us. Not that it makes her any less dead. But don't compare.

Sent: December 11, 2010 at 11:56 a.m.
From: Cecily Murphy
To: Suzie London

So you're triple negative too? I've been wondering.

Sent: December 11, 2010 at 12:02 p.m.
From: Suzie London
To: Cecily Murphy

No! Don't compare! Or read the stupid statistics! Don't feed the statistics. Starve them of meaning. To paraphrase you: don't make the statistics feel special. Live in your moment. Your journey.

Sent: December 11, 2010 at 1:06 p.m.
From: Cecily Murphy
To: Suzie London

OK, OK! I promise! I'm normally pretty good about avoiding that stuff online, but I've been Googling quite a bit before finally meeting my oncologist tomorrow. It's so weird that it's so long before you meet the oncologist. She's like the wizard, behind the curtain this whole time.

Sent: December 11, 2010 at 2:02 p.m.
From: Suzie London
To: Cecily Murphy

Ask for ticket out of Oz. One way. Brain, heart & courage included. But, of course, it's no use asking the wizard: she'll say it's up to you. She's just there to give you statistics about the flying monkeys and sell you tornado insurance (chemo).

Posted December 13, 2010 at 2:23 p.m.
Cecily Murphy

Oncologist appointment: three hours long. Much to do before chemo starts. Port surgery, tests, etc. Turns out, I do get to choose my poison. Well, I get 3 options. Will have Jane read 20-page document listing "side effects" and summarize. She reads briefings all day, she can hack it. I would get side effects from just reading about them!

Sent: December 13, 2010 at 5:50 p.m.
From: Suzie London
To: Cecily Murphy

Which chemo? I want the Mr. Rogers Neighborhood chemo. There weren't no sweater vests in sight during my last round. They do give you a choice. Read all the choices carefully, and remember the person selling you these drugs is extremely likely to have benefited financially from selling you these drugs. Maui, golf trips, etc. The chemo companies go aaaallll out for their real salesmen: the oncologists. You don't have to be in a trial if it's not right for you. You don't have to be a drug company's test monkey. You don't have to be in chemo if it's not right for you. Make sure you read the benefits carefully, and take a nice, stiff shot of whiskey and really read the side effects. Liquid courage. It's important you go in knowing. Oh, and losing your hair means more than the hair on top of your head. Eyebrows, eyelashes: say goodbye. But it's awesome you don't have to shave your legs. As for other areas: that goes too!!!! If you really miss it, you can get a Merkin. Google Merkin right now. :)

Sent: December 13, 2010 at 6:32 p.m.
From: Cecily Murphy
To: Suzie London

Re: Merkin. Holy moly! I think I'll pass on the pubic wig, although the pink one was kind of cute ... I'm exhausted. I saw Dr. SPO for a tissue expander fill-up right before my three-hour appointment. Where do I buy fake eyebrows? Or just Sharpie them in? Most things in life don't live up to their hype. Cancer, however, does. This ship is crazy.

**Sent: December 13, 2010 at 6:40 p.m.
From: Suzie London
To: Cecily Murphy**

You can slow down the schedule for your "fill-ups." I used to call the tissue expanders the "evil bricks." It sounds like Dr. SPO doesn't have a light touch. If it's hurting, tell him to slow the fuck down. If you want to skip a week, skip a week. They're probably rushing to do as much as they can before chemo starts, but it doesn't matter how far they get. Heal. It's ok to just heal a few weeks. Plus, the fill-ups are sooo much easier if you do them after chemo, closer to your 2nd reconstruction surgery.

How big are you going, anyway? You can always B-have and stay with your B's but you don't have to B-have. You can C how the other half lives: the half that gets free drinks! That's what I did. It's D-batable whether bigger is better, and you DDefinitely DDon't want a DDisaster, if you catch my drift.

**Sent: December 13, 2010 at 6:48 p.m.
From: Cecily Murphy
To: Suzie London**

Ha! I hadn't even thought about going bigger! I was just focused on getting put back together, making the surgeons clean up after themselves. You're right. I could expand a little, maybe. B+. Or C-. C sounds intriguing—especially the part about the free drinks! But, remember, mine would be attached to someone lacking in the "feminine charms" department, so I doubt they'd have the same effect yours have!

My profile picture is deceiving. It was taken at a christening when I was dressed up, wearing makeup, with my hair done. This is how I look every day: hair pulled back into hasty ponytail because I don't know what else to do with it, glasses, lab coat. I doubt a C cup would suddenly turn all the boys' heads! Strange how it never occurred to me. I've been in "get through this" mode. It also didn't occur to me to slow down the process. They just hand me the appointment cards, I enter them into my calendar, and show up when told to. I love having your perspective on this. I'm sure Dr. SPO won't like it. He's so bossy. Most of the time, the plastic surgeons do this part, but he won't hand me over until he's done with all the drains and the fill-ups. Maybe the plastic surgeon will be more collaboration-minded. Whoever this Dr. Cachella is, I've only met her twice and both times I was whacked out by whatever the anesthesiologist had given me.

Sent: December 13, 2010 at 6:59 p.m.
From: Suzie London
To: Cecily Murphy

Oh, you don't really have to go bigger. Just know all your choices going in. You're right. Size doesn't matter. But if you ever wanted them, it's like God's candy store threw open its doors and said everything's free! It's pretty freaking awesome. You watch all your colleagues paying for them: suckas! You had to save all your tips at TGIFridays for years, and you could have had cancer instead! Jealous much? Ha!

I read a story somewhere about Marilyn Monroe. The reporter interviewing her asked if they could go for a walk, but was worried she'd get mobbed because she was so famous. She said, "Norma Jean isn't famous." And they went out walking and nobody recognized them. Then she turned to him and asked, "Want to see Marilyn?" She didn't do anything but change her posture, her attitude, and her confidence level, and suddenly, she was recognized. She didn't change a thing on the outside. It's all attitude. So, no, the C's don't get all the credit when I get past the velvet rope. But I'd be lying if I didn't admit they're awesome for hustling drinks.

Chapter 9

May 22, 2011, 3:00 p.m.

"Suzie had breast cancer." Cecily approached the statement carefully, as though stalking a rabbit in the backyard. "Five years ago."

Brad nodded slowly. "God gave my sister many hardships."

"She is, was, very brave. It's sad that she didn't win her battle," Cecily said. And, taking the opportunity, added, "with cancer."

Brad nodded again, turning his face away, looking like he was concentrating hard on patting the dog.

Wendie had been standing in the arched doorway to the kitchen, leaning into it like a narrow shadow. Cecily had been focused so intently on Brad she hadn't noticed.

"Yes and no," Wendie said, shaking her head. She wore a tan blouse with a bow collar and a straight brown knee-length skirt. The outfit reminded Cecily of a Pine Hill PTA member who planned Halloween parties to keep kids from the horrors of trick-or-treating: razor blades in apples and whatnot. Pine Hill suited Wendie fine, Cecily concluded at first glance. Her fluffy brown hair framed her narrow face, the ends turned in sharply in a perfect line at her chin. She was the type of woman, Cecily guessed, who styled her hair to go to the grocery store, like Cecily's mother.

"Brad's right," Wendie continued, stepping into the room and placing her hands on her husband's shoulders. "God gave her many challenges. But Suzie died from complications due to alcohol and drug abuse. I'm sorry," she looked at Cecily and Jack as though seeing them for the first time. "I'm Wendie, Brad's wife. You probably know that, if you've seen the show. But it seems like you ... haven't seen the show?" She squinted at them quizzically, as though she found this curious.

"Cecily Murphy and Jack Schwinn," Jack said, standing and offering his hand. Cecily followed suit. They shook Wendie's hand—cold, limp, and bony.

"I'm sorry for your loss," Jack repeated.

"Thank you," Wendie acknowledged, as though to a waiter. "Because of the show, we've been meeting a lot of fans. It's strange having strangers know what's going on in your life, having opinions about your problems. Not that you're strangers to Brad, of course. I'm sorry. It's hard to get used to. Wouldn't you say?"

Brad nodded. "It's been a blessing, in some ways, but ... yeah."

"It's been a difficult week, I'm sure," Jack said.

"Difficult year," Brad confirmed.

"May I get you some tea? Something to eat? The TV people sent us all this food."

Cecily and Jack shook their heads. "No, thank you." Cecily watched the dog eye her again, and squirmed in the couch cushions, positioning herself to avoid another dog-nose invasion.

"Here, I'll just grab a few things from the kitchen. Sophie, get your nose out of there now." Wendie whistled a sharp, quick note. The dog sat, motionless for a moment, considering his options, then stood up and followed her into the kitchen.

"Brad," Cecily started. "I have some questions for you. They're a little bit ... personal. I hope you don't mind. Suzie was such a huge support to me the past year during my cancer battle and I was stunned by her death. I had no idea."

Brad's eyes filled with tears. Oh no, Cecily thought. No crying. Not ready to cry.

"Thank you," said Brad, pinching the bridge of his nose between his forefinger and thumb.

Cecily nodded slowly. She had seldom been thanked for announcing her intentions to intrude.

"Thank you so much," Brad repeated. "You have no idea how wonderful it is to hear positive things about my sister. Usually when we hear from Suzie's friends, they're looking to get their money paid back, or they're not ... singing Suzie's praises."

"Oh," Cecily said. I'm not in the mood to sing Suzie's praises either, frankly, Cecily thought. She didn't tell me anything about this *Dr. Dick* business, or dying, or liver failure. Or anything.

But she sat in Brad's living room, intruding on Brad's grief, and she had no business piling her own issues onto Brad's plate, which seemed full enough. She wished Jimmy were here. He and Brad had been close once.

The silence opened up in the room, expanding into its own universe. With Brad an arm's length away, Cecily didn't think she could bridge the distance between what she wanted to say and what he needed to hear. She'd have to try.

Cecily inhaled deeply and exhaled her words in one breath. "Suzie was funny and smart and loving and giving and generous and so good to me and ... Brad?" She finally took a breath, but it caught in her throat. "I didn't know she was going to die. She didn't tell me. I didn't know a thing about this television show or about 'complications due to alcohol abuse.' I was led to believe she died of cancer. No, that's not correct. I was led to believe her cancer had recurred. And that she was fighting it; we were fighting it. Together!" Cecily's throat closed over her words and her eyes stung. Jack picked up her hand and held it between his hands on his lap. She liked this odd habit: holding her hand with both hands, as though one wasn't enough.

Brad sighed, crossed his arms, then looked at the ceiling. "OK. Can we go over this piece-by-piece? This sounds complicated. But, that's how God made her. Complicated." He smiled a little, then frowned again and glared into the middle distance, which from his vantage point was the overgrown hedge out the window. Cecily felt a pang of guilt, heaping her anger and confusion on Suzie's freshly grieving brother.

Wendie walked into the room balancing a tray with a delicate porcelain teapot and four petite china cups painted with ivy. In the center of the tray sat an arrangement of store-made and expensive-looking frosted sugar cookies. Wendie set the tray down on the coffee table, then turned to sit in the rocker.

"We don't have to—" Jack began, but Wendie waved her hands at him dismissively.

"No, no. You're fine. Help yourself to the tea and to the cookies. Cecily, please." She motioned toward the cookies.

Cecily wasn't hungry or thirsty, but she picked up a teacup and the teapot and poured herself a cup.

"I appreciate this, your hospitality and willingness to speak with me about Suzie. She meant a lot to me. That's why I'm asking. I'm not trying to dredge up any difficult memories. I just, well—" Cecily shrugged lamely and finished her sentence in her head: You're here. In your family's house. And I'm here too, for some reason. And I have questions.

Brad nodded. "Please. Feel free to ask. Our life is an open book now," he said, and Cecily and Jack both caught the note of sarcasm.

"Starting with that," Jack leaned forward in the sofa and took a cookie. "How did Dr. Dick get involved with your family?"

"How did Hollywood find us, you mean?" Brad rolled his eyes. "Suzie, of course."

"But Suzie hated reality shows! She hated Dr. Dick! Hated him!" Cecily set her teacup down and stood up. She couldn't think while the sofa cushions tried to suffocate her. Dahlia wouldn't have approved of pacing in a grieving family's house, but she was through pretending this was a normal house call.

"Let's ... start at the end. Just for a moment. Regardless of the alcohol situation, did Suzie have a recurrence of the cancer she fought five years ago?"

Brad's whiskers and eyebrows seemed to fall limply on his face as he frowned. Wendie was sitting on the rocking chair in the corner with her legs crossed, biting her thumbnail.

Finally, Wendie said, "Well, I suppose it's possible that the cancer recurred. At some point. Somewhere."

Cecily exhaled. "Did she ever mention anything about it?"

"No," Wendie said.

"No," Brad said.

Cecily stopped pacing and stood quietly, considering this. Watching her, Jack stopped chewing his cookie. Outside, a lawnmower roared to life.

"But," Wendie added, "that was typical of Suzie. To not tell us things."

Brad's watery blue eyes leaked one heavy tear. "Towards the end, when her drinking got much worse, she saw us as the enemy. I understand the disease well. It lies to you. The Lord Jesus Christ saved me years ago, but I never succeeded in saving my little sister. I prayed. I prayed for the Lord to save her."

"I'm so sorry," Cecily's knees bent to the floor and she found herself kneeling next to Brad's chair, gingerly touching his arm and staring at the floor, unable to look up at his face. He grabbed her hand and squeezed it with a bear grip. This time Cecily didn't try to pull away, and just allowed her knuckles to collapse in on themselves in Brad's grip. It was the only part of her that was being held together at all, and they sat like this silently for a long moment.

Sent: December 16, 2010 at 2:12 a.m.
From: Suzie London
To: Cecily Murphy

Hey, East Coast. I'm listening to Guns 'N Roses. Remember when we used to jump on your parents' bed to "Sweet Child O' Mine?" I used to scream this song. About Jason Buckman. I want to have another crush. I'm crushing on crushes.

Sent: December 16, 2010 at 2:17 a.m.
From: Cecily Murphy
To: Suzie London

I'd love a crush now! I kind of have one. I don't know. This is a stupid and impractical time to have a crush, to say the least. I used to have that song on cassette. I completely forgot about jumping on the bed! I remember your soundproof basement and how we used to blast REM and Michael Jackson and dance and dance. Seven years old and you could moonwalk. Man, I was jealous!

I'm stressing about chemo. I know it's a month away, but I had to go in for another appointment with the oncologist today—I had to take the tour of the "infusion center" and take "chemo class," which was useless, except to make me realize, OK, this is actually happening to me. So now I'm just working on some chemo research.

Sent: December 16, 2010 at 2:18 a.m.
From: Suzie London
To: Cecily Murphy

Been there, done that, thrown up all over my shoes, and going back for more. I'm like the Marines. With whiskey. Researching what?

Sent: December 16, 2010 at 2:22 a.m.
From: Cecily Murphy
To: Suzie London

Drug absorption from plasma concentration versus time and urinary data following the administration of a drug via intravascular routes. Then trying to figure out how long I'll be out of work after each dose based on these figures. Yes, I am a nerd. I'm guessing you are NOT thinking about this as your chemo approaches. :)

Sent: December 16, 2010 at 2:25 a.m.
From: Suzie London
To: Cecily Murphy

No. Thinking about shaking doctor and asking why she poisons me. Wouldn't you love to trade places with your doctor for a day? I'd say, "Well, good morning. How's about a needle in your ass and then for dessert, some nice poison?" I'd report her to the psych ward if met with resistance. Ha! I'd ask her, with sad doggy eyes: "Why aren't you liking the poison?"

It's poison, Cecily. That's Lie #1 the oncologist tells you. Some things about it I'll never tell you. We'll just do the positive, and the positive is this: you'll get through it.

Sent: December 16, 2010 at 2:29 a.m.
From: Cecily Murphy
To: Suzie London

It's a fine line between poison and medicine. What makes poison medicinal and what makes medicine poisonous is simply the dose. Drug makers look for selective toxicity. They try to find something unique and essential to a problematic cell, like functioning or reproduction. In a perfect world, the drug will kill the part of the cell you want it to and nothing else. But in the real world, the most you can hope for is for a drug to prefer to kill one thing, and hope the other things it wants to kill are small and nonessential.

Sent: December 16, 2010 at 2:45 a.m.
From: Suzie London
To: Cecily Murphy

There's always collateral damage. Like my shoes. Apple juice doesn't stain your shoes when you puke on them. I regret always going for the cherry Slurpee from the Slurpee machine at the "infusion center." Yes, doesn't "infusion center" sound sweet? Nothing like: poison center, torture chamber, hall of pharmacological horrors, and say goodbye to lunch-ville. I have bigger regrets than shoes: not going after Stevie Nicks, Rolling Stones, the true greats. I never worked with the true greats. I let that whole part go after I met Jace.

How was chemo class? You're getting the port put in, right? Get the port. Getting mine next week. I used to watch them stab the old people over and over trying to get a vein. Don't know why the old people never get ports. All the young people did. Maybe because they kind of look like tattoos from an angle.

Sent: December 16, 2010 at 2:56 a.m.
From: Cecily Murphy
To: Suzie London

They do? Really? Chemo class was not informative ("Everyone's different!") but pretty entertaining. Woman next to me was very concerned about infection control measures re: pets. "Can I kiss my horse? Can I pet my horse? Can I brush my horse?" I had to leave for my next appointment, so I'll never know, sadly, the rules governing the level of intimacy one can safely have with one's horse during chemo.

Sent: December 16, 2010 at 3:05 a.m.
From: Suzie London
To: Cecily Murphy

LOL!!!! You don't want to know what she's doing with her horse. That horse and her, they've got a "special" relationship. I had to do chemo class last time ... this time, I got off for good behavior. It's kind of like the "alcohol education" classes they make you go to. You go around the room and tell people why you're there, but instead of saying, "I got hammered at DreamLand and I don't know why I'm here, but I had an awesome time doing it," you say, "Ovarian. Eggs. With a side of hash. And, what I did to get here, I don't fucking know."

Sent: December 16, 2010 at 3:11 a.m.
From: Cecily Murphy
To: Suzie London

They said one interesting thing: we can't use chemicals on our hair for one year after chemo. I thought about you when they said that. You and your wild hair statements.

Sent: December 16, 2010 at 3:18 a.m.
From: Suzie London
To: Cecily Murphy

Yeah ... I remember them saying something about that at chemo class, but I called bullshit on that one. I haven't had brown hair since Pine Hill. Right now it's this midnight black with blue highlights: fly! I'm going to change them to pink in your honor: supa fly! I'll post a picture. This lady in my chemo class said: "What about perms?" I was like: "Don't get a perm!!!!!! Are you kidding? Is it 1989?" She was so shocked so they told her: "Maybe your hair will grow back curly anyway? It happens." And I said: "And don't get a perm then, either."

Sent: December 16, 2010 at 3:21 a.m.
From: Cecily Murphy
To: Suzie London

I hope that lady thanked you, talking her out of a perm! Who would you work with tomorrow, if you could? Why don't you, again? Now.

Sent: December 16, 2010 at 3:26 a.m.
From: Suzie London
To: Cecily Murphy

Trying is trying, but I will. Tom Petty. Listening to "Wildflowers" right now. Tonight, I'd say Tom Petty. Download Wildflowers (the whole album) and listen to it for me. It's beautiful. He is one whose songs just get better and better.

Sent: December 16, 2010 at 3:27 a.m.
From: Cecily Murphy
To: Suzie London

I will.

Chapter 10

May 22, 2011, 4:45 p.m.

In the car, Jack suggested they stop at Nick's Fish House, a beer and crab shack on the Patapsco River with an expansive outdoor deck facing the Hanover Street Bridge. Cecily, tired, didn't enthuse but didn't argue. People—doctors, family, friends, Jack—relentlessly force-fed her throughout chemo, the world's longest stomach flu. She let them. Chemo had been a ruthlessly efficient diet. She now had to jump on the scale to get it up to three digits. Weighing 97 pounds gave her veiny, old-looking hands and sunken cheeks—a feature Cecily dubbed "cancer face." She wasn't thrilled about her 13-pound weight loss, and especially despised being told she was "lucky" to have lost so much weight. Generally, the people who said that had never heard her puking her guts up in the bathroom for days on end.

Her digestive system had now recovered from the onslaught, but her appetite was slower to return. She didn't voice this to many people for fear of getting slapped by friends on diets, but she had as much enthusiasm for food as she did for doing laundry. *This again?* She'd ask herself every morning. *Didn't I just do this last night?* She hoped eating would be pleasurable again soon, but in the meantime, she could make a decent show of eating french fries at low-key, low-ambition Nick's. Beige food had been good to her.

So had fresh air. Cecily contemplated a seagull that flew in over the porch railing, landed on the deck and strutted confidently toward a french fry. Another seagull soared to a landing on top of the fry, and the two birds squawked loudly at each other until the waitress chased them away, sweeping her foot in their direction as she balanced a tray with two cans of National Bohemian intended for Cecily and Jack. The deck was nearly empty, save for the scavenging seagulls and a few old men at the sawgrass-roofed bar in the center of the deck, watching the Orioles lose on ESPN.

Cecily thanked the waitress and took an indifferent sip of her National Bohemian, a tasteless yellow lager that used to be produced locally but was now manufactured elsewhere.

"Are we getting crabs?" Jack asked.

"It's a little early in the season for crabs."

"But we could pound them. With these mallets." Jack liked the wooden crab mallets, which he thought looked like toys rather than serious dining implements. He was less fond of the Old Bay Seasoning, a red, crumbly mix that clung in large chunks to Baltimorean blue crabs. In addition to setting fire to your mouth, it stuck to your fingers and stung every cut, scrape or hangnail. Jack wondered why people didn't wear gloves for this endeavor. When he asked Cecily about this before, she'd called him a tourist.

"Pounding is good," Cecily agreed. "Maybe I need to pound."

Jack reached for her hand and held it between his own. "You might need to cry."

She looked up at him, surprised, and asked, "How do you know I haven't cried yet?"

"I just know you. And you haven't cried all day, even when Brad was crying. *I* almost cried when Brad cried."

"But how do you know me? Because of what I say about myself on Facebook? Half the stuff people say on Facebook isn't even true. I mean, it *is* true. But it's more like they're presenting a version of themselves they want other people to see. How do you trust someone to be who they say they are?"

"I just know you from being with you, and the rest ... I don't know."

"She wasn't anything she said she was. Where there weren't outright lies, there were lies of omission."

"What I think might make this easier is if you ..." Jack said, politely waving off the waitress who had returned to take their order, "put together what Suzie said, what Brad said. Once you see where the discrepancies are, we can ask why. We can go further than Brad—ask her friends, ask people who knew her."

"You don't want me to just drop it and forget about it?"

"No, why would I?"

"That's what Cait keeps telling me to do," Cecily said.

"Well, Cait's wrong. You need to work this out. You might even need a spreadsheet, in Excel," Jack winked at her.

Cecily's stomach felt like it was grinding glass. Suzie had actually had the nerve to accuse Cecily of over-caution. Cecily had been nothing but open and honest since day one of her diagnosis. Too open. Too honest. She'd let more people in than she should have. She'd paid for this. Her house had been robbed, she'd been swindled and now used. Used for what?

"I can't walk around like an idiot anymore. I can't just assume everyone I meet has my best intentions in mind. I am just as accountable for this situation as Suzie London."

Jack sipped his beer.

"And that's why I can't sit around here," Cecily swept her arms to indicate all of Nick's deck. "Blaming people. Dead people in particular."

"OK."

"And that's why I'm going to Los Angeles. As soon as possible," Cecily concluded.

Jack paused. On the television, the announcer called out: "Pop fly to left field." The men at the bar groaned.

Timely, Jack thought. "Why?" he asked.

"Due diligence," Cecily said. "I failed in my due diligence. I guess I can forgive myself for that, considering the circumstances. But I can do it now. Plus, I've never been, and someone once told me that everything is beautiful in Santa Monica. I'd like to see if that's true, and what else might be. If anything."

****

**Posted December 17, 2010 at 6:02 a.m.
Cecily Murphy**

Going wig shopping this weekend if anyone wants to join. Looking for: 1 Lady Gaga, 1 blue mohawk, 1 Cher, 1 Baltimore Hon beehive, and 1 wig a la my "normal" haircut, which Cait claims is just a longer variation of hers (Tired Suburban Housewife #3). Thanks!

**Sent: December 17, 2010 at 6:08 a.m.
From: Suzie London
To: Cecily Murphy**

No don't get wigs. I'm sending you wigs, I have them.

**Sent: December 17, 2010 at 6:54 a.m.
From: Cecily Murphy
To: Suzie London**

Suzie! How's your port? How did surgery go?

**Sent: December 17, 2010 at 1:08 p.m.
From: Suzie London
To: Cecily Murphy**

God it sucks this time. Can't lift arm or turn head without being stabbed in neck. My surgeon was Britney Spears. It feels like they got something wrong. Fucking Britney. It feels like it's going up my neck this time, and I have a fever. People shouldn't do this twice. Screw me once, shame on you. Screw me twice, shame on me. It's all about the comeback, according to Chris Rock. They're not interested in curing me, they're all "Daddy needs a new jet ski, bitches! Come and get your drugs!"

**Sent: December 17, 2010 at 1:12 p.m.
From: Cecily Murphy
To: Suzie London**

Suzie London, do not start talking that way. Dr. Britney Spears may not be a very good port surgeon, but you'll get it fixed. You'll fight this. You said we'd fight. You said we'll do this together.

Tell your surgeon this is a device that's supposed to improve your standard of living during chemotherapy. At what point does the benefit to detriment ratio reverse for this thing? If it's not benefitting you, you'll get it taken out. Tell her to fix it, or take the dang thing out at no cost to you. She works for you, not the other way around.

**Sent: December 17, 2010 at 10:13 p.m.
From: Suzie London
To: Cecily Murphy**

Oh, Cecily. I'm just messin' wit' cha. I'm just bitchin'. Totally bitchen, man!

**Sent: December 18, 2010 at 12:15 a.m.
From: Cecily Murphy
To: Suzie London**

Sorry! I'm sorry. I hate it when people tell me not to bitch when I need to bitch. You can't be positive all the time. This sucks. You can bitch all you want. You've earned it. I have to get to bed ... pre-op with my port surgeon tomorrow morning. Believe it or not, Dr. SPO doesn't do ports. Oh God, what if my surgeon sucks?

**Sent: December 18, 2010 at 12:17 a.m.
From: Suzie London
To: Cecily Murphy**

Yours won't suck. Except, if she looks like Britney Spears, flip a chair over and run.

Posted December 18, 2010 at 9:21 a.m.
Cecily Murphy

Pre-op with port surgeon. Port is inserted under skin next to collarbone, so you don't have to get stuck with needles every day and burn out all your veins with chemo. Doctor said port is hidden on most but on me it will stick out a little, a triangular lump. Hmm. I could say I was abducted by aliens? Or am a member of Star Fleet? Surgery next week.

Posted December 20, 2010 at 9:04 a.m.
Cecily Murphy

From my boss's email: "We have good biodiversity, grouped by species, of beer for your enjoyment." Ah, the joy of holiday parties at an environmental research center.

Sent: December 20, 2010 at 9:14 a.m.
From: Jack Schwinn
To: Cecily Murphy

When is your office holiday party? Do you hold it every year in a different museum? If it's in the Air and Space Museum, I'd like to volunteer to go. That would be awesome.

Sent: December 20, 2010 at 9:52 a.m.
From: Cecily Murphy
To: Jack Schwinn

This one is just my lab; it's more of a Friday happy hour. Very casual. No spouses/guests. We don't dress up or anything. The larger Smithsonian employee party requires dressing up, finagling a date, and posing for group pictures—it's usually in the castle. I played the Cancer Card on that one. Said I was tired, but really lacked the emotional energy: date-finding, dress-finding (dress I can wear over surgery ... stuff). I'll take you to the Air and Space Museum anytime you want, though. It's mind-boggling. I could live here forever and never see everything in the collection.

The Truth About Suzie

Sometimes on my lunch break, I'll walk over to the Natural History Museum (my favorite lately). In the dinosaur exhibit, there's a two-story column listing all the eras of the earth's 3.5 billion year history: Protozoic, Mesozoic, Jurassic. Down near you, the pole is sparse of content. Then your eye follows it up, scanning thousands of years with every inch. "Single-celled organisms appear." Three quarters of the way up the pole, it says, "First dinosaurs appear." It goes up. And up. And up. And almost all the way up, three inches from the top, it says: "Man."

Tens of thousands of years, all of human history is just the top three inches in the two-story pole of Earth's four billion year history. I could look at that pole for hours. It makes my problems feel so small. I move my eyes all the way up, through the ages, and everything bothering me becomes insignificant. This too shall pass, life moves along. It sounds silly, I know, but it's comforting to me the way that church is comforting to some people. Anyway, I'd love to give you the tour of my favorite parts of the Smithsonian, both public and non, but I'm not doing the holiday party thing this year.

The only party I'm actually looking forward to is Michele's. It's not really a holiday party; it's a birthday party for her dog, Spike. With an international theme because he's a mutt. You're assigned a country and have to bring a dish native to that country. It's optional to dress in indigenous garb. I got New Zealand this year. I can't figure out what they eat: Hobbit food? Should I bring second breakfast? It's all Michele's staffer friends from Capitol Hill—you've never met a bigger bunch of policy wonks in your life—and there's a ferociously competitive geography quiz. You can win a framed picture of Spike. It gets ugly. You have to turn in your cell phone so you can't cheat on Google.

Sent: December 20, 2010 at 10:08 a.m.
From: Jack Schwinn
To: Cecily Murphy

Sounds like you need a date to this party who's good at geography. Coincidentally, freakishly difficult geography quizzes are my forte. We'll team up and win you that picture of Spike.

Sent: December 20, 2010 at 10:12 a.m.
From: Cecily Murphy
To: Jack Schwinn

Thanks, but you really have no idea what you're getting yourself into!

Sent: December 20, 2010 at 10:13 a.m.
From: Jack Schwinn
To: Cecily Murphy

I'll take my chances.

Chapter 11

May 22, 2011, 6:30 p.m.

After their early dinner of beer, fried clams and fries, Cecily and Jack drove back to his apartment and opened their laptops. Jack researched plane tickets to LAX and hotels in Venice Beach, and filled out an overly complicated vacation request form from his company's intranet site.

Cecily extracted all of Suzie's emails from her Facebook account into a Word document and ferreted out names: she needed last names, contact information where she could find them, clues. She combined the story Brad shared with any semblance of a fact she could ferret out of Suzie's emails. All this knowledge combined to form very little in the way of a solid hypothesis, but it put Cecily in a comfortable mindset—the start of an inquiry.

October
- I stupidly announce cancer diagnosis on FB
- Suzie contacts me, says she's in radiation. Where? What hospital? Doctor names?

November
- Brad's son Peter suspended from school.
  (Peter=Brad's son from pre-Wendie "days of booze and prison." Brad and Wendie have 2 other kids: a boy & girl.)

- Suzie claims to be "songwriter, actress, singer, artist, set designer, stagehand, dog walker, singing telegram deliverer, primary muse." Where? Tiki Tata Lounge mentioned.
- Names dropped: RuPaul, Satan's Ejaculation???
- Lisa? Friend. Cinematographer/Photographer. No last name.

December
- First mention of Dragon Lady
- According to Brad, Suzie lands in ER at UCLA for alcohol poisoning/possible overdose. Brad notified by Suzie's boyfriend, Jace. (Suzie calls Jace her ex-boyfriend.)
- Brad's family travels to LA. Suzie tells him alcoholism has taken its toll, and she has six months to live. Brad is not her next-of-kin, so he can't make decisions for her. Brad pissed about this. He wants her to get tests, MELD score, placed on transplant list: whatever's needed. Suzie leaves hospital one morning against doctor's orders, in middle of testing.
- Wendie and kids go home for Xmas. Brad stays in LA to convince Suzie to go back to UCLA: offers to pay, to make all arrangements, offers to let her stay with him, offers to get her treatment for alcoholism. Suzie tells him to go home, and she will "do what she has to do."
- Brad says, when he said goodbye to Suzie, he believed it would be the last time he saw her alive.
- Early December: Suzie told me she was going to chemo, had port surgery. Said she went to hospital for port surgery: could have been overdose?

January

- Suzie AWOL end of Dec. through early Jan. Comes back, says port is out. "Going freestyle," "I fired the oncologist I hated." Dragon Lady?
- Jace is Jason Frost!!! Jack points out: She could be lying about that too. But, I do have those autographed CDs.
- Suzie helps me through the worst week of my life.
- Jan. 14: said she had beers with Jace—while supposedly in liver failure?

February

- Brad contacted by Dr. Dick staff member re: Peter. Brad says they used Suzie's name as a reference.
- Peter's intervention is staged, featured on Dr. Dick's show.
- Dr. Dick suggests intervention for Suzie: Suzie refuses.
- Suzie mentions intervention to me in rambling email. Implies it was Brad's idea.
- Shaves her head. For me. Sends me wigs.

March

- Brad's family filmed for two weeks in Pine Hill.
- Suzie asks me to find Gretchen Garrett, starts talking about healer, God, etc.

April

- Brad and Suzie's father found in Portland, OR, by Dr. Dick's staff. Brad's family and father reunite. Suzie refuses.
- Suzie said they added another round of chemo for her.

Wait, no. I said that. She just said she's "not done."
She talks about survivorship, gives me advice, like I'm
going through it alone. Did I really not see this? Am I
this dense?

- Mentions Dr. Dick and intervention, circuitously as usual. "Well, if you get treatment," Dr. Dickhead says, and I interrupt him and say, "There's an 85% chance I won't get better and a 100% chance you'll be richer." I suppose that all happened in February?

May

- May 1st: I last heard from Suzie. She said goodbye, and I didn't even see it.
- May 3rd: Suzie admitted to hospital for last time.
- May 13th: Suzie dies at 4:22 p.m.

Cecily reread her list and said aloud, "Well, some things are clear. Mainly how dense I am."

Jack was trying to buy the plane tickets using his airline miles, which Cecily had expressly forbidden. "Just research," she'd told him. "You're not paying for my airline ticket, and you don't want to come. I won't be at my best."

"I don't care about you being 'your best,'" Jack had scoffed. "Have you ever been to Venice Beach?" he asked. She hadn't. "Have you seen *The Doors*?" he asked. She had.

"That'll help," he'd told her.

"Do we want to add tickets to Universal Studios to our vacation package," Jack read aloud.

"Jack!" Cecily stared at him, exasperated.

"Sorry," Jack said. "Not a vacation. No Universal." He paused. Cecily interrupted before he could ask. "No Disneyland."

"That's in Anaheim," Jack said dismissively. "But I'm looking at these surfing lessons ..."

The Truth About Suzie

And this is all I need, Cecily thought. But her next thought surprised her: Suzie would have told him to go for it.

"Wait a second," she said aloud, not to Jack, and not with regard to surfing lessons. She Googled UCLA and read about their oncology department, then clicked on the gynecologic oncologists' page.

"Looking up to see if Suzie's doctor—I know, this is a waste of time. She never told me her doctor's name, but I just want to see something," Cecily mumbled.

"Mmm," said Jack, reading.

"Oh my God," Cecily said. "Oh my God."

"What is it?"

"I found the Dragon Lady."

"The what?"

"Suzie called her oncologist the Dragon Lady. Look," Cecily said, turning the laptop around to face Jack.

In the picture, an unsmiling woman stood against a beige wall with dark eyes and dark hair sharply pulled back. She wore a white lab coat and slumped forward in a way that foreshortened her neck and made her head appear to be photoshopped onto her shoulders. The picture allowed no guesses for her age, which could have ranged anywhere from 35 to 65.

Under her picture, a name was written. Dr. Ella Drago. And under that, her specialty: gynecologic oncology.

"Dragon lady?" Cecily asked.

"Dragon lady," Jack answered. "Huh. That's ... possible. We'll never know though. Because of HIPAA, Dragon Lady can't even tell us if Suzie was a patient. Nor can anyone at the hospital."

"The cancer support center. She went to a cancer support center and did yoga with a bunch of old ladies."

"That's a possibility. And the healer probably isn't bound by HIPAA," Jack noted.

"All I know about the healer is that it's a 'she' who is deathly allergic to wasps," Cecily said. "But Drago. Do you see that? This is possible."

Posted December 20, 2010 at 11:00 a.m.
Cecily Murphy

Today: collect water samples at Middle River, echocardiogram at GW, oncology appointment, then gym. I love that cancer only gets a few measly hours of my days now. The rest of my hours are MINE! I'll rephrase: the rest of my hours are not Property of Cancer. The real fight is peeling that sticker off yourself every day.

Posted December 21, 2010 at 6:24 p.m.
Cecily Murphy

Home from port surgery. Long but fine! Haven't been allowed to eat since midnight last night ... starving! Eileigh wanted to bring me dinner, so she's bringing it in now ... oh, she brought me two donuts and a banana! Krispy Kreme!!! LOVE her.

Posted December 21, 2010 at 6:52 p.m.
Suzie London

In case of emergency, shatter glass.

Sent: December 21, 2010 at 6:59 p.m.
From: Cecily Murphy
To: Suzie London

What's going on? Is port better?

Sent: December 22, 2010 at 1:22 a.m.
From: Suzie London
To: Cecily Murphy

I'm gonna call you "Bootstraps." Cause you just pull yourself up by your bootstraps.

Sent: December 22, 2010 at 7:00 a.m.
From: Cecily Murphy
To: Suzie London

Um ... OK. When does chemo start? Is port better?

Sent: December 22, 2010 at 11:36 p.m.
From: Suzie London
To: Cecily Murphy

Morphine is good. 24 hours in hospital: tests and shit. They say port is "in the right place!!!" but they don't care 2 rats what's wrong with it. If this isn't cleared up by tomorrow, I will have port shoved up someone's ass. Ahm'onna blow this taco stand! "Just relax, Miss London, this won't hurt a bit!" yeah right! I'm going to start charging them for my blood. I swear they're selling it. I give you my blood, you take it off my bill: you likey? They were supposed to start two days after Xmas. Sick of Xmas. Too much Kristmas Krap on muzak. "Santa Claus is Coming to Town" is creepiest Xmas song ever. Think about it: he knows when you are sleeping. He knows when you're awake. He knows if you've been bad or good, and he's standing in your shower with an axe.

The horoscope writer for the *LA Times* hates us Geminis. Rothner brought me the papers/tabloids tonight and this is my horoscope: "That carefree feeling of utter confidence that things will work out in the end may mislead you." Dear Gemini: you think everything's going to be OK. But it's not. F-you. Sincerely, Wednesday.

Hey you've got chemo too, when's that

Sent: December 22, 2010 at 11:42 p.m.
From: Cecily Murphy
To: Suzie London

Oh God, I'm so sorry to hear this port thing has been such an ordeal! I start 1/13. They're still feigning innocence on my likely side effects. If I hear, "Everyone's different!" one more time, I'm going to pull a Suzie London on them! :) They gave me five prescriptions for nausea meds alone ... there's a clue! They haven't pushed back your chemo start date? They couldn't wait till after New Year's?

Sent: December 22, 2010 at 11:43 p.m.
From: Suzie London
To: Cecily Murphy

Oh, I'll have New Year's regardless! I'm gittin' lit up like the Hollywood sign. ON the Hollywood sign.

Sent: December 22, 2010 at 11:44 p.m.
From: Cecily Murphy
To: Suzie London

Are we allowed to drink on chemo?

Sent: December 22, 2010 at 11:45 p.m.
From: Suzie London
To: Cecily Murphy

They can't take away my special Drunk Fu powers! I forgot, which one of us is Thelma and which is Louise?

Sent: December 22, 2010 at 11:46 p.m.
From: Cecily Murphy
To: Suzie London

You're definitely the one with the chutzpah in this operation. Louise? Going to bed now: feel better, sending positive thoughts/love!

Sent: December 22, 2010 at 11:46 p.m.
From: Suzie London
To: Cecily Murphy

Thelma. Good night!

December 23, 2011, 11:30 p.m.

Jack had never met Michele, but he knew Jane from Cornell. Jane had been Cecily's roommate since freshman year, and she seemed to be at least partially responsible for Cecily's disinclination to hang out with the boys in the microbiology department. Jane dragged Cecily to sorority rushes and fraternity parties—places unlikely to be frequented by the shy herd that roamed the science and technology quad. Twenty-two-year-old Jane was an English major with pre-law ambitions and a bit of a wild streak, her blonde straight hair worn long, her belly button ring flashing in the strobe lights at parties.

Jane's claim to fame on campus was allegedly saving the life of the drummer from the Kings of Leon after they played on the fraternity quad during Spring Riot. Jane, waving a six-pack of Genny Light, had lured the drummer away from the stage after the first set, just moments before a Psi U pledge plunged from the fraternity's roof into the drum set, destroying it. The pledge, pressed into a full-sized mattress sandwich secured tightly with duct tape, was physically unscathed. When the police finally succeeded in cutting the duct tape away from the two mattresses, the pledge emerged from his cocoon pumping his fists in the air to elicit cheers from the crowd before he was wrestled down and handcuffed. The drummer, watching this scene from six feet away, stood horrified at the carnage of his instruments, then turned to Jane, awestruck, and said, "You saved my life." Jane knew an opportunity for an anecdote when she saw one and kissed him. The Kings of Leon never returned to campus after that day, but their lawyers did.

Jack found Jane, and most of Cecily's college friends outside the microbiology department, intimidating. They were New York and New Jersey girls: loud, brash, forward, prone to cornering you at parties then dashing off when something shiny appeared in their peripheral vision. In settings that didn't prominently feature beer bongs and shot luges, the girls were less likely to overload the senses. But then Jack had never been the fraternity-joining, party-loving guy in college. By age 20, he had built a TiVo from scratch. He ran six websites that earned him an average of $22 per week. Each. He had upgraded the security access on his student badge, so he could gain entry to the sports complex pool for midnight lap swimming. Hacking wasn't foolproof. Occasionally, a dining center employee swiped his ID card and said, "Hey, this says you're a janitor, not a student."

Even when given the opportunity to share the full, rewarding life he believed he led behind his quiet façade, he found that yelling over the music at pretty girls was never worth the effort. (Pretty girls—of whom Cecily was by far the prettiest, the smartest, the cutest, the funniest.) "What?!" Cecily would yell back, cupping her ear. Then, finally, earnestly, she'd wiggle her thumbs, miming the sign for "text it."

Cecily's college world was never a place Jack enjoyed visiting. But now he was older, wiser. Not just another twerp from Cecily's biology class that she'd dragged along. He had a salary. He knew—knew for a fact—gainful employment was a big selling point for women now. The tables were turning in favor of the nerds, albeit more slowly for some nerds than others. But Jack had spent the past summer attending the weddings of friends who had graduated along with their virginity from Cornell. If there was hope for them, there was certainly hope for Jack. The nerd revolution had begun, and Jack was taking up arms.

****

Cecily pulled Jane into Michele's roommate Ben's room. "Sorry," she motioned to Ben, who was entertaining a group of three women with his vintage record collection.

"Jack has been talking to Michele for a bit," Cecily raised her eyebrows at Jane.

"I've noticed," Jane took a swig of her beer.

"You have? Should I be worried?"

Cecily noticed she was peeling her beer bottle again. She smoothed the label down. Jane had gone to a lot of trouble to find a brand of New Zealand beer for Cecily to bring to the party. Speights. Not bad, but nothing worth a 24-hour plane ride. Good thing Jane only had to travel to Adams Morgan to find this.

"Definitely," Jane said. "Michele can be terrifying. Oh, you mean ... flirting or something?"

"Which guy is Jack?" One of the girls, dressed in a sombrero and clutching a Bananarama album to her chest, asked.

Jane pointed. "Over there. Skinny, brown hair. Bad facial hair." Cecily tried to wrestle Jane's finger down to her side.

"He's cute," the girl on the floor approved.

"He'd be cuter without the facial hair," Jane replied.

"Totally," the girl nodded. "Look at that cute smile, though. He's smiling a lot. He thinks that girl's funny."

Cecily marched straight into the kitchen to interrupt Michele and Jack.

****

Michele had cornered Jack in the remodeled kitchen of the Dupont Circle townhouse she shared with three well-trained and deferential men, two of whom were gay and used to date, but now publicly professed to having a "complicated" relationship on their Facebook profiles.

Michele swirled the ice in her whiskey glass and fixed her glacier-blue eyes, which always sported impeccably applied makeup, on Cecily's new little crush. Cute, she thought. She prided herself on being a decent judge of character, and settled in for a lengthy interview.

"We haven't met. You're Cecily's friend, Jack?" she asked.

"I am," Jack replied. "And you must be our hostess, Michele." He knew because Cecily had described her to him: "Picture Ann Coulter, with slightly less sociopathic rage." Cecily had also warned him not to mention Michele's striking resemblance to the tall, blonde, gaunt Coulter, who happened to be Michele's arch nemesis.

Michele had once given Coulter a birthday card with a prescription to Valtrex in it. Coulter had retaliated by picking up Michele's nametag at a NATO dinner and wearing it prominently while patting Tony Blair on the bottom. Cecily couldn't remember the crux of their issue with each other, but was reasonably certain it involved some worthless guy. Or rather, some guy Cecily perceived as worthless but likely wielded power in some area important to both women. Politics was just high school with nicer purses, Cecily had explained.

Jack smiled, remembering this, and continued, "Great party. Excellent beer selection."

"Thank you. I'll take credit for it even though you're drinking my friend Scott's beer. Beer-making is his girlfriend. Speaking of girlfriends, how did you and Cecily meet?" Michele noted the alarm in Jack's expression with delight. Skittish, she thought. This will be fun.

"In college," Jack said, eyes scanning the kitchen for Cecily.

"Oh. Great story," Michele said, hands on hips expectantly.

Jack realized escape was not an option. "OK, it actually is a great story. It's epic."

"Your eyes met across a crowded room?" Michele asked. "Go on."

He smiled, exhaling a little bit. He actually did love telling this story. "Yes, but we were both wearing troll wigs and footie pajamas at the time."

"No!"

"You really didn't hear this story from Cecily?" Jack asked, a little disappointed. Maybe Cecily didn't even remember this.

"Not at all," Michele shook her head.

"Oh," Jack said, a little deflated now. "Well, I tell this story all the time. Anyway. It was Halloween, freshman year. I was Thing 2, from Cat in the Hat—"

"See, that's awesome. Straight guys are so lazy about Halloween. And women are so slutty about it. How many versions of slutty nurse and slutty cat and slutty slut can you do before you realize that hey, it's fucking cold in Ithaca in October. If I want to flash my bits, I'll do it in June."

"Yes ... er ... anyway. So Cecily was Thing 1. Thing 1! It was amazing. I took one look at her, and we just cracked up. We talked all night," Jack smiled, thinking, it was so fantastic. Until I took her back to my room to watch Raising Arizona, which happened to be our favorite movie, and she fell asleep before I worked up the nerve to even put my damn arm around her. Which is, he thought dismally, exactly how I landed in the Friend Zone.

"You knew. You just knew. That's so—"

Jack, panicked, interrupted her. "I knew we would be friends. Do you need another drink? There's some New Zealand lager downstairs that's pretty interesting."

He dashed down the basement stairs a few moments before Cecily made her way through the crowd to the kitchen.

Michele raised her glass to Cecily. "I think I scared your date."

Cecily winced. "Oh no. Please don't scare him. He's so, so nice."

"I know. You like him. He's cute. Not at first. At first, he's kind of nerdy looking. But he's got good eyes and a terrific smile, adorable dimples. It's the kind of cute that grows on you. He's a little skinny, but I'd hit that," Michele threw in that last line just to mess with Cecily, because people with unexpressed crushes on each other are so easy to rattle.

"Please don't!" Cecily glared and slapped her arm.

Michele laughed, "What kind of monster do you think I am?"

"One that's had five drinks. You get really handsy. Oh my God, he's bringing you another one."

"Take it for the team. I need to find Deb's friend Marcelino. He's Italian, and he plays bass in a ska punk fusion band. Dibs. If I can find him again. Hey, where's Spike?"

Jack's relief was tangible when he saw Michele retreat from Cecily. As he walked up to her, Cecily motioned for him to toss his extra beer to her.

"Here, I'm Michele's designated drinker for the hour. Sorry about Michele. She's—"

"She's like the female Bangladello."

"Wow, you're right. Have they ever met?"

"They can't have—a wormhole would have opened up in the universe."

"A loud wormhole. We should make sure it never happens."

"Speaking of loud, do you want to go outside and talk? Or no, it's probably too cold. That's OK."

"No, I'd love to."

On the tiny porch that jutted out into the alley, the smokers gathered, politically incorrect and exiled. Cecily and Jack held their breath as they passed the sullen group of three, taking a seat on the last open piece of porch furniture, a sort of chaise lounge, canvas covered and rusting at the legs.

Jack looked up at the sky. "You can still see the Geminid meteor shower tonight. Probably not from downtown DC, but you never know. Did you hear Ian Bennington is coming to town to talk about an asteroid he discovered?"

Cecily shook her head. "I throw away the alumni magazine now. It's too depressing. I start looking at our class news ..." She shivered in the cold, and drew her hands up into her coat, holding her beer through the sleeves of her jacket.

Jack smirked. "Yeah, it can be hard, living in the shadow of Bill Nye the Science guy." He threw his leg over one side of the chaise and leaned back. "Here," he motioned for Cecily to lean back against him. She cautiously scooted back, and he wrapped his arms around her. "There," he said. "Warmer? And we can see meteors. Maybe. There's a lot of light, but no clouds."

Cecily leaned back, her head against his coat. She sat there for a minute, encircled, looking up at the stars. Because she knew Jack couldn't see her face from here, she allowed herself a quick smile.

"No, I just mean I've been sidetracked. I'm off wrestling this stupid bear while everybody is busy making their mark, getting married, having families, doing all the stuff you do before you hit the brick wall of old age and cancer. And I'm doing it now. It's the timing of it that just feels ridiculous. As well as frightening." She paused, "A little."

"A lot frightening. And a little ridiculous. But you're here, aren't you? I'm here. New Zealand's best is here. You're not too thrown off course. And next year you can write to the alumni newsletter about all your accomplishments, and then add, as an afterthought, 'oh and I did all of that WHILE I was fighting cancer.' How 'bout them asteroids, Ian Bennington?"

"Suck on that, Bill Nye," Cecily smiled again. "It's not all the cancer. It's getting steered into management. I feel like the lab mascot sometimes, the way I keep getting sent to all these Women In Science management seminars. They're not bad, I don't mind them. It's just these forces moving us forward: a lot more out of my hands than I thought it would be. I thought I'd have a lot more ... control over the direction of things." She paused and quickly added, "I'm not complaining, I'm just ... surprised."

"I know what you mean. I've bumped from New York to Baltimore to ... I thought I'd steer my career, but it seems like it's steering me, or rather, just kind of shoving me up and down the East Coast, like a shuffleboard puck."

"Yes! That's it! I couldn't explain it."

The back door opened again and Jane's head peered diagonally out. Cecily suddenly saw herself and Jack through Jane's eyes—how they must look, entwined on the lounge chair.

"We're driving away the recreational smokers," Cecily laughed, sitting up. "They think they're interrupting something."

"That's terrible," Jack said, sitting up with her. He leaned in slightly, his right arm moving behind her, running lightly down her back. His left hand landed at the base of her cold cheek behind her ear, and he slowly turned her face toward his, now so close she could feel his breath on her eyelashes.

Cecily stood up so quickly she almost sent Jack backwards over the chaise. I can't have this, she thought, shaking. I can't do this. There are bricks. Bricks in my body. Brick red scars. All over me.

Jack stood up a moment after her. "I'm sorry," he said, clearing his throat. "I'm not really good at ... interpreting ..."

Oh no, Cecily thought. He thinks it's about him. Again. Quickly, before she could think and screw it up again, she threw her arms around him. Or rather, she performed the post-mastectomy version of this, which involved carefully lifting her elbows up to the edge of where the pain started, moving her arms forward to the pain threshold, then mashing her body into his, bulldozing him with her cement slab-like expanders. Oh lord, Cecily thought, as she maneuvered her clumsy arms around, if I were trying out for the "spontaneous, romantic gesture" team at the Olympics, this would be a major fail.

Fortunately for her, Jack was not on this or any other Olympic judging committee. He caught her arms, and before his luck could change again, kissed her.

Sent: December 24, 2010 at 8:22 a.m.
From: Jack Schwinn
To: Cecily Murphy

At BWI waiting in epic security line. Can't believe we were robbed of 1st place on the geography quiz, but I can deal with 2nd. It just makes us stronger, hungrier next year. Your friends know how to put on a good time. I'll be in Durham 5 days. I'll call you. You ladies should come up to B-more for NYE.

Sent: December 24, 2010 at 8:25 a.m.
From: Cecily Murphy
To: Michele Geraci

What happened after I left? Sorry we had to leave on the early side. I had a blast, but I get tired so early now and Jane is overprotective and bossy. Want to hang out with those guys in Baltimore NYE?

Sent: December 24, 2010 at 11:06 a.m.
From: Michele Geraci
To: Cecily Murphy

Jack left right after you did, if that's what you're asking. And yes, everybody saw you hooking up on the porch. Excellent work, Murphy. @NYE: we'll discuss our options.

Chapter 12

May 30, 2011, 5:00 p.m.

Ceci,

Safe travels. No matter what you find in California, please remember none of it changes what happened when it counted. I understand why you have to ask the questions you're asking, but be prepared if you don't find the answers. Or if you don't find the answers you want.

I'll miss you, but I'm excited for a few days to throw my socks on the coffee table without remorse. I'm also going to invite Marcelino to stay the weekend ...! If security tries to steal your wig shampoo at the airport, just use the taser I slipped into your carry-on.

Love,
Jane

****

Cecily and Jack disembarked at LAX behind a Mexican family who had been blessed with the recent birth of triplets. The triplets hadn't enjoyed air travel, and Cecily kept her iPod ear buds in until she stepped onto the blue carpet of the airport and away from the horde of furious babies.

Almost as soon as she turned her phone back on, it rang. Cait's specific ring—which Cecily had changed to Flight of the Bumblebees. Cecily felt it adequately reflected her sister's mindset. Even before she answered, Cecily sensed the phone call sounded angry. Correctly.

"So. Mom has to tell me you're going to LA today? Why don't you tell me things?"

"Cait, I'm walking through an airport. Can I call you back? And, also, I don't understand why any of this is your business."

"Are you kidding? Anything dragging you down and taking your focus away from your recovery is my business."

Cecily took a deep breath, and since she was 3,000 miles away, felt empowered enough to snap back, "I don't know, Cait. Maybe it's just not. You're over-protective, and you've been obnoxiously so since my diagnosis."

"No, I'm just regular protective. Not overly. Do you remember the stories Mom told us when we were young? The ones that prepared us for this?"

"Sorry, but this is no fairy tale, Cait. And nothing prepared me for any of this, as it turned out."

"It was my job, in the story, to protect you. I've always known this would come and when it did, it was my job to step in. And Suzie London stepped in instead. And look what she's gone and done."

Cecily thought of Brad, who saved himself, was fighting to save his son, but ultimately couldn't save his sister. She remembered summer night sleepovers with Suzie: Suzie occupying the top bunk (always), Cecily on the bottom. They drifted asleep listening to Cait, Jimmy and Brad outside playing kick the can. Cecily and Suzie had always been so jealous that the older kids were allowed to stay up until the sun was gone and the fireflies came out.

All this time Cecily was jealous of Cait, Cait was jealous that Cecily and Suzie had each other.

"Cait, I'll call you later," Cecily snapped, and dropped her phone back into her purse.

Jack pointed at the palm trees out the window, visible just past the tarmac. "Look! Cec! Palm trees," he said, tossing Cecily's carry-on horizontally across the top of his wheeled carry-on. Cecily nodded, trying to shake off her sister's brief interruption.

Jack's small bag was his only luggage. Cecily normally travelled light as well, but traveling with wigs was like traveling with pets: they required special care and feeding. At the very least, she couldn't just shove them in a duffle bag without an hour of repercussion with the wig brush. She still wasn't completely comfortable with her shorn head. When it was hot and humid, typical for May in Maryland, she'd eschew the head coverings, but she'd get questions, as though she'd plastered an "Ask Me About My Chemotherapy" bumper sticker across her forehead. Since airplanes were generally kept as frigid as Cecily's lab, she had no qualms wearing what she called her "regular day" wig and what Jane called "Big Red."

One thing she liked about Jack was his antipathy toward her wigs. The minute she entered his apartment, he'd ask her to take it off. He said it wasn't about the wig's appearance—he admitted it looked fine—but that Cecily acted differently, more formal in it. "It's like you're putting on your ... socially palatable face when you have it on," he'd explained. "That's not the right word. I just like regular-grade Cecily." It was comments like these that made Cecily understand how close she was to the edge of falling for him. "As opposed to industrial-grade?" Cecily had teased.

After a harrowing and pungent 15-minute taxi ride up Highway 1, Cecily and Jack were relieved to find themselves standing under a two-story palm tree in front of the Hotel Edwin.

The sidewalk of Pacific Avenue teemed with people who would look like interplanetary visitors in DC. The people who passed them in swarms were less dressed, more tattooed, more beautiful, more frightening, and more exotic than Cecily had ever seen.

"Is it all you imagined?" Jack asked, watching a tall, hairless man covered completely in tattoos roller skate past them.

"More," Cecily answered, trying to not stare at a girl wearing nothing but nipple tassels and a thong bikini bottom standing next to a board advertising henna tattoos. "This was Suzie's neighborhood, eh?" Suzie was right. She had gotten kind of prudish.

"You want a henna tattoo while we're here?" Jack asked, piling the rolling bags onto each other and maneuvering them into the revolving door of the hotel.

"I might surprise you." Cecily followed pensively, still staring and nearly tripping over the bags.

Their room on the ninth floor had marble floors, sparse modern furnishings, and a glass and chrome balcony overlooking the Pacific Ocean—as blue, bright and sparkling as the website promised.

Cecily took off her wig as soon as the bellman left, slid the glass doors open and stood against the glass-enclosed balcony, trying to make herself lean forward on the rail, her heart beating fast as she looked down at her feet hovering over the street below. Glass-enclosed balconies were *de rigueur* on this street, in this city. Beyond and between the next row of buildings, the Pacific Ocean could be seen in snippets, through more glass balconies, shining silver on blue along the horizon. The breeze was salty and cool.

Jack walked up behind her, looped his arms around her waist and kissed her neck. "Do we have an agenda for today?"

"Of course we do," Cecily said, smiling. "But we can start with yours."

****

Jack's agenda took longer than anticipated, and by the time they re-emerged from their cocoon, the sun hung low over the ocean and threw long shadows into their room.

"I've never seen the sun set over the Pacific Ocean before," Cecily said, propping herself up on one elbow in bed.

"Really?" Jack asked.

"Have you?" Cecily asked him back. "Oh, yeah, you have. With Diana," she teased.

Jack threw a pillow at her head. "Not with Diana. But I've been to LA before. But even in LA, Venice feels like a different city."

"I want to see the beach," Cecily said. "I want to see where Suzie lived, and I want to start there."

"Whatever you like," Jack said, pulling her back into his arms. "Do you realize this is our first vacation together?"

"I hadn't really thought of it as a ... vacation. More like a trip." Cecily worried whether their afternoon had set the appropriate tone for their mission. Her intent and her boyfriend stood at cross-purposes. It didn't help how good he looked in the waning light, half covered in white sheets.

"OK, a trip is fine," Jack said. "It's still part of the story we'll tell at cocktail parties years from now. The first trip we took together was to California. That's where we conceived—"

"No," Cecily laughed, despite her determination to set their trip's trajectory back on course. "No conceiving. No future cocktail parties. Get dressed. I want to see this beach. Or experience it. Suzie would say experience."

Sent: December 25, 2010 at 9:30 a.m.
From: Cecily Murphy
To: Suzie London

Merry Christmas, Suzie!

Sent: December 27, 2010 at 7:20 a.m.
From: Cecily Murphy
To: Suzie London

Good luck today: I'm thinking of you.

Sent: December 28, 2010 at 6:12 a.m.
From: Cecily Murphy
To: Suzie London

Suzie? You OK? How did chemo go? Did it start yesterday?

Sent: December 29, 2010 at 11:22 a.m.
From: Jack Schwinn
To: Cecily Murphy

Hey, I'm back in town. Given any thought to New Year's Eve up here? I'd love to see you.

Sent: December 29, 2010 at 11:31 a.m.
From: Cecily Murphy
To: Jack Schwinn

How was your trip? How are your parents and brother? Melissa was juggling a few ideas for NYE; I took myself out of the conversation because I'm not a huge New Year's Eve fan. It's amateur night—all the drunken idiots. And then every place charges double or triple their usual cover, and random—really random—guys try and jump on your face at midnight, and for the next two weeks the ellipticals are full at the gym because of New Year's resolutions. And then I get all angsty about my non-resolute resolutions. At least I have a nice, clear resolution this year: get through chemo. That's straightforward enough.

Sent: December 29, 2010 at 11:35 a.m.
From: Jack Schwinn
To: Cecily Murphy

Then let's ditch and do something on our own. My New Year's resolution is to dazzle redheads with my wit, charm and dashing good looks. I should delete that, but instead I'm just going to hit send.

Sent: December 29, 2010 at 11:37 a.m.
From: Cecily Murphy
To: Jack Schwinn

Redheads? How many redheads are on the Jack Schwinn 2011 hit list?

Sent: December 29, 2010 at 11:38 a.m.
From: Jack Schwinn
To: Cecily Murphy

It depends. We'll see how it goes.

Sent: December 29, 2010 at 11:39 a.m.
From: Cecily Murphy
To: Jane McCann and Michele Geraci

See attached. Jack is hitting on me. Yes?

Sent: December 29, 2010 at 11:45 a.m.
From: Jane McCann
To: Michele Geraci and Cecily Murphy

Are you trying to make me vomit? He's adorable. You guys are adorable. Blech. Are we doing lunch today? Burrito cart on K Street is closed down ... local news said a woman found a chicken head in her chicken burrito last week. Gross. Let's try the new Indian place on 15th.

Sent: December 29, 2010 at 11:52 a.m.
From: Michele Geraci
To: Cecily Murphy and Jane McCann

Oh for the love of God, people. Get a room.

Kidding, Cecily. Glad this is happening now. Something nice before something less nice. Plus, you guys hooked up at my house, so I get the fix-up credit.

Sent: December 29, 2010 at 11:54 a.m.
From: Jane McCann
To: Michele Geraci and Cecily Murphy

Is the fix-up credit some sort of tax deduction? Because I'll take credit for it too. I dressed Cecily that night. I made her show off the new ladies. Ceci, I can bust out of here in 10 minutes. (Get it? Bust?) (Sorry! Too easy ...)

January 8, 2011, 5:00 p.m.

Cecily knew her next-door neighbors' names were Fantasia and Charlene, but needed Jane's help to apply the correct name to the correct woman. She could, however, recognize the pair on sight from a block away.

No matter the weather, Fantasia and Charlene occupied their front porch amid an array of beer bottles, cigarettes and Cheetos bags each evening before heading out to an undisclosed location they called work. The ladies subscribed to a "less is more" philosophy of fashion, and they owned spandex tube dresses in every hue saturated to Las Vegas levels.

On a typical day, Cecily would flash a mildly frightened smile at her neighbors as she returned home from work each afternoon. Cecily usually clomped her boots on the pineapple welcome mat and, occasionally, sighed in relief as she closed the door against their cigarette smoke. Cecily and Jane had devoted many hours to speculating on their neighbors' lives and livelihoods. They'd pegged Fantasia as the younger, agreeing that Charlene's age might fall anywhere between her mid-forties or mid-twenties, as Charlene applied makeup like a transvestite disguising a psoriasis flare-up.

At 5:00 in the afternoon, the gray disk of light at the top of the Metro escalator promised no warmth above ground. Cecily arranged her scarf, preparing for her brisk, two-block walk. The Metro tunnel was moderately populated at this time of day, but quiet. On the escalator up to the surface, commuters either charged to the top or paused on the moving staircase to use their smartphones. Cecily loved hearing the whoosh of trains in the tunnels under her feet. Step in and be whisked away, she thought. She was growing nervous about her upcoming chemotherapy sessions and had wasted her workday clicking back and forth between news and celebrity gossip websites, trying to assign blame for her anxiety on some exterior event. There were plenty of potential scapegoats: the economy, political scandals, the mere existence of Kim Kardashian. Nothing, not even the Kardashians, seemed worse than the side effects of chemo, which her oncologist listed for Cecily's review in a 10-page document. Double-sided and single-spaced.

And Suzie. What had happened to Suzie? Suzie was supposed to start chemo on December 27, and Cecily hadn't heard from her since. Suzie hadn't even been on Facebook. That doesn't bode well, Cecily thought.

Today, the sound of Cecily's long black boots clacking on the sidewalk gave her tremendous satisfaction. Maybe I'll go to the gym, she thought. Run it out on the elliptical.

Absorbed in thought, she automatically turned down Warren Street. The neighborhood surrounding her Metro stop, Tenleytown, featured 60-year-old oak trees planted along the quiet side streets. The trees shaded the 1940's era townhomes that housed an eclectic mix of families, American University students, and other renters like Cecily and Jane. The brick townhouse Cecily and Jane called home was old, cantankerously wired, and a bane to its owner, who was frequently consulted for plumbing emergencies, untimely appliance demises and ant infestations. Cecily and Jane, not financially responsible for its upkeep, found the old house utterly charming.

Toward the middle of the street, Cecily noted Fantasia and Charlene's porch presence, and checked out their sartorial couture du jour: minidresses. A bold choice for January: one hot pink, one canary yellow. Eye-catching, Cecily thought, in the way that fish hooks can be eye-catching. She wondered what today's shoes would be. As she continued down the buckled sidewalk, something about the scene before her struck her as off. She realized, from four houses away and across the street, that Fantasia and Charlene were not sitting on their front porch, but Cecily's.

Uh-oh, Cecily thought, sour dread rising up in her stomach. Briefly, she reviewed which neighbor was which so she'd get their names right when she asked them to please smoke on their own porch. Maybe there weren't enough places to sit on their porch anymore with all the beer bottles and ashtrays lying around.

But as Cecily fixed what she hoped was a conciliatory smile on her face and headed up the front walk, she realized that Fantasia and Charlene, deeply engaged in conversation, were sitting on top of something. Someone. And smoking, as she had guessed.

"Oh my God!" Cecily yelled, aware that her mouth was hanging open, but not caring.

"Hey there, Ceci!" Fantasia called out. "Come here, girl! We got somethin' for ya."

"Do you, now?" Cecily's boots clanked up the porch steps.

The someone lying facedown under her neighbors' two miniskirted derrieres groaned and squirmed, and was rewarded for his—it looked male—efforts with a thwap upside the head by Charlene's thick forearm. Cecily had never noticed how muscular Charlene was: she was a big girl to be sure, but strong looking with broad shoulders and a corded, muscular neck.

Charlene raised her black, painted-on eyebrows—jarring next to her orange tan and large halo of bleach-blonde frizz. "This one broke your back window," she said, adding, unnecessarily, "We caught him."

"You did," Cecily confirmed, muffled, because her hands hovered over her mouth. Then, realizing Fantasia and Charlene expected acknowledgement, she added, "Thank you. For ... stopping the breaking."

Appeased, Charlene smiled, nodded, and took another drag on her cigarette. Fantasia chimed in, "Oh, it broke, he just didn't get in. We pooled him out," Fantasia said, slapping the backs of the alleged perpetrator's denim-clad thighs, "Ass firs'."

"We know he was goin' after drugs, but he not sayin' nuthin' to us. We's all: no sir, Ceci need those drugs. She sick. What low-life piece a turd steal drugs from ladies who sick?"

"What ... what?" Cecily stuttered. "What drugs? Can we—has someone called the police?"

Fantasia and Charlene raised their eyebrows, looked at each other and laughed. The figure facedown on the gray wooden porch boards tried to move, and once again, Charlene slapped his head.

"Next time, I don't go open hand!" she bellowed at him in her indiscernible accent.

"What drugs?" Cecily asked again. "How did you find this person, and why do you keep talking about drugs?"

Fantasia scrunched her features up into the center of her face. "Watchoo mean? Drugs is Oxycotton, chile. Everybody know a cancer patient get Oxycotton. This is why you keep that shit quiet. Jane telling us y'all ben Facebookin' that shit. We tellin' her you don't go round like dat. Folk come after you drugs."

"That ... wasn't my mom's reasoning for not telling people about cancer. When did Jane say this?" Since when was Jane buddies with Fantasia and Charlene?

"Jane doin' our taxes," Charlene said. Cecily looked around, confused. Charlene and Fantasia pay taxes? And Jane nearly failed tax law in law school.

"And," Charlene continued, "she helpin' us file a retraining order genst Ralph."

"Okay," Cecily nodded as though this all made sense. So they're "retraining" Ralph. "OK. And now ... there's this man that you're sitting on. This isn't Ralph, is it?" She nodded again, as though to say "go on." The lump of squashed man on the porch moaned softly, almost melodically. Perhaps Cecily imagined it.

"Huh? He ain't Ralph! We heard a smash and come out back, and dere dis one got a hammer. I jumped the railing and tackled him. He look like one a Jane's boyfrens."

From Cecily's vantage point, now standing over the captive's limp body, she could see the truth in this. Jane did have a type. Cecily called it "Smarmy, Arrogant Congressional Staffer." If the man had an unusual, multi-syllabic name like "Sebastian" or "Benedict," Jane was even more susceptible to their dubious charms.

"We watch CSI wid da rapists, and da one wid Miami Vice, and we thinkin' the same thing," Charlene said. Fantasia nodded.

"He know about tha drugs. Everybody know about tha drugs. You a target," Charlene said. Fantasia nodded emphatically. "Oxycotton," she said.

"But I don't have Oxycontin. I only have codeine. Oh, and I guess some leftover Percocet. And Xanax. And Ativan." She paused and shivered in the cold. "And ... nevermind. I have drugs. Can we seriously call the police? I'd like to go inside and see the window." And call a company to put bars on it, she added internally. Bars all over the first floor. All over the house.

Cecily had never experienced a house robbery before, only car break-ins. Her previous car, an old, wheezing Jeep with canvas sides, had been slashed repeatedly until she stopped locking the doors and locked the steering wheel. After that, she had to leave a Post-It on the dashboard: "While you are trying to find something to steal in my car, please refrain from smoking." The would-be thieves never did stop smoking while ransacking her empty glove box, and Cecily suspected that homeless men were sleeping in the backseat, so Cecily traded it in. That, she believed, was simply part of urban living. The house robbery was far scarier—even scarier that the invader was still here, apparently dragged through the side yard to where he now lay, facedown on her porch.

The intruder now lifted his head with difficulty and rotated it toward Cecily, his face red as a pimple. He looked as though he'd been crying. His nose dripped and his brown eyes watered. Recognition dawned slowly, but Cecily realized Fantasia and Charlene were right. Or could be. She knew the perp! He wasn't one of Jane's romantic interests, however. Cecily had met him at Michele's. He was a friend of ... who again? She couldn't remember. But, Fantasia and Charlene were right again, she *was* Facebook friends with him.

He was a Morning-After Facebooker, the sort who friended people after meeting them at a party. Cecily generally ignored these friend trollers, but remembered having a conversation with this person. Come to think of it, their conversation had been about drugs. There was actually a chance that Fantasia and Charlene, TV crime show fans, could be correct.

Cecily blinked incredulously as she recalled their conversation. She'd been telling Charlene's captive how she felt like a 90-year-old woman at the pharmacy these days, and how she had to invest in a giant, weekly pill sorter. He had laughed. That asshole laughed, Cecily seethed. While he was planning to find my house and rob me. Of my drugs!

"Joe? Joe from Michele's party?" Cecily yelled. She dug into her black, cross-body shoulder bag for her Mace. Too many pockets! She seethed inwardly. Finally she pulled it out and realized she'd never used it before, and had to read the directions, printed in 3-point type on the compact, lipstick-sized canister.

"Oh, eff it already," she sighed. "Charlene, hit him, please."

Charlene complied, fulfilling her earlier promise to use her fist next time.

The assailee cursed and spat on the porch. Charlene took her fist up again and brought it down hard on his ear. His head thumped the porch boards ominously.

"He dead?" Fantasia asked.

"Naw," Charlene scoffed, then craned her neck over to look at Joe's face. She pried open a closed eyelid with one black fingernail. "He aiight."

Fantasia and Charlene then stood up in unison before Cecily had time to look away. She paid for her slow reflexes with a brief view of Fantasia and Charlene's thongs. Cecily shuddered.

"I'm calling 911," Cecily announced. Fantasia and Charlene protested, insisting they could "take care a him," but Cecily insisted. "Yes, ladies," she said. "It's the right thing to do," now wondering how many bodies were buried in her neighbors' backyard.

"Oh EFF THIS. I am on hold. I am on hold with 911," Cecily stormed. Fantasia shrugged, unphased by this information.

"'Your call is very important to us,'" Cecily repeated the automated message for her companions' benefit. "Can you believe this? 'Please hold until the next available'—what is this, the frickin' cable company? This is 911, for Pete's sake!" Fantasia shook her head and said, "Mm, mm. Shameful." She brushed off her mini-dress. The shoulder straps' miserable chore of containing Fantasia's chest was taking a toll on the spandex strings, which now lengthened to the point where they exposed more faded-green-tattooed flesh than seemed reasonable or comfortable in January.

Cecily covered the speaker of her phone and offered Fantasia and Charlene her coat, noting that Fantasia's breast tattoo was not a witch hat, as she'd previously believed, but a Mickey Mouse wearing a sorcerer's hat. Oh: Fantasia. I get it now, Cecily thought.

"I ain't cold," Charlene remarked. Fantasia laughed loudly. Cecily shook her head at the ineptitude of emergency services in the district, now listening to "Copa Cabana" on the 911 switchboard's hold music.

Behind them, Joe stirred, but nobody noticed until he leapt to his feet, darted past them, jumped down the stairs and ran into the street, where a moving car appeared and screeched to a skidding stop in the same instant, inches from Joe's waist.

Joe stared at the driver. Jane, the driver, stared back at him, her heart beating like hummingbird wings.

In that moment, Charlene launched her body into the air and tackled Joe from behind, her chest slamming his top half onto the hood of the car. Without missing a beat, she lifted herself up and started punching him alternately, methodically, with both fists. Jane screamed and held down the car's horn. Cecily pulled open the driver's side door, causing Jane to scream more loudly until she recognized Cecily. Cecily pried Jane's hands off the horn with one arm, holding the phone against her ear with the other in case the hold music stopped and she reached a live human being. At that moment, she did.

"911, what's your emergency?" the operator asked.

There is one hooker, wait, now two hookers, beating up a dude who broke into my house on top of my roommate's car in the middle of the street, Cecily thought, but she said, "I've been robbed.

And we caught him. 5110 Warren Street. We caught him. Please send the police."

Charlene looked up at Cecily, her fist poised over Joe's head. Joe was either unconscious or pretending to be. Jane stared open-mouthed at the blood that ran down the hood of her white Toyota.

"Ambalansh!" Charlene yelled.

"And an ambulance," Cecily added into the phone. She nodded, then hung up.

"Cops won't show less summon's hurt or kilt," Charlene explained. She nodded at Cecily. "Damn, girl," she said. "You lucky you got us."

Cecily, wide-eyed, nodded in return. "I sure am," she agreed, and shuddered when she realized she believed it.

That night, at the direction of the police officer who showed up an hour and a half after the ambulance, Cecily and Jane each set a goal to purge 100 friends from their lists, just in case this had been, as Charlene and Fantasia had insisted, a botched drug robbery.

"They call it a 'frenema,'" Jane told Cecily.

"Who's 'they?'" Cecily asked.

"I don't know. I just know we should have been doing them regularly, on a schedule. Like every time we go to the dentist or something."

"Maybe you need to. I'm not a friend hoarder like you," Cecily retorted.

Jane denied hoarding, but succeeded in eliminating just 59 marginal acquaintances out of 864. Cecily scrubbed her online parlor clean, de-friending 211 non-friends and would-be drug thieves: somewhere between one-third and half of her friends. (She'd stopped counting years ago. Jane knew her number at all times and wished Facebook had an un-friending alert feature. She liked to keep regular tabs on her status with ex-boyfriends.)

The women still didn't know if Joe had really robbed them for drugs, but they were pressing charges to find out, and Fantasia and Charlene were right about some things. There was too much information out there on the Internet, and apparently one couldn't be too careful about the people with whom you shared your life.

Chapter 13

May 30, 2011, 7:00 p.m.

Cecily's green sundress billowed in the warm ocean breeze as she and Jack walked down the Venice Beach boardwalk. Even in the waning hours of sunlight, the crowds lingered, the air filled with the sounds of competing drum circles, guitar players, vendors calling out to the tourists and Hare Krishnas chanting. Tourists outnumbered locals, and could be identified by their Midwestern-looking attire and by their gawking at the carnival players surrounding them.

As Cecily and Jack sat on a bench facing the ocean sharing a gelato, Jack noted, "This place is a circus. Literally. Look." Jack pointed to the gymnastics equipment set up on the beach, then a group of 20 or so people surrounding five jugglers. "Did you see what they were juggling?" Jack pushed his sunglasses up his nose then took another bite of their neon green ice cream. Cecily shook her head.

"A human skeleton. Hopefully fake."

"I feel overdressed," Cecily mused, staring at a gaggle of tall, lean, blonde girls in bikinis and knee socks, roller-skating down the boardwalk. She wondered if she should be hyper-vigilant about sunscreen or if she could bare more of her pale skin to the California sunshine. Her sundress exposed her shoulders, but her large floppy sunhat protected the soft new growth on her head. She decided her shoulders should be safe from the wide brim of the straw hat, and edged out of the shade on the bench toward Jack in the sun.

A Spiderman wearing nothing but a blue thong and body paint walked up the beach toward the boardwalk, waved to her and blew her a kiss.

"I think Spiderman has a crush on you," Jack said.

"No, look. He's doing that to everyone. Thongs are big here. Look at those women over there. Wait, I changed my mind. Don't look." Jack laughed, and pretended to try to look over her.

"Are you lying about kiwi gelato being your favorite?" Cecily asked him. "I mean, seriously. We can't have everything in common."

"You can not seriously question my commitment to kiwi gelato. Kiwi gelato is up there with pad Thai. Test me. See what I order first in the restaurant. I'll do everything first. Then decide if I'm copying you. Personally, I think you're copying me."

"Are we eating around here?" Cecily noticed a small kebob cart, and wondered if that might be where Suzie got her late-night kebobs, the ones she claimed were made of people. She looked around for nearby bars. "She said she'd pass the kebob stand on the way back from the bar," Cecily said absently.

"Hmm? No. Something tells me we don't want to be here when this place puts its night face on," Jack said, watching two unwashed, unshaven men shove each other down the beach about 50 yards away from them. As a crowd gathered, the older of the two men (wearing a kimono) spit on the younger man who seemed to have just one tooth, gleaming gold in the sunlight as he yelled incoherently.

"Maybe that's performance art," Cecily said, thinking the skeleton jugglers hadn't looked much different.

"The cops don't seem to think so," Jack said as he watched two buzzcut police officers approach the men. "Whoa, dude! Don't resist! He's got a ... taser. Too late." He tossed their empty gelato cup in the trash can next to them.

"This place is so beautiful," said Cecily, closing her eyes and listening to the ocean crash and churn in the distance, unhurried. "I mean, crazy, but beautiful. I can see why Suzie chose here. Come on.

I've never been in the Pacific Ocean. Let's go stick our feet in the water."

"I'll race you," Jack said, standing up.

"My sandals have heels," Cecily pointed out. "And I'm not really sure if I want to walk barefoot in that sand yet."

"Good point."

"Plus, I don't want to embarrass you."

"Oh, you wouldn't win," Jack said and took off running.

Cecily sprinted behind him, laughing. "Cheater! My shoes!" she yelled ahead. "It's my shoes." Her heels sank into the hot sand with every step and she stumbled, but kept running toward the ocean, so far away at low tide she could barely see the white line where the waves broke and the surfers bobbing above.

She caught up with him when she reached the wet sand, grabbed his hand, out of breath, and kept walking toward the ever-receding surf.

"You'll get your shoes ..." Jack panted, "wet ... ruined."

"Tired already?" Cecily teased, adding, "My shoes will survive."

"I was hoping you'd say that," Jack scooped her up over his shoulder like a sack of grain.

Holding her hat down with one hand, pulling her dress down to cover her underwear with the other, she tried to pound Jack's back with her elbows. "Jack, if you throw me in ..."

He dropped her as quickly as he'd picked her up. Her head spun as the remains of a wave crept up to their feet. Cecily knelt down to slip off her sandals and stepped into the Pacific Ocean for the first time. The water was warmer than she expected, and, for some reason, this was an enormous relief to her. She'd been apprehensive, coming here. She smiled up at Jack from under her hat.

It was easier with him, she realized. Everything was easier, even just the simple act of smiling. She tried it again. Was that really all there was to it, all this time?

Sent: January 9, 2011 5:30 p.m.
From: Jack Schwinn
To: Cecily Murphy

Are you OK? Got your message. Will call when boss leaves vicinity.

Sent: January 9, 2011 6:22 p.m.
From: Cecily Murphy
To: Jack Schwinn

We're fine. I took down your post because I didn't want to breed panic in the reading masses, i.e. my family. (It's exhausting doing my own public relations. Maybe I should hire a firm.) We've told our parents, of course. In just 24 hours, Jane's parents and mine have gone out and gotten us a security system. We couldn't talk them out of it. Jane is livid about it, but truthfully, I like it. It's a little embarrassing taking things from your parents in your late twenties, but yeah, I like the new alarm system. I won't lie. The robbery freaked me out.

So, physically, we're fine and safe. Psychologically, I'm less trusting, less likely to drag the recycling bin out to the curb after dark. I've ditched 200+ Facebook friends or, rather, voyeurs. I still can't get what's come over Jane. She is over at Charlene and Fantasia's house right now, helping them file a restraining order against Prince Charming (Ralph, the ex-boyfriend whose idea of "communicating" is yelling and pounding on their windows). She's also helping them with their taxes.

And, she is trying to get onto Sen. Boxer's domestic violence task force project at work, which is an about-face from appropriations, where she's been working since law school. She says it's my cancer. It's made her realize she's coasting, that life is too short to not pick your teams, AND that it's the cancer that's made everyone's motives more clear to her. I told her, look, you don't even have "the cancer." "The cancer" is not getting credit for this or for Charlene and Fantasia's stunningly efficient Duffs of Doom. The cancer can bite me. Sorry. I'm having an ungrateful day. I don't show the ungrateful side to many people. Not that you wouldn't get it. Nevermind. I'm going to stop typing now. Do you really want to visit me when I'm like this?

Sent: January 9, 2011 7:05 p.m.
From: Jack Schwinn
To: Cecily Murphy

Sorry. Still at work. "The cancer" can take credit for a few epiphanies of mine too. And you can tell me anything you want. You're not as frightening as you think you are. (And for that reason, I'm glad to hear you have the security system.) I'll take the 11 a.m. to Union and then the metro to your house. I'll get there around 12:15. I'll pick up Thai food for lunch at Union Station.

Sent: January 10, 2011 at 10:45 p.m.
From: Cecily Murphy
To: Suzie London

I haven't heard from you in weeks, so I have to assume your energy is all being directed toward managing chemo. Just wanted to let you know I'm thinking about you and I sent you a mix CD. You can listen to it for your second chemo. It's all songs from the years you and I were born: 1981 and 1982. Such great music to choose from: Don't Stop Believin', I Love Rock 'n Roll, Eye of the Tiger, Physical, 867-5309, Hey Mickey. Listen to it during chemo and I'll listen to mine. I feel prepared for it now. You're probably getting ready to go into your 2nd round. I don't want to bug you when you're feeling bad, but I'm a little worried I haven't heard from you since your first treatment. How is your port? Did you get it fixed? How did chemo go?

Sent: January 10, 2011 at 11:57 p.m.
From: Suzie London
To: Cecily Murphy

Hey Cecily. Port is out. I'm going freestyle. I had my unconventional chiropractor work on me. He couldn't help me so he refused to take my money. Can you imagine that? Imagine a doctor not charging you because they didn't fix you!! My oncologist would be SOL. Could you imagine?? My healer is helping me now, and wow, my energy has taken a big turn for the better. So much, much better. Love the mix CD, can't wait to get it! Things will go fine this week, you'll do awesome, you'll see. I'm proud of you for being so strong. You always were the rebel.

Sent: January 11, 2011 at 12:03 a.m.
From: Cecily Murphy
To: Suzie London

You say that a lot. And I'm not really. I follow directions. I read the directions. I did my homework when I got home from school. What do you mean by rebel? You're the rebel—running off to California and having this glamorous life. That's another good 80's song: Glamorous Life, Sheila E.

Sent: January 11, 2011 at 12:10 a.m.
From: Suzie London
To: Cecily Murphy

Rebelling is forging your own path. It's the Cecily way. You're a self-contained unit. See, you have vertical ambition. You're going up, you'll always go up, but you're still every bit a rebel. You're like Jace: focused. Sometimes I wish I could be like that, but then I wonder what I'd miss if I just focused on one aspect of art, film, acting, music, life. I love it all. My ambition is horizontal and I'm not talking about the casting couch. I mean I try to experience as much as I can, soak up everything. Horizontal ambition looks to some people like no ambition: like you're going nowhere, but it's going everywhere. There aren't even enough hours in the day for it.

Sent: January 11, 2011 at 12:16 a.m.
From: Cecily Murphy
To: Suzie London

Oh boy. Now I'm embarrassed. Here you are calling me a rebel and you know what I'm listening to right now? My four-year-old niece Eileigh has recently gotten me into ... Taylor Swift. What can I say? I'm not proud. I don't admit my musical inferiority to many people: only you, because you and I used to dance to Kriss Kross together, so I dare you to judge. :)

Sent: January 11, 2011 at 12:21 a.m.
From: Suzie London
To: Cecily Murphy

Daddy Mac'll make you jump! Jump! I'll take you to the Rock & Roll museum in Cleveland, Ohio. They have Tom Petty's songwriting notes. Lyrics written on napkins and coffee spilled all over his notebooks. Jace and I went there five years ago—it was like finding my church at last.

Sent: January 11, 2011 at 12:22 a.m.
From: Cecily Murphy
To: Suzie London

Suzie, who's Jace? Can't find him on your Facebook page.

Sent: January 11, 2011 at 12:52 a.m.
From: Suzie London
To: Cecily Murphy

Trust me, he's there! He is, was, and will never be my One and Only. (Insert violins.) Ha! I'm shitting you. He ain't no Lionel Richie song. He's either an ex-boyfriend with financial benefits or an ex-benefit with boyfriend tendencies. You have to use triple reverse psychology to explain it. I lost Gretchen, my best friend, over him. (more violins, please.) We said we'd never fight over a guy, and we did. Stupid, stupid. I was morbidly romantic when I was 17. In the end, it never even mattered. Stupid Jace. I'd never met anyone who had the same brain. We found the same things funny. We'd look at each other and just start laughing. Nobody else in the room knew what we were even talking about.

Someone took a picture at a bonfire at the beach: it's right on my page, you can see it. It was a cold night and we were bundled in blankets. He sat behind me with his arms and legs wrapped around me. I should have been lying back but I was craning my neck around to look at him. He was singing to me. I Want You, by Elvis Costello. Download it now. Kind of a creepy song the way Elvis sings it, but the way Jace sang it, it was beautiful. I told him he belonged in a museum so life couldn't tarnish him, and he said I belonged in a convent so men couldn't tarnish me, and that's when Lisa took the picture.

I was on the beach at Santa Monica last time with Jace. He showed up at my house on his motorcycle and told me his day belonged to me. Not his heart and soul, mind you. Just his day. I took it. It was enough. I said, Santa Monica, that's where we'll waste your precious afternoon. It was sunny and warm and windy. He sat behind me again and sang into my hair. Oh, I had hair that day. Blowing around in the wind. We smoked a joint or two and talked and made out and I thought, this is enough, isn't it? It has to be enough. Just loving. Even though he has no idea what love means. Even though you know he's here because of your "health problems" and he feels guilty, just like you thought you always wanted him to be. But it's not love, it's pity, all stirred in with lust and regret. But it has to be enough because it's my happy place.

It was the day I wrote you. I'd been thinking about your post for days, just haunted by it, and when I got home from the beach, I just did it, I wrote you. I figured you could write back or not, that I did my part, that I answered whatever fate had been calling me to do. There was something about that day: the sand, the waves, Jace kissing my eyelashes in the sun, it made me not optimistic, really. But optimistic enough. That day, at least, it was enough.

Sent: January 11, 2011 at 12:59 a.m.
From: Cecily Murphy
To: Suzie London

The way you describe him, kind of like he's better than you. It's not something I'm used to hearing from you. Whoever he is, this guy in the blanket on the beach (the picture is a little blurry, but I'll grant he's pretty cute) he's not better than you. I see that a lot here in DC. My roommate and some of my friends work for Congress and these guys they hang out with: they think they're rock stars or something, and Jane is so "lucky" to date them. Wait, you're in LA. Is Jace an *actual* rock star?

Sent: January 11, 2011 at 1:10 a.m.
From: Suzie London
To: Cecily Murphy

You know him as Jason Frost. Or you don't. He's more famous than he thinks he is but less famous than his sycophants tell him he is. He's more successful than famous, I'd say. He's a success. He earned it. I'll send you his albums. Autographed. Yeah, baby. I said autographed. I can make it pay.

Sent: January 11, 2011 at 1:25 a.m.
From: Cecily Murphy
To: Suzie London

OK, successful is right. I just Googled him. He's HOT, too. That beach picture doesn't do justice. But Suzie, he's not better than you. It sounds like he thinks he's better than you, or you think he is. It's unequal. It's not enough.

Sent: January 11, 2011 at 1:31 a.m.
From: Suzie London
To: Cecily Murphy

Don't think I don't know how to get what I need. I just know what to expect from people. I'm no withering daffodil. Jace even wrote a song about it, after he cheated on me with Gretchen. It's called *She Hates My Guts*. Download it now. No, don't. I'll mail you the whole album. You remember that old bitch who lived between us: Mrs. Douglas? She told everyone in the neighborhood my mom was a worthless drunk. I flooded her living room for it. After that she shut her mouth. After that I wasn't a stupid kid anymore. That stunt made me a playa: it put me in the game. I was old enough to say, shut it, bitch, or else. And I was only nine. Nine years old.

You know what I need right now? To expand my horizons. Let's go on a trip! I've never seen Montana. We can rustle cows and stay on a dude ranch. You're Lefty. I'm Shorty. "You Can Sleep While I Drive," Melissa Etheridge. You know that song? Download it now.

Sent: January 11, 2011 at 1:36 a.m.
From: Cecily Murphy
To: Suzie London

Oh my God. I had no idea. About Mrs. Douglas. I told on you, Suzie. I got you in trouble.

Sent: January 11, 2011 at 1:39 a.m.
From: Suzie London
To: Cecily Murphy

And I hated you for it!!!! But on some level I didn't, because I wanted her to know it was me. Not Mr. Random Mayhem (my brother.) Me = not random. Pissed off.

Sent: January 11, 2011 at 1:43 a.m.
From: Cecily Murphy
To: Suzie London

Remind me to never piss you off! Well ... again.

Sent: January 11, 2011 at 1:45 a.m.
From: Suzie London
To: Cecily Murphy

I wouldn't survive one minute without what Jace calls "Suzie justice." Imagine me with my movie announcer voice: "In a world ... where justice ... is a dim memory." But honestly, I don't have that kind of anger anymore. I'm not going to sit here and tell you I'm a better person. It's just kind of evolved into not caring what people think about me. I'll cut-paste you the lyrics to *She Hates My Guts*. Watch out: Q Magazine (UK rag) called it "shock rock." Fuh! Not even! He left the good stuff out, IMHO.

She Hates My Guts *music/lyrics by Jason Frost*
    She stole my U2 bootleg tapes
    took them to a laundromat
    sent them through the spin
    said it was the best buck she ever spent
    and her favorite sin.

CHORUS:
    This chick is killing me.
    She hates my guts.
    What did I do, what did I say?
    She just hates my fucking guts
    And I love her anyway
    She bleached the word "whore"
    into the grass in my front yard
    We didn't know till the grass died
    My roommates were fucking pissed
    I think I have to move and hide

CHORUS

> The kittens on my doorstep
> a new one every day
> took them to a shelter close to here
> I had to keep the last two though
> was looking like a pervert, like Richard sodding Gere.

CHORUS

> She slept with my drummer, bass guitarist,
> tour manager—a girl
> She just did that to piss me off
> She's not into that she says
> She just knew I'd want to watch.

CHORUS

CHORUS

FADE

Sent: January 11, 2011 at 1:56 a.m.
From: Cecily Murphy
To: Suzie London

HOLY COW!!! Now I really can't wait to get these CDs. Amazing you can still get them autographed after what you did to his lawn. The watershed issues, Suzie! What are you doing to California's watershed?? And speaking of charming famous men, always wanted to ask you this … how did you meet Seal?

Sent: January 11, 2011 at 1:56 a.m.
From: Suzie London
To: Cecily Murphy

I didn't just meet him. :)

Sent: January 11, 2011 at 1:57 a.m.
From: Cecily Murphy
To: Suzie London

Nuh. UH. NO WAY. Shoot, is it this late? Gotta go to bed. But when I wake up I want details IN my inbox!

Sent: January 11, 2011 at 1:58 a.m.
From: Suzie London
To: Cecily Murphy

Way! Good night!

Chapter 14

May 30, 2011, 8:30 p.m.

"I don't know much about alcoholism," Jack said, sipping his beer at Zengo, an Asian-Mexican fusion restaurant he'd found online. Jack and Cecily had taken a cab to dinner on the Third Street Promenade in Santa Monica, a tree-lined pedestrian mall near the beach.

"Except what I've seen on TV. The only experience I've had with it was in high school, working as a bus boy at the University Club at Duke. The wine cooler system broke. It was summer and it got up to 92 degrees in there. We had to throw out 100 bottles of wine. We took them out to the dumpster, and all the homeless people in town showed up like we had a megaphone yelling 'free wine!' It was like a convention out there. But the wine was rancid, pure vinegar. We realized we were going to kill homeless people if we kept tossing bottles, so we had to pour out all the wine by hand. We stood at the dishwashing sinks for hours, dumping rancid wine. As I was taking out the trash that night, a man grabbed my arm. He just looked at me and said, 'Please.' I told him I couldn't help him. But that look. And the 'please.' Please give me rancid wine. If that's not an illness, I don't know what is."

"She didn't believe she was an alcoholic. She said she didn't 'marinate in victim sauce' like her brother."

"If you're on reality TV, maybe you're embracing so-called victimhood, but at least he's moving toward something that resembles living. Suzie was just running screaming toward death,"

Jack regretted saying it. He watched Cecily closely over the top of his glass. She seemed a bit fragile today. She was on vacation one minute, on a mission the next.

Cecily took the first sip of her drink and made a face. "That's different," she said, giving the verdict on her sweet and sour margarita. Thinking about Suzie, she added, "She ran straight towards everything else I guess."

"It's fusion," Jack said. "I thought you'd like it because Asian and Mexican are your two favorites."

"Together, they *are* quite a pair. But different is good. You ordered squid. I never would have ordered squid. Especially as an appetizer."

"See? I don't copy you. I'm full of surprises."

Cecily felt calmer tonight as the sun sank behind Jack's head into the Pacific Ocean. Maybe it was the drink, maybe because Santa Monica resembled the Los Angeles of her imagination: sunny, clean, with movie theaters everywhere. It was different, but familiar. The stores were all the same as they were back home and a few of the restaurants, too. When they stepped out of the cab on the edge of Palisades Park, she recognized the beach from *BayWatch* and the amusement park out towards the pier from *Lost Boys*.

"Her address is about four blocks from our hotel. But we don't have to go to her house tonight," Jack suggested.

"I want to meet the roommate. Rothner. He's a drag queen. You know that, right?"

"I know. He's the one with the wigs. If we go tomorrow, he apparently works nights, why don't we wait till the afternoon?"

"Sounds good."

"And that gives us all morning?"

"We can start with her neighborhood, and ask around at the coffee shop where she used to check in on Facebook."

The waitress arrived with their food: Peking Duck tacos for Jack and salmon with guacamole and soy sauce for Cecily.

Jack thanked the waitress and raised his glass.

"To life," he said.

Cecily smiled and clinked. "And surprises."

Posted January 11, 2011 at 10:22 a.m.
Cecily Murphy

One phase of reconstruction is done, on schedule, even with the delays I enforced (thanks, **Suzie London**). No stabbing today at Dr. SPO's office. Was almost confused: that's kind of our thing. I come in. He stabs me. But now I get a nice long reprieve filled with ... chemo.

Posted January 12, 2011 at 9:11 a.m.
Cecily Murphy

Big shout out to **Jane McCann** for driving me to pre-chemo bloodwork today. And to **Jack Schwinn** for lending me his portable DVD player. I'm all set for tomorrow morning: bring the chemical crazy (knock wood).

January 12, 2011, 6:00 p.m.

Cecily didn't want to do the dishes. It was technically her turn, but she knew Jane would never push it. First of all, Jane, like all her family and friends, now treated her like an unexploded bomb wrapped in pink ribbon. Secondly, Jane didn't care whether the dishes were done or not. Jane thrived in squalor, and only cleaned up after herself when parents or male friends were due to visit. Cecily had learned to eke out a peaceful existence with Jane over the years: dealing with clutter, phone messages written on what appeared to be important pages ripped from Jane's textbooks, and even Jane's cat, Vermin. Cecily named the cat after the fleas that colonized the sofa minutes after Vermin's daring street rescue. (Daring, in Cecily's opinion, because Jane had no business handling stray cats without proper gloves and eye protection.) Jane was too smart for stunts such as these and, in Cecily's opinion, too smart to fail the Bar, which Jane also managed to accomplish, spending her summer Bar prep time reading romance novels in a bikini on the back porch. Despite her more trying qualities, Jane was smart when she wanted to be, fiercely independent, generous, funny and sociable. And she encouraged Cecily, who considered herself an introvert trapped in the life and times of an extravert, to edge outside her comfort zone, just often enough.

Cecily lay on the ancient sofa, thinking about what had transpired on this spot over the years and whether Jane had remembered to give Verm his medication for his urinary tract infection. How could she live with this disgusting cat during chemo? How was life going to work at all? Independence from her mother's maudlin weeping exacted a price. And hadn't Jane hooked up with Richard Lain on this couch just a few weeks ago? Cecily turned to her side and with her "good" arm (today it was her left), pressed herself into a sitting position just as she heard Jane tromp up the porch steps with her baggage: a briefcase and a purse large enough to smuggle a medium-sized collie. Fortunately, no new pets resided in Jane's bags today.

"Hey!" Jane called, kicking her boots off in the foyer. "How're you feeling?"

"Good," Cecily lied. "I was just about to do the dishes and stick one of my mom's casseroles in the oven."

"I'll do that, go lie down," Jane waved a dismissive hand at her then dumped her bags on the massive, faux-marble dining room table that came with the house. The brown, tan, and gold speckled monstrosity occupied three-quarters of the dining room and belonged in a museum of 1970's neo-baroque horrors in furniture design. Cecily was certain the Smithsonian would open such a museum, if it didn't exist already. Jane adored it on sight, naming it "Big Brown" and arguing that it was so awful it was actually cool. Guests at their dinner parties agreed, debating possibilities of the table's storied past: a ping-pong table in Donald Trump's basement, maybe? Cecily had grown to love it too, albeit more reluctantly. If it can't physically be removed from the house without the use of a chainsaw, she reasoned, they might as well enjoy it. Plus, the plastic made it so easy to clean.

Jane opened the freezer and stuck her head inside. "Ooh, your mom made us pierogies! Let's have those! Want pierogies?"

"Sure," Cecily said, standing up and hobbling into the kitchen. "I can make them."

"You go upstairs now, or I'll call your sister to come get you," Jane kicked the low freezer door shut with her socked foot.

"Look," Cecily sighed, leaning against the counter. "This is very nice of everyone. But this is not a sprint. It's a long haul. We're only in the beginning, and I don't know how to put this, but I want to save my favors. I don't want people to get caregiver burnout right when the bad part is about to start."

Jane smirked as she smacked their too-heavy cast iron skillet on the stove coils. Cecily winced, thinking of their security deposit. "Nobody's going to burn out or lose patience with you. Nobody. Trust us. Swipe the Cancer Card. Yes, your swipes are unlimited. You are not a swipe abuser. It's not in your nature. The opposite, in fact. Go to bed. You don't look so good. Get a quick nap, and I'll wake you up in half an hour when these are ready."

****

Over pierogies and a salad, Jane and Cecily dissected Jane's love life, specifically Richard Lain, whose appeal completely eluded Cecily. It was the first time since the robbery that Cecily and Jane had eaten dinner together at home, lending a sense of occasion to the routine, a christening of the new dining room window. Jane even lit the candles in their large, silver candelabra, and Big Brown reflected orange candlelight off its shiny acrylic surface.

"I refuse to believe you see anything in this guy worth dating."

"Dating someone from work is like shopping in the same store every week. They keep the nuts here, they keep the fruits—well, they keep the fruits hidden, at least during the day. There's nothing, new, exciting. Richard's like boxed wine. He's cheap, but the label is pretty. I can get drunk with him, but he's not going to impress me."

"Then why waste your time?" Cecily asked.

"What else would I be doing, sitting home scrubbing the toilet?"

"No, you definitely wouldn't be doing that."

"I love going out. If anyone wants to go out, I'm game. I'm not dead yet," Jane froze. After a pause, she spat out, "Oh crap. Am I allowed to say 'dead' now?"

Cecily rolled her eyes. "Say dead, for God's sake. Say dead until you're dead, Jane."

Jane smiled in relief, her big, radiant smile, the one that showed all the teeth Jane pointlessly fretted over for being too large. "You allowed to drink wine today?"

"I haven't taken a pain pill since last night," Cecily thought aloud, leaning back in her chair. "I probably shouldn't, though, because I'm going to cave and take one tonight."

Jane pushed her chair away from Big Brown, walked into the kitchen and returned with a bottle of Pinot Grigio and two glasses. "Nonsense. White wine with pierogies, right?"

"Absolutely. I think. Bring it."

"So, that's one problem with the dating pool at work," Jane continued. "No variety. And, then, I'm going to be 28 next year."

"March. Two months."

"Thanks. I guess because we spent all our vacation time and money this summer going to weddings, the single boys are nervously edging toward the exit doors. Like we're going to grow claws and fangs and start coming after them. Commitment! Marriage! Babies! They're all weird now. Everything comes with a caveat. Before Richard would even hook up with me he sounded like the legal notices at the end of the pill commercials. 'Richard Lain's participation in any extracurricular activities does not guarantee future participation in said activities.' Shut UP, you loser! You're with a girl who's willing to make out with you. You're lucky to be here! Act like it!"

"Any views expressed herein by Richard's Richard do not reflect the views of Richard himself, and should not—"

Jane ran out of the room to spit her mouthful into the kitchen sink. She wiped her mouth and took a deep breath. "Damn you, Cecily, I was drinking! Anyway, it's so ridiculous because nothing could be further from the truth. Do we want to be sucked out of the city through the Metro tunnels and dropped into a depressing suburb? God no! We pity those people. Melissa never comes out anymore. She's got her crazy real housewives of northern Virginia with their competitive engagement parties and book clubs and, oh my God, the showers. If I ever consent to marry one of these clowns someday, you may not throw me a shower. Wedding. Baby. Any occasion."

"Deal," Cecily said, absent-mindedly. There was a long, companionable silence during which the two friends sat with their own thoughts. Then Cecily said, "Artists. Musicians. That's who you need to be dating. Branch out. Find someone who's fun, smart, great in bed and needs a sugar momma."

Jane smiled, "I like it. But I can barely sugar momma Verm."

"You'll quit," Cecily said, now a little tipsy off the three ounces of wine. "You'll open your own practice, specializing in the defense of Congress members accused of wrongdoing. Your market is limitless. A new crop of criminals arrives every two years."

"Yes! I'll advertise at the DNC: 'Have you been accused of perverted sexual acts banned even in Nevada?' And at the RNC: 'Have you been accused of securities fraud or selling political influence?' To both of them I'll do: 'When you were arrested, did you ask the police, Hey, don't you know who my daddy is? Let Jane McCann work," Jane paused, pointed her wine glass at Cecily, and added, "for YOU.'"

Cecily laughed. "You'll need an 800 number. 1-800—"

"BAD BOYS," Jane finished.

"DUMB ASS!"

"You'll be rich!"

Cecily's phone rang.

"It's Jack!" Jane sang, raising her eyebrows.

Cecily ran over to the couch and picked up the phone. "Huh," she mused. "It's my oncologist's office. Someone's working late."

Posted January 13, 2011 at 6:19 a.m.
Cecily Murphy

Bloodwork came back bad. V. high white cells: matched previous blood report they thought was fluke. No chemo today. Next step: bone marrow biopsy, to test for leukemia. V. scared.

Sent: January 14, 2011 at 1:54 p.m.
From: Cecily Murphy
To: Suzie London

Suzie,

I don't know where you are and how you're doing. But I'm scared over here. I'm putting on a brave face, but I'm really, really scared. And my stupid oncologist isn't returning my phone calls. She actually makes my cocky, sexist surgeon look like prince charming. He always returns my emails within five minutes, calls me on weekends, 10 p.m., 6 a.m., you name it. The oncologist calls me "Celia" and I swear she couldn't pick me out of a lineup. Not to mention she does not. Return. My. Freaking. Phone Calls. So frustrated! I just have some simple questions about typical leukocytic responses to some of the pre-chemo meds they had me on and whether those could be factoring in to my bloodwork scores. But no. Only the stupid, worthless counselor will talk to me. I'm climbing the walls and she's babbling on about therapy and Zoloft. Are you kidding me? I just have a medical question, nobody who is able to answer it will deign to do so, and I need Zoloft? I need an answer. That's all!

I hope you're doing well. I think of you, every day. Hope you're resisting the lure of the cherry Slurpees, for the sake of your shoes.

Sent: January 14, 2011 at 5:30 p.m.
From: Suzie London
To: Cecily Murphy

Everything will be OK. I know this much: you don't have leukemia. I read your post and I was like bullshit. I've seen people with leukemia. They're sick-sick, not like breast cancer where you can't believe you're sick because you feel fine. You don't feel fine with leukemia. There are clues. When you're sick with that, it's not that subtle.

I'm doing better. I fired the oncologist I hated. You need to fire yours too. There are millions of doctors willing to take your money, right? You need to find someone you like. Who answers your calls.

I read your update at Skateland, turning in an exquisite and nuanced performance as Snow White on sparkly pink roller skates with neon rims, for a gig, a birthday party for a nine-year-old girl who spent the whole time texting on roller skates. Mayhem. I was thinking about it, well, I was in character, so Snow was thinking about it, and she—we—came up with my Theory of Inverse Proportion With Regard to ... I'm still working on the name but here it is: This first year, your Year 1 of Cancership, is going to be the year you go to the doctor frequently, and the doctor will find weird things, frequently. At this point your fear will be the highest, but the likelihood of It Being Cancer is probably lowest, because you're being watched so closely. I wondered, as they kept finding stuff in the middle of my treatment: are these things that always existed in my body BC, never before documented because of their complete lack of interesting-ness, or is this the omen of the Apocalypse, the sign that all hell is breaking loose? For you, the cancer wasn't in your lymph nodes, and the odds of having two cancers at the same time are slim. See? You didn't think I was this smart. I used to read about this stuff. Not this time, but last time I did. This time I'm lazy because I have you to read about it for me. :)

Tell those mof's they can kiss your grits. Is it wrong to go to your AA meeting drunk? I have to go but I had a few beers with Jace this afternoon. I hate AA. The only thing I ever got out of it was the Serenity Prayer: God grant me the courage to live my life on my own terms, to change the things I can, and throw out the things I can't. I got that. And a few random hookups ... that I also threw out for overstaying their welcome.

Sent: January 14, 2011 at 6:47 p.m.
From: Cecily Murphy
To: Suzie London

OK, now I'm more worried about you. Are you drinking when you shouldn't be?

Sent: January 14, 2011 at 7:32 p.m.
From: Suzie London
To: Cecily Murphy

Don't worry about me: I'm doing great. I should really be in Al Anon, not AA, but tell that to the judge. I'm working a LOT, I've been going to my healer. She's helping me achieve clarity, understanding and peace. And helping me manage pain and nausea and all that crap. I'm doing great. You, though. You need to try on some new oncologists. Oh, and talk to the nurses. The nurses know more than doctors 99.9 percent of the time.

Sent: January 14, 2011 at 7:47 p.m.
From: Cecily Murphy
To: Suzie London

OK ... I guess if you're feeling well enough to work and have a beer, that doesn't sound too bad. That is, if you're using "tell that to the judge" as a colloquialism, and not referring to an actual court case. I really don't know about this healer business, that sounds sketchy, but I believe you about nurses. Nurses are in the field, on the ground. They're foot soldiers. They collect information and yes, it's anecdotal, but aren't all theories born from that? If it's not published, it doesn't exist for doctors. Nurses are five years ahead of the doctors, especially when you're dealing with unknown variables. I trust nurses because they're the ones seeing what happens with their own eyes. If I looked sick to them, I'd have an easier time believing I was sick. But they're always telling me I look well, I'm recovering nicely. I feel well. I don't feel sick in my blood. I don't feel ill.

When's your next treatment? Are you still on the 3x a month schedule? Has your hair gone yet? Twenty pages of potential side effects, any random combination can hit people like scattershot: how do you even plan for something like that? It drives me crazy.

Sent: January 14, 2011 at 7:47 p.m.
From: Jack Schwinn
To: Cecily Murphy

There you are! Sorry for cornering you online (I hate this new instant message feature. It seems like I'm invading your privacy: I am.) I just wanted to let you know 1) I am here for you and 2) I can be there for you in 40 minutes or less, depending on Beltway traffic. It's always more fun to watch Battlestar Galactica with a friend. Chang didn't believe me when I told him you got me the Battlestar DVD for Christmas. He was with me when I bought the Battlestar DVD for you, so he thinks I bought it for myself and told everyone I was getting it for my "girlfriend at band camp." For the win: what movie is the quote from?

Sent: January 14, 2011 at 7:49 p.m.
From: Cecily Murphy
To: Jack Schwinn

American Pie: too easy!

Sent: January 14, 2011 at 7:51 p.m.
From: Jack Schwinn
To: Cecily Murphy

I knew you'd write back if I threw movie trivia at you. Seriously, though, can I see you tomorrow?

Sent: January 14, 2011 at 7:52 p.m.
From: Cecily Murphy
To: Jack Schwinn

Only if you swear we're not going to wallow. Just Battlestar. No wallowing. No thinking, no worrying.

Sent: January 14, 2011 at 9:21 p.m.
From: Suzie London
To: Cecily Murphy

But with the healer you get free a henna tattoo with every crystal ball reading. And she's gonna git those witches that caused my disease!

It's not like you think at all!!! Healers are one of the remaining few scholars of ancient earth and life wisdom. What's all this modern knowledge getting us? Freedom from suffering? Not hardly. Hopefully only few will suffer like you and I, waiting for the phone call, will we live or die? (I didn't mean for that to rhyme it just did.) (I kind of meant to, halfway through writing it. That might go into a song.)

And I'm not cutting on your work, because I think you're strong and smart and brave and good, but really, how is the Chesapeake Bay doing these days? Despite all your efforts to save it, with your knowledge and your measuring, it's still going to die, isn't it? As a toxic waste dump. I'm not cutting on your work. Your good work, your science, is the pick of the pack, the yin of the yang. (Now I can't stop with the stupid word play.) But my healer's wisdom goes back to a time before money was god and God was god. It's good shit and worth every penny Jace pays for her.

**Sent: January 14, 2011 at 9:50 p.m.
From: Cecily Murphy
To: Suzie London**

Didn't mean to come off as healer-phobic. You're right about the Bay. It has 50-100 years, tops, depending on how stupid we are. I get your point. What's the point of knowing how to prevent algae blooms if a factory can just write a check to a politician and make that knowledge go away? But I do like to think earth science was not a completely pointless Master's degree. For instance, I can even tell you which mushroom species you'd enjoy most. Although I suspect you already know that. :) Also: glad to hear Jace is helping you out. I worry about you, out there on the West Coast, so far away.

Chapter 15

May 31, 2011, 8:00 a.m.

The next morning, Cecily awoke with her arms and legs sprawled over Jack who was sitting up in bed with his laptop open.

He leaned down and kissed the top of her fuzzy head. "My little Borg," he said, grinning.

Cecily was not generally averse to Star Trek references, but she didn't like the Borg comment while she was feeling vulnerable and exposed in her bra, and pulled the sheet up to cover herself. When? She asked herself. When will I ever let him see this part of me? When reconstruction is done? When the caution tape comes down? Once again, she chastised herself for the ridiculous timing of this. What a great time to bring my sex life back from the dead, Cecily thought, when half my body is off limits. How could Jack put up with her? Why would he want to?

"Are you hiding again? Come out," Jack said. "I'm on Facebook. Brad set up a Facebook page, Suzie London RIP. It's getting lots of likes and hits. From people with last names. I don't know how many of these are Suzie's friends or how many of these are fans of Dr. Dick—wow! Seal! Is that the real Seal? It couldn't be."

Cecily threw the sheet off and climbed up the mountain of pillows behind Jack to peek over his shoulder. "It could be," she said. "She knew him." She smiled. "In the biblical sense."

"No way!" Jack laughed. "That looks like both of them in that picture."

"She's so beautiful," Cecily sighed. "Look at her skin, her eyes. She's radiant."

"Have you posted anything to this page?" Jack asked.

"No," Cecily said, leaning her head on his shoulder. "I don't know what to say yet."

"We'll figure it out," Jack said. He looked at his watch. "But we'll need coffee."

"Soon," Cecily agreed. "What was in those margaritas? I shouldn't have had two."

"If you didn't, you wouldn't have gone dancing on the beach with me," Jack said, leaning in to kiss her. "And then we wouldn't have done this—" he rolled on top of her and kissed her, longer.

Cecily laughed. "Yeah, and then the cop wouldn't have come up behind us and told us to get a room."

"Like we were crazy teenagers or something," Jack kissed her again.

"Except you'll never get to second base with me," Cecily mumbled into his stubble.

"Second base is overrated," Jack said, kissing her neck.

"Doesn't that bother you?" Cecily pushed him away. "Come on. That's got to be annoying."

"Cecily," Jack rolled off of her and sat up. "Sometimes I think you don't know me at all. I'm not pressuring you to show me something you don't want to show me. I don't want to pressure you to do anything you don't want to do. Do you want to know the truth?"

Cecily nodded.

"What you have here, now," he gestured to her bra, "your scars, your evil bricks, whatever you call them. They're more beautiful to me than anything that was there before them. You know why?"

Cecily shook her head.

"Because they mean you survived."

Cecily's eyes stung with tears. "You're not really serious."

"I'm more serious than I've ever been. You could do anything there. You could plant two sunflowers there for all I care, and I'd love them because they're part of you, and I love you."

Cecily flushed all over. She hid her face in the pillow but she was smiling.

"That's not ... normal ... for a boy," Cecily shook her head. "Boobs are important to boys."

"Then all the other guys can have all the boobs they want. I want Cecily Murphy. Alive. With me. Now. I won't have her any other way."

Cecily was quiet for a minute. "I guess I will have semi-normal boobs eventually. Soon. I guess. But then I won't have a uterus once Dr. Sharp Pointy Objects gets through with me. Do you see the trouble you're taking on? I'm losing body parts right and left. I'm a mess. A leper."

"You were trouble from the day I met you, Thing 1. I think it's the red hair," he ran his hand over the thick red sprouts of curly fuzz that covered her scalp. "Please. Can you trust me?" He was serious now.

"Well," Cecily sighed. "Yes, but I'd be a lot happier about trusting in general if I could figure out where I ever stood with Suzie London or where she stood with me."

"In the past, now," Jack said, picking up his laptop from where it had fallen to the side. "But on this page she's still alive. This was a great idea for Brad. I think he could use the support."

"Can I see?" Cecily asked. "I want to look for a Lisa."

"I did. The videographer/photographer, right? There are quite a few Lisa's offering condolences," Jack said.

"Hmm," Cecily said, scanning. "It looks like most of these people are just fans of the show. Oh, wait! There's one of my classmates from Pine Hill, Jenny. Huh. No, she just saw the show too. Yeah, I don't know how much help this will be ... except for maybe confirming the Seal story. Wow. That's really him."

****

They chose the coffee shop Suzie talked about online; the one she said was right around the corner from her house. Cecily just wanted to walk by Suzie's house, take it in, even if they wouldn't disturb Rothner until the afternoon.

Although it wasn't even 9:00 a.m., Cecily and Jack both reached for their sunglasses as they whirled out of the hotel's revolving door into the bright sunlight. It was mild for the early hour, promising them a hotter day ahead. Following the map drawn by the hotel concierge, they turned left and continued to the end of the block where they zig-zagged through the streets of Venice, moving further away from the beach through mixed-use residential neighborhoods.

"Where are the canals?" Jack asked.

Cecily looked at their tear-off map of the Venice neighborhood. "South of us," she said. "We can walk by them on the way back, or we can turn west and walk back through the park."

Cecily counted every liquor store they passed. She didn't know why. This statistic proved nothing. But she thought it was notable that she'd counted five by the time they turned onto Beech, a short, one-block street connecting two busier streets. Beech Street was lined with shrubs that formed a barrier around the half-dozen or so squat, boxy apartment buildings and condominiums.

Halfway down the block Cecily stopped at a pink stucco building. "Forty-one," she said. "This is it."

The three-story building was split in two, the two sides facing each other with a connecting cement stairwell. The paint peeled off the mailboxes that stood against the left wall. Cecily and Jack read the names: "Rothner, 2B," Cecily read aloud.

"Excuse me?" a voice behind her said.

Cecily and Jack turned around to face a beefy, African-American man about Jack's height with black hair cut tight to his scalp. He appeared to be sweating through his white pinstriped button down shirt although he had his suit jacket off and slung over his shoulder.

Standing on the bottom step of the staircase, he appraised Jack and Cecily as cautiously as they appraised him.

"We're looking for someone named Rothner," Cecily ventured.

The man squinted at them, then acted like he hadn't heard, continuing down the walk without looking at them. Jack moved aside. Cecily thought of moving aside, then didn't.

"Not interested," he said, stepping around Cecily at the last possible second.

Cecily felt like an excitable puppy being chastised for making a puddle on the floor. "Wait! I want to talk to you about your roommate, Suzie London." She thought the name would slow him. It didn't.

From behind his back, Cecily heard him call out, "Whatever she owe you, I don't got."

"No, it's—" Cecily scampered down the path, her bare calves grazing the hedges as she tripped in front of Jack. The man stopped walking and abruptly turned around to face them.

"Whatever this is, I suggest you leave it be. Leave her in peace. She finally in peace. I gotta go to work," he said and started walking again.

"I'll walk with you," Cecily offered.

The man made a sort of growling noise and slowed down enough to turn around and face Cecily again. "I'm not walking!" he half-sang.

"I'll drive you," Cecily said, then realized she couldn't do this. "In a taxi?" she added uselessly.

The man's phone buzzed. He flipped it out of his pocket like a pistol. "You got David. Yes. No! Tami's got that segment! Oh yes she is! Well, she can go fuck a duck because it's right there on the calendar. Look it up. I know. She crazy. Look. Lemme call you right back, I got Suzie stalkers."

Jack looked amused, but Cecily took offense. "I'm not a stalker," she huffed.

"Then kindly get out of my way," the man motioned to the red Prius parked at the curb behind her. He had expressive eyebrows and might have been wearing eyeliner.

Jack took her arm and moved her out of the way. The man stepped in and opened the car door. "Wait!" Cecily called. Jack stepped in front of her: "Honey, don't—"

"No, this is not the first time you call me honey," Cecily said. "This is not going to be a thing."

Rothner rolled his eyes, shook his head and lowered himself into the Prius.

Desperate, Cecily called out, "Did Suzie London have cancer?"

The man paused, his hand on the door handle. He let go and sat back into the bucket seat in the car

"Are you kidding me? This is going to be my Monday morning?" he asked a feathered God's eye hanging from the rear view mirror. Looking up, he asked Cecily, "What business is that of yours, lady? Who the fuck are you?"

"I was a friend of hers!"

"If you was a friend a hers, you'd know better."

"I live in DC. I'm from Pine Hill. I came all the way out here. She helped me on Facebook. I saw her on *Dr. Dick*. I need to know."

"DC? Wait a minute: you're Cecily?"

"Yes!"

"Well, why didn't you say so? What is wrong with white kids these days! Do you not introduce yourself? What did your momma teach you 'bout manners?"

Jack answered, his hands resting on Cecily's shoulders, "She's a little overwhelmed."

"Are you really Cecily? Suzie said you was some kind of genius."

"She did? Did she talk about me?"

"Did she talk about you?" Rothner shook his head in disgust. "She sent you my old wigs. Yes, I know all about you, Cecily. I'm glad to see you're ... feeling better. This must be ... either your brother or the guy who wants to get on you, but you won't let him."

Cecily's eyes widened and she thought she heard Jack laughing quietly behind her. "Thanks. Thanks for that," she crossed her arms and looked down at the man, definitely Suzie's roommate, Rothner.

"Oh, we all sensitive now for going 'round asking 'bout private medical information about my roommate. Suddenly you all Miss Sensitivity."

"Wow. You're charming. You're in the hospitality business?" Cecily asked.

Jack cleared his throat. He didn't want to be this direct, but needed to salvage the conversation between Cecily and Rothner. "We heard about *Dr. Dick*. Cecily's been very upset over this, and we're trying to clear some things up. Did Suzie have cancer when she died? Because she told Cecily she did."

Rothner stood up and stepped out of the car. He would not, as planned, make it to work in time for the 9:30 a.m. staff meeting. He sighed and looked up at the sky. "You gone," he mumbled up into the air. "And you still trouble."

He looked at Cecily and Jack, then rubbed his forehead with his thumb and index finger. "I think they're officially calling it 'complications due to alcoholism.' She was an active alcoholic. No way you didn't know 'bout that. And the drugs."

"Was she at UCLA when she died?"

"Yeah, she died in the hospital," Rothner said, his voice softening.

"Alone?" Please say Brad was there, Cecily thought. Brad hadn't told her much about the end, and she still hadn't watched the show.

"I don't know."

"You don't know? Weren't you her friend?"

"She was in a coma for 10 days. Her brother took her off the machines. Once she was off the machines, it happened fast. Look, I loved Suzie. I let her stay with me while she was crashing back down to earth. I didn't charge her rent. I've been in the business my whole life. I get tired of watching my friends douse themselves in alcohol and light up. Setting yourself on fire doesn't make you a star. It's hard to watch. You got no idea. I'm sorry you didn't know the whole story. You lucky that way. You don't have strangers coming up and blaming you and shoutin' opinions an' ignorance at you. You don't know nothin'."

"I know I know nothing! That's the problem! I didn't blame you. Nobody's blaming you."

"You don't know nothin' 'bout me, and it look like you don't know nothin' 'bout your friend. I suggest you go elsewhere for what you lookin' for." Rothner turned and clicked open the car door again.

"Sorry. I'm sorry. I'm so confused." Cecily started heaving quiet sobs from her gut. Jack held her upright as she cried.

Rothner looked annoyed, then softened towards her. "Oh, sweet fancy cat pants. I'm sorry. I shouldn't be talking this way to a lady with cancer. Now you're makin' me feel bad. I'm sorry. You had a rough time. I know. Com'ere. Give Rothner a hug. You look like you need a hug."

"I – oof," Cecily couldn't speak in Rothner's engulfing embrace. He held her for a long time, until her sobs quieted down and she stood quietly hiccupping into his damp shirt, made translucent by her tears. She was grateful she hadn't bothered with mascara before they left the hotel room.

Jack took the reins of the inquiry. Cecily was in no shape for it. "Is there any possible way Suzie had a recurrence of cancer? Work with me. I have a theory here. We know she had cancer a few years back, breast cancer. She stayed with her brother in Maryland. We know she came back to LA after that. While she was living with you, did she go to the doctor a lot? Did she say anything about the cancer recurring?"

"Really, I dunno. She went to the clinic a lot. But of course she did. She had a lotta shit going on. Poor girl." Rothner hugged Cecily tighter, thinking of Suzie.

The Truth About Suzie

Jack ran his hand through his hair and continued, thinking aloud, "And her medical records are sealed, of course. HIPAA privacy laws and all."

Rothner released his grip on Cecily, who inhaled fresh air gratefully. Rothner said, "Can I ask you somethin'?" He paused. "Why is this important to you?"

Cecily answered before Jack could. "She told me she had cancer while I did. Then I saw her die on TV of liver failure. Was she lying?"

Rothner looked thoughtful. "Suzie truth and the world truth wasn't always ... connected. She experienced the world different. Still, she wasn't a liar."

"That clears everything up," Cecily mumbled.

"Let me ask you something. Why is her exact diagnosis so important when she gone? Suzie is gone. The winds came and took her away that day and the world ain't been the same since."

"What would you do if you were me? I just want to know if she was ... real. What would you do?"

"She was all too real, honey. Know that much. Be grateful she chose you as her friend. Be grateful to be alive today. Be grateful to God and leave the rest be. Go home. Go home and be with this boy here, coming across the country with you. Appreciate that. Put that boy out of his misery."

Jack smiled. "She already did."

Cecily rolled her eyes and glared at him. "Really?" she asked. *So this strange man knows all about my love life, but doesn't know his roommate's medical information?* She shook her head.

Jack stopped smiling and focused. "Is there anyone else we can talk to? Besides her brother. We've spoken with her brother. Anyone in LA, I mean."

Rothner said, "Not anyone you'd want to seek out. Trust me on that." He opened the car door then stopped short.

"What?" Jack asked hopefully.

"OK," Rothner shook his head, as though trying to talk himself out of what he was about to say. "I can help you, maybe.

Give me your contact info. Phone number, hotel. I might be able to send some stuff over when I get to the office."

"What stuff?" Cecily asked.

"Transcripts, tapes. That kind of thing. You got access to a DVD player?"

"Yeah," Cecily said. "But, I'm lost. What are you maybe sending over?"

"Transcripts. *Dr. Dick*," Rothner said.

"You ... work for *Dr. Dick*," Jack said, nodding his head slowly in understanding.

"Segment producer. You didn't know that? Well, of course you didn't. Since you never saw the show. Watch the show. That could clear things up. I produced two a her family's segments."

Cecily felt the hairs on her arm stand on end. "You ... produced her death?"

"God no, woman. I hate hospitals. Suzie wanted me to, but I couldn't go. Tami produced the segment where Suzie passed away. She'll do anything."

"That's horrible. I think it's horrible," Cecily said, quietly.

"Honey, you missing something here: it's what Suzie asked for. And it's just show business. That's all that is. It ain't all wigs and high heels and makeup, love. I've worked in reality TV since it was invented. I've seen and done everything a person can see and be seen doin'. One a my segments on *America's Most Wanted* made someone check into a motel room in Virginia and kill themself, according to the family's lawyer," he paused, glancing at Jack and Cecily's stunned expressions. "They settled out of court. Shame Suzie never told you 'bout that. She scratched the underbelly a this town."

"But you can," Jack pressed. "Tell us, I mean."

"Look, I'm late for a meeting. I'll send over the tapes and transcripts. Watch 'em, then call me if you still got questions."

Suddenly, Cecily remembered. She looked up into Rothner's lovely dark brown eyes. "Jason Frost," was all she said.

"Good luck getting through to him," Rothner rolled his eyes. "He all 'famous' now." The word "famous" was accompanied by air quotes.

"She was dating him?"

"You could call it that," Rothner conceded, one leg creeping into his car again.

"How would we reach him?" Jack asked.

Rothner finished climbing into his car. He called out before he shut the door, "I don't know. He took her phone when she passed. It was his—or, he was paying for it. I gots to go."

He shut the door, pulled out of the parking space, and drove off down the quiet street.

Posted January 18, 2011 at 6:17 p.m.
Cecily Murphy

Bone marrow biopsy: Nurse Pennie held my hand, talked about her newborn grandson. She glared at the doctor each time I flinched, told him: "Easy! She FELT that." God bless nurses! Results to Mayo Clinic: back in 2+ weeks.

Posted January 19, 2011 at 6:08 a.m.
Cecily Murphy

Has become master of diversion in test-result limbo. Jane and I convinced landlord to let us scrape Laura Ashley wallpaper off bathroom wall to keep me occupied and useful. Under the paper, we uncovered an entire mural drawn by a kid with a magic marker. The theme? CLOWNS. Jane's greatest fear. The clowns have lurked under the wallpaper, for YEARS. Must exorcise as well as re-paint now!

Posted January 23, 2011 at 7:09 a.m.
Cecily Murphy

Biopsy results are in, according to receptionist at GW. Waiting for call from oncologist.

Posted January 23, 2011 at 7:19 a.m.
Cecily Murphy

Bone marrow cancer-free! Apparently just weird. Treatment back on course. Exhale. Exhale. Exhale. Just realized I have not breathed for a week and a half. Chemo will start (hopefully)(?) next week.

Chapter 16

May 31, 2011, 9:30 a.m.

They reviewed Cecily's lists on her laptop over coffee and sesame seed bagels at the bagel shop that capped the street.

Cecily took in the dimly lit room, scattered with small tables and smelling reassuringly of coffee and yeast. Behind the counter, the tattooed barista with spiky, dyed-black hair and a large looped nose ring used five colored chalks to elaborately illustrate the day's specials. Cecily wondered if the specials lived up to their presentation. The girl drew without looking up, winding spirals around the letters, sweeping her chalk into shapes that became curlicues and butterflies and slices of pecan pie.

"Those are lovely," Cecily said over the counter, nodding to the chalkboard as she grabbed more napkins for their table.

The barista smiled, revealing bright white teeth. Everyone in California had such white teeth. "Thanks," the barista said, looking up. "I'm just messing around."

"Are you an artist?" Cecily asked.

"I guess so," the barista said, tilting her head and thinking about it.

"My friend," Cecily began, taking a deep breath, "was an artist. She used to come into this shop every morning."

"Are you talking about Suzie?"

"Yes!" Bingo. They'd found the right place.

"I miss Suzie every day," the girl said wistfully. She looked around the shop, empty except for Jack and Cecily. "She gave me a lot of good advice."

"What kind?"

The girl stepped back and appraised Cecily.

"I'm Cecily Murphy." Cecily stuck out her hand, taking Rothner's advice to introduce herself before peppering strangers with questions. As badly as that interview had gone, Cecily found herself relieved to find there was at least one person who felt protective of Suzie.

The girl gave Cecily's fingers a cursory little tug that sufficed as her handshake. "Regina Dannenfelser."

"Nice to meet you, Regina. I was a friend of Suzie's from back east, and she said she'd come to this place to write because it was quiet."

The girl smiled. "Yeah, quiet," she said. "There are five other coffee shops within two blocks of here. And bagels, well, carbs are villains now. Everybody wants to go to Starbucks and Jamba Juice. Still, it's not usually this empty." Regina looked at the clock on the wall. "The morning crowd is come and gone and we get the mommies coming in after Stroller Strides around 10:00 a.m."

"Ah," Cecily said. She turned to Jack, walked over and sat down at the table. "She wrote a poem about this place. Maybe it was a song. Something about deciding what to put on a bagel. I remember a line: 'It's difficult to know when cabbage is appropriate.'" Jack smiled and took another bite of his bagel.

"She would leave when the mommy groups came in," Regina reminisced as she smudged her finger across a green chalk leaf, softening its edges. She blew on the chalkboard. "I think it was because of her ovarian cancer. She didn't like to be reminded."

Jack and Cecily stood up so fast Cecily's chair fell over behind her. Regina, startled, dropped the chalkboard and ran to the cash register, pulling a phone out of her pocket and holding it at the ready.

"Suzie told you she had cancer?" Cecily approached the counter slowly.

Regina reached under the counter. "Yes?" she asked, wondering what these people wanted.

Jack grabbed Cecily's shoulders and pulled her away from the counter. "You're cornering her," he whispered in her ear.

"I'm not!" Cecily hissed under breath.

"I can hear you," Regina reminded them, stress making her voice high and tinny.

"I'm sorry," Cecily said. "Suzie didn't tell many people she had cancer. You're the first person in LA we've met who knew this. We were ... startled."

Regina seemed to accept this. She backed away from the counter and picked up her chalk again. "Well," she said. "You startled me a little there too. Sorry to startle you then." She laughed a little, nervously, under her breath.

"Did she ... talk about it?" Cecily asked quietly.

"In a weird way. She would talk about being broke from the doctors and how they kept wanting to take her body parts and how she was going to travel when she was done with this. Not really specifically, but more in the way of telling stories. She liked to tell stories."

Cecily nodded. "I know what you mean." She picked up her coffee and sipped it thoughtfully. "How did you find out when she passed?"

"I watched on *Dr. Dick*," Regina said. "She told me it would be on."

Cecily's mouth fell open a little. "She died of alcohol poisoning on that show."

Regina nodded sadly. "No doubt about it. At the end, she looked terrible. She carried her coffee cup, and it was shaking so hard I was sure she'd spill it all over herself. She wouldn't accept help. She ordered the same bagel four times a week for two years, but the last six months she didn't touch it. Girl had a lot going on."

Posted January 27, 2011 at 9:17 p.m.
Cecily Murphy

Needs a ride to & from chemo next Thursday. Jane will be on travel & I'm not allowed to drive self. Advice: if you drive me TO chemo, there's less of a chance I'll vomit in your car, so I'd sign up for the 1 p.m. slot instead of the 6 or 7 p.m. slot. Any takers? There's a free drink attached to this, not to mention good karma.

Sent: January 27, 2011 at 9:19 p.m.
From: Caitlyn Murphy Doyle
To: Cecily Murphy

Why are you posting on Facebook that you need a ride? I'll take you there, stay with you, and drive you home. Ask me first, please! Oh! Is this about Jack? Would you rather have Jack drive you?

Sent: January 27, 2011 at 9:22 p.m.
From: Cecily Murphy
To: Caitlyn Murphy Doyle

No. I didn't ask you because I thought you'd have Cooper at home. You can't bring Coop to the infusion center.

Sent: January 27, 2011 at 9:25 p.m.
From: Caitlyn Murphy Doyle
To: Cecily Murphy

I can get a sitter for Cooper next week. Please, Cecily, let me. I want to help out, I need to help out, and you won't ever let me. I'm thwarted at every turn: "Suzie told me about that already; Jane can drive me."

Anyway, thanks for picking Eileigh up today while we were at the hospital with Cooper. Hopefully these new asthma meds they gave us will prevent more days like today ...

Sent: January 27, 2011 at 9:28 p.m.
From: Cecily Murphy
To: Caitlyn Murphy Doyle

Don't get a babysitter! Sheesh! I appreciate it, but there's simply no need. Three people have volunteered already. Turns out, everybody wants a good excuse to leave work for the afternoon. Don't know what you're talking about, "thwarting." Flattered & a little embarrassed by all the attention and help. I'm fine. Thank you! I'm fine.

Posted January 30, 2011 at 4:01 p.m.
Cecily Murphy

Yay! Jane's trip postponed. Now she can drive me to chemo AND keep me from punching oncologist, who I'm dumping for not returning calls or answering questions. After weeks of this, I asked Dr. SPO to call her, get answers for me, then call me back. He did. And got back to me in 10 minutes. HA sucker. I beat the system! Thursday is Dump Your Oncologist Day, and I will celebrate with gusto.

Sent: January 30, 2011 at 4:11 p.m.
From: Jack Schwinn
To: Cecily Murphy

Dump Your Oncologist Day has always been my favorite holiday. My offer to drive you, both ways (and trample you at Scrabble) still stands if Jane falls through.

Sent: January 30, 2011 at 4:17 p.m.
From: Cecily Murphy
To: Jack Schwinn

You're fantastic, but I'm not letting you drive from downtown Baltimore to downtown DC and back on a weekday when there are six hours of rush hour to contend with. You can come down to visit anytime you want, but do yourself a favor and take the train. How about this? If I'm up for more Battlestar Galactica this weekend and you aren't working, feel free to come sack out on the couch with me again. That was so nice last weekend. You really helped me chill. Thanks again.

Posted February 2, 2011 at 6:11 a.m.
Cecily Murphy

Chemo. Take two.

Posted February 2, 2011 at 7:03 p.m.
Cecily Murphy

Home. 7-hour appointment. Had reaction to chemo (fever, throat closing) so bumpy start, but fixed quickly. Oncologist apologized for 45 minutes. OK, but still exploring options. Feel surprisingly OK, so far.

Posted February 3, 2011 at 3:37 p.m.
Cecily Murphy

Day 2. Foggy and groggy. Could push through it. Or not. Multi-tasking ability impaired. Jane banned me from driving. Stomach stuff not great, but have 5 meds at my disposal, including a $40 pill that I take 1x daily for 1st 3 days. Will push back on nausea, try to eat well, but will let grog-fogginess have its way for now.

Sent: February 4, 2011 at 9:22 a.m.
From: Cecily Murphy
To: Suzie London

I'm so sick, I'm going to die. Chemo is like hiring a rabid, drunk chimp to run security at an event—ransacking, tossing glassware, billy-clubbing good cells, bad cells, all cells. My prescriptions are helping me cope until the chimp tires and stumbles back out, but can't wait to resurface from this whacked out cocktail party. How do you do this? Why are you so well, and I'm so sick? I can't even sleep in. I woke up at 6 this morning.

Sent: February 4, 2011 at 2:00 p.m.
From: Suzie London
To: Cecily Murphy

It's not like this all the time. It's just like having the flu for a few days. You'll feel better even as soon as tomorrow. I promise. We promised each other we'd fight. This is the fight. In your head, right now. The bell has rung, the fight starts now. I'm sick too, sweetie. I'm so sick too. Do anything you have to do to feel better. Remember when we used to catch fireflies and eat honeysuckle? Why were we in such a hurry to grow up, pay bills and do our own laundry? Why didn't I take a few more years of that? Sleep through the worst of it. I hate it when you take the nausea pills and they just make your stomach worse. Whiskey is better, but she can be a trickster bitch too. Sleep through the worst of it: don't push through. You're a push-through kind, but I'm giving you permission to lay down this load and become one with the bedsheets today. Lie down, open all the windows, and breathe.

Sent: February 4, 2011 at 2:21 p.m.
From: Cecily Murphy
To: Suzie London

You are wonderful. Just had to say that.

Posted February 5, 2011 at 8:59 a.m.
Cecily Murphy

Today I feel OK. Yesterday was hard: a "don't-know-if-I-can-really-go-through-with-this" day. But then Cait, Eileigh and Cooper spent the afternoon piled on the couch with me, which turned it into a "there's-no-way-I-CAN'T-go-through-with-this" day.

Posted February 6, 2011 at 5:33 a.m.
Cecily Murphy

Call me crazy but I'm going to the gym today. Dad got me a gift certificate to a trainer, and I'm going to check this out.

Feel like Boba Fett, Star Wars Ep. III, post-Sarlacc Pit. But it feels better to move than to give in, at least in the a.m. So this could be good. Or a spectacle ...

Sent: February 7, 2011 at 9:28 p.m.
From: Jack Schwinn
To: Cecily Murphy

Can I take you out to dinner this weekend? Or bring you Thai food with strict orders that it must be eaten in sweat pants? We've got to keep you eating, you know.

Sent: February 7, 2011 at 9:40 p.m.
From: Cecily Murphy
To: Jack Schwinn

I'm sorry. I really overdid it today and am regretting it now. I'm just not going to be up for it. Thank you, though. I appreciate it!

Posted February 8, 2011 at 10:17 p.m.
Cecily Murphy

Day 7, I love you! Well, with a two-hour nap after work and one dose of anti-nausea meds. Which, BTW, were originally purposed as anti-psychotics. How did they figure out how to cross-purpose those? Schizos doing better on chemo? Or chemo patients going schizo? Either way, it's win-win: not nauseous and may become more normal w/ repeated use.

Posted February 9, 2011 at 7:53 p.m.
Cecily Murphy

Aunt Lil brought over cupcakes from Caroline's. I chose mine, took a bite: tasted fish. Thought, hmm. Must be the chemo. Gave it to Lil, asked what she tasted: "Fish," she said. Uncle Merv, Mom, Cait, Dad all tasted it. Fish. With poppy seeds. & vanilla frosting. So, if you go to this cupcake joint, don't tell them to "surprise you."

Sent: February 9, 2011 at 9:35 p.m.
From: Jack Schwinn
To: Cecily Murphy

So … let me get this straight. Fish cupcakes are OK, but me bringing over Thai food (your favorite) is not?

Sent: February 9, 2011 at 9:39 p.m.
From: Cecily Murphy
To: Jack Schwinn

Aunt Lil is in town from Philly. She's my aunt. I'm just not up for anything that's not absolutely required of me. This is hell, Jack. Please, do me the huge favor of not taking this personally. Please.

Sent: February 10, 2011 at 6:55 a.m.
From: Jack Schwinn
To: Cecily Murphy

Hi. Can we just pretend I never sent that email? I'm sorry. You're right. I'm really stupid. That was Exhibit A of "Why Drunk Facebooking Is A Bad Idea." I'd just returned from happy hour with Chang and Bangladello, taking a fair amount of crap about you, I might add. And how I'm hanging out with them on Valentine's Day. Sorry again.

Sent: February 10, 2011 at 7:02 a.m.
From: Jane McCann
To: Cecily Murphy

Are you at work already? How are you getting up so early? Any word from Jack? Can't believe he didn't email again last night or call. This guy: his timing is awful. What is he thinking?

Sent: February 10, 2011 at 7:39 a.m.
From: Cecily Murphy
To: Jane McCann

I wish I could sleep in, but for some reason I'm waking up earlier than ever: my blood is swimming in chemicals, and they don't want me to sleep.

Re: Jack. Yes! He apologized! See attached: this was about Valentine's Day! I forgot this weekend was Valentine's Day! I didn't realize I was giving him a Valentine's Day "sorry-I'm-too-tired" blow-off. I thought it was just a regular "this-isn't-a-great-weekend" blow-off. I feel terrible! But, you're right, whatever this is, the timing couldn't be worse. I think I need to put this on hold until chemo's over. And maybe reconstruction. I don't know. It's not fair to him, but it's not fair to me to expect relationship-type stuff in the middle of all this. Actually, putting it on hold for six months is not fair to him. And not to be completely shallow about this but I'm going to be BALD soon, and seriously: going bald in the beginning of a relationship? I don't know if I can do it.

I feel so guilty for getting myself embroiled in this when I knew the timing was soooo wrong. I've got to call him and tell him this is just a bad idea.

Sent: February 10, 2011 at 7:44 a.m.
From: Cecily Murphy
To: Jack Schwinn

Jack, no worries. I'm sorry too. We should probably talk. I'll call you today.

Chapter 17

May 31, 2011, 10:00 a.m.

"Well, if Suzie's barista is sure of it, then it must be true," Jack rolled his eyes under his sunglasses, balancing his coffee and bagel in one hand as he fished through his jeans pocket to make sure he still had their hotel key.

"OK, OK, I hear you," Cecily was more excited than Jack had seen her in weeks. "But she did tell someone this story besides me and that's huge. That's huge. And you know who would definitely know? Jace. I just know, Jace would know too."

"Yeah, but how are we going to get hold of Jason Frost? 'He all famous now,'" Jack said, imitating Rothner.

"Do you even look at my Excel documents?" Cecily asked. She reached for Jack's hand as they walked the four blocks back to their hotel. "I listed my ideas for reaching Jason Frost. And we just got another idea from Rothner: call her cell phone. Jace has it."

As they walked through the high-ceilinged hotel lobby, the young, blonde front-desk clerk called out to them. "Room 612? I have a package for you. A bike courier dropped this off, just 30 seconds ago." She handed them a large manila envelope with a business card stapled to the flap. David Rothner's. The logo on the front of the envelope read: Amerivision. Dr. Dick's production company.

They opened the envelope in the elevator to find a thick, stapled manuscript printed on pink paper and a DVD in a plastic sleeve. The date was printed on the disc: DD 2/11/11.

"It's not the segment you don't want to see," Jack said quickly. "Let me read the transcript first."

As Jack studied the package contents on the bed, Cecily set up shop on the balcony, laptop open to an email containing Suzie's cell phone number. She watched the sun dance on the ocean beyond the rooftops. The air was so dry, so warm. She could live here. Finish her treatment with the Dragon Lady, maybe. The binder-snapping dragon lady: no thanks.

She took a deep breath in and dialed Suzie's cell number. Strange how calling felt so old-fashioned. An automated voice told her Suzie's voicemail was full. Ah, I don't even get to hear your voice, Cecily thought.

Jack walked out and handed her the script. "Here, you can read this. She only makes a cameo. It's not too awful."

"I called her phone. It went straight to voicemail, and it's full. Damn it. I don't think Jason's checking the messages."

"Huh. OK, start here," Jack said, opening to the tenth page. "I'll look up those cancer support centers in Venice."

"And look at the document titled *Jace*!" Cecily said.

Opening his laptop on the bed, Jack called out: "Is this it? 'Find his agent. Ask Rothner. Go to one of his concerts.' Is this all we got?"

"No," Cecily said. "Look at page two: logistics. He's playing at the Metro Dome tonight and tomorrow."

"That's lucky."

"We're in LA. Jace lives here."

"How do you propose we accost him at the concert?"

"Go early and stand at the stage door."

"Like groupies?"

"Sure," Cecily shrugged. "If that fails, I'll throw him my bra with my room key stapled to it."

"Somehow I can't picture that happening."

Posted February 11, 2011 at 9:15 p.m.
Suzie London

People with bad ideas and a whole lot of official authority. Well what do you know? No more authority. Ha, I'm legal ward of myself, and free, and American, and I dare you to try to take it away, I dare you.

Posted February 11, 2011 at 9:15 p.m.
Cecily Murphy

's mom asked me if I'd scored medical marijuana yet. I was like, uh, no? And you're asking because ...?

Sent: February 11, 2011 at 9:35 p.m.
From: Suzie London
To: Cecily Murphy

Really, Cecily. Score some mary jane for your mom! I'll send her some. Pot is not really illegal here. One of my pot guys walks around the boardwalk with an actual flowerpot on his head, with a painting of a marijuana leaf on it. He sells right out of his backpack. This other guy is in a thong bikini and a necklace of shark teeth, and sits there with a sign: ASK ME ABOUT MY MARIJUANA CROP. It's a lie, though. It's not homegrown. He sells this nasty Nicaraguan hash laced with PCP and it's nothing like true herb. You want the good stuff, organic, you must get off the boardwalk, go into Santa Monica.

I went walking on the beach in Santa Monica yesterday dressed for the weather. 65 degrees. Within 5 minutes, the temp plummeted to East Coast Winter. February tiptoed away and hid for a few hours, then jumped out from behind the curtains: GOTCHA! Screw you, February. I was wearing capris.

Remember School House Rock? I used to sing it in the car with my brother in the back-facing seat of the station wagon. Remember those tripped out station wagons with the wood panels? Rad. We used to sit in the very back seat and give hand gestures to the car behind us. And we'd flip ourselves backwards over the tops of the backseats whenever my mom braked. Why don't they make those station wagons anymore?

We sang: "*Interjections! Show excitement! And emotion! They're generally set apart from a sentence by an exclamation point. Or by a comma if the feeling's not as strong. So if you're happy: whee! Or sad: aw. Or frightened: eek! Or glad: yay. Excited: WOW. Or mad: Fuck! An interjection starts a sentence right.*" I learned more from School House Rock than I did in school. So I sang to Brad: "Interventions! Show excitement! Over nothing! They're generally staged by attention whores who have nothing better to do and assholes who have wives with pointy, pinched, constipated faces. An intervention starts your week off right." Did you know you can download all the songs off iTunes??? Go do it now! We can do our multiplication tables! Very useful waiting tables: figuring out how many bags of hash I could buy off the cook based on expected nightly tips. Math is good. You're right, Cecily Thelma, science is for girls. Girl power!

Sent: February 12, 2011 at 8:49 a.m.
From: Cecily Murphy
To: Caitlyn Murphy Doyle

WTF is this? See attached. I thought my life was drama with chemo, but the past few weeks Suzie's been busy imploding. She's freaking me out. I'm too f-ing tired and chemically unstable to know what to say. I've got my own problems: I haven't had a clear thought in weeks. I'm going to get fired because I keep screwing up at work. If you forget one step or do it at the wrong time, the whole experiment gets tossed— months of work down the drain, literally. This is so stressful, always second-guessing myself, making lists for things I used to do automatically.

Sent: February 12, 2011 at 9:16 a.m.
From: Caitlyn Murphy Doyle
To: Cecily Murphy

Do you want me to come by today? At Gymboree w/ Cooper. Listening to that horrible clown song. Grown woman across room dancing w/ clown puppet. Doubt you are messing up work, even on chemo. Suzie addicted to drug & alcohol & having interventions staged on her behalf. OK to de-friend, u know. Surprised u didn't de-friend after cop gave you lecture on friending Internet people, w/ her blatant drug background, problems.

Sent: February 12, 2011 at 9:20 a.m.
From: Cecily Murphy
To: Caitlyn Murphy Doyle

She's in LA, so little chance of her breaking into my house. Plus: Cancer. That's the connection.

Sent: February 12, 2011 at 9:23 a.m.
From: Caitlyn Murphy Doyle
To: Cecily Murphy

With Suzie? Hardly. She's dealing w/ lifetime of abusing her body. We're dealing w/ DNA. Probably. (Mom is on me to take test.) But it's just a disease. It's not who we are. This is just a short, short chapter in our lives. You're taking care of it. You're doing a great job & we're all so proud of you. Focus on you! Don't get dragged down in her drama.

Sent: February 12, 2011 at 9:28 a.m.
From: Cecily Murphy
To: Caitlyn Murphy Doyle

Addiction's a disease too. Probably just as inherited as my cancer. Maybe Suzie has more diseases than I do, but we still have cancer at the same time. I'm not saying I feel obligated to go forth and save her right now. I'm just saying ... I don't know what I'm saying. Can't keep thoughts in brain! Ugh! You're probably right.

Sent: February 12, 2011 at 9:38 a.m.
From: Caitlyn Murphy Doyle
To: Cecily Murphy

Love you Cec. Let me come over later and make you dinner. Check out Cooper!

Sent: February 12, 2011 at 9:43 a.m.
From: Cecily Murphy
To: Caitlyn Murphy Doyle

Too cute!!! Look at those cheeks! Cooper's daycare nickname will be either "Cheeks" or "Drools Excessively." Wipe off the front of his shirt! That kid is going to drown in his own saliva.

I'm OK, Cait. I don't need anything. Don't come over. I feel so guilty everybody wants to rearrange their lives for me.

Sent: February 12, 2011 at 9:46 a.m.
From: Caitlyn Murphy Doyle
To: Cecily Murphy

Not rearranging. Called "love." Out of here in 10; talk then!

Sent: February 13, 2011 at 4:52 a.m.
From: Suzie London
To: Cecily Murphy

Sang tonight with Rothner. I spent the whole day painting then got on stage at Tiki Tata. I sang "La Vie En Rose" with a hibiscus in my hair and a dress that reminded me of a red polka dotted Esther Williams bathing suit. I don't know French, so I made up my own French words. In the fifties, I would have been described as a strumpet. Only in LA. Come out here and visit me. Please. I'm tired and we could have a Yahtzee tournament.

Sent: February 13, 2011 at 6:22 a.m.
From: Cecily Murphy
To: Suzie London

I'd love to. But unlikely. How are you up on stage singing?? How do you have the energy? All my energy goes into the littlest things now. Get up. Get dressed. Eat something so I can take my pills. Use my special toothpaste that really does work against mouth sores. Are you getting mouth sores? They terrified me, but they disappeared when I used the toothpaste the nurses told me about. I go to work. I have lists now, because I'm so slogged down in chemical mire. Stuff I knew doesn't live in my brain anymore. Everything has to be written down. I can do it, I can really do it, but that's all I can do: it, and nothing more. Yesterday, I missed my Metro stop because I fell asleep—at 4:30 p.m.! I woke up at Farragut North downtown and thought: I can get off the train and fight my way back onto a packed train going back out of the city, or I can sit here and nap against the train wall until the train goes to the end of the line and comes back. And I stayed! Hour and a half to get home! Anyway, I just need everything to go smoothly for this regular-living stuff to work, and that is too much to ask most days, so it's stressful. My friends, my wonderful friends, put together this thing called a care calendar: it's a website where you sign up. People come over and do laundry for me, and cook and clean. It's amazing. I try to send them home, because I can do it myself, but they won't hear of it. And the (horrible) truth is, I couldn't get through this without them. Even my next door neighbors, who scare the crap out of me, have put aside their busy schedule of pounding Schlitz on the porch to drop off strange dinners at my house, i.e., two cans of tuna and a bag of Funions. But it all definitely helps. Because I go to bed at 7 p.m. And stuff piles up. Suzie, I worry about you. Who is taking care of you?

**Sent: February 13, 2011 at 3:14 p.m.
From: Suzie London
To: Cecily Murphy**

I am. And you are. And sometimes I let Jace. I don't like a lot of cooks in my kitchen. They spit in the soup. I mailed you wigs. Kick ass wigs. Pink, blue, GaGa, Katy Perry, Dolly Parton (that's your gig). A big box. It should arrive in the next week. Rothner helped me put purple sparkles in the pink one: he is turning me into a drag queen. What would a female drag queen be called? Dolly Parton? She's so freaking awesome.

Sent: February 13, 2011 at 5:45 p.m.
From: Cecily Murphy
To: Suzie London

Thanks for the wigs, but Suzie, I'm serious. What is going on that your brother is staging interventions? You can't just throw that out there.

Sent: February 13, 2011 at 6:17 p.m.
From: Suzie London
To: Cecily Murphy

You're right. It's like PETA throwing coffee on you and you weren't even wearing real fur. This is H&M, motherfuckers! And I'm wearing vegan shoes and you're wearing leather Birkenstocks! Hate PETA. Anyway, yes, sorry to throw my family shit on you. Love is a many splendored thing, but family is a multi-headed beast. Brad was an alcoholic. My mother was an alcoholic. Brad thinks everyone who has a beer needs to be in rehab, and at one point I believed in that shit. But I don't marinate in victim sauce anymore.

I am in pain. Duh. My brother doesn't really get that pain is a large part of my life. And I do everything I can to manage my pain, including but not limited to: drinking (gasp!), acupuncture (well, letting my friend Marci who is an acupuncture trainee practice on me), sessions with my healer, and Pratyahara yoga with the old ladies at the cancer center. I was there today. Pratyahara is learning to withdraw from your emotions: very powerful stuff. I can sit there and meditate but to be a great yogi you have to turn off your senses: I can't get there. I love the smell of the wooden barn we're in, the sound of the space heater in the quiet room (the old ladies are always cold when it's 70 degrees out). I'm supposed to go there to tune out my senses and learn how to live in peace with less than peak physical conditions, but I actually go there to take a nice, long sense bath. The woman who sits next to me smells like mothballs. My eyes are closed but I know it's her sitting down next to me and I smile. I try to do the "distantly observe" thing. I did it once: I came in one morning afraid. You know the fear I'm talking about. The fear that's born when a doctor snaps your binder shut and shoos you out the door and you're left going, wait, is that supposed to be a joke? Did she just read me someone else's test result? I want a recount! So instead of screaming at the doctor, "yeah, you heard me, I want a recount," I went to Yoga Nidra and laid down, and I was shaking all over. I followed all the exercises and the mantras, shaking and sweating, and then as I got quieter I found a hallway in my brain. Dark and echoey. I was scared but I walked down it and there was a door at the end of the hallway. I opened the door, and inside, there was a little girl screaming. I said: oh, it's you making all this racket in here. And I leaned down and I hugged her and calmed her down. Only then did I stop shaking.

Sent: February 13, 2011 at 6:59 p.m.
From: Cecily Murphy
To: Suzie London

Wow. That's intense. Maybe I should try Yoga Nidra. Family is weird and hard. Not nearly as difficult and complicated as yours. But there is some in-fighting between my caretakers. It's surreal. Negotiating the family is one aspect of this experience I was surprised to find difficult. I had placed my family in the "benefit" column, where they belong, of course. But I'd neglected to acknowledge what a burden it also is to deal with the family drama. Some of which is caused by my illness, some of which is just the regular background noise. It's still stuff I have to deal with. When I feel fine, it's not hard to deal with. But when I'm sick, it's one more issue in a pile of them.

Cait's the hardest. She gets jealous. Of Jimmy. Of people who I think she sees as taking her place in my life. I have to remember to be careful with her, to appreciate her, because I don't think she feels appreciated. But I do, and what I need from her now is to just Know That without me having to seal it in blood every day. I don't have the energy to prove it. All I can do is say thank you. I think Cait puts a lot of her burdens on herself, but I'm not convinced Jimmy and my parents don't play into the dynamic too. All growing up, Cait led the charge onto the battlefield where the issues of makeup, skirt length, and bra usage were negotiated, daily. I was born knowing that was her job. But Jimmy was different. He didn't battle, he just shined. He got a lot of positive attention that maybe Cait didn't. And don't get me started on my mom: she is a Superfund site! Her mother died of breast cancer, her sister battled it twice, so this is clearly bringing up terrible memories for her. My mom is usually a rock, but throughout this she's been a mess. She cries all the time. She burst out crying when I was trying on my wig. It's not wildly helpful. I feel resentful. Then I feel guilty about it, because I know she doesn't want to be a mess, and I know she also must be reliving her mother's death. So I try to be strong and blasé, for her. And then I feel resentful again. It's like this never-ending cycle of resentment and guilt over feeling resentment.

I'm sure Brad loves you, and is just trying to help and protect you the only way he knows how. I also wish my family was able to support me in the way I need to be supported but I guess nobody gets exactly what they need. Maybe it's the universe's way of telling us we have to go find it.

Chapter 18

May 31, 2011, 10:00 a.m.

Cecily let the pink document sit in her hands for a moment, feeling its weight. She took a slow breath in, held it, then released.

Hello again, Suzie, she thought. Let's see what you were really doing in February.

> **PART I: THE LONDON FAMILY RETURNS**
> DR. DICK: We've met two members of the London family who have struggled with addiction issues. Brad London asked us if we could help a third member of his family—his younger sister, Suzie. Welcome back, Brad.
> BRAD LONDON: Thank you Dr. Dick.
> DR. DICK: And thank you for being here today, Suzie. Suzie London is a dog walker, is that correct? And a singer for the band ... I can't say the name of this band on television. The censors would go crazy.
> SUZIE LONDON: Too bad. We were hoping to get some publicity out of this.
> BRAD LONDON: Suzie, come on. You're not in a band. Please take this seriously.
> DR. DICK: Brad, we'll start with you. How would you describe your relationship with your sister?
> BRAD LONDON: Um, tough. I guess. My dad took off when Suzie was in grade school. Our mom kind of

imploded after that, and we were sent to live with our aunt.

DR. DICK: Brad, for those who missed the last episode, explain what you mean by "imploded."

BRAD LONDON: Her alcoholism got worse. And she had a nervous breakdown. Her sister sent her to the hospital and took us to California to live with her. I left after six months, dropped out of school. I was angry and just lost. We had no parents, no home. I wanted to go back home, to the way it was, even though it was bad. Suzie was too young to understand, really. But when she got a little older, she got angry. I wanted to get a job and take care of her, but I was a total screw-up. I couldn't handle life on my own. I thought I could, but I was so wasted I didn't pay enough attention to her, and then she was gone. She left when she was 15.

DR. DICK: To me, it sounds like you blame yourself for Suzie's situation.

BRAD LONDON: I do.

DR. DICK: And we're going to talk about that more. But now, I want to hear from Suzie. Suzie, how would you describe your relationship with your brother?

SUZIE LONDON: Completely [redacted.]

DR. DICK: I'm going to have to ask that you not use foul language on the air. If you do, I'll have to ask you to leave. Do you understand?

SUZIE LONDON: Of course I understand. Why do you think I'm doing it?

DR. DICK: Suzie, you seem to be angry that you're here. Is that the case?

SUZIE LONDON: It is, Dr. Dick. It is the case. You're quite the detective.

DR. DICK: I want to make clear to the audience that Suzie

London is free to go. We are not holding her against her will, are we Darla? [laugh]

[Audience laughs.]

DIRECTOR: No, Dr. Dick.

SUZIE LONDON: No. In fact, I contacted this show in December. About Peter. According to one of your segment producers here, you were trolling for alcoholic families to help. To give them a free trip to rehab in exchange for being on your show. I thought it was just crazy enough to save Peter's life. So I said, go ahead. God knows Brad and Wendie are in over their heads. Give them a free trip to rehab for Peter.

DR. DICK: Suzie, may I ask why you are so angry to be the focus of today's show, rather than as a support person for Peter?

SUZIE LONDON: You may. First, my brother lied to me.

BRAD LONDON: Suzie, I—

SUZIE LONDON: Second, I'm not an alcoholic. I respect my brother and his sobriety. I'm proud of him for turning his life around. I don't have his life, though, and I can't follow the same path. I know he wants me to, but it's just not possible.

DR. DICK: Why do you think Brad believes you're an alcoholic?

SUZIE LONDON: Because I drink. And he doesn't. And everyone who drinks is an alcoholic in Brad's book.

DR. DICK: When we come back, we'll discuss a day in the life of Suzie London.

[AUDIENCE RESPONSE]

[PROMO CLIP]

****

PART II: THE LONDON FAMILY RETURNS

DR. DICK: *We're speaking with Suzie London, sister of Brad London who is the patriarch of our 2011 Therapy Family. Brad believes Suzie's drinking is out of control, and he wants her to commit to rehabilitation.*

DR. DICK: Suzie, how much do you drink per day?

SUZIE LONDON: Well, it's hard to say.

DR. DICK: If you had to guess.

DR. DICK: Five drinks? Would five drinks be fair to say?

SUZIE LONDON: You can say anything you want. Oh, except [redacted.] You can't say [redacted.]

DR. DICK: OK, Darla?

[SECURITY enters stage right.]

[SUZIE LONDON stands up.]

SUZIE LONDON: I'll be going now. See ya, Brad. Fame suits you.

[SECURITY escorts SUZIE LONDON backstage.]

SUZIE LONDON: [off mic]: Enjoy the attention! This is what I get for [?]

DR. DICK: So. You asked me, Brad, how we dealt with uncooperative guests and now you know. And now I know why you asked. [laughs]

BRAD LONDON: Can I go back there with her? I need to talk—

DR. DICK: Of course you can. In just a minute. Now, would you say your sister drinks five alcoholic beverages a day?

BRAD LONDON: I … I don't know.

"Is that it, after she walks out?" Cecily asked, folding the script back and tossing it on the bed.

"Yeah."

"But Rothner said she asked for the Dr. Dick show to film her at the end. Why? Could this girl just do one single thing that made sense? Ugh! How hard would it have been, just to say, hey, Cecily, this is goodbye. But, no. It's like she enjoys pulling the rug out from under people, and you know what?" Cecily's voice was rising. She started pacing again.

She was so angry she'd lost her point. She looked down at Jack. "I'm angry," she concluded. Weak, but it would have to suffice.

"I know," he answered. "I'm sorry. I've called two places that sound promising: Hopewell House and Caring Bridge."

Cecily marveled at him. "Aren't you freaked out that I'm all freaking out?"

"That's why we're here. You're angry. And you need answers." He paused. "Do you need a hug?"

"Yes," Cecily said, sheepishly. "Yes, I do."

He stood up and hugged her, and they stood that way for a long time before Jack started talking again. "So, these cancer centers are bound by privacy rules, they said. They said they weren't allowed to give me names of their clients or former clients."

"But the clients themselves can give me their names," Cecily said, stepping back. "And, when we were scaring the bagel shop girl, we found out Suzie is far more likely to tell her problems to strangers than to those closest to her."

"Kind of like you," Jack said. "With Facebook."

"A little like me, I guess," Cecily said. "I hadn't thought of it that way, but yeah, it is easier to spill your guts when there's a degree of anonymity to it. Which means she could have been telling me the truth the whole time."

"She didn't," Jack reminded her. "She didn't tell you she was going to die. That's a pretty big omission."

Sent: February 13, 2011 at 9:59 p.m.
From: Cecily Murphy
To: Suzie London

You still online, West Coast? I just finished breaking up with a boy. No, that's imprecise. I staved off a boy. Four miserable days of phone tag and interrupted conversations and brick walls. He wanted a relationship, and I'm going into chemo and I have bricks in my boobs, scars all over my chest, and I'm going to be bald, rumor has it. I don't want a boyfriend now. It sucks. It sucks. It sucks. Because I really did want a boyfriend, BC, and how often do I come across actual, awesome boyfriend candidates? Not often. But it had to be done. And it sucks. Did I mention it sucks?

Sent: February 13, 2011 at 10:10 p.m.
From: Suzie London
To: Cecily Murphy

What did he do? Cheat? Lie? Put on your underwear and dance to Kool & The Gang? Drink your last beer? Complain the yogurt isn't organic? Fuck boys. They all look like they'd make good boyfriends, but how many turn out to be?

Sent: February 13, 2011 at 10:12 p.m.
From: Cecily Murphy
To: Suzie London

He didn't do anything. I'm just reluctant. No ... careful.

Sent: February 13, 2011 at 10:12 p.m.
From: Suzie London
To: Cecily Murphy

And by reluctant and careful you mean scared?

Sent: February 13, 2011 at 10:14 p.m.
From: Cecily Murphy
To: Suzie London

God, you sound like my roommate and my friend Michele. See, I thought you of all people would understand.

Sent: February 13, 2011 at 10:23 p.m.
From: Suzie London
To: Cecily Murphy

I do! I struggle with it too. Keeping your soul open and receptive enough to lay your fingertips on his face and say: ah, you. I found you, my kindred, the pit of my peach, even though now the pits of my peaches are plastic and my insides are swimming in microwave rays. And balancing that need with the even more real need to protect what's left. I struggle too.

I think I said the same thing to Jace before chemo last time.

I might have given Jace too much hell. No not really. It was the appropriate amount of hell when you factor in the Hep C scare. Goldilocks hell: juuuust right.

But it took its toll on me is what I'm saying. I was the collateral damage. I'm so good at that. It's on my resume: fluent in self-fuckery. If you want to protect yourself, do it, but make sure you're actually protecting yourself and not protecting your fear. That's all.

Sent: February 13, 2011 at 10:27 p.m.
From: Cecily Murphy
To: Suzie London

I know you struggle with it. At least Jack is way too shy for cheating! Well, I guess you can't make definitive statements about who people really are. Who knows? But the bottom line is: there's only so much you can ask of a person. I can't ask him to take on this burden.

Sent: February 13, 2011 at 10:29 p.m.
From: Suzie London
To: Cecily Murphy

So what you're talking about is fear of disappointment, but reversed. Fear of his disappointment in you.

Sent: February 13, 2011 at 10:30 p.m.
From: Cecily Murphy
To: Suzie London

Huh. I guess you're right. But it's just that I can't make any promises.

Sent: February 13, 2011 at 10:32 p.m.
From: Suzie London
To: Cecily Murphy

I know the feeling. Staying fluid, I called it once. Maybe I stayed too fluid, or had too many fluids. If you made a mistake or not, I'm not the one to ask. I'm still trying to figure out how I got on this square. Life is one hell of a confusing hopscotch game.

Sent: February 13, 2011 at 10:33 p.m.
From: Cecily Murphy
To: Suzie London

It is one hell of a hopscotch game. You always won, though. Hopscotch.

February 13, 2011 at 10:38 p.m.
From: Suzie London
To: Cecily Murphy

You'll win this one, CCM. Hands down, double dutch, without a scratch on your Tretorns. Don't stress about this one. I bet he goes crazy until you change your mind—men like the chase—Jace did. He took it as a challenge, and then once I said yes, he instantly reverted to his old pain-in-the-ass ways. So if he doesn't chase, bullet dodged. Either way, you're golden. As for sex, you don't need it right now anyway, and once you do again, well, I've never met a woman who's had to pay for it.

Sent: February 13, 2011 at 10:40 p.m.
From: Cecily Murphy
To: Suzie London

LOL! Oh right! Option A: this boy. Option B: paying for it!

Sent: February 13, 2011 at 10:40 p.m.
From: Suzie London
To: Cecily Murphy

What does your sister say?

Sent: February 13, 2011 at 10:41 p.m.
From: Cecily Murphy
To: Suzie London

Cait?

Sent: February 13, 2011 at 10:41 p.m.
From: Suzie London
To: Cecily Murphy

No your sister Jimmy.

Sent: February 13, 2011 at 10:44 p.m.
From: Cecily Murphy
To: Suzie London

I don't know. I never tell her about this stuff. She's got a pre-fabricated opinion about everything. I'm glad she's a teacher, because it puts her natural bossiness to work for good instead of evil.

Sent: February 13, 2011 at 10:59 p.m.
From: Suzie London
To: Cecily Murphy

I remember her bossiness. I was my own boss, which I liked and didn't like. I wanted a regular dinnertime and a toaster oven that worked. But then Brad grew up and Found God, and he's bossy now too, and you know what? Turns out I wasn't missing anything. Now, instead of him being off somewhere, it's all: "Let go and let God, Suzie." And I'm all, dude, I've been emancipated since I was 15. Emancipated.

Spiritually, emotionally, physically. If you want to dance the 12-step, dance it: enjoy. But I am and will always remain a free person. Free to be you and me! Remember that record from 3rd grade social studies?

Sent: February 13, 2011 at 11:05 p.m.
From: Cecily Murphy
To: Suzie London

Yes, but only the title song! Freedom. I'll go to bed dreaming of it. Freedom from cancer, freedom from my genes, freedom from my sister's unsolicited advice, the weight of my mom's sadness. That's what it is: weight.

Sent: February 13, 2011 at 11:09 p.m.
From: Suzie London
To: Cecily Murphy

Me too. Weighted down with Doctor Pity Face. Oh no, here it comes. Pity Face. You know you're screwed when you get Pity Face. But after this, we'll go to Alaska and raise sled dogs and race in the Iditarod. The freest of all free agents, racing across the snow, the wind in our faces. We'll have a new crop of puppies every year and we'll name them after David Bowie songs, our Diamond Dogs.

Sent: February 13, 2011 at 11:12 p.m.
From: Cecily Murphy
To: Suzie London

Love it! XO Goodnight!

Chapter 19

May 31, 2011 10:45 a.m.

The first thing Cecily noted about the house was its Victorian architecture, which stood out like a pore on a magazine model between the modern storefronts that flanked it. Painted a pale yellow, it attempted to blend into its whitewashed surroundings, unobtrusively sitting back from the street behind a small garden with a brick path leading up to the wooden front porch.

"Do you think this is it?" Jack asked, after commenting that it didn't look barn-like enough to fit Suzie's description.

"It won't hurt to ask, I guess. Keep in mind Suzie wasn't a literalist."

The wooden front door, open about a foot, revealed a high-ceilinged hallway with wide, dusty floorboards and walls papered in pastel stripes. A broad staircase took up most of the entryway. To the right, an office door stood open. Bells over the front door announced Cecily and Jack's arrival when they pushed it open, and a middle-aged woman walked into the hallway to greet them before they reached the office door.

The knowing look on the woman's face caused Cecily to remember she had forgotten her sun hat back at the hotel.

"Welcome," the woman said. "I'm Eileen Buford. Is this your first visit to Caring Bridge?" Cecily and Jack nodded and introduced themselves.

Eileen took hold of both of Cecily's hands and led her, walking backwards as though Cecily couldn't see, into the office.

"Please have a seat," she said, motioning to an antique-looking olive wool couch that would have looked at home in a Midwestern mortuary. The late-morning sunlight illuminated the dust in the air. Jack sneezed.

"Excuse me," he said.

"God bless you both," Eileen answered.

Oh no, Cecily thought. She thinks we're here for—

"The services we offer here at Caring Bridge are free and completely confidential," Eileen began her spiel, handing Cecily a folder.

"We—uh, thank you," Cecily said, accepting the folder and looking to Jack for an idea that might free them from orientation, from wasting this woman's time. She always felt slightly like a trapped animal when receiving concern from strangers over the cancer.

"Is it …" Cecily interrupted when Eileen took a breath. "Is it OK if we just look around? The yoga class gets out in a minute and we just wanted to have a quick word with the teacher. Ask her some questions."

"Or some of the other clients," Jack added quickly.

"Of course!" Eileen smiled warmly. "You should know that all of our instructors are licensed and have years of experience working with cancer patients. Indigo is teaching today. She'll be able to answer any of your questions."

Cecily and Jack stood up. Free, Cecily thought.

Not so.

"I can walk with you to the barn, where we hold our classes, and tell you about our other programs" Eileen chirped, flitting around Cecily and Jack as she prepared to leave the office.

"Barn," Cecily repeated to Jack, eyes wide and smiling.

Jack nodded.

"Oh, it's not a real barn—it's more like a log cabin. It's lovely. You'll see."

The sweet smell of sawed wood greeted them as Eileen swung open the French doors that separated the "barn" addition from the old house. Sunlight poured through the skylights in slats on the wooden floor. Broad, built-in, wooden benches lined the walls, large enough to nap on. To the right, a narrow hallway led to a log-cabin kitchen, where three women of retirement age stood around a steaming chili pot on a stovetop on a granite island.

"I could live here," Cecily said.

Eileen nodded. "That's the idea," she said. She greeted the ladies and introduced them to Cecily and Jack.

The tallest woman, thin and regal with a scarf wrapped like a turban around her pale head, hugged Cecily, who was a little stunned by the gesture.

"Bless you, you're so young," she said. "I'm Anna."

"You missed yoga, but you didn't miss Anna's chili," a short woman in an ironed tracksuit told Cecily. "It gives me gas, but it's worth it," she added, lilting slightly to the side as she nodded to herself.

"Thank you," Cecily said, smiling in surprise.

Eileen cleared her throat. "By the way, how did you find out about Caring Bridge?" she asked.

"A friend. Suzie London," Cecily answered.

The air sizzled like Cecily had lit a match. The ladies starting talking all at once. The short woman, whom Eileen had introduced as Karla, took Cecily's hands.

"God bless Suzie London," she said, a tear resting on the reddened rim of her eyelid, magnified in her large glasses. "She saved us from verbally abusive yoga."

Eileen dropped her forehead into her hand and shook her head.

"She ... what?" Cecily asked, surmising from Eileen's reaction that this was not Eileen's fondest memory of Suzie.

Karla shook her head. "It was awful. We had a yoga instructor—"

"Who no longer works here," Eileen quickly interjected, laughing nervously.

"Thanks to Suzie," Karla nodded crisply at Eileen, who shrank slightly at this rebuke.

"That reminds me," Eileen said. "I'm just going to go find Indigo, our yoga instructor this morning. Why don't you tell Cecily and Jack here how much you like Indigo?" The ladies shrugged. Indigo wasn't their favorite.

Despite Eileen's assurances to Jack and Cecily about her staff, Indigo was turning out to be a problem employee. Eileen suspected Indigo of dealing marijuana and using her job at the center to find clients for Indigo's girlfriend, a self-styled healer whose services were as expensive as they were lacking in any accreditation recognized by the State of California. She had been in the office speaking with one of the attorneys on their board about how to go about terminating her.

Eileen's mission would be futile. Indigo was safely hidden behind the greenhouse, smoking a joint before teaching her next class, Meditations II.

A woman with short, dark hair, who reminded Cecily of a Chia pet, rubbed her hair absently and said, "Suzie got rid of our last bad yoga instructor. Tossed her out. Cold. I'm Beaulah, by the way." Cecily took her extended hand, cold to the touch.

"Horrible teacher," Karla nodded. "A screamer."

"A bad fit," Anna nodded, adding, "She didn't adapt her teaching style to the needs of the population she was teaching."

"Suzie made her adapt," Karla added. "Her name was Sheila? Or Shiloh? She kept yelling at me, 'You're doing it wrong! Hook your ankle behind your tricep!' And I said, 'ma'am, I've only done that one time in my life. And it was in 1969 at a party with a gentleman named Corky who claimed to be a distant cousin of JFK—and I will never ever get my body to do that again, even if I wanted to.'"

Cecily turned her face away and tried to hide her smile.

"It's OK to laugh at Karla," Beulah said, matter-of-factly, "We all do."

Karla continued, oblivious to any interruption, "She kept yelling, 'Don't look in the mirrors! What, you think you all look like pretty ballerinas?'"

Anna said, "And that's when Suzie stood up."

"She did. She just stood right up," Karla verified. "She seemed so tall."

"Because we had our feet behind our heads," Beulah giggled. "I was so excited. I thought: get her, girl!"

Karla continued, "Suzie walked right up to her, poked her finger right in her bony little chest—right here! Like this!" Karla demonstrated by inserting her finger between the bones of Cecily's clavicle. "And Suzie said, 'You need to leave. And never come back.' Just exactly like that. And the yoga teacher opened her mouth. And closed it. And opened it. And closed it. Like a fish." Karla demonstrated the fish face for Cecily and Jack. "Then the yoga lady said, 'They don't pay me enough for this c-r-a-p,' and she scooped up her bag and her flip flops and walked out."

"And Suzie taught the rest of the class," Karla finished. "It was beautiful."

"She should've been a teacher," Anna added. "She had such a gift."

"The gift of bossiness," Karla agreed.

"And love," Anna added.

"Bossiness with love," Karla agreed again.

"Sometimes it's the same thing," Cecily said, smiling a little.

"There was no public service for her although that silly Dr. Sicko show was public enough," Karla shook her head regretfully.

"Dr. Dick," harrumphed Anna. "The girls and I were talking about a service. We don't know what church she belonged to, if any."

"She said it was a church in Cleveland," said Karla.

"No, Karla, she was talking about the Rock and Roll Museum." Anna shook her head, pursing her lips together in exasperation. Cecily pegged her as the possible Suzie expert in the group.

"I didn't know where to send flowers," Anna continued. "There was a note on the board saying her brother had started a memorial fund for her through Susan G. Komen. But no address for family members. I wanted to send a card, although, I guess Komen sends a card when you donate."

"I still think we should have a service here," Karla said, inadvisedly ladling chili into a bowl. Don't do it, Karla, Cecily thought. Don't mess with your digestive system; it's taxed enough.

"We sort of did," Beulah said. "Kaylee dedicated our Yoga Nidra to her that day. We all guided her spirit to the light."

Anna asked who wanted coffee. Cecily said she'd have some, and as Anna glided around the kitchen, she asked Cecily the usual questions. Karla and Beulah sat down at the counter to listen.

"What kind of cancer, may I ask that? How did you know Suzie?"

The women told Cecily they also had breast cancer (Anna was metastatic), and that Cecily and Suzie were far too young to deal with such things.

"What kind of chemo did you have?"

"How fast did you lose your hair?"

"Did you lose your nails?"

"What about your toenails?"

"Does this look infected to you?" Karla held up her bare foot.

"Karla!"

Jack tuned out as the women traded war stories. He had no need for the status of the woman's toenails, but Cecily seemed interested.

"See?" Cecily said, taking off her shoes. "They're kind of growing back, but not very quickly."

"Oh, they look wonderful. Look at that. No, they're coming back very quickly," Anna said. She held up her sandaled foot. "I'm a few more months out than you and mine just started coming back in."

Jack wandered into the hallway to read the bulletin board. Flyers offered nutrition seminars, house cleaning services, pet walking services ....

Dog walking.

Jack ripped the flyer down. "Cecily!" Jack called. "Cecily, look!"

The women were now comparing eyebrows, deep in conversation.

Jack tapped her on the shoulder and waited patiently.

Cecily and Anna looked up. "What's up?" Cecily asked.

"This flyer," he waved it at her. "Suzie!"

Anna reached out and took the flyer. "Oh, this makes me so sad," she murmured. "Yes, Suzie walked our dogs for free. Well, if she liked you," Anna smirked, clearly remembering something. "She didn't like Tom."

Karla nodded, covering her mouth with her hand to hide her smile.

"I miss her," Anna said. "I miss doing yoga next to her. I was always late to class and Suzie would always save me a spot."

Mothballs! Cecily remembered Suzie telling her about the woman who smelled like mothballs. She stepped closer to Anna sniffing. Mothballs! The smell had never before brought her pleasure, but it was a link to Suzie, finally. She closed her eyes and inhaled.

When she opened them, everyone was staring at her.

Sent: February 14, 2011 at 6:27 a.m.
From: Cecily Murphy
To: Suzie London

Suzie: help!!! Hair falling out!!! Already! Woke up with a mouthful of it and looked down and it's all over the pillows, everywhere! No! No! Stay on! Stay on! I thought I had another month before this happened—that's what they said in chemo class! Stupid, worthless chemo class!

Sent: February 14, 2011 at 6:31 a.m.
From: Suzie London
To: Cecily Murphy

That IS fast. Don't wait. Time to shave your head.

Sent: February 14, 2011 at 6:31 a.m.
From: Cecily Murphy
To: Suzie Murphy

What?! I can't.

Sent: February 14, 2011 at 6:32 a.m.
From: Suzie London
To: Cecily Murphy

Make it fun. Like when we were kids and we cut our Barbie's hair. Except poor Barbie's hair never grew back or got the toothpaste out. I'll go first.

Sent: February 14, 2011 at 6:35 a.m.
From: Suzie London
To: Cecily Murphy

Here it is: my new mullet.

Sent: February 14, 2011 at 6:35 a.m.
From: Cecily Murphy
To: Suzie London

Are you crazy?! What are you doing?! Put the scissors down!

Sent: February 14, 2011 at 6:40 a.m.
From: Suzie London
To: Cecily Murphy

Yes. I'm crazy. No, I won't put the scissors down. Here's my perfect, even bob—if I tilt my head to the side. Now you go Cecily. You can do this too!

Sent: February 14, 2011 at 6:40 a.m.
From: Cecily Murphy
To: Suzie London

Wait. Wait. Why is my hair falling out first? You started two months before me!

Sent: February 14, 2011 at 6:45 a.m.
From: Suzie London
To: Cecily Murphy

That is pretty fast to lose your hair. My hair hasn't gone anywhere lately. But, it's gotta go eventually. Look, I'm Billy Idol!

Sent: February 14, 2011 at 6:46 a.m.
From: Cecily Murphy
To: Suzie London

HOLY SHIT, SUZIE!!!

Sent: February 14, 2011 at 6:47 a.m.
From: Suzie London
To: Cecily Murphy

Come on, Cecily! Scissors ahoy! Don't just sit there and cry as your hair comes out. Chop it. Take control. Grab this mofo by the nuts and GO.

Sent: February 14, 2011at 6:48 a.m.
From: Cecily Murphy
To: Suzie London

OK.

Sent: February 14, 2011at 7:12 a.m.
From: Cecily Murphy
To: Suzie London

OK. Look at this ... not bad. I think it's a bob.

Sent: February 14, 2011 at 7:14 a.m.
From: Suzie London
To: Cecily Murphy

Fabulous! Now the mullet. Or the Princess Diana!! Do the Princess Diana!!

Sent: February 14, 2011 at 7:14 a.m.
From: Cecily Murphy
To: Suzie London

OK.

Sent: February 14, 2011 at 7:28 a.m.
From: Cecily Murphy
To: Suzie London

I hate this!!! I hate this!!! I have BRICKS in my BOOBS and I'm a FREAK and I HATE THIS!

Sent: February 14, 2011 at 7:32 a.m.
From: Suzie London
To: Cecily Murphy

Are you done? Because you've been secretly dying to wear my hot pink wig. It will be at your house in two days. I wish I'd sent it earlier. Time for Billy Idol. Then grab your electric razor and I'll show you how to do the Sinead O'Connor look. Sinead is as far as I go today. I looked hot with my Sinead last time. You will too. It's a tough look to pull off but I totally see you pulling it off.

Sent: February 14, 2011 at 7:35 a.m.
From: Suzie London
To: Cecily Murphy

Come on, Cecily! Nothing compares 2 U! Do it!

Sent: February 14, 2011 at 7:42 a.m.
From: Cecily Murphy
To: Suzie London

OK. Wow. You do look hot with a Sinead O'Connor. You look like Demi Moore in ... what was that movie when we were kids? We saw it together. Why is it, Suzie, that before you contacted me on Facebook, I only remembered the times when we weren't friends and you remembered all the times we were? Jane has an electric razor. She's going to freaking kill me when she wakes up.

Sent: February 14, 2011 at 7:44 a.m.
From: Suzie London
To: Cecily Murphy

"There is no objectivity in truth. There is only your truth." My healer said that. She is one crazy smart bitch. I WANT TO SEE THE MOHAWK. Get Jane's clippers and show me the Mohawk!

Sent: February 14, 2011 at 8:12 a.m.
From: Cecily Murphy
To: Suzie London

There. What do you think?

Sent: February 14, 2011 at 8:14 a.m.
From: Suzie London
To: Cecily Murphy

I think you're brave and beautiful, the same you've always been. But now it shows more. Go put on your wig before you freeze to death. Then get the wig cut today, on your head. You'll do fine. Christ it's late. Or early. I'm going to bed before Rothner wakes up and sees the hairy bathroom.

Chapter 20

May 31, 2011, 10:45 a.m.

When their coffee finished brewing, Anna led Cecily and Jack to the back porch, a large wooden deck about a foot off the ground with no rails to block the view of the backyard, a shady lawn lined with hostas, rhododendrons, and palms. Anna swept the tree debris off the picnic table, then set their coffee mugs down. Beulah and Karla had remained inside, eating their chili at the counter and cruising Pinterest on the iPad on the counter.

"You were close with Suzie," Cecily ventured. "Because you were both metastatic?"

Anna nodded. "We were both in the breast cancer group, and we talked about forming a new one for the metastatic ladies." She laughed. "Suzie wanted to make us pink satin jackets like the Pink Ladies in *Grease*! Oh, she made me laugh. So full of life—right up until the end."

Cecily wondered if Suzie hadn't thought of Anna as a mother figure, since her mother was taken from her so suddenly. Why hadn't Cecily known any of this when she was younger? It was one of those topics the adults didn't discuss in front of the children. Would it have changed anything if she had known? Would Cecily, 10 or 11 years old, stepped up to the plate, set aside the three-year-old Go-Go's scandal, set aside her fear and distrust, and been an actual friend to Suzie London? The way Suzie, in her unique way, had been a friend to Cecily: pulling Cecily under the fence at Pine Hill pool, concocting all of their games, showing Cecily a new way to see their small world? There were two kinds of friends—those who stretched your boundaries, and those who reinforced them. As a child, Cecily had believed there was only one.

"Did you know that Suzie was getting sicker?" Jack asked, as Cecily appeared to be deep in thought, staring out over the hostas toward the greenhouse.

Anna nodded slowly. "We talked about coping." She paused. "I'm also terminal."

But she is so put together, Cecily thought. She has such wonderful posture and carries herself with the dignity of someone who is capable of ruling, if not a small country, then at the very least her own life.

"I'm so sorry," Cecily stammered, with Jack stammering the same a beat behind her.

"Thank you," Anna said, smiling and nodding. "There's no need to be sorry, however. I'm feeling good, and I'm going into an experimental trial at UCLA. God bless these doctors. They never give up on you. I hope you never said I'm sorry to Suzie." Anna raised her eyebrows.

"Oh! Oh no! I'm sorry for saying I'm sorry!" Cecily blurted, horrified at herself.

Anna laughed. "Breathe, dear. Deep breaths. Don't be sorry. I'm grateful for your sympathy and your empathy. I'm talking about Suzie. She loathed sympathy." Anna regarded Cecily closely. "Are you OK?"

Cecily willed herself to inhale and exhale normally. Suddenly she laughed. "Oh my gosh. I'm becoming one of those people—afraid of saying the wrong thing!"

Anna smiled. "Yes, I end up feeling bad for the people I tell, having to come up with something 'appropriate' to say on the spot. It's so stressful for people! That's why I don't tell many people. Suzie was the same." She laughed suddenly, a high-pitched giggle that sounded like a tiny bell ringing. "Well, unless you crossed her. Then she told people to punish them. But she hated sympathy. Pity, she called it. She fought it her whole life."

"I didn't know," Cecily said. "About Suzie. That she was dying."

Anna stood up, walked over to Cecily and hugged her. "Oh, darling. Now *I'm* sorry. See? Now we can be sympathy equals." She smiled. "There's nothing wrong with sympathy. But I could never convince Suzie of this, so don't feel left out. In fact, if you did know, I'd think you were here because she owed you money."

"Jesus. People come looking for her here?" Jack asked.

Anna laughed again. "No," she said, waving her hand dismissively. "She always said stuff like that. She liked her tough-girl act. I think she had tough times definitely, but she was all bark."

Cecily paused, thinking of how to word this. "Can I ask you some questions about Suzie's last six months?"

"You may," Anna replied, sipping her coffee. "But I don't know how much help I can be. And Meditations Class starts in 15 minutes."

"We don't want to keep you," Jack said. "First, though, did you know any of Suzie's friends? Her brother?"

"No, though I knew she had them."

"Do you think," Cecily didn't want to ask this, but she winced and continued, "Suzie really had metastatic disease? Do you think she died of cancer?"

Cecily could barely look at Anna. If she could have gotten away with it, she would have watched the woman's reaction through her fingers.

Anna, however, simply looked thoughtful. "Those are two very different questions, you realize. I know she had metastatic disease. We had the same oncologist."

"Dr. Ella Drago?"

"You've heard of her?"

"Sort of." Cecily smiled. "Suzie had a nickname for her."

Anna smiled. "Yes. Yes she did."

"But you don't think Suzie died of cancer?" Jack prompted. "Is that what you're saying?"

The Truth About Suzie

Anna readjusted herself in her chair. "When you're given the news that your cancer has metastasized, again, there are choices to make. You can keep on your present treatment course. You can get second, third, fourth opinions. You can turn to alternative medicine. Or, you can stop fighting, have a nice Christmas, and do what you can do with whatever time you have left."

"So this was in December, for Suzie?" Cecily asked.

"Yes. After her port surgery. The port was bothering her neck. They went in, did tests, and found that her lymph nodes, well ..." Anna paused, pressed her lips together tightly. "She was so damn young, God." She addressed the sky. "I'm a great grandmother, but she was so young.

She told me ... well ... this stuck in my head. She said, 'I never believed I was indestructible. It's just so hard to believe my future could be erased in such a regular moment. A Wednesday morning, sitting in a hospital gown, eating Jello, reading my horoscope, waiting for my discharge papers, then the doctor walks in and game over. Game over."

"Anyway," Anna continued. "It had spread. They told her they couldn't guarantee the chemo would help anymore and sent her home. They just handed her her discharge papers and sent her home. Terrible week. I've been very lucky, being in this study. She asked what I'd do. I said I'd get the chemo. She said no. She was going to try alternative treatments. Her own plan. Indigo has a girlfriend who's a healer. I said that's fine, but you're going to have to stay in treatment, at least nominally, to have access to pain management and hospice. Then she asked me if I was a Dorothy Parker fan. I was. I am.

And she said, 'Well, Anna. Like Dorothy said: 'Candy is dandy, but liquor is quicker.'"

Sent: February 19, 2011 at 6:07 a.m.
From: Cecily Murphy
To: Suzie London

I'm willing to bet you're awake—the hours you keep, girl! How do you do it on chemo? I guess your work schedule is not your typical 9-5. How are you doing? How are things with your brother?

This may be urban legend, but my nurse said if I take Claritin (allergy med) for three days before chemo & five days after, I won't get bone pain from Neulasta, aka NeuNasty. Started too late last time ... no more rookie mistakes! Have you tried this, and if so: A.M. pill or P.M.?

Sent: February 19, 2011at 10:10 p.m.
From: Cecily Murphy
To: Suzie London

I got the wigs! Thank you so much! I love them! Man, they're fun! The purple one is my favorite! No, the pink. No, the Katy Perry blue one. The Dolly Parton one is ... more fabulous than I could've ever imagined. Jane and I invited our next-door neighbors over for dinner tonight, and we tried all the wigs on all evening. So much fun! It's so funny. I never thought I'd have you to help take care of me during this time. I thought I'd just hunker down, close my hood around my face, and plow on through. But it's amazing—all these former strangers (or friends that became strangers and became friends again)—we all take care of each other. I never dreamed I'd have Fantasia, Charlene, Jane and I all wearing different color wigs in the living room, hanging out with takeout and cans of Schlitz. But that's what this experience does, right? It turns everything upside down. I love the wigs. They're the greatest gift. And yet, they aren't even the greatest gift you've given me. Are you really just going to go around LA with a Sinead O'Connor in February? I guess the weather is much warmer so it doesn't matter as much? Don't you need these?

**Sent: February 19, 2011 at 11:32 p.m.
From: Suzie London
To: Cecily Murphy**

Honey, I live with a drag queen. Rothner is a drag queen. Did I not tell you that? I have access to wigs. I don't wear them much though. I like looking like a biker bitch. It keeps the riff-raff off my porch. Also, I like going to Jace's performances disguised and having him find me in the crowd.

**Posted February 24, 2011 at 12:19 p.m.
Cecily Murphy**

Good news: better at managing chemo effects/meds this time. Bad news: this weekend still sucks, and like **Suzie London** said, they are trying to kill me! Good news: just a few vile days and the rest are better. Like having the flu at predictable intervals, as Suzie also told me. Predictable is always better than the sucker-punch. Meds, try to sleep, water by the gallon, try to eat = done.

**Sent: February 28, 2011 at 6:24 a.m.
From: Cecily Murphy
To: Suzie London**

Did you get my email about Claritin? Do you take it? I had to describe chemo to my niece. She was full of questions last night. I love talking to her like she's an adult. Eileigh loves it, and it drives Cait crazy. I told her—literally, I said this to a four-year-old: "Chemotherapy is an industry-standard treatment regimen that is scientifically proven to either work or not work. Whether it will work for you is completely unknown, unknowable and outside the current parameters of science." She just looked at me and said, "Well that's silly." She's awesome.

Sent: February 28, 2011 at 3:42 p.m.
From: Suzie London
To: Cecily Murphy

Once that poison is out of your system, there's nothing but peace. Never heard of the Claritin, but try it, why not? It's legal too. You like legal.

Posted March 2, 2011 at 6:08 a.m.
Cecily Murphy

Well met again, Day 7! I know I'm feeling human again when I look around my room & office and see the toll of my week off from housework. I highly recommend the Claritin. It worked this time! Or I think it worked: same thing!

Sent: March 4, 2011 at 5:21 a.m.
From: Suzie London
To: Cecily Murphy

What's up, East Coast? You're online early.

Sent: March 4, 2011 at 5:24 a.m.
From: Cecily Murphy
To: Suzie London

You're online late!

Nothing much. I found out I'm not allowed to do my annual OB/GYN appointment during chemo. Yay! No dentist either! Only certain medical professionals are allowed to harass me at this time. The rest can just get in line.

I'm checking out the new Facebook timeline. It's weird. It makes life easy for your stalkers. It's your autobiography, but with input from all your friends as well.

Sent: March 4, 2011 at 5:28 a.m.
From: Suzie London
To: Cecily Murphy

It's recapping your life, the way you want it. Writing your memoirs for you, written in ether. Written in the stars ... love that song. Download it now. And on Facebook you can delete your posts and other people's posts that piss you off: that's nice. I hate getting pity posts on my page. It's like mocking someone with a kindness mask on. LA is like Facebook. People keep or discard you with one glance. It's a relief in a way. You don't have to explain anything ... even the doctors do it. I've gotten skinny again, but here anorexia rules with a whip, all the girls are doing it, and my skin can pass for a self-tanning accident. I've seen girls look worse than me on purpose. You can pass through undetected. Only Jace is allowed to feel real bad for me, and I like that. But I keep him on his toes enough that I don't know how he even has time.

Sent: March 4, 2011 at 5:36 a.m.
From: Cecily Murphy
To: Suzie London

Never thought of them as "pity posts" or being mocking. Interesting. I should update my timeline: "In October, 2010, I was diagnosed with cancer. And Suzie London found me, and she had cancer too. We grew up a house apart and we're both insanely too young to have cancer."

How weird is that? Suzie, I think of this all the time. I really do believe there was a cancer cluster. And yet, I know it's genetic. It doesn't even matter that science can't find proof of the cancer cluster. I still believe there's something involved, but since there's no proof it's more faith than science. Maybe I am religious after all.

Sent: March 4, 2011 at 5:41 a.m.
From: Suzie London
To: Cecily Murphy

I'm naughty and you're nice. I gave myself cancer and you didn't. You were born this way, baby.

Sent: March 4, 2011 at 5:42 a.m.
From: Cecily Murphy
To: Suzie London

Don't be ridiculous, Suzie!

Sent: March 4, 2011 at 5:45 a.m.
From: Suzie London
To: Cecily Murphy

Some people do give themselves cancer. There are risk factors outside of genes, you know. I want a do over. I look at my timeline and I want to do over entire years, particularly the years between ages 15-25. Or not even a do over. If I could just go back and give myself a hug, and say love your life, love it, cherish it, don't waste a minute of it. Don't listen to Dr. Hollasch: he's full of shit. And do not, do NOT, try crystal blue persuasion.

Sent: March 4, 2011 at 5:49 a.m.
From: Cecily Murphy
To: Suzie London

I wouldn't do over this time in my life if you promised me a million dollars and world peace at the end of it. Maybe if you threw in ending worldwide child hunger. Then I might. And I would NEVER try something called crystal blue persuasion—that sounds like a hippie mob weapon.

Sent: March 4, 2011 at 5:51 a.m.
From: Suzie London
To: Cecily Murphy

Ha! It might be. So tired, but have to stay awake. Too much work to do.

Sent: March 4, 2011 at 5:52 a.m.
From: Cecily Murphy
To: Suzie London

What work do you have to do?

Sent: March 4, 2011 at 5:55 a.m.
From: Suzie London
To: Cecily Murphy

Dog walking schedule. Bills. Jace wants me to see a financial planner. I don't see why. He seems happy busting my balls about my finances and he does it for free. Why pay someone else to do it? Also homework from the healer.

Sent: March 4, 2011 at 5:55 a.m.
From: Cecily Murphy
To: Suzie London

Healers give homework?

Sent: March 4, 2011 at 5:56 a.m.
From: Suzie London
To: Cecily Murphy

Don't all doctors? You gotta take your temperature every day, take your Dexameth.

Sent: March 4, 2011 at 5:59 a.m.
From: Cecily Murphy
To: Suzie London

Yeah, I guess so. So what's healer homework? Rub essential oils on your feet and stick garlic up your nose? Sorry, I'm being healer-phobic again. Even Dr. SPO is more open-minded than me in some ways. He's a big fan of complementary medicine.

Sent: March 4, 2011 at 6:02 a.m.
From: Suzie London
To: Cecily Murphy

Yes, not just for hippies anymore! I know you're getting a Rasputin-type vibe from all this, but I assure you she's totally legit. Karmic soul work. And for me, lots of it.

Sent: March 4, 2011 at 6:02 a.m.
From: Cecily Murphy
To: Suzie London

Oh, Suzie, Your karma is fine. Don't let anyone tell you differently.

Sent: March 4, 2011 at 6:03 a.m.
From: Suzie London
To: Cecily Murphy

Sometimes souls have competing needs. It's complicated. It's not that my karma is bad. I have to heal my relationships with my soul partners. My healer says we travel with soul partners from life to life to teach each other things, and they all switch around, fulfilling different roles and relationships among your friends and family. I was like, oh shit, I could have been Jace's mom in my past life? She said, exactly. And I said, OK, that is completely disgusting. But I got it. I get it.

Sent: March 4, 2011 at 6:04 a.m.
From: Cecily Murphy
To: Suzie London

OMG! Sooo ... while we're on the topic of karmic maintenance and repair, can you answer me a few questions I've been curious about? Like jail, for instance. Were you really in jail?

Sent: March 4, 2011 at 6:05 a.m.
From: Suzie London
To: Cecily Murphy

Oh God yes. You've never?

Sent: March 4, 2011 at 6:05 a.m.
From: Cecily Murphy
To: Suzie London

No. Can't say that I have. Why were you?

Sent: March 4, 2011 at 6:06 a.m.
From: Suzie London
To: Cecily Murphy

Hmm, well, not counting juvie offenses of hormonal mayhem, a couple of d & d problems (drunk and disorganized), then the PETA crap.

Sent: March 4, 2011 at 6:06 a.m.
From: Cecily Murphy
To: Suzie London

But you said you hate PETA!

Sent: March 4, 2011 at 6:08 a.m.
From: Suzie London
To: Cecily Murphy

Uh, YEAH. Those fuckers left me rotting in jail after I freed the dogs from the monkey rodeo for them.

Sent: March 4, 2011 at 6:08 a.m.
From: Cecily Murphy
To: Suzie London

Monkey rodeo. That has got to be an auto-correct.

Sent: March 4, 2011 at 6:10 a.m.
From: Suzie London
To: Cecily Murphy

No auto-correct: monkey rodeo. They dress up the monkeys in cowboy outfits, spurs, hats, they ride dogs and round up goats. Those dogs needed my help. It's degrading to be ridden, for a dog.

Sent: March 4, 2011 at 6:12 a.m.
From: Cecily Murphy
To: Suzie London

Just the dogs? How about the monkeys? Or the goats? Or the spectators, even? It's hard to tell who's the most degraded in this scenario.

Sent: March 4, 2011 at 6:21 a.m.
From: Suzie London
To: Cecily Murphy

Nah, the monkeys are having a blast in their little outfits and kicky hats. It's hard to degrade a primate. They're shamelessly ridiculous creatures and so good at degrading themselves. The ultimate bio-degradables: primates.

I was in it for the dogs. I freed them, and the goats, though technically it was felony theft. Who knew goats were worth so much? The word "felony" scattered PETA like mice back into the walls. They didn't come get me like they said. Fuckers. After that, I borrowed a really real-looking fake fur coat from a friend and wore it to their meeting. People cried and threw coffee at me. The dry cleaning was expensive. But worth it.

Sent: March 4, 2011 at 6:24 a.m.
From: Cecily Murphy
To: Suzie London

Oh my God, Suzie. It's like you beg for trouble. Beg for it. Has it ever occurred to you to not act on your vengeful impulses?

Sent: March 4, 2011 at 6:24 a.m.
From: Suzie London
To: Cecily Murphy

No.

Sent: March 4, 2011 at 6:25 a.m.
From: Cecily Murphy
To: Suzie London

Really? You never thought, "I wouldn't be here getting a mug shot if I didn't do that," or "Maybe there are more constructive ways to go about expressing my displeasure."

Sent: March 4, 2011 at 6:26 a.m.
From: Suzie London
To: Cecily Murphy

Never.

Sent: March 4, 2011 at 6:26 a.m.
From: Cecily Murphy
To: Suzie London

Really?

Sent: March 4, 2011 at 6:26 a.m.
From: Suzie London
To: Cecily Murphy

Really. When I take a stand, I take a stand. I only harm those who harm me.

Sent: March 4, 2011 at 6:26 a.m.
From: Cecily Murphy
To: Suzie London

But like you say: collateral damage. There's always collateral damage. To you.

Sent: March 4, 2011 at 6:27 a.m.
From: Suzie London
To: Cecily Murphy

If the world wants to punish me for what I've done, it's free to do so, and it does. I don't get angry about it. I know the costs going in. I'm willing to pay.

Sent: March 4, 2011 at 6:28 a.m.
From: Cecily Murphy
To: Suzie London

You think it's brave. Or self-sacrificing.

Sent: March 4, 2011 at 6:30 a.m.
From: Suzie London
To: Cecily Murphy

No, it's honest. It's the only way I know how to be: honest. Everything else gets lost in ego and intention and rhetoric. I've read your Facebook posts: you think that's being honest: telling people what they want to hear? "I'm doing fine! Move along! Nothing to see here!" There's nothing honest about Facebook.

Sent: March 4, 2011 at 6:32 a.m.
From: Cecily Murphy
To: Suzie London

It's that obvious, huh?

Sent: March 4, 2011 at 6:38 a.m.
From: Suzie London
To: Cecily Murphy

It's obvious to me. I don't think it's a bad thing. In fact, it's a damn smart way to relate. You don't owe people front row seats to the workings of your soul. If you want to show your audience some pluck and resilience, go ahead. They eat that shit up. Seriously, I admire you for it. What do I always tell you? You're a self-contained unit. So am I.

Chapter 21

May 31, 2011, 1:30 p.m.

Jack and Cecily sat on the beach in Venice, a foot apart, like bookends facing the ocean. Cecily wanted to process, decompress after their talk with Anna, whose contact information sat in the pocket of Cecily's pink dress.

"So," Cecily said, digging her feet into the sand and piling it on with her hands. She suspected, but didn't care, that the sand was going to stick all over her because her special chemo SPF 1,000 sunscreen was interchangeable with Elmer's glue. "We've met Suzie London's brother and roommate. The two closest people to her didn't know she had cancer. Then we meet two complete walk-ons, random friends. And they say she had cancer. Then, Anna offered what I consider proof: they had the same oncologist and Suzie openly discussed her plans with her. What isn't clear to me is whether Suzie just gave up after finding out she was terminal, and said, 'I'm drinking myself to death.' I got the impression she was fighting her own battle, going to the healer, and using alcohol, and whatever else, as her pain management plan. 'Liquor is quicker' though. That sounds so ..."

"Suicidal," Jack murmured under his breath.

"I take issue with your terminology," Cecily said, as though defending her thesis. "I think Suzie didn't choose to die. She just chose how. Maybe. I still don't get why she died on Dr. Dick though."

"Well, that Dr. Dick thing seems to have snowballed away from her pretty fast. Dr. Dick outright lied to her. Maybe they ambushed her again."

Cecily nodded. "No. Rothner told us she asked to be filmed. God, she's confusing. Was."

"But you're convinced of the cancer now," Jack said.

"Yeah, and that's good, I guess. Not good, but informative. I'll take informative."

"See, I don't think it's good at all."

"What do you mean?"

"All this time, when you were worried she was lying, I was worried she wasn't lying," Jack said, his elbows hooked over his knees, his eyes on the ocean.

"What? Why? That's crazy," Cecily stared at him until he met her gaze.

"I thought you wanted proof. That recurrence, metastasis, didn't happen. That it was all a big lie."

"What? What on earth would make you think that?"

"I know you. Your pride isn't so delicate it can't survive a lie. You never took Suzie literally anyway. It's the fear that's a monster. You won't move forward, you won't look ahead past the rest of this until there's some sort of guarantee it won't come back."

"You're sitting here telling me that I wanted Dr. Dick's version of events to be the true one." Cecily couldn't believe what she was hearing.

"You did. A little bit."

"I didn't. A lot."

"Admit it. You're a commitment-phobe."

"Commitment-phobe?! Are you talking about us? How did this suddenly become about us? You're a commitment zealot!" Cecily charged back.

Jack sighed and looked out at the ocean again. "You're the only one I want to convert."

"Well, go hand out your pamphlets somewhere else. I've got too much on my plate."

"I can help take it off your plate."

"I don't want to be that to someone. A burden. Sand in your toes." Cecily shook out her feet.

"How could you possibly burden me? You make my life better. Ask Chang. I've been a completely different person this summer."

"Jack, no. I'm not done. I've got reconstruction. I've got surgeons hovering over me asking me to make a choice about the hysterectomy. Not to even mention it could come back, anywhere, anytime. It's an aggressive strain. There's a 25 percent chance!"

"See? Recurrence. That's it. That's what's holding you back. That's all it is."

"Nothing's holding me back. And if it is, it's because of my relationship with you, not my relationship with cancer. We're just not on the same page."

She regretted saying this as the words formed, but didn't know how to backtrack.

Jack pressed his lips together and was silent a moment. "OK," he finally said. "It's OK. Can you answer me, honestly, though? Do you love me?"

"Yes," Cecily groaned. She hadn't wanted to say it the first time under inquisition, under oath.

"And I feel the 'but' coming," Jack pressed.

"But I don't want to be in love now. This happened too soon. I feel like I tripped and fell."

Jack rubbed his forehead with his hand. "See, for me, it wasn't soon enough. It was so much later than I wanted it to be and now, I finally have you. I love you. And you don't want this. I don't get it. You won, Cecily. You won your battle with this disease. But what's the point of winning if you won't move past it?"

He stood up in one motion and started walking toward the ocean, arms crossed.

Cecily debated whether he wanted her to follow him. He walked purposefully at first, then slowed down. Now, she thought. She clambered to her feet and ran down the beach after him, her feet burning in the sand.

"Ouch!" she yelled. "I'm not wearing shoes! Can we move to the wet sand?"

Jack looked like he would remain there, feet secure in his flip flops, staring at the ocean, then he looked back at her, rolled his eyes and moved forward 10 feet onto the wet sand.

Cecily stood in front of him, angling to get him to look at her. The wind tried to snatch her hat, and the waves roared behind her, picking up spray in the strong breeze. "I do want this! Come on, Jack. I don't want to fight. Don't be like this. Can't we just wait and see? Or, sorry, not wait—just see? I'm just feeling rushed here."

"I'm not trying to rush you into anything, Cec. It's not that. I'm sorry. I just feel like you have one foot out the door."

Cecily smiled. "You've got it backwards. I've got one foot in the door. I'm not skittish, just slow. I admit, I was skittish before. During chemo I was a flight risk. Now I'm just slow."

As Jack considered this, the creases in his forehead smoothed a bit. He wrapped his arms around her waist and looked down into her eyes. "So when you go through your next round of surgeries, you're not going to push me away again?"

"No," Cecily promised.

"Promise?" his eyes searched hers, intent, though a smile hid behind them. He's a serial optimist, Cecily realized. How was I lucky enough to find one of those?

"I have to live my life based on what I want, not what I fear. Suzie taught me that. But I'm working on it. I'm working through it."

"Fair enough. I can live with that."

Cecily exhaled in relief, giddy with it, engulfed. "But," she added, smiling, "I reserve the right to shove you away at any time, for any reason. This is an at-will dating state."

The wind picked up and gusted around them, carrying Jack's laugh, lifting Cecily's hat, lifting her dress and thwacking her thighs with it. As Cecily frantically tamped down her clothes, Jack calmly brought his lips to hers and kissed her as the sand and salt swirled around them.

Sent: March 14, 2011 at 2:51 a.m.
From: Suzie London
To: Cecily Murphy

Watching "Short Circuit." Ally Sheedy, Steve Gutenberg & walking Commodore 64 styled with E.T. firmly in mind. Cinematic gold. This part's my favorite: the bad guys want their robot back because it contains a nuclear bomb. So they're shooting at it. I miss the 80's.

So here's what I learned tonight: Performing at Tiki Tata With Headgear: An Education. This will be useful to you. Take notes. 1) Wigs reach tropical temps right after lights go on. 2) No need for wig tape: mic headset will keep wig on. 3) BUT mic + big wig + small head = possible launch conditions for mic AND wig. 4) Dishwasher trumps washing machine for wig glitter glue removal. 5) Scarves keep cool & make exotic turbans! 6) But tend to slip down over eyes. Blind dancing + elevated stage = YouTube sensation.

Sent: March 14, 2011 at 7:49 a.m.
From: Cecily Murphy
To: Suzie London

How do you have this exciting life on chemo? I would fall asleep on stage. Not that I should ever be allowed on stage. My singing voice is similar to that of Jane's cat when he's outside looking for love—and forget dancing. I look like I'm being tasered. I think it would be fun though. Especially with the fabulous wigs. Although, who knows? You might think that attending a Women In Science symposium on effective lab management strategies is the height of excitement. There are free donuts, after all. But you would get stared at in the pink wig. I know this from experience. Kidding!

New issue today: I woke up, looked in the mirror, and WTF? I look like I slid face-first down a steep, astro-turfed mountain last night. Toaster oven face. Really? The pathetic thing is I wanted to see this guy this weekend, but now I have to put a bag over my head until whatever this is clears out. I'm not typically a high maintenance type of girl. I'll never be accused of being fashion-forward, I'm not even sure where I keep most of my makeup (it might still be packed from our last move), but I do have standards. Looking human is important to me. In general, and also on the rare occasion there's a boy of some importance in the picture, which is stupid. I actually broke up with him, sort of. I told him to go away so he wouldn't have to look at my ugly, bald head and toaster oven face. No, I'm kidding (sort of ...). We're friends. It's completely better this way. No expectations, no stress.

I could watch Short Circuit today. I'm taking a sick day. This is only my second one since I started chemo. I'm trying to save all my sick time for my next surgery recovery. But it's not because of the face situation. I think I got my sister's family's cold. I was hoping that wouldn't happen, but then, I caught Cooper *licking* our remote control last night and then drooling on it, so it was kind of inevitable. That kid has epic salivary glands. Sat up all night watching temp hover at 100. 100.5 is the magic number that sends us to the hospital, right? Now I'm 98.6. White cells, you rock! Chemo is Thursday. Will they or won't they, because of the cold? Only time & Airborne will tell, I guess.

Sent: March 14, 2011 at 11:51 p.m.
From: Suzie London
To: Cecily Murphy

Temporary: word of the day is temporary. And, you're underestimating the sexiness of your baldness. Boys AND girls love the Sinead head.

Do you remember Taffy, the Nazemis' senile dog, the one who would lie in the street all day? Taffy didn't give a fuck. She was 16 years old and she just wanted to lie her old butt down on the warm asphalt. She didn't care about cars. You could honk all day. She wasn't gonna move. My mom would get out, pick her up, move her to the sidewalk, and by the time she got back in the car, Taffy would be back in the street, beached. I've always aspired to have Taffy's dogitude: it's my street. You're just living in it. See, a bald head is sexy as hell but you have to own the sexiness. You have to find everybody else curious for having hair. It's your world: they're just living in it.

Feel better. Make tea from ginger root and cinnamon. And don't look in the mirror until you can look at it through Taffy's eyes.

Sent: March 14, 2011 at 11:55 p.m.
From: Cecily Murphy
To: Suzie London

Love it!!! But, I kind of don't want to tell you this: my brother ran over Taffy when he had his learner's permit. It was maybe a year after you left? Maybe I shouldn't tell you this. In his defense, Taffy literally walked right under his back tire. He had no idea what he'd done.

Sent: March 14, 2011 at 11:59 p.m.
From: Suzie London
To: Cecily Murphy

TAFFY!!!! I'll kill him. I'm kidding. I never claimed Taffy was canine Einstein—just free in her own world. An undervalued state of being, except in traffic situations.

Chapter 22

May 31, 2011, 5:00 p.m.

Cecily and Jack planned to leave the following morning on a 7:35 a.m. flight out of LAX.

It was a quick trip, and even though Cecily was just beginning to adjust to her jet lag and the pleasantly low humidity levels, she would be glad to board the plane and return home. Her talk with Anna prompted Cecily's first big cry on the beach that afternoon. Now, in the shower, scrubbing off all the sand, she wondered if she was up for trying to meet Jace tonight at the Metro Club. She wondered if Jack was right that she had never wanted the truth about Suzie, but rather a cleaned up version of the story, like the one Cait tells Eileigh. She wanted a happy ending for Suzie, and for herself—proof that Suzie was OK, that she would be OK, and that she hadn't failed as a friend.

Cecily looked down at the foreign mounds that would pass for breasts until her next reconstruction surgery. Evil bricks, Suzie had called them. She cupped her hands around them, and her hands felt alien, cold flesh. She had no more feeling in her breasts. Suzie told her she'd be grateful, but she wasn't. Cecily felt guilty for not feeling grateful. For one, she was alive. And second, her next surgery would certainly be easier because of the lack of feeling.

But now, she had Jack. Jack who claimed to not care about this. Did he care about uteri? What about later, when babies might be dreamed of, discussed? I'm getting way, way ahead of myself, Cecily thought. But whatever lay at the end of the tunnel, she had promised Jack, and herself as well, she'd stick it out and see. He was right after all. The fear was the monster, the anticipation of unknown future quantities.

And as for tonight, Cecily wasn't even sure if they'd be able to reach Jace with their half-baked plan. Derived from watching *Almost Famous*, the plan involved finding the stage door at the Metro and sitting out back until the stretch limo pulled up and the shiny superstar emerged in dark glasses, smiling and waving. And then, Cecily surmised, they would be tackled by bodyguards.

Suzie's Facebook pictures provided some evidence that Suzie hadn't been lying about knowing Jason Frost, although Cecily knew that Jack suspected as much. The pictures Suzie posted from her phone were aggravating to behold: often unfocused and always perspective-challenged; they featured faces too close up or too far away.

But even if Cecily didn't have solid photographic proof, Suzie had sent Cecily three Jason Frost CDs, autographed by Jason Frost himself. Those could be faked, Cecily thought. But Rothner confirmed it, with his vague comment about Suzie dating Jason Frost: "I guess you could call it that."

The best evidence for the real nature of Suzie and Jace's relationship was in Jace's song titles. If one used the songs as a roadmap of their relationship, they'd spent years torturing one another for sport. Suzie's name was right there in the titles. On his first album, "F*ck L*ve," there was a song called "London Bridge" about a girl who loved, cheated on him, and left. His second album, "Love On the Rocks," contained a remake of "London Calling" by the Clash. That album featured a number of remakes: Cecily loved Jace's rendition of Bryan Ferry's "Slave to Love," however, she had made the mistake of playing it on her iPod during infusion. Now, as she tried humming it in the shower, the song proved impossible to extricate from her memory of chemo, a memory that nauseated her even at a few month's distance. She gave up and sang her way through the songs she remembered from F*ck L*ve. "She Hates My Guts" had a catchy tune.

Jack knocked on the door as she toweled off. "You decent?" he asked.

"Yeah," Cecily answered, pulling her small towel hastily around her torso to cover its tangentially attached parts. Someday, she'd show him the new breasts. But Jack wasn't pushing for it, and Cecily wasn't ready. "Almost," she added. "Almost."

Posted March 17, 2011 at 7:01 p.m.
Cecily Murphy

Chemo #3 down! Three-quarters done! Great news: my white cells were so good they let me skip Neulasta (white cell growth shot) this time! So instead of 3 nasty meds, I'll only get side effects from 2! And Neulasta is the worst of them (bone pain), so I will send something nice to my white cells to thank them. I think they like OJ & Airborne.

Posted March 19, 2011 at 3:15 p.m.
Cecily Murphy

To celebrate my white cells going unassisted for 1st time during chemo, the tiny cold I had earlier this week roared back to life in the form of bronchitis, strep & vomiting. Courtesy, I think, of the petri dishes known as my niece and nephew. :) And here I thought Day 3 of chemo couldn't get more exciting. Tomorrow's goal: stay out of hospital!

Posted March 20, 2011 at 2:22 p.m.
Cecily Murphy

My day is not awesome. But my blood counts are. And, fortunately, the latter is all that matters. Treated and released!

Posted March 21, 2011 at 6:30 a.m.
Cecily Murphy

You're probably wondering what my roommate's darling cat was doing during all the medical brouhaha this weekend. Verm took the opportunity to stage a coup against my wigs—

toppling, dragging, and arranging them into a sort of nest in the corner of the bathroom vanity. Where he now sleeps. Nothing says, "I'm my best self!" like going out in hair that's been chewed by cats.

**Posted March 21, 2011 at 3:34 a.m.
Suzie London**

He glowed in the dark with incandescent truth under white hot gobos
She was too delicate to keep him long
Dissolving when touched, scattering like seeds
But he
He sat on a barstool, closed his eyes, held his guitar
In one flick of the wrist he could plant a thousand trees
And burn a thousand more.

**Sent: March 22, 2011 at 3:06 a.m.
From: Suzie London
To: Cecily Murphy**

Congratulations on making it through your week. Is the boy who keeps posting on all your updates this week your boy-of-some-importance—the one who cannot see the toaster oven face? Flirting is always allowed no matter what stupid cancer says.

[cancer] Life [cancer] is no life. Last week you said you might be "religious after all." Please elucidate. Imagine me on your doorstep with a clipboard, taking notes.

**Sent: March 22, 2011 at 6:13 a.m.
From: Cecily Murphy
To: Suzie London**

What? 1st: boy is Jack Schwinn. Well, you've obviously read his name. Friend from college. I need a stock response for all the questions I get about him, like an NIH grant proposal acknowledgment: "Thank you for inquiring about Jack Schwinn. Your comment that he has been somewhat attentive to Cecily on Facebook has been received. Please print a copy of this acknowledgement for your records."

Yeah, this is the guy from before chemo. Yeah, he posts a lot on my updates, but—and this is a big but—he also has an attentive female on his page, of late. Friend him, and check it out. Her name is Diana. Fortunately, she's in San Jose, California. Unfortunately, she posts on his page every single day and he responds to all of them, all the time. So I'm not the only person he's attentive to.

Check out her profile picture. She's maybe 22, tops, and she looks like a too-young Gwyneth Paltrow. Did I mention she's too young? Ugh! If only I had a little more time to pull myself together (I'd settle for eyebrows, just "having eyebrows" would do!) I could, I don't know … compete with that? I don't want to compete. I'm just focusing on getting well, and if he wants a girlfriend, why shouldn't he have a girlfriend? Why would I begrudge my friend a love interest? I don't care. Anyway.

2nd: re: God. No. Sorry. Wouldn't that be nice …

Sent: March 22, 2011 at 3:01 p.m.
From: Suzie London
To: Cecily Murphy

Liar!!! #1: you SO care about California Gwyneth, or you wouldn't be checking out her FB page. #2. I think you're a God-believing person. I feel it.

Sent: March 22, 2011 at 6:13 p.m.
From: Cecily Murphy
To: Suzie London

Re: #1 In my defense, I only checked out her page once. OK, twice. Re: #2 Why the God drill today? We're half-Jewish, half-Catholic, and 100 percent atheist. You know that. Or you did.

Our family celebrates a very secular-type Xmas and very little else. My dad's the world's laziest Catholic, and according to my Aunt Lil, my mother dropped Judaism when she learned that her breast cancer gene was a trait distinctive to the Ashkenazi Jews of Europe. Lil thinks my mom is nuts. As a child, I never understood or cared about any of this, and consequently, I never took sides. I believe having a religious foundation and culture is good for people, but I guess in the end, I'm my mother's daughter. Cells trump heritage. We're just a collection of chemicals when it comes down to it. I don't believe people are a special species. Either all living things have souls or none of us do. Life is life: the opposite side of death. Nothing mystical about it. We're just a carbon chain reaction, the result of a completely random recipe that's probably replicated in endless variations on millions or even billions of planets. But most of all, we're 99.9 percent genetically identical to two species of chimpanzee. Why the clipboard? Why the notes?

Sent: March 22, 2011 at 8:01 p.m.
From: Suzie London
To: Cecily Murphy

You, my friend, are, by definition, NOT an atheist at all, but rather a pantheist. You believe that God is not IN everything but rather IS everything. It's very pagan, actually. That's some very ancient wisdom there.

I'm collecting ideas. I'm starting to believe in God. God is a Facebook friend you've never seen in person, the original frenemy. I had an experience a few years back. My friend Lisa—the photographer—had a poltergeist in her house. Don't laugh—she was sleeping and the vacuum cleaner turned on by itself. It wasn't plugged in!!! Crazy, right? I told her that was some freaky shit, but if she wanted, she could send the ghost over to my house to do some vacuuming. She was like, no, this thing has got to go.

So she went to see this psychic woman in Beverly Hills, and I went with her. This was ... 2003 maybe? BC. The psychic woman was this rich Hills mom: blonde, tan, skinny, fake boobs, the works—not what I expected, but all the other psychics I'd been to were more of the roadside, toothless, meth-addict variety. I came because this alleged psychic was the wife of a record producer, and I thought, hmm, maybe I can slip her a CD while she's getting rid of the ghost of June Cleaver.

We went to her house and stood in this Disneyland-size foyer with white marble and she came out and she shook Lisa's hand, then she shook mine. She jumped back, like she'd been electrocuted. The kids were running around in their pajamas and the maid was trying to chase them, and she just stood there, eyes all wide. It was not an act. She was shocked. She said good night to the kids, then she turned to me and said, "What's going on in here?" And she pointed to my belly. I got the biggest chill down my spine and said, "What! Nothing!" And she said, "It's your womb. Is everything OK?" And I was like, holy shit. She knows! From shaking my hand, she knows about Adam, my stillborn son. I had a baby at 5 months. I was 16. I'd never talked about it. The people who knew, I cut out of my life. My ex married me when I got pregnant and I had the marriage annulled the day after Adam was born. My two-month marriage. A miscarried marriage. Never looked back. He couldn't have saved me anyway. We had nothing but that baby and we were so young. We had no business playing grownup, but at the time we were so convinced we could.

But now I get what the psychic was saying: get your ass to the gynecologist because you're gonna have cancer, girl, and not just where they find it first. She saw the future, not the past. Or, maybe she saw nothing, and my hand was cold. Or maybe she was scamming me, trying to impress Lisa. She didn't need to though. She went and put the smack down on Lisa's ghosts. Lisa filmed it.

The psychic went all ape shit and screamed down something in Lisa's shower. It was off the hook! And after that, no more vacuum cleaners. So you can believe it or not, but I know one thing: Lisa's an artist, a truth teller. In LA, there are "truth" sellers and truth tellers. So I'll leave it up to you. I know from experience that vacuum cleaners don't run themselves, though I wish they would.

What do you say when people say, "I'll pray for you?" People always say that. My brother and his wife claim to pray for me, but they are praying for fame and money and to get little, sordid messed-up Suzie out of their lives so they can look perfect in their church group. My roommate Rothner prays for me. He really does. I tell him, "Yeah, good luck getting me in good with your God. I've got a REJECTED stamp on my ass." But I like that he does it.

Sent: March 22, 2011 at 9:22 p.m.
From: Cecily Murphy
To: Suzie London

I like it too, that Rothner's praying for you. I wish I had more faith so I could say I prayed for you too. It's better than standing there knowing someone's in pain and not having anything to give them. That's why I wish I were religious, sometimes. It gives you something you can give to people when they're hurting. I will also take any prayers offered to me. A little kindness and positive thoughts are always welcome. I'm sorry to hear about your son. I can't even imagine.

Sent: March 22, 2011 at 9:40 p.m.
From: Suzie London
To: Cecily Murphy

Don't be sorry. Some phenomena are not meant to be. I like what you said about death just being the flip side of life. We fear death our whole lives, but what if all this time, death is actually better? And people are on the other side just laughing at us. "Death is where it's at, chumps!" they're saying. Hey that should be a song. That's totally a song.

Sent: March 22, 2011 at 9:42 p.m.
From: Cecily Murphy
To: Suzie London

Write it! Maybe it'll get picked up by your record-producer-wife-psychic!

Sent: March 22, 2011 at 9:43 p.m.
From: Suzie London
To: Cecily Murphy

Death is where it's at, chumps. It's either a rap or a show tune.

Posted March 23, 2011 at 6:18 a.m.
Cecily Murphy

Feels better at LAST! What do you know, it's Day 7 again. Day 7 likes me, and I love it back. I would not wish that last week on my worst enemy (Asian Tiger mosquitoes or the person who invented Autotune.)

Sent: March 23, 2011 at 9:22 p.m.
From: Suzie London
To: Cecily Murphy

Andy Hildebrand invented Autotune. He was an Exxon oil scientist who studied music. I've read 60 percent of all musicians use it, but I know a bunch of studio engineers and I think it's closer to 98. It's why any asshat with a stylist and a plastic surgeon can make a record these days. I need a favor.

Sent: March 23, 2011 at 9:23 p.m.
From: Cecily Murphy
To: Suzie London

Anyway.

The Truth About Suzie

Sent: March 23, 2011 at 9:24 p.m.
From: Cecily Murphy
To: Suzie London

DAMN auto-correct! I wrote "anything!" This phone makes me sound like an asshole: like I need that! At grocery.

Sent: March 23, 2011 at 9:24 p.m.
From: Suzie London
To: Cecily Murphy

Anyway ...

Sent: March 23, 2011 at 9:25 p.m.
From: Cecily Murphy
To: Suzie London

:)

Sent: March 23, 2011 at 9:26 p.m.
From: Suzie London
To: Cecily Murphy

Did you know Gretchen Garrett? Are you friends with her on Facebook? Your friend list is private: how did you do that?

Sent: March 23, 2011 at 9:28 p.m.
From: Cecily Murphy
To: Suzie London

Vaguely remember her ... don't think I'm FB friends ... let me check. Re: privacy controls—no idea. Jack set them for me after robbery.

Sent: March 23, 2011 at 9:30 p.m.
From: Cecily Murphy
To: Suzie London

No. Not friends w/ Gretchen.

Sent: March 23, 2011 at 9:31 p.m.
From: Suzie London
To: Cecily Murphy

Do you know anyone who can find her?

Sent: March 23, 2011 at 9:33 p.m.
From: Cecily Murphy
To: Suzie London

Prob. not. Not too many friends from your class. What about people in your class?

Sent: March 23, 2011 at 9:35 p.m.
From: Suzie London
To: Cecily Murphy

I don't really have anyone I kept in touch with from Pine Hill, except you and Gretchen.

Sent: March 23, 2011 at 9:39 p.m.
From: Cecily Murphy
To: Suzie London

Friend 'em anyway. "Friend" as verb = loose term. But happy to ask around.

Sent: March 23, 2011 at 9:40 p.m.
From: Suzie London
To: Cecily Murphy

Thanks. Ask about Gretchen. Please. What are you buying?

Sent: March 23, 2011 at 9:42 p.m.
From: Cecily Murphy
To: Suzie London

Saltines! I go thru a box in 3 days!

Sent: March 23, 2011 at 9:43 p.m.
From: Suzie London
To: Cecily Murphy

You go girl! Saltines + peanut butter = keepin' it real on chemo.

Chapter 23

May 31, 2011, 7:00 p.m.

Their cab ride took them up Vine Street through the heart (or the unwashed boxer shorts) of Hollywood—lined with porn shops, liquor stores and garbage. Then, suddenly, over the course of one block, neon lights blazed ahead, heralding the tourist area.

"Look to your left," Jack instructed, and Cecily caught a whirl of neon lights, palm trees and crowds packing the sidewalks. "That's the section of Hollywood Boulevard with the Chinese Theatre, the Egyptian Theatre, the Walk of Fame. The tourist places. Want to see any of those?"

"I am curious about the Walk of Fame, I guess," Cecily leaning her head back and smiling, thinking of Suzie London. "Can we ditch the cab and go see?"

"I wouldn't. Not at night," Jack said. "It's not the best neighborhood to walk around, and it's so packed, you can't see anything anyway. We can go tomorrow before our flight if you want."

Cecily shook her head. "Nah. It's just a bunch of names written in cement. I can't imagine it would be that interesting."

"It's not. Although the footprints and handprints in front of the Chinese Theatre are kind of cool." Jack said. "If you want, I can write 'William Shatner' on one of our towels back at the hotel, and we can both walk over it."

"Thank you!" Cecily smiled, leaning in to kiss him. "Change it to Harrison Ford and that'll do it for me."

"Isn't he a little old for you?" Jack raised his eyebrows.

"I was a huge Raiders of the Lost Ark fan. Jimmy got me into Indiana Jones and Star Wars. Why, who would your celebrity five be?"

"My what?"

"You know, the five celebrities you're allowed to hook up with when you're in a relationship."

"None," Jack said. "You."

"Oh, that's adorable. But really, who?"

"OK, maybe Halle Berry from Batman. Rebecca Romijn from the X-Men. And Dr. Amy Mainzer."

"Who?"

"The astrophysicist from the History Channel. She's on that show, *Universe*."

"Nerd!" Cecily laughed.

"She looks a lot like you!"

"Wait. She came to the Smithsonian for one of the space symposiums last year. She's borderline real. You can't have someone you might meet on your list!"

"Fine, I'll clear my list. My list is deleted."

"Aren't you going to ask me about my list?"

"I don't want to know who you're thinking about when you're with me. I like to pretend you're thinking about me."

"Jealous even in the hypothetical!"

"Never jealous," Jack straightened up, trying to look serious, but his dimples betrayed him. "Just realistic. I'm dating the most beautiful woman in the world. I can't expect other men not to notice you. Do you know how many guys you have drooling over you on Facebook?"

"Zero?" Cecily speculated. "Unless you count Michele's dog Spike, who, yes, is my Facebook friend, and sometimes I do think he's flirting."

"At least half a dozen," Jack told her. Cecily, smiling, shook her head. Jack nodded.

"No, no," Cecily said. "You might be thinking of my gay male friends. They flirt with everyone."

"I know. I was excluding the gay ones."

"You're crazy," Cecily laughed.

"You're missing the scenery," Jack said. "Look," he pointed. "Genuine Hollywood hookers."

"I can see hookers at home, next door," Cecily countered. "Though I did find out that, technically, they're dancers. At a fetish club."

"How do you know? You said they were cagey about direct questions."

The cab swung into a right turn without braking and screeched to a stop, tossing Cecily and Jack forward against their seatbelts and back against the hard seat back. "Metro! You're here," the cabbie hollered without turning around.

Cecily gasped her answer, still catching her breath, "Jane did their taxes. And 'cagey' was more descriptive than I knew, apparently."

Jack dropped two twenties into the cab driver's outstretched hand, and thought about disputing the fare, which had climbed at a suspicious rate while Cecily and Jack had been ogling Hollywood Boulevard. In the interest of getting himself and Cecily out of the cigar-smoke encrusted cab, he let it go.

They found themselves standing in front of a small, grungy theater that seemed to be shedding its black paint on the sidewalk before it. Half the marquee lights were burnt out. In the middle, small, black letters spelled out JA ON FROST 2NITE.

As he stuffed his wallet in the back pocket of his jeans, Jack remarked, "I was expecting something bigger, flashier. Hollywood-ier."

"Are we in Hollywood? Or Pasadena?" Cecily asked, looking around. Jack shrugged. Cecily continued, "I read about this on Jace's web page. Musicians, even famous ones, play in these small clubs while working on their albums, I guess to drum up interest. They sell out fast once they're announced. Britney Spears did this while she was making her comeback album. Jace is here twice this week. I tried to buy tickets online, but you have to show up in person. It's semi-secret—just advertised on his webpage and nowhere else."

"I suppose we can buy our tickets before it gets crowded," Cecily said.

There were about 10 people lined up in front of the ticket booth, most of them occupied with their phones. Cecily peered in to the dark, empty ticket booth. Behind her, she felt a tap on her shoulder. She turned around and faced a buxom, teenaged girl squeezed into a tank top with a giant gold peace sign necklace sitting on top of her bosom as though it were a shelf.

Sights such as these made Cecily panic about her choice to go larger during reconstruction. *Dang Suzie London, making me feel all ... empowered! What if I end up with a knick-knack shelf bolted to my chest?* She dismissed the irrational thought, quickly shaking her head to peel her eyes from the girl's chest. *I've become a chest leerer*, she thought. *Weird.*

"The line starts back there," the girl stuck her thumb out over her shoulder and snapped her gum.

"Oh I know, I was just trying to see if there was a sign that said when they opened."

Cecily peered around the blonde girl's head, and noted that the line was longer than she'd previously thought. She could see from this angle that it wound around the corner about 20 yards down.

"Do you know when it opens?"

The girl, tired of talking to a line cutter, dropped her chin back into her chest and went back to playing Angry Birds on her phone.

Cecily walked over to Jack who was looking at his phone. "Come here," she motioned for him to follow. She pointed toward a narrow alley, about four-feet wide, that separated the theater from the mattress store next door, then ducked in. Jack followed her, dubious.

"I don't think you're going to find the mythical stage door back here," Jack called behind Cecily, who navigated her way around garbage cans and swept her eyes down to scan for rats. She wondered whether LA rats were as large, ubiquitous and menacing as their DC counterparts, and almost walked right past a wider alley that ran perpendicular to the narrow one.

Jack, still behind her, called out for her to stop, his voice echoing against cement walls. Cecily looked up and realized she now stood in the middle of an intersection. To her left, half a dozen cars were parked up against the buildings, leaving a narrow drive area in the center of the alley. She turned down this road, dark and smelling of garbage and car exhaust. When she passed the cars, she saw a green door, right where she guessed it would be.

In front of the door sat a man on a barstool, engrossed in his iPhone. The man was bald, round, and wore a black t-shirt and jeans. Clothes that said, to Cecily: I'm with the band. As Cecily approached, quickening her step, she could hear Jack behind her, running.

"Wait!" he called.

The man looked up to see the two of them. He had the darkest, bushiest eyebrows Cecily had ever seen off a Muppet and a face that seemed squished, somehow, onto his neck.

"You guys with tech? Got your passes?"

"No," Cecily said, hesitantly, then immediately wished she'd said yes, because the man lost interest in them, and went back to whatever fascinations his iPhone held.

"I'm looking for Jason Frost."

The man snorted. "You ain't gonna find him here. Clear off." He smiled sarcastically, then jerked his thumb in the direction from which they came. "You're trespassin'."

A walkie-talkie crackled to life in his back pocket. "Lou. Come in, Lou."

The man twisted his torso, lifted his rear-end off the stool, then appeared to speak to his butt, with his hand on the Motorola button: "What?"

The walkie-talkie crackled again. "Jace here yet? Rick can't do nothin' without him here."

Lou regarded Cecily's now-bright smile, then Jack's wary expression. Hmm, he thought. Usually Jason Frost just had girl groupies. Jason's appeal had widened. Lou yawned, then performed his job again. "Git," he said. And, because he was feeling ambitious, added, "Scram."

"So, Jace isn't here yet?"

"He goes in another door," Lou raised his eyebrows in innocence and shrugged. "Unda tight security." Lou was referring to himself, although, as the flesh spilling over the sides of the barstool could attest, he was anything but tight. "Don't know nothin'. Sorry, can't help ya."

"OK, thanks!" Cecily said brightly. She hooked her arm through Jack's and they walked back toward the narrow alley, Jack mystified by Cecily's acquiescence.

"What are you planning?" he whispered.

"Duck!" Cecily ordered, leaping like a gazelle behind a black GMC truck.

"Uh, OK," Jack followed her, not leaping. He peeked out from behind the SUV's black tinted windows. The bouncer hadn't seen them, engrossed as he was in texting his two girlfriends. "Now what?"

"Now, we wait," Cecily said in a dramatic whisper.

"I don't think he can hear us," Jack pointed out, speaking in his regular conversational tone.

An army green Toyota hatchback turned into the alley. It pitched across the potholes, chopped pavement, and gravel to stop in front of the man on the barstool. Jack watched from behind the car.

"Then, when his car pulls up—" Cecily was saying.

"Cecily."

"We run up and say, really quickly, we need to—"

"Is that Jason Frost?" Jack took Cecily's shoulders and positioned her so she could see down the alley.

Lou was standing now, leaning into the car on his elbows, his walkie-talkie in hand. At the wheel was a man with thick, straggly, black hair and five-day stubble. One arm rested on the steering wheel as he talked to the man on the barstool.

"That's not him," Cecily said.

"I think it is. I'm going in," Jack said. He walked briskly toward the car, breaking into a bit of a run as Cecily yelled, "Stop! No!"

The bouncer stood up and looked at Jack, then shook his head in annoyance. "No, sir," he told the advancing groupie.

A trailer-sized black SUV with black, tinted windows rumbled down the alley and came to a stop behind the Toyota. The door opened, and Jason Frost stepped out.

There was no mistaking him. Cecily took in a quick breath. Suzie was right. He had that evasive "it" everyone talked about, but nobody was willing to define for her. Like Suzie in her shortest OP shorts, he didn't just wear, but improved, form-fitting, black-leather pants and a tight t-shirt that read, "FML." He had shiny dark hair, piled into a curly pompadour on his head. Even in the dim alley he wore dark Ray Bans.

A lanky guy with a long braid climbed out of the car behind him, carrying a guitar case and bobbing his head in rhythm with his iPod ear buds.

The next thing Cecily saw was the bouncer reaching out and grabbing Jack's shoulders.

"Stop!" Cecily ran up to them, yelling. Jace and the bodyguard paused and looked up at her. "Jace, I need to talk to you." She was panting—six weeks out of chemo, and her exertions fell short. Her arms and legs shook from a combination of the adrenaline rush and hypoglycemia. "I was friends with Suzie London," she panted.

"Were you now?" Jace eyed her sarcastically, with a faint trace of an English accent. He regarded Jack with outright suspicion. "Suzie had quite a lot of friends."

"I have some questions. I'm—"

Jace wasn't listening. He examined Jack as though he was a rare specimen. "Who are you then?" Jace addressed Jack. "Suzie's friend, eh? Hard up for cash, are we?"

"No, I'm—"

"Do you have any idea," Jace asked, lifting his sunglasses and circling Jack to get a better look at him. "Any idea a'toll, what it's like to be in love with a woman who just pushes you away?"

"Yes," Jack answered, surprised.

"Put him down, Lou," Jace instructed. At this, Cecily realized Jack's feet weren't touching the ground but rather hovering two inches above it. Lou was tall, standing up, almost impressive. Jack's feet dropped to the pavement.

Jack exhaled slowly, sizing up Lou from the corner of his eye. He didn't want to take that on in front of Cecily.

"You, lad," Jace jabbed his finger into Jack's brown The Doors t-shirt. "I'll talk to you then." Jace nudged Lou, who had settled back into his seat and pointed at Jack. "I want that one."

Cecily felt her jaw go limp. "Excuse me?! Who do you think you are? You can't just pick and choose people like they're cupcakes—"

But Jace apparently could do just that, and, as Jack shrugged apologetically at Cecily, the bouncer lifted him up by the collar and shoved him through the grimy green door after Jace.

The man carrying the guitar case, still wearing headphones, paused politely to let them through.

Cecily crossed her arms and glared at the bouncer. Lou settled back into his bar stool, took out his phone again, and started typing.

"Are you serious?" she asked.

"Shoo."

"I'm not a groupie!"

"You'd've had a better chance gettin' in if you was," he answered, not looking up from his phone.

"What, am I supposed to flash my tits or something? Is this how women get in to see rock stars?"

The bouncer looked up, eyebrows raised, hopeful, interested.

Cecily ineffectually glared.

The stage door burst open and ejected Jack, flushed and panting.

"Holy shit!" Jack could hardly contain his excitement. "I just saw Travis Barker! Travis Barker was in there! Oh my God!"

Cecily looked at the bouncer, still typing on the phone. "Go on," the bouncer said, without looking up. She shook her head in disgust.

"Travis Barker!" Jack was repeating at Cecily, as though imparting lifesaving knowledge at a critical moment.

"What happened in there?" Cecily asked.

"I don't know," Jack said, taking a deep breath. "I just followed Jason Frost to his dressing room, and there was Travis Barker! Sitting there! On the sofa! Jason asked if I had cigarettes and I said no. Then he asked if Suzie owed me money and I said no. Then he flicked his head, and this guy who came out of nowhere threw me out. It was AWESOME."

Cecily stared at him, arms crossed. "OK, fanboy. What now?"

"I need to call my brother," Jack said, fishing his phone out of his pocket. "He's gonna freak out."

The bouncer looked up again. "I'm tired of looking at you," he told Cecily. "If you want to go inside, get a fuckin' ticket." He eyed Jack with disdain. "And chill that one out before he pisses himself."

"DUDE," Jack was saying into the phone. "You will not BELIEVE what just HAPPENED to me."

Cecily hooked her arm through Jack's and led him up the alley.

The line now wound down the block, around the corner, down another block, and around the corner again. Cecily claimed a space at the end, and checked out the people lined up in front of her, all waiting to see the man who had just abducted her boyfriend and returned him with Stockholm Syndrome. In front of her, a college-aged looking girl in tight, shredded jeans stitched together with safety pins talked on her phone while her friend, in a pink zebra print minidress paired with Doc Martens ran her hands through her short, metallic blonde hair.

Cecily tapped the shoulder of the girl in the zebra dress.

"Excuse me," she said. "Do you think the tickets will sell out before we reach the front of the line?"

"OMG," said the pink zebra girl, snapping her gum. "You have to start standing in line the second they announce it. Used to be you could walk in to a Jason Frost show pretty easy, but he's working on a new album about his dead girlfriend, and apparently it's over-the-top shit and now look at this." She gestured around them. "We're not gonna get in, and we were, like, his first fans. We found him long before all these other *posers*."

Two guys in dark hoodie sweatshirts and baggy jeans turned around to scoff at her.

"Dude," one of the guys laughed. "The tweenagers are callin' us posers."

The girl in the zebra dress glared. Her companion, now off the phone, joined her. Riot at the Metro, Cecily thought. She slipped out of line, pulling Jack, who was still on the phone with his brother, behind her.

"Tiki Tata," she said, thinking aloud.

"What?" asked Jack. She didn't know if Jack directed this question to her or his brother, Paul.

"I have questions for Rothner still," Cecily said, maybe to herself. "We'll never get in here, and I don't know if that's the best use of our time anyway. I'm getting a cab and we're going to the Tiki Tata."

"Sure," Jack said into the phone. He hadn't heard her. Well, Cecily thought, won't he be in for a surprise then.

Posted April 3, 2011 at 5:52 a.m.
Cecily Murphy

Hands swollen & itchy. Chemo, you're just full of surprises this round. When this is over, I'm going to read the list of side effects and check off what I actually got. Maybe that'll make me feel better, to see what I didn't get. "Hey, I didn't grow a second head! And I still have toenails!" Knock wood!

Sent: April 3, 2011 at 6:01 a.m.
From: Suzie London
To: Cecily Murphy

Do not fuck with your toenail karma!!! Delete your post! I'm just messing wit' you. How you doin'?

Sent: April 3, 2011 at 6:03 a.m.
From: Cecily Murphy
To: Suzie London

Hi. I woke up in a bad, bad, bad mood. I'm drinking coffee and making a list of things I hate. In Excel. The chemicals are talking through me today. There's poison in my brain seeping out. So I caught it on paper. There is nothing as lovely as a list, in Excel, where it can be sorted into categories. Probably you're going to say yoga would be better, but Excel spreadsheets are my yoga.

Sent: April 3, 2011 at 6:10 a.m.
From: Suzie London
To: Cecily Murphy

It's good to get the negativity out, however you must. Toxins fester in your brain and your body. I could give you a karma volley. I'll sing "My Favorite Things." I don't remember the words though: "Junebugs and doormen and whiskers on kittens, something and something and girls with white mittens. These are a few of my favorite things!"

Sent: April 3, 2011 at 6:15 a.m.
From: Cecily Murphy
To: Suzie London

You are one of my favorite things! You actually made me smile.

Sent: April 3, 2011 at 6:19 a.m.
From: Suzie London
To: Cecily Murphy

I'll give you one for your Excel list. It's rampant in LA: people who spend an entire party texting. This has got to be the most annoying phenom ever. A plague of rudeness.

Sent: April 3, 2011 at 6:22 a.m.
From: Cecily Murphy
To: Suzie London

Agreed! I'll give you a local one too: Congressional staffers who think they're celebrities because they work for the group of idiots collectively known as Congress. They appear in my bathroom from time to time as overnight guests of my roommate Jane, who's too good for them and smart enough to know better. There's one hogging the shower right now as I'm waiting to get in.

Sent: April 3, 2011 at 6:25 a.m.
From: Suzie London
To: Cecily Murphy

Kick him out! And humorless prigs. I hate humorless prigs. I read all your posts and I think DC is just LA for nerds. Or LA is DC without white pantyhose. What is up with white pantyhose on women in DC?

Sent: April 3, 2011 at 6:27 p.m.
From: Cecily Murphy
To: Suzie London

I swear I don't know, but Jane owns white pantyhose!!! OH: passive-aggressive sympathy trollers on Facebook. I.e. "Sigh." Or: "Cried all night." Or: "Worst day ever." Prompting a frantic wave of concern: "What happened?" "Is everything OK?" "What's going on?" Post about it, or don't post about it: don't be coy. If you want sympathy, just ask for it. "This happened, it sucked, and I need love."

Sent: April 3, 2011 at 6:29 a.m.
From: Suzie London
To: Cecily Murphy

People who use Facebook to flaunt purchases. To quote the great Douglas Coupland: "Shopping is not creating."

Sent: April 3, 2011 at 6:30 a.m.
From: Cecily Murphy
To: Suzie London

People who use the condescending phrase "Bless her heart." Only Southern women do this, to other women. Oh, and United Healthcare!

Sent: April 3, 2011 at 6:31 a.m.
From: Suzie London
To: Cecily Murphy

AKA Screw-U-nited Healthcare! Cramps.

Sent: April 3, 2011 at 6:34 a.m.
From: Cecily Murphy
To: Suzie London

How do you still have cramps? Didn't the chemo kick you into menopause? It did to me, right away. They said it would take a while, but … it didn't. Just like my hair.

Sent: April 3, 2011 at 6:36 a.m.
From: Suzie London
To: Cecily Murphy

See? Chemo's good for something. Look ma, no cramps.

Chapter 24

May 31, 2011, 8:00 p.m.

In the cab, Cecily leaned her head against Jack's shoulder. Bracing her head on something, or someone, helped stem the nausea that was either a lingering side effect of chemo or of riding in the always-fragrant LA cabs.

"Jace was exactly like I thought he'd be," Cecily told Jack's shoulder. "Exactly what Suzie described—or didn't describe."

"That was awesome," Jack repeated for the umpteenth time, adding, loud enough for the cab driver to hear, "I met Travis Barker."

Cecily smirked and closed her eyes, but realized that made the nausea worse. "Your story's changing, hon. Before, you said you saw him. Now you've met him."

"Being in the same room is meeting!" Jack argued. "Wait—where are we going again?"

"The Tiki Tata Lounge."

"Right," Jack nodded. He paused. "Why?" He started typing on his phone. Cecily figured he was texting Chang about the Travis Barker sighting.

"I want to talk to Rothner again. And I want to see where Suzie sang. And Jack, before you tell everyone you met Travis Barker, are you sure it was Travis Barker? Bald men look all the same to—Well, I guess I'm one to talk."

Jack raised his eyebrows, still ensconced in his phone. "I'm not texting. I'm looking up Tiki Tata. And it was 100 percent Travis

The Truth About Suzie

Barker. I've seen him before. Blink 182 was my first concert. I still have my t-shirt. And, oh, look at this," he said, showing Cecily his phone, then reading aloud:

"'Our featured performer, Kiana, who hails from Bangkok, performs Monday through Thursday, nights when no reservations are required.' That's good. We can just walk in. 'Our other girls, Countess Davida, Lola, Lemon Drop, Gilda, and Budgie, perform with her depending upon the night.' Do you think Countess Davida is our man? Er, woman?" Jack asked.

"I can't wait to find out."

The Tiki Tata stood out—even on a block in Venice Beach crowded with bars and clubs.

They knew they'd found their destination a quarter mile before they reached it, as the neon lights that flashed the Tiki Tata's name could likely be seen from space.

They fought over who would pay the cab fare. They'd agreed to alternate expenses, per Cecily's insistence, but Jack wasn't cooperating.

"You don't need to show off for me. I know you have a better job."

"Yeah, I probably make more money at this time, but I don't think I have a 'better' job," Jack argued. "My job's a Dilbert cartoon. You're doing useful stuff."

The cabbie, uninterested in the esoteric details of their employment situations, cranked the music—Middle Eastern wailing—to kill the conversation and entice them to simply deposit the money into his outstretched palm.

Jack won again. Cecily let him win because he hadn't brought up her medical bills this time.

The club charged a $20 cover, but let Cecily in free for no apparent reason. Maybe, she thought, it was a reward for taking off her wig before she came in.

"It's my Brigitte Nielson haircut," Cecily whispered to Jack as they followed their host/ess, a tall man dressed as Dorothy in *The Wizard of Oz*, if Dorothy had an enthusiasm for glitter.

The club was pink: dizzyingly so. Pink lights, pink walls, pink curtains over the stage, pink neon signs in the shape of palm trees.

On second look, another theme emerged as well. "Fuzzy pink pillows shaped like breasts," Cecily noted.

"Is this your first visit to the Tiki Tata?" Dorothy had a sugar-sweet Midwestern accent as she motioned for them to sit in a round, pink, velour-covered booth that surrounded a sparkly, black Formica table with a raised red disk in the center. Cecily and Jack, staring at the table, said it was.

"Tonight's drink special is the Mohican Mai Tai. You can order it," Dorothy nodded to Jack. "But you," she raised her meticulously plucked eyebrows at Cecily. "You're too small. It would go straight to your head and next thing you know, you'd be up there on stage." She smiled at Cecily, her horse-like teeth glowing white.

A challenge, Cecily thought.

"Well, in that case, we'll take two," she said to Dorothy.

Dorothy winked. "Atta girl! Dinner menus?" They nodded. Cecily's nod was vigorous, remembering the previous night with the margaritas and her half-eaten, half-Mexican, half-Thai dinner. The Mai Tai would need some cushioning.

As Dorothy sashayed away in her five-inch ruby platforms, the lights dimmed, and a voice that brought to mind cashmere, sequins and chest hair boomed out over the half-empty bar, hushing the loud, drunken voices in the room.

"Honored guests of the Tiki Tata Lounge, please turn your attention to the stage, as the performance is about to begin. The management would like to remind you there is no flash photography allowed. And now, it is my pleasure to introduce ... the Countess Davida!"

Patti LaBelle's *New Attitude* blasted out on the speakers, sudden and loud. One bare, hefty leg emerged from behind the curtain. It hovered in the air outstretched for a moment and flexed its purple high heel before planting it on the stage, sudden and hard, as though trying to kill a fast-moving roach. After a long moment, shiny, lacquered fingernails ripped the curtains open, and Countess

Davida emerged, sporting a purple feathered headdress, a purple leotard with a sequined peacock design and four-foot feathers fanning out from her considerable rump.

The crowd, still sparse in this early hour but containing one bachelorette party in the corner, screamed and cheered. Jack and Cecily, who both recognized David Rothner, gave each other a high-five.

Cecily, clapping, yelled over the music to Jack, "I don't think I'll ever understand cross-dressing. I have to wear panty hose sometimes, to Women in Science workshops. There's no worse feeling than being encased in nylon. Like a sausage. Why would you do it if you didn't have to? Plus, the expense of it: hair, makeup, clothes. Being a woman is 100 times more expensive than being a man."

"Better karaoke nights?" Jack suggested, showing his dimples.

A waitress clopped up to them in white, knee-high boots. Nancy Sinatra? Cecily guessed, taking in the server's mod minidress and straight, long, blonde hair.

As Nancy bent her knees to carefully place their drinks in front of them, Cecily asked her, "Is there any way we can get the Countess, over there?"

"Of course!" Nancy answered, producing a pencil out of her hair and a small notebook out of what must have been her bra. "I'll put in an order. Mild, medium or spicy?" Nancy asked.

Cecily blinked. "Pardon?"

"Your lap dance. Mild, medium or spicy?"

"Spicy!" Jack answered.

"Spicy's extra," Nancy said, looking down her furry black eyelashes at him.

"Then no," Cecily said, tamping down Jack's hand as he tried to give Nancy another bill. "We'd just like to talk to him. Her?"

"Buzzkill!" Jack whispered in her ear. To Nancy, he said, "Medium is fine."

Cecily rolled her eyes and laughed. Dear Suzie, she wrote mentally, I just ordered a lap dance from your roommate.

Cecily was half into her drink and well into a hubcap-sized plate of nachos when the Countess Davida sauntered over to their table. Rothner half-smiled when he saw Cecily and Jack, and thanked them for coming to the show.

"This is awesome," Jack said, gesturing to the room, the nachos, the drinks. "Best drag show I've ever seen. And I met Travis Barker tonight!" Cecily had to give him props for enthusiasm. He was up for anything and unintimidated in a room full of men wearing lip gloss.

"Thank you," Rothner said. "This is my other life. I can let down my hair. After I put it on." He smoothed down his glittery, black afro. "Thanks for your email. Glad you got the package. I's wondering if you'd turn up. I thought you'd have questions."

"Oh, I do," Cecily stirred her drink with her straw. Due to the drink's strength, she couldn't remember them, however. "We've had an interesting day. I think your roommate was a complicated girl."

Rothner threw his head back and laughed for half a minute. "Thanks, tips!" he sputtered between guffaws.

"I understand what she was angry about. Her body was a ... dartboard for doctors for so long. I've only been doing this ... six months now? And I'm already sick of the fuckers. Her family was fucked up. Oooh," she paused. "I'm saying fuck a lot," she said in an exaggerated whisper.

Jack laughed. "You're so drunk off half a drink! Cheapest date ever!"

"I'm not!" Cecily protested, sipping the grain alcohol hidden behind a sweet mango nectar facade.

Rothner shook his head. "Honey, you drunk. You cussing so much you sound like Mel Gibson sweet-talking his girlfriend."

"We talked to some people today. We found them in a yoga center. They said she had a recurrence of cancer, and it happened last September, and she had radiation, and then they said it spread." Cecily hiccupped. Maybe I need to stop talking, she thought. But she didn't. "And she was terminal. And she dropped out of treatment and drank herself to death. Liquor is quicker, she said."

"It sure is," Jack commented.

"What do you think of that?" Cecily asked Rothner.

"I dunno," Rothner's deep-set eyes looked improbably serious underneath glittery, purple eye shadow. "Anything's possible wit our girl. But Suzie was an alcoholic. I got this feeling you want to paint her innocent, or a ... victim of circumstance, and girlfriend was anything but. She was an active playa, always. It's possible there was cancer, but if it was, her addiction was giving that evil beast cancer a run for its money. That's what I saw, day in, day out. She put away four liters of vodka a week when I took her in."

"Holy fuck," Cecily marveled. She told Jack, "I'm saying fuck a lot." Jack nodded.

Rothner pushed Cecily's glass toward the middle of the table, telling Jack, "Watch this one and her booze. Half a drink, and she at Defcon 3. Just to compare. Cecily, you drank one shot of—I don't know—prolly grain alcohol in there, and your head looks like one a those bobble head dolls."

"Nooo," Cecily argued. But when she shook her head, she noticed her eyes didn't want to point in the same direction.

"I took Suzie in knowing all this. All this. Knowing I couldn't help her, because she wasn't asking for no help. I thought, two things can happen. One day, this girl is gonna wake up an ask me for help. And I'll thank God in heaven, and I'll help this beautiful girl. This girl who saved my soul with her good heart, her laugh, her songs. Or, one day, she gonna take the vodka taxi on outta here."

"How did she end up on Dr. Dick?"

"I told Dick about her. An I put the bug in Brad's ear. We argued. He said he ben tryin' to help his sister for years, but she had to buy in or it couldn't never work. I knew he was right, but she was lookin' awful. Pale and bony and yellow and grey. You ever see a girl dyin' of poison? It's awful. I had to do somethin'. I told Dick I had more alcoholics for him in the London family. He said, 'Bonanza.' And I got promoted."

Cecily hiccupped loudly. "What? Why?"

"Dick thought the idea for Therapy Family was mine. But it was Suzie that gave it to me. It was a hit. Still is. Brad and Wendie bumped up our website hits to where they got the marketing people shittin' theyselves. Wendie's got an agent. She pitching reality shows. Fer serious. Suzie was pissed about the February show. I told her, honey, you open the door to your big, fat alcoholic family. You gotta take the bad with the good. And the good of it is it could save your own damned life if you let it."

"Why did she want to go back on Dr. Dick? You said she did that willingly, but she walked off the set. I saw her. She said she wasn't gonna let them exploit her or turn the cameras on her when all she wanted was a free trip to rehab for Peter. Do you want a sip of my drink?" Cecily offered.

"No thanks, ladybug," Rothner pursed his lips together. "Isn't it obvious? The last show was for Peter. She did it for Peter."

"Huh?"

"If you watched her last show," Rothner continued. "I sent it over."

Jack looked up frantically. Cecily side-eyed him. "You said it was just the one show on the DVD and transcript."

"Uh," Jack said. "Have more of your mango thingie."

"We'll talk later," she mouthed largely at Jack, then turned to Rothner. "Well, I didn't see the last show. Because my boyfriend is hiding it from me. Tell me."

"She stopped fightin' us. She said, 'If you can't be a good example to someone, you can be a horrible warning.' She said if she gonna die, maybe she could stop Peter from following her footsteps. Cameras followed her a week or two before she went in the hospital. Tami and I produced. Suzie was hammin' it up. She talked at the camera, she gave advice to Peter, and Emma and Logan." Rothner paused at Cecily's quizzical look. "Brad's youngest ones. We gave hours and hours of outtakes to the family. They awful and sad."

"But I'm willing to guess," Jack interjected. "That the most awful, and the most sad parts are what made the final cuts onto the show."

"Well, ain't you the budding TV executive over here?" Rothner raised his pruned eyebrows at him. "You can have my job, honeybunch. If you agree to be my sugar daddy, of course."

"No thanks," Jack looked a little frightened for the first time since setting foot in the Tiki Tata. "Cecily, that's why I didn't want you to watch it. Not because I'm patronizing you. But because we didn't have all the information yet."

"The protective vibe!" Rothner nodded and winked at Cecily.

"You could also call it patronizing."

Rothner caught someone's eye behind them. "Hey, girlfriends. I'm getting the eye back there. I suppose to be workin'."

"Well, we did pay for you," Cecily pointed out. "Give us a lap dance."

With one loud heave, Rothner pulled himself up on their table, and, balancing on his knees, ran his hands up his dress, his bra, through his hair, and raised his arms high. He started swaying to the music, which Cecily recognized as Shannon's *Let the Music Play*.

Jack scooted further into the booth, taking himself out of Rothner's range of motion. "I didn't think he'd actually do it!"

"Shut up and enjoy the view, tiger," Rothner purred. "Or I'll touch you." Rothner erupted laughing.

Cecily swayed along with Rothner, tried to imitate his pops, locks and grinds and failed. "If she really did have a recurrence," Cecily asked, her straw hanging from her bottom lip. "Why didn't she tell you, Rothner?"

Jack cleared his throat. "Would you have treated her any different if you knew her cancer had returned?"

"Hell yes!" Rothner exclaimed, right as the music stopped. The drag queen performing on stage in a one-shouldered, powder blue unitard abruptly stopped spinning on her stomach. Cecily's gut recoiled at the sight. The curtains snapped closed on stage, and an intermission was announced. Rothner hopped off the table, and landed gracefully on both feet with no wobble, despite his towering high heels.

"I would've sent her right home to her people. Her brother took care of her last time. He was aside himself wanting to help. We all was."

"There's your answer, Cec," Jack said. "Suzie told Cecily the thing she hated most was … what did she say? Something about tomato sauce?" He didn't need the second half of his drink either. "What is IN this thing?" he asked Rothner.

Rothner shrugged. "Sumpin' that'll jack my tips." He looked up, and saluted the bartender. Then he leaned forward coyly, twisting his shoulder to give Jack and Cecily a view of his verifiable cleavage. Cecily happily dropped a five into his bra. Jack looked away and held his breath until the ordeal was over.

"Marinating in victim sauce," Cecily answered. "It was incredibly selfish but also unselfish. She wasn't lying when she said she hated Dr. Dick."

"Yep," Rothner nodded and helped himself to a nacho. "The show and Dick Dortches personally. I hate to break it to you, baby love, but you ain't gonna make it as a detective if you didn't even watch all the shows she was on."

"That's OK with me," Cecily said. "I don't have the stomach for it. I just miss her is all. I didn't know what else I could do but come out here and meet you and Jace and just understand her life."

"And sing," Rothner said. "Sing praise to God for Suzie's life. Come with me."

Rothner took Cecily's hand and led her on stage.

"Wait, Rothner?" Cecily asked. "How did you meet Suzie London?"

"Let's just say she saved my life once. Just like you said she did for you. What you gonna sing?"

"Do you have anything by the Go-Go's?" Cecily asked. "You know, Vacation, all I ever wanted? Or, how about some Madonna? Something you can jump on a bed to?"

"Like a Virgin, Kevin!" Rothner chirped into the microphone in falsetto, and in ten seconds, the music began. He handed the microphone to Cecily, who took it, wide-eyed.

"'I made it through the wilderness,'" Cecily sang, off key and flat. "Somehow I made it through-hoo ..."

Sent: April 3, 2011 at 7:45 p.m.
From: Cecily Murphy
To: Suzie London

Thanks for cheering me up this morning. Feeling better now. I'm babysitting at my sister's. Cait had to go in for a second mammogram and an ultrasound because they saw a "blob." It's ridiculous how bad mammography is. It's like a Rorschach test. They tell you, "Mammography won't work well for YOU, your breast tissue is DENSE." Every woman I know who's had a mammogram has been told they have dense breast tissue.

Could it be then that dense tissue is the rule rather than the exception? Could it be that a typical characteristic of breast tissue is, in fact, a high density? It's like requiring people to wear gloves to protect their eyes. "These won't work well for YOU because YOUR eyes happen to be situated on your face."

OK, fine, no. Mammograms ARE better than nothing. But is "better than nothing" really the best science can do? All this time, I thought science was so advanced, and I was part of it! Part of the revolution, understanding the universe! And it's like, really? Mammograms don't ... reveal breast cancer? That sucks. Sorry, still in my mood, apparently!

Sent: April 3, 2011 at 8:02 p.m.
From: Suzie London
To: Cecily Murphy

Yeah, I love that and I love "getting treatment" for addiction. My nephew here is resistant to getting treatment!!! Oh no!! You mean, he doesn't want to spend 10 grand on a 15 percent chance of getting "cured" of his addictions? Because that's their "success" rate: 15 percent. Oh how they talk. "Well, if you get treatment," Dr. Dickhead says, and I interrupt him and say "There's an 85 percent chance I won't get "cured" and a 100 percent chance you'll be richer."

But this is different. Breast tissue gets less dense as we age. It's a shitty tool, yes, but it gets less shitty as we age. Remember that. You can't go getting cynical on medical care like I am. You can't pull a Michael Stipe, losing your religion. Remember, Cecily, I've diagnosed you as a pantheist, not an atheist. One of the best things about pantheism is how open you are to the mysteries of life and the universe. You have this great open heart, wide to the world and beautiful. People will disappoint you, and you'll want to close your heart off to the world, and I want you to promise me that won't happen. You'll keep your heart and your mind open and your face up to the sun.

Do you remember that game we used to play: "Would You Rather?" Would you rather have to wear a sombrero for an entire year or turn plaid every time you stepped into the sun?

Sent: April 3, 2011 at 8:18 p.m.
From: Cecily Murphy
To: Suzie London

OMG, I'd forgotten about Would You Rather! OK. Do I have to shower and sleep with the sombrero on?

Funny you should say I'm so open. I'm having boy problems right now. Or rather the boy is having problems with me, and he's, ironically, accusing me of being too closed off to taking chances. I don't see how it's his business. He's been flying out to San Francisco for weekend trips lately, not weekday trips, which would be business trips, but weekend. AND he hasn't told me about them (and, yeah, I find out this stuff by reading his Facebook page. I'm not proud.) I think there's a girl involved. California Gwyneth. Which, you know, good for him! Moving on! So I don't need him complaining I'm all closed off. Apparently I'm not closed off enough. (We still have moments.)

Sent: April 3, 2011 at 8:35 p.m.
From: Suzie London
To: Cecily Murphy

Everyone should take more chances than they do. We're all mortal, so where's the risk? Oh, except for herpes. Gotta avoid the herp. Which boy? Same as before? Sleep with him and put him out of his misery! You'd be surprised how quickly they stop pining for you after they get what they want.

Yes, you do have to shower and sleep with the sombrero on.

Sent: April 3, 2011 at 8:55 p.m.
From: Cecily Murphy
To: Suzie London

Sorry. I had to put the kids to bed. OK, I'd rather turn plaid. Turning plaid wouldn't inconvenience me, only people who looked at me. Wearing the sombrero would inconvenience me and the people looking at me. Interesting theory about men ... :)

Sent: April 3, 2011 at 9:00 p.m.
From: Suzie London
To: Cecily Murphy

Me too. But because I'd look hot plaid. Who wouldn't? Now—would you rather forgive or forget someone who has popped up out of your past, someone who hurt you? And you're not allowed to change your mind later.

Sent: April 3, 2011 at 9:01 p.m.
From: Cecily Murphy
To: Suzie London

Aren't you supposed to do both? I'd say forgive privately (for the benefit of me, not them) and forget publicly.

Sent: April 3, 2011 at 9:02 p.m.
From: Suzie London
To: Cecily Murphy

Braziliant. Now that is an excellent answer. Did you find Gretchen?

Sent: April 3, 2011 at 9:04 p.m.
From: Cecily Murphy
To: Suzie London

I asked around. Nobody's heard from her in years. I looked on Facebook, Twitter (my roommate's account), Google + (that place is like walking around a ghost town. They should add echoes for ambience: "Hello ... hello ... hello ..."), LinkedIn, YouTube, Instagram, Pinterest, Google: nothing.

Sent: April 3, 2011 at 9:05 p.m.
From: Suzie London
To: Cecily Murphy

OK. Thanks.

Chapter 25

June 1, 2011, 1:00 a.m.

Cecily and Jack lay in their hotel bed, naked except for Cecily's ever-present bra. Instead of falling asleep, they'd started talking again, whispering confessions about their romantic histories until they realized there was no reason to whisper. The secrets that seemed privileged before seemed so negligible when spoken at a regular volume, and they laughed and talked and glowed in the bright moonlight. Jack revealed that he'd had more sex this month than he had in his entire life combined. To Jack's surprise, Cecily couldn't have been happier (or more amused) about this. She drilled him on his assertion that she was his first love, the first one he'd considered "real."

"You've never been in love? Not even once? I don't believe you," Cecily smiled hugely and rolled away, pretending to be in a huff. She loved this.

Jack spooned up against her. "I've had crushes. Requited and not. But I've always known how things would end and why at the beginning of every relationship. So I never wasted my time."

"So how do you predict we'll end?"

"Concentrate and ask again," Jack said, nibbling her ear, which tickled.

Cecily squirmed and laughed. "So it's more like a Magic 8 Ball type prediction?"

"As I see it, yes."

"You're a goofball."

"I can't believe how not horrified you are at my inexperience."

"You don't give me anything to be horrified by. You're so patient and awesome and intense. And I can't believe how non-horrified you are by my hair and my current breast situation, so we're even. Finally, we're even on something. I love it! And I love being your first 'real' girlfriend, although I think six months with Emily counts as real."

"Emily was using me to pass chemistry, so no: not real. Although I was the only guy in chess club to go to the prom with a non-relative, so I guess I should be grateful for that."

"I wonder if Suzie would consider our friendship real, considering she never told me anything real. It was so one-sided."

"Are you sure you want to watch the last Dr. Dick? Do you want me to watch it first?" Jack asked her.

"I've been avoiding it too long. It's just a puzzle piece. That's all it is. I've been so afraid it's going to make me cry. Of course it's going to. I can do it. And Rothner said it was tastefully done."

"Rothner had peacock feathers coming out of his ass," Jack pointed out. "Don't get me wrong. I like him. He's good folk. I'm just saying he may not be the final word on tasteful."

"It may help me file things in my brain. And when the rest of my life is up in the air, that's so important. I lost my guide. And it feels like I'm on our victory tour without her. I miss her."

Cecily paused, swimming in her own thoughts. "I've lived two-thirds of my life without her in it. She was gone but not missing. Now she's gone and she's missing. They buried her without my knowing. Why did she have to dig everything up, why did I have to? We could have left well enough alone, and then she'd just be gone. That's selfish, I know."

Jack ran his fingers through Cecily's soft inch of hair, which made her look like a post-punk Audrey Hepburn. He couldn't believe Cecily was so self-conscious about it; it was so beautiful and soft, and smelled like ripe peaches.

"Because everyone—everyone—needs other people to get through," Jack said. "I think that's something you and Suzie both struggled with. I think that's what you had in common most."

"I know. But she didn't get through, and I did. And it's not fair. She always drew the short stick." Cecily grimaced. "How did she continue to be my friend when it looked like I was winning my battle and she wasn't? How did she not get bitter? How did she not hate me for everything? For living? For staying to grow up in Pine Hill while she left? Looking at myself now, through her eyes, I just look like an obnoxious little snot. A couple times she seemed bitter, I guess. But, wow."

She sat up, pulling her knees into her chest. "I need to watch the tape," she said softly. "I don't want to, but I have to."

Cecily climbed out of bed, and scooped her nightshirt off the floor. She pulled it gingerly over her head as her computer booted up. I'm not made of glass, she chastised herself. Jack rifled through the piles of paper on the desk and produced the disk.

Jack clicked through the first two chapters: Dr. Dick speaking with an actress about eBay addiction.

The 2011 Therapy Family logo filled the screen, then Suzie's face. Her eyes bloodshot, her voice slurred. She was drunk and yelling at the cameraman,

"*Oh don't worry about that! You'll fill in the blanks with the music. You'll use the ridiculous 'she-a-drunk-girl' music, and then, can I lie down? When I lie down, the music will get sad and serious. It's a very special Dr. Dick. Like the child molesters on Diff'rent Strokes. Look at me, viewers: your worst fears realized. My kid won't end up like that. Thank God we're not this [bleep.]*"

Cecily squeezed Jack's hand. It was worse than she'd guessed. Suzie's hair was one inch long, matted and spiked. Despite its disarray, it made her blue eyes look huge, haunted. Her bones jutted out from under her skin and her long tank top, the only piece of clothing she wore. Her clavicles prominently topped her ribs. You could count the ribs under the baggy and ineffectual top, which appeared to be on inside out and an afterthought. No pants.

Cecily turned her face away, wincing. "What are they doing, filming her like this? Why is she letting them? IS she letting them? Did Rothner do this?"

Suzie's voice on camera made Cecily turn back.

"*I want you here. Peter might watch me and take something from it. I don't let people feast on me. But I'll do it for people I love. Here, Peter, look at me, a mess. It's the only thing I have left to give. What are ... if I feel sorry for myself? [Bleep] you. I don't. Millions of people each day are born with [bleep] or create their own [bleep.] Screw you. I'm getting out of this, and I'm getting out of here. I'm free. I'm free to go.*"

She swiped a pile of newspapers off a brown couch and dumped herself into the cushions, her arm twisting improbably beneath her. "*But I'm gonna lie down first. Do you have a blanket?*" To someone off camera she said, "*And that's why I want you here too. Get in there in the kitchen and make me some fruit salad! Clean up the bathroom too. And wait! Wait! Can I say one more thing? Can I? Ceci, if you see this, I don't—GET the [bleep] off my dog. No, that's my dog. I walk him. He doesn't like you. He doesn't like you.*"

"Turn it off," Cecily said.

"Wait," Jack held up his hand. "We're back to Dr. Dick now, with Brad and Peter." He looked over, and reading Cecily's face, added, "I'll listen on the headphones?"

Cecily nodded, crossed her arms, turned away, and took slow breaths to aerate the anger. They treated Suzie like a joke. Imagine, Cecily thought to herself, if I had seen that earlier, if I had turned on the TV and saw that. She shuddered.

Jack touched her arm. "Cec, she's back on. Here. I'll pause it. She's in the hospital. You didn't miss much with Dr. Dick and Brad. They were just talking about Peter's problems and the genetic roots of alcoholism."

"Did they talk about putting Suzie in pants before filming her?"

"I know," Jack said. "And this part is going to be awful too. She's in a hospital bed."

"Deep breaths," Cecily said.

"Deep breaths," Jack repeated. He unplugged the headphones and pressed play.

Once again, the screen filled with Suzie's face. She seemed calmer than before, sedated and swimming in a translucently thin hospital gown. An enormous IV punctured her arm with clear liquid journeying from a bag on a pole through a tube into her skin. Her skin looked jaundiced, her lips cracked and dry, her eyelids drooping. Suzie was straining to listen as somebody off camera spoke to her.

"*Tuesday. I need to be out of here Tuesday. I have a gig.*"

A woman's voice off camera asked, "*What gig?*"

"*I have to walk the dogs,*" Suzie said. "*I need a computer too. WiFi. Cec, if you see this, I need to talk to her too. It's going too quickly now.*" Suzie paused, inhaled. She looked directly into the camera lens and continued, "*It was going to be the ultimate rock opera, but it's a reality show. Ah well. You don't control it. I tried to give you a free fall from fear. Wait. No. A fear-free fall. I wanted to give you freedom from fear. It seemed like a good idea at the time.*" Suzie laughed a little, then coughed, then convulsed. Jack and Cecily heard urgent voices off-camera, then the camera swung and focused on the floor. On the bed, they could still hear Suzie crying or laughing or coughing or all of the above. Finally, the microphone near her picked up words.

"*I'm sorry,*" Suzie whispered, then coughed. "*I just want to say I'm sorry. I—stop that! [Bleep] leaning on my [bleep] IV. To Brad. And to Jace and to—it didn't—woman, if you touch my [bleep] IV one more time, I will shove that boom where the sun don't shine.*"

In spite of herself, Cecily smiled. The scene cut away. "Got it, Suzie," she said, to nobody in the room. "Message received. Same way you always send them. Ass backwards and full of attitude."

"Look at this!" Jack pointed to the screen. "They brought the dogs to her! They gave her her dogs."

Suzie's face illuminated Jack's computer screen, her smile as wide as her face, dogs in her lap, under her bed, on her bed, bumping into each other, knocking around the IV pole and whining to get on the bed. "*Pandemonium*," Suzie said to the camera. "*My favorite.*"

Dr. Dick's face replaced Suzie's, announcing that Suzie had slipped into a coma the next day. Cecily was finished with him, and before he could finish his inauthentically earnest speech, ejected the DVD from her computer.

She told Jack, "I'd hang up the phone with you and go write her on Facebook this time of night, sometimes. Now I go on Facebook and it's like walking into an empty room. A noisy empty room, but still empty."

"What happened to her Facebook account?" Jack asked, spreading out on the bed and hooking his hands behind his head.

"I don't know," Cecily said. "Maybe I'll write to her and find out. Right now."

Sent: June 1, 2011 at 2:38 a.m.
From: Cecily Murphy
To: Suzie London

I know this is crazy: writing to your Facebook page. It's my portal to you. Where do the emails go, once you're gone? Into the miraculous vacuous I guess. Sometimes you just need to howl into the wind.

I'm here in your neighborhood. I love it. I see how you woke up every morning wanting to take a bite out of all of this. There is so much to see and do. I loved the Tiki Tata Lounge. I'm beginning to develop some horizontal ambition myself. (No, not that kind! Your definition!) But I miss you more here, and I feel like I'm on our victory tour, alone. What did we say we'd do? Dollywood. Cattle rustling. Cruise. Raising hell, Thelma and Louise style. Oh, and RuPaul.

Sent: June 1, 2011 at 2:39 a.m.
From: Suzie London
To: Cecily Murphy

You're "here?" LA you mean?

Let's meet. Maybe I can help you. Or vice versa.

Chapter 26

Sent: April 4, 2011 at 6:01 a.m.
From: Cecily Murphy
To: Suzie London

According to my calendar, this should be your last day of chemo!!!! You didn't even say anything last night! Six chemo sessions in the can. Congrats, girl. And I'm only a few weeks behind you! (Well, five, because of the delayed start).

Sent: April 4, 2011 at 6:09 a.m.
From: Suzie London
To: Cecily Murphy

Not my last day, but getting close. Three weeks, probably. I'm behind you in some ways. I've been reading your Facebook posts. You have a lot of good friends. You are a good friend. You send thank-you notes on nice stationary. I've not been a good friend always. I have some karma to repay.

Sent: April 4, 2011 at 6:15 a.m.
From: Cecily Murphy
To: Suzie London

They added another chemo? You're a wonderful friend. Everybody has karma to repay to someone. Don't they? Don't beat yourself up right now. Not now, when you've come so far. What happens after your last one? PET scans? You just survived another six rounds of chemo. You're a fighter. You're a rock star. You're my absolute inspiration.

Sent: April 4, 2011 at 6:21 a.m.
From: Suzie London
To: Cecily Murphy

Ay yi yi. Haven't gotten into it with the Dragon Lady lately. I was talking to my healer yesterday, though, who says I'm a young human soul, a learner. I told her I'd rather be an old animal soul than a young human soul. It seems a more humane way to live. Eating grass. Or disemboweling squirrels, if I come back as Peanut, this dog I walk. If there's a way to become reborn as a firefly, I'd choose that. A summer life.

Sent: April 4, 2011at 6:23 a.m.
From: Cecily Murphy
To: Suzie London

What's your follow up? With the oncologist, of course, not the healer! Why did they add a chemo session? Are they addressing a specific issue or is this just the treatment protocol?

Sent: April 4, 2011 at 6:41 a.m.
From: Suzie London
To: Cecily Murphy

I guess I'll find out. My hospital has a program called "survivorship." My old hospital had one too. Survivorship has its challenges! They said brightly. It does. I truly hope it doesn't for you. I hope when you finish, they tell you to go away and never come back. You will NOT go through this twice.

Sent: April 4, 2011 at 7:02 a.m.
From: Cecily Murphy
To: Suzie London

And you will not go through this three times. I think they're just estimating the number of chemo sessions I get in my case. They're not even going after anything specific. It's not like they have any insight as to what's really going on. What

I'm fighting here is a ghost: a potential for cancer, not an actual cancer cell. Chemo in my case seems overkill at best, recklessly unethical at worst. Actual chemo benefits can be summed up in fractions of percentages, but nuking an anthill is the standard of care. It's all they've got. I woke up to swollen fingers and the feeling that I might lose my fingernails. My fingernails! What were you saying about extraneous body parts? Those aren't terribly extraneous to my mind! And I realized I had to start taking my Claritin again for chemo on Thursday. Does anyone ask why, ever, except for you? This week, I'm going in and I'm asking why. I need fingernails. I just do. So one more for you, one more for me (after this week, so, actually, two, but I like the sound of one. OK, I'm lying to myself!) Then we're done, right? And we go on the cruise? Or to the dude ranch? At the very least I'm going to see you sing at the Tiki Tata Lounge!

**Sent: April 4, 2011 at 7:40 a.m.
From: Suzie London
To: Cecily Murphy**

You're allowed to lie to yourself going into your third round of chemo. In fact, there are very few better times to lie to yourself. I can't tell you what's next. I just take it as it comes at me, bumping down the stream.

Hey, since I'm here and you're there, I wanted to give you your survivorship preview. You know, before you send me the email freaking out about it, ha ha. It's not what you think it is. It's going to be test after nerve-wracking test. But once again, just like in January, your fear will be high, and the likelihood of Everything They Find Being Cancer is low. Why? Ask your hair. The chemo managed to seek and destroy every single hair cell on your body down to your nose hairs. Do you think it missed something? It sure missed nothing in your stomach. That shit was a system-wide nuclear bomb. Only the cockroaches and, God willing, your sense of humor, survived the attack. Fast forward to five years from now, the magical

Five Year Mark. You barely remember chemo. You've attached your beautiful, expensive wig to the end of your Swiffer and use it as a mop. (After driving over it with the car, over and over again). You're so used to going to the doctor and having Things found. You're blasé about it. You're too cool for school. Ironically, it's by the time you've learned to manage your fear that your fear is (somewhat) (not totally) (but slightly more) warranted.

Walking that line between vigilance and fear is your next great challenge. You have to live your life based on your dreams, not your fears. It would be so great if I could tell you where to hide from this monster, but the reality is you'll have to face it every time you go to the doctor. But when the doctors find something, you're safe. When they find nothing, you're happy. There are a few safe/happy spots, a few logs to cling to in this crazy game of Frogger. You fight cancer this year. Next year you fight fear. I know you're sick of fighting. I'm sick of fighting. But if you don't, suffering wins. And you're not a sufferer. Your life will not be bracketed by suffering. We can't choose much, but we can choose that much.

Sent: April 4, 2011 at 7:51 a.m.
From: Cecily Murphy
To: Suzie London

Huh. I never thought ahead to that. I kept thinking: we're almost through this! Almost. While you're 100 percent right, I don't like thinking of "survivorship" as a phase. I'd rather have it just be an ending: "end of chemo." OK, you're done! Everything's OK now! Goodbye!

Sent: April 4, 2011 at 7:53 a.m.
From: Suzie London
To: Cecily Murphy

I'd like that too. It's not all that bad. I'm just telling you all at once. Chemo required some Thelma and Louise.

"Survivorship" only requires some Laverne and Shirley. Shameezle. Shamazzle. Hoxonbread incorporated!

Sent: April 4, 2011 at 7:58 a.m.
From: Cecily Murphy
To: Suzie London

Not sure that's what they were singing! I can do Laverne and Shirley. Thank God, because chemo is cumulative. I feel worse now this cycle than I did the past three cycles combined. I just need some Gettin' Through. Chemo brain is no joke. My brain is fried.

Sent: April 4, 2011 at 7:58 a.m.
From: Suzie London
To: Cecily Murphy

Amen, sister.

Sent: April 4, 2011 at 7:59 a.m.
From: Cecily Murphy
To: Suzie London

Shoot. I have to get working here, but can I ask you something about your recurrence? How far out was it? How did you know? How did you find it?

Sent: April 4, 2011 at 8:08 a.m.
From: Suzie London
To: Cecily Murphy

Nope, you can't ask that. You want to stress about it. Not allowed. You can see my boobs again if you want to, but I draw the line at the recurrence story.

Have a great day at work. Remember what Dolly Parton once said, "Home is where you hang your hair." Dollywood is going to be a whistle stop on our cross-country train tour. It's going to be fabulous.

Posted April 4, 2011 at 8:24 a.m.
Suzie London

Inventory. I light a candle, watch you sleep, consider your bones, then slip out before you wake.

Chapter 27

Sent: June 1, 2011 at 2:52 a.m.
From: Cecily Murphy
To: Suzie London

OK, my heart just stopped. This is Jason Frost. Isn't it?

If you are Jason Frost (the one whose albums Suzie sent me and the one I met earlier tonight), you need your own email address. Have you read all of my personal emails to Suzie? Yuck.

Cecily Murphy

Sent: June 1, 2011 at 2:57 a.m.
From: Suzie London
To: Cecily Murphy

Dear Cecily:

Sorry for the scare. Yes, it's Jace here. Thought you knew Suzie gave me her Facebook account to manage. She gave me a bunch of stuff to manage and she didn't prepare super well. Planning was not her strongest suit. Fortunately, paying bills is mine. I'm figuring stuff out. Suzie told me about you. I haven't gone through and read her personal emails, no. This just popped up in my inbox. I switched her Facebook notifications to my email address this week. It hadn't occurred to me to go through her emails. I resent the implication.

Were you the cute little punk Audrey Hepburn girl in the alley today?

Sorry again,

The Truth About Suzie

Jason Frost

"Rothner is right. You need to work on introducing yourself when you meet people," Jack yawned. He'd been awakened by Cecily's scream nearly 20 minutes earlier and, once he ascertained there was no murderer in the room, shuffled over in his boxers. He opened a bottle of water from the mini-bar, and used it to take an aspirin. "Want one?" he asked. Cecily declined. She had better meds than aspirin if she needed them, which she didn't. Her father had always told her there's no point getting rid of a headache when you could get rid of what was causing the headache.

Jason Frost was a headache. He had invaded Cecily and Suzie's sacred email space. And even their time: 3:00 a.m. West Coast time, Cecily thought. But ...

Sent: June 1, 2011 at 3:01 a.m.
From: Cecily Murphy
To: Suzie London

Yes, I was the "punk" (chemo hair, not buzz cut) whose boyfriend you temporarily kidnapped. I'm here because I want to know what happened. You can read my emails with her as long as you don't look at the pictures. If you do read them, you'll see that I was kept in the dark on a number of issues. I'm hoping you can help shed a little light on them. Would you be willing to talk to us?

Sent: June 1, 2011 at 3:02 a.m.
From: Suzie London
To: Cecily Murphy

Of course. Playing again tomorrow night at the Metro. Come to the back door again, but, this time, tell me who you are and we'll get on fine. -Jace

"I'll change our plane tickets," Jack said, reading over Cecily's shoulder.

Posted April 7, 2011 at 5:52 p.m.
Cecily Murphy

Chemo #3 is in the can. Told Jane at the infusion center how stupid I've become on all these drugs, and how I didn't have those brain cells to spare in the first place, but she pointed out: "Enjoy it. Being rendered temporarily more stupid is other people's problem, not yours." :) She's right. Sorry, whoever I didn't call back last week.

Posted April 8, 2011 at 9:52 p.m.
Cecily Murphy

Slept all day. No Neulasta again! Must have tiger blood & Adonis DNA like Charlie Sheen, but got stern lecture on adding Ensure to my diet. "It's not bad," the nurse argued, "if it's very, very cold and you put it in a very, very cold glass and hold your nose." A ringing endorsement!

Sent: April 8, 2011 at 9:53 p.m.
From; Suzie London
To: Cecily Murphy

Jesus Christ don't believe her

Sent: April 15, 2011 at 7:02 a.m.
From: Cecily Murphy
To: Suzie London

Hey you! Long time no write! Last chemo grew fangs and destroyed me. Back to work. Can't believe I caved & took 1 full week off work this time. Have lobster claws for fingers now. Fingertips too swollen and sensitive to open cans, turn door handles. Forget about car doors or jar lids, those make fingernails bleed. Called doctor about this. He said it's normal, want more drugs? No, want ETA for Lobster Claw departure. Or oven mitts & duct tape. How are you holding up?

Sent: April 20, 2011 at 3:13 a.m.
From: Suzie London
To: Cecily Murphy

My healer gave a seminar today about self-knowledge, self-projection and the capacity to be alone. It was in a park. During the introduction, a wasp landed on her neck and stung the shit out of her. She always says animals come to us because they are our spirit guides. Their presence has meaning. It's our job to find that meaning. I think the meaning of a wasp on your neck is God's way of saying fuck you. I mean, not to dismiss centuries of indigenous wisdom, but really.

So while the ambulance was taking her away (she's allergic to wasps ... her face had swollen up like a float in the Gay Pride parade), she told us to write down our ideas and share them with each other. And we stayed. (Because there were no refunds.) Anyway, it felt important for me to share some stuff we talked about. I especially learned a lot from a dude named Stan, who let me braid his long, gray ponytail while we were meditating.

Stan thinks our generation has been given too many access points. The miraculous vacuous, he called it. We don't fully understand or know how to manage and maintain our boundaries. It's a destabilizing experience.

It's too easy to form connections based on created selves, as opposed to real selves. The virtual mirror distorts us, or rather we distort it to reflect what pleases us about ourselves and hide what doesn't please us.

Or, does this virtual mirror of ours actually create the real self? I can be Googled, therefore I am.

The miraculous vacuous reflects back the illusion of infinite access, the seductive more, better, faster. The illusion tells us there's no price. The truth is, there is always a price. By choosing, selecting the self we interface, we're naming that price, even as we pretend it doesn't exist. Choosing always creates loss, choosing is loss.

I had to write this down to remember it. I smoked a lot of dope today. You probably guessed that. Love you girl. Believe it.

Chapter 28

June 1, 2011, 8:00 p.m.

Cecily dragged. Normally a brisk walker, she arrived in the alley behind the Metro sluggish and towed by Jack's outstretched hand.

They'd spent the day sightseeing in Beverly Hills. Rothner had sent over tickets for a tour of the Getty Museum with his package of Dr. Dick materials. Cecily smiled in her wig as they took touristy pictures overlooking the city from the hilltops. She reminded herself to not slump against the stone wall of the Getty's terrace, and envisioned her wig combusting into flames in the relentless LA sun. She couldn't articulate why she needed to wear the wig that day, though she admitted to Jack that sometimes a typical-looking head cover made her feel less conspicuous, open and vulnerable to comments. Some days she was up for it, some days she wasn't.

Jack noticed the drag on his hand, but paused before bringing it up, as Cecily's lingering fatigue from chemotherapy irritated her. "We don't have to go. It's been an eventful few days," Jack said, falling back into step with her, kissing the top of her wig, then spitting out a piece of poly-nylon hair. But Cecily insisted. No concessions for fatigue.

The bouncer they'd met the night before sat on the same barstool as they approached the green back door of the Metro. Cecily still wore her wig, hoping to deflect comments from Jace. She hadn't enjoyed being called "punk." Plus, maybe the bouncer wouldn't recognize her in her long red hair.

He did.

"You people," he said, shaking his head. "You've got to go."

"We were invited," Cecily countered. "And told to wait here."

"Sure, sweetheart," the bouncer chuckled. He reached for the walkie-talkie in his back pocket.

Uh oh, Jack recognized the change in Cecily's demeanor. She really hated being patronized.

Cecily clutched the top of her wig and ripped it off.

The bouncer raised his eyebrows and chuckled again.

Cecily pursed her lips, flummoxed. "That didn't work the way Suzie said it would,"

Cecily murmured to Jack. Jack patted her shoulders. "He saw you with it off yesterday. You didn't have shock value in your favor."

"You crazy," the bouncer laughed. "You're my favorites now."

"So you're going to let us stay and wait, like we were told to?"

"Keep your hair on, lady," the bouncer said, then laughed at his own wit. He shook his head, still laughing, and went back to texting on his ever-present phone.

Cecily and Jack sat on the curb and watched as cars slowly rumbled along the gravel through the back alley, some of them stopping in front of the green door to unload their wares. A large order of Chinese food arrived, then a huge speaker balanced on the shoulders of two men in black t-shirts and tight jeans.

The bouncer made himself useful, opening the door both times. Cecily and Jack continued to wait.

"You're spaced out," Jack said, poking her. "You sure you don't want to go back to the hotel?"

"What? No! I was just thinking about one of Jace's songs: *She Hates My Guts*. I wonder how she left things with him. She dumped all her responsibilities and records on him, like her phone and her Facebook account. He was her next of kin. I wonder if that was because she loved him or because she hated him. Because I think she felt both, combined, like samples in a centrifuge: a spinning blur. What are you left with after that?"

"Isotopes," Jack answered.

"Yes," Cecily mused, oblivious to his teasing. "I wonder what isotopes Jace was left with, aside from dizziness." She shook her head. "Never mind. I'm being weird."

A black Range Rover pulled up in the alley and blocked out the sun above them. They stood up from the curb and brushed off their clothes.

Jace stepped out of the car, leather pants shiny and tight as before, sunglasses obscuring his eyes. Another man tumbled out behind him carrying a guitar case, opening the green door and dashing inside without a glance at Cecily or Jack.

"Was that Travis Barker?" Cecily asked.

Jack rolled his eyes at her. "Travis Barker plays drums," he said.

"Hipster," Cecily retorted.

"Uh," Jack pointed at himself then Jace, who chatted up the bouncer in a casual manner that belied his lateness. "Who's the hipster?"

Jace looked up and saw them, came over and draped his arms over their shoulders. "Cecily! Boyfriend! Come along, then, eh?" he asked.

Cecily couldn't resist firing a gloating look at the bouncer who just shook his head and laughed.

As they stepped through the door into the black hallway, they were swarmed by people in black t-shirts and headsets. Jace sauntered through the commotion, nodding and answering questions, deflecting all attempts to stress him out, until they reached a grungy black door with a tin foil star attached with scotch tape.

He opened the door for Cecily and Jack, motioned them inside with a small half-bow, then followed them in, closed the door and stood against it.

"Chaos," he said, exhaling loudly. "Have a seat," he motioned to the couch, a mod-style bench on four peg legs upholstered in synthetic orange.

Jack searched the room, which was lit only by the lights surrounding a window-sized mirror on the wall. A partition with a mural of a tiger hid the back half of the room, which was littered with takeout containers, candy wrappers, and used, half-empty glassware. "Where's Travis?" Jack asked, sounding more hopeful than he'd wanted.

"Travis?" Jace's tone was mocking, then his expression turned serious. "He's not playing with me tonight," Opening like a parachute, Jace dropped his long, lanky frame into a swivel armchair next to the mirror at the counter. He swung the chair around to appraise his two guests, crossing his legs and letting his Doc Marten dangle.

"You look beautiful, Cecily."

"Thank you." A celebrity knows my name, she thought to herself. A stranger. She was glad she wore the wig.

"Truly. Better than your Facebook picture."

"Thank you. Sort of."

"Oh, no offense, it's just, you know, your Facebook picture, you're wearing this brown dress that makes you look like a school guidance counselor who has to spell out the word S-E-X."

"That was taken at my nephew's christening."

"Ah. A nice Christian girl, I see. Mind if I smoke?" He pulled a pack of American Spirits and an old-fashioned lighter out of his pocket and flicked it, then picked up a can of Febreze off the counter and sprayed the air liberally. "Bloody smoking restrictions. Don't get me wrong, I love Americans. They're right spunky, but they can be such hysterics. So screechy, they are. 'What about the children?'"

Cecily didn't know what to say to this. She didn't particularly enjoy the smell of cigarette smoke, but here they were in Jace's dressing room with Jace, and she didn't want to be labeled a screechy hysteric by a rock star. She was cool. She could hang. This wasn't her first time at the rodeo. No, it was. And she guessed it showed. The stupid picture with the brown dress had given her up.

"Actually, my sister's in-laws are Catholic—enough about me," Cecily was flustered now.

"You have questions. I have answers," Jace began. "I have questions. Maybe you have answers. Ladies first."

"Why didn't Suzie tell me she was going to die? Did you know?"

"Well. You get right to it," Jace said. He paused. "Yes, I knew."

"When?"

"December of last year."

He tapped the counter absently, then, seized by some unexpressed concern, started rummaging through a stack of papers.

"God damn it!" he yelled. Cecily jumped. Jace leapt to his feet, then taking two long-legged strides, flung open the black door, and yelled down the hall, "Belinda!"

From the black hallway a beautiful, blonde-haired girl of 18 appeared. Groupie, Cecily thought, then saw her microphone and clipboard—and finally, her look of resigned dread. Definitely not here by choice, Cecily concluded.

"May I help you Mr. Frost?" she asked flatly.

"Where's tonight's set list?" he asked, drilling his blue eyes into hers. "If I don't have it, I know the band doesn't, and they haven't seen the new phrases on *Gone*."

"I'll check on that, Mr. Frost," she said, her voice a raspy whisper. She caught Cecily's eye on the way out, then slipped away.

Before the door clicked shut, it opened again. "I'm sorry," the girl addressed Cecily and Jack on the sofa. "Can I get you something to—"

"SET LIST is your priority, Belinda," Jason Frost yelled.

He turned to Cecily and Jack, his scowl performing a quick feat of gymnastics by flipping into a smile. He nailed the landing. The smile was as warm and genuine as anything he'd shown them before the set list tempest.

"Events and promotions intern," he chuckled, and picked up his cigarette. Cecily tried to crack her frozen smile into a chuckle and failed. Jace stood up. "Suzie was one of those, once upon a time. I can take care of you. What do you drink?"

He walked over to a small, black refrigerator gleaming under the counter, kicked open the door with a flick of his boot, stood before it with his hands on his knees and sighed.

"Jack Daniels, Grey Goose both straight and gay varieties, Kahlua," he listed. He leaned down and picked up the Kahlua bottle. "Kahlua? Not mine."

"What are the gay varieties of Grey Goose?" Cecily asked. "Just out of curiosity."

"Pomegranate," Jace answered, leaning down to read the label of an icy clear bottle half full of pink liquid. "Definitely homosexual. Not that there's anything wrong with that." He cleared his throat. "It's pink," he added, as though that would help her decide.

"I'll have a Jack Daniels," Jack said.

"Nothing for me, please," Cecily said.

Jace searched the room, picking up three oversized shot glasses, and wiping them out with his shirt. Cecily cringed.

"I've spent the last month in the recording studio, and I only leave it to play here and try out my new songs on whoever wants to come out. The record company promotes it, and the fans seem to like them, the new songs. I think they're rubbish. Not the fans, the songs. I can't stand any of them. I can't stand myself, cashing in on my grief. What used to be my sanity is now a consideration for my manager. Should this one go on the album? Will it pay for my manager's girlfriend's new tits? Oh sweet Jesus in a jelly jar, I'm such an arse! Why am I always talking about tits to a breast cancer patient?"

Cecily tried to shake her head. "No, it's OK! You don't need to … bring Jesus into this. Or apologize." She felt a little loopy, and noticed he was filling three glasses with whiskey.

"Here, drink this," Jace instructed, handing her a glass. "You too," he added to Jack.

"You're bossy," Cecily noted. The statement held neither unkindness nor charm, just scientific observation. "Suzie is bossy. Was."

"Indeed," Jace said, raising his glass. "To Suzie."

"To Suzie," Cecily and Jack repeated.

"Who is likely busting God's balls right now," Jace said, and threw the shot down into his upturned mouth.

Jack sipped his drink, then noticing Jace's smirk, threw back the shot as well, choking for a good 10 seconds, during which he waved off Cecily's Heimlich offers.

"So," Jack said, pausing to cough again. "December, you said."

"Yes, mm hmm. They found a tumor in her ovaries. In the fall. They took it out and gave her radiation. 'They,' the mysterious 'they.' They're not unnamable gods. Dr. Elgin, I believe. She was nice. And Drago, that vile Drago woman. Anyway, I went through and read your emails," he paused, looking up under his eyelashes endearingly. "Only after you invited me to." He paused again, lowering his eyelashes again. Cecily realized he was trying to curry her favor. And was he even a little bit nervous? Maybe.

"Now I realize," he continued, "Suzie could be belligerent when faced with the direct question. She never answered you straight about anything. Please don't take that personally. She does that. Did. She has her reasons. Had. Her reasons. And a very stubborn nature. Beautiful women often do, do they not, chap?" The question was directed at Jack.

Jack nodded, still nervous. Jace poured another shot of Jack Daniels for Jack and himself. He raised the bottle for Cecily, but noticed Cecily was still clutching her first shot, almost as though she were trying to balance the liquid in front of her chest.

"Exhale, love," Jace told her. "Sit back a little, relax. Take that shot, and I'll pour you another." Cecily complied, tossing back the shot and feeling the acid fumes of whiskey burn down her throat and up her sinuses. "I'm not going to sit here and tell you I'm an angel either. I'm trying to make some things right. And I feel like I can do that if I help out some of the people that maybe got run over by the Suzie express. She wasn't a careful girl. Extraordinarily gifted. Really, smart as shit. But sloppy, you know?"

"Sure," Cecily murmured, as two men opened the doors and peered in. One of them, tall, lanky and spectacled, looked like one of

Cecily's biology professors. The shorter one, fair, shaggy and smelling like bong water, spoke first.

"Thanks for showing up, dude. Sound check is done. We had to finish with Lawrence, so I don't want to hear any bitching about sound tonight. Or lights. It's all done to Lawrence's specifications. Not yours."

"Thank you, Rick," Jace smiled up at him. "You're a prince among men. What's up then, Duncan?"

The tall man spoke and seemed less annoyed than the first. "So, uh, that's all you're going to give us? Just lyrics?"

"It's a solo piece. Go. I'll be out in a second to go over it with you. Go work on trying to get in Belinda's knickers for a couple minutes, or take up smoking. All the Europeans are doing it." Jace said.

The door closed behind them.

"You call the shots," Jack stated.

"Well, yes, I am the rock star, so they tell me," Jace said. "I'm told that's one of the perks. Deferential treatment and all." He laughed. "Not hardly."

Smoke poured out of his mouth along with his words. When he finished one cigarette, he lit the next. "Suzie hated these," he held them up, as though to explain.

Cecily couldn't decide if she was surprised to learn this or not. Not surprised, she decided. The only other ardent pot smoker she'd known beside Suzie (Michael of the Appendicitis Incident) found other kinds of smoking either stupid or redundant.

Jace reminded Cecily slightly of Michael. Was it something about his looks? Yes, he got better looking the more you looked at him. His long, wavy hair hung unwashed off his head, framing a boyish face: his blue eyes with possibly mascaraed lashes eager to charm, his lips seemed as big and soft as sofa cushions. He pulled it off. And the leather pants, which squeaked slightly as he shifted in his chair.

"I'm still working on tense confusion. Suzie is now a past tense verb, but all day I write about her in the present tense. I wake up every morning amazed I'm still here and she's not. Some days, it's crippling. I can't get out of bed. I let the phone ring and ring. I go through all the motions. It's scary to me how easy it is to fake my way through a day. I want to shake people. Don't you realize you're talking to a zombie? It doesn't matter. The shows matter. The record matters. The money matters. I've made it to a decent place. People want to meet me. People look at me and see dollar signs. They see my future, where I can keep a lot of people floating in cash and cocaine. I look at me, through their eyes, and I think, why not? Why the fuck not? I've got nothing else now.

And these shows ... everyone's in suspense, seeing what I'll do next. It's coming, they say, the platinum. I'm on the edge of it. I just want to put down my guitar calmly, stop singing and give them all the finger. Maybe I won't lay the golden egg. My career used to be the most important thing to me and now I think, Christ, I had her for the few years she was allowed to roam this planet, and I was preoccupied the whole time. Maybe I'll just go to Cabo. I need a vacation, but I'm afraid to stop. I'm afraid to stop moving. Honestly."

"You really loved her," Cecily said, marveling.

"Are you fucking kidding me? She was my wife. She was my wife in every sense except the legal one," Jace said. "She was a roaring pain in my arse and now—gone."

"How did you meet?" Jack sat on the edge of the couch, looking up at Jace like he was an exotic animal in a zoo.

"Do you want the story approved by my publicist? They made me get a bloody publicist. I met Suzie when I first moved to the states. I was 21 and she was 18. Really, she was 17, but apparently that's illegal here, so I have to say she was 18. What, do they think I was going to card her before I shagged her? I was touring with my band, the Sexcentrics. We started as a Sex Pistols cover band, but I quickly grew out of it, and started writing my own music, as did our bassist, Nigel.

The band split when I was offered a solo contract. That's the publicist story. The band really split when Nigel got so fucked up on meth, he threw a lawn chair at my head and spit in our drummer, Trevor's, face. So, being in a band is not for me. Nigel's OK now, so I hear. Five stints in rehab, and now they're doing electric shock therapy. Holy fucking hell." He exhaled a mouthful of smoke.

"But me and Suzie were together from the minute we met and we were never not together after … except when we weren't. Except we always were, mostly."

"Makes sense," Cecily smiled.

"Have another shot, it gets better," Jace said. He picked up the bottle of Jack Daniels and tipped it over her glass until Cecily gasped and said, "Enough!"

"I didn't get the impression you guys were together," she said carefully, letting the fumes from the brown liquid settle into her nostrils for a few seconds. Once she acclimated to the smell, she tossed back the shot: her second. She was counting tonight.

"Well, we didn't live monogamously ever after, I suppose. Not in the traditional, Tory sense," Jace concurred.

"It was more than that. I got the sense that …" Cecily paused, waiting for the second shot to give her either the courage or the bad manners to continue, "… she didn't think you loved her."

Jace nodded, quiet. He took a drag on his cigarette, considered the ceiling, uncrossed and re-crossed his legs. Finally he said, "Yes. Yes, I know that."

"But that's all fodder for my therapist now. I think I found her too soon. When I came to LA, I thought: I'll meet lots of fabulous women, I'll have all these experiences. I met Suzie the first week, and I thought she was the archetype—free, beautiful, smart, fearless, half-naked all the time. Well, I was wrong. Nobody was like her. I was completely wrong. It was just her. I'd been so lucky and I had no idea. So boy meets girl, boy falls in love but is an idiot, boy shags a starlet or two, boy has a Hep C scare, girl throws boy's guitar into pool. It's not the stuff of fairy tales, no. And it's my fault. I know that. I spent the last few years making it up to her, but it wasn't enough … maybe. Or maybe it was the timing. The moment I woke up to what an arse I'd been, my career suddenly, through no fault of my own, started to exist. I'd pounded the pavement for years, playing these dismal clubs night after night, just plugging away, and then one day Richard sodding Geffen's in the audience, and he says, "I'll take a look at you, then." And just like that, I'm signed to a major label, and they're telling me I'm the next BFD. And there's Suzie, through it all, telling me 'I told you so.' All these girls want to get with me now, and it's so obvious, oh my God, they're like heat-seeking missiles. They're terrifying, really. The military could repurpose them to find Osama Bin Fucking Hussein or whoever they're looking for now. All they'd have to do is tell these birds he has a yacht and, for a blow job, they can use it all summer. And Suzie was never like that. She was never like that."

His voice cracked, and he stared at the ceiling again. Jack and Cecily exchanged glances.

"Was she suicidal?" Jack asked. Cecily raised her eyebrows at him and, using her eyes, eyebrows and various head bobs, communicated silently her thoughts: Really? He just spilled all that, and that's what you say?

"I'm sorry for your loss," Cecily said. Suddenly, she realized it was the first time she'd said that and meant it. Up until then, Jack had performed the social niceties. She was finally beginning to see Suzie in a more global context, not as a conundrum for Cecily to solve. She seemed real, now, finally.

"Thank you, Cecily," Jace held one hand up to his face and outstretched a pinky to catch an errant tear that threatened to smudge his mascara (confirming to Cecily that he, indeed, sported eye makeup.)

Jace turned to Jack. "Suicidal. Always. Although I don't think actively. I just think if you wake up every morning and pour yourself a six-ounce jelly glass of vodka, you have to have at least some awareness you might not see sunset one of these days."

Jack, emboldened, continued: "Did she drink herself to death intentionally, do you think? Or was she using alcohol as a pain management tool with all these medical problems? I don't mean to be dissecting her like this. I know it's distasteful to say these things.

It's just, it will really help Cecily to understand what happened to her friend and why."

"I know that's why you're asking, and that's why I'm answering you honestly. And honestly, I don't think there's a difference really."

Cecily asked, quietly, staring at her empty shot glass. "Did she fight? I just need to know if she fought, or if she'd checked out. That's what's important to me. Not the diagnosis. I just need to know if I was fighting alone all this time."

"Oh, Cecily. You weren't fighting alone." Jace stood up and stubbed out his cigarette. He walked over, took Cecily's two hands, and lifted her off the couch to standing. He hugged her for a long, long time, and had Jace not been crying quietly, Jack might have objected.

They stood and cried until Belinda opened the door, peeked in, and said, "Mr. Frost. You're on, sir."

Posted April 28, 2011 at 7:02 a.m.
Cecily Murphy

Could it be? That there's a finish line in my sights?

Posted April 28, 2011 at 9:52 p.m.
Cecily Murphy

BEST DAY EVER. DONE WITH CHEMO. DONE WITH CHEMO!!!!!! I AM FREE. I AM FREE OF CANCER!!!!!! (Er, cancer treatment. And hopefully, cancer). THANK YOU, GOD!

Posted May 1, 2011 at 2:51 a.m.
Suzie London

I closed my eyes and reached
someone to dream with
someone to know what I know
it escaped so quickly
like it always does

slipping through my fingers like a dandelion seed in the wind
Blame the seed
blame the wind
blame your clumsy, grasping hand
But don't fear to reach again.

Sent: May 1, 2011 at 12:01 a.m.
From: Suzie London
To: Cecily Murphy

Happy last chemo day. Told you you were a God person, you damn hipster you. There's a song I want you to download. Go do it now. It's called "Say Goodnight Not Goodbye." It's an old one. So pretty. I've been listening to it all night and crying, it's so beautiful. Go do it now. We'll listen to it together.

Sent: May 1, 2011 at 7:01 a.m.
From: Cecily Murphy
To: Suzie London

Sorry I missed this. I was asleep. Thank God for sleep. And for these nausea meds. I downloaded your song. It's so sad, Suzie. Beautiful, but so sad.

Sent: May 1, 2011 at 7:02 a.m.
From: Suzie London
To: Cecily Murphy

Imagine me dancing, when you imagine me. I love you.

Chapter 29

June 1, 2011, 9:00 p.m.

Belinda presented Cecily and Jack to the stage manager who bravely and assertively cleared a space for them in the front row, wielding his clipboard as a weapon when teens refused to yield. The band waited patiently, tuning their instruments, waving at girls who screamed their names.

Jace walked on stage moments later. The lights dropped, and the shrieking reached levels of hysteria normally reserved for life-threatening emergencies. Now Cecily was tired. The screaming, not to mention the crying and the hugging backstage, were taking a toll. She wondered if she would last the whole show.

Jace circled his guitar strap around his shoulder sat down on the stool in front of the microphone and sang. The song, all the songs, summoned a flicker of Suzie back into life, briefly illuminating the silhouettes of Cecily's memories. Jace's voice was Elvis Costello, Bruce Springsteen and Ben Folds, and it was as honest as a bell ringing. He seemed incapable of singing a false note, as every word he poured into the microphone evoked truth and pain and love. He stopped between songs to greet the audience, and he was a natural at it.

"I wrote this," he told the room, hot and damp with anticipation and sweat, "sitting on the beach at Santa Monica, listening to Jackson Browne, watching the sun go down, smoking a joint, my arm wrapped around my girl. Hang on to it. That wave will crash, and then it's gone."

The Truth About Suzie

The crowd ate up his pain, accepted it like a gift offering and held their hands up for more. Even the songs Cecily thought were awful (and there were a few) didn't sate the crowd's hunger for more songs, more Jace.

Jace told the band the next one was a solo piece he'd reworked that day. He strummed a few chords, and the crowd quieted in response to his mood. He sang:

I don't want you working
I only want you here
Why do you never buy organic yogurt?
What happened to the beer?
I organized your medicine
It took me half an hour
Did dishes, found your remote
Put your houseplants in the shower

I wake up and once more you're gone
Gone, gone, you're still gone
All my plans, all ripped up
Gone, gone, you're still gone

I'd take you to an island
We'd make love and laugh all night
Or I'd just stare in your eyes
Your brother says I'm not that bright
I don't care what people say
I don't care about my brain
Right now I just need you here
Only you can ease this pain

I wake up and once more you're gone
Gone, gone, you're still gone
All my plans, all ripped up
Gone, gone, you're still gone

They shine a flashlight in my eyes
They cajole me and they sneer
Do you realize you're talking
To someone no longer here?
I want to smack his face and say
That's ironic son,
The person I was when she left
Is just as dead and gone

I wake up and once more I'm gone
Gone, gone, I'm still gone
All my plans, all ripped up
Gone, gone, I'm still gone

"Not one for the album," Cecily whispered to Jack.

"It needs a little work, but he just wrote it today," Jack said, rapt, head tilted back and looking straight into the hold of Jace's guitar as he slammed down the first few chords of *The Honesty Song Is Brought To You By Our Friend Jack Daniels*, Jace's biggest hit yet and a crowd sing-along. Cecily screamed in anticipation.

"Shot 1!" Cecily screamed with the crowd.

Jace replied, *"Her? She's just a friend."*

"Shot 2!" the crowd screamed. Jace replied. *"Last time we talked? Ahhh ... last weekend."*

"Shot 3!" Jace sang along with the crowd. *"I never got your text."*

Shot 4: I was gonna call you next.

Shot 5: Yeah, so when we had our fight

Shot 6: I slept at her place that night

Drop our problems in a bath of booze
Watch them explode, watch us lose
Buried a diamond deep in shit
So deep we cannot deal with it.
So deep we cannot deal with it.
We cannot, will not deal with it.

The shot verses and chorus repeated one more time, getting louder until Jace finished with a flourish, smacking his guitar. "Jason Frost, out!" he yelled, waving at the crowd, leaving them to erupt in protest.

"Can we stay for the encore? I know you're tired," Jack asked, but Cecily, staring longingly at the empty stage and clapping for Jace's return, didn't hear.

May 5, 2011, 1:00 p.m.

The Orioles' first game of the year against the Yankees would be played on a hazy, humid Saturday afternoon in May, and Jack had asked Cecily to go with him. Jack made it his personal mission to attend every Yankees game. Not because he was a Yankees fan: on the contrary. His own hometown team, the Durham Bulls, was a farm team that fed into the Orioles, so he had a much easier time adopting the Orioles upon his move to Baltimore.

But during Orioles-Yankees games, the seats at Camden Yards undulated with a sea of blue, Yankees blue. It was easier and, improbably, cheaper, to see the Yankees play in Baltimore than it was to get tickets in New York. Jack had ordered the tickets figuring that if Cecily said she wasn't up to it, he would go with Bangladello, a Mets fan who also hated the Yankees. They'd wear orange to protest the extreme yuppification of baseball, of Yankees seats so scarce their fans had to commute to different cities to see their home team.

Cecily arrived on his doorstep with her old Orioles cap, a Cal Ripken jersey and an agenda. She'd spent the week slumped at her desk at work, her hands and feet aching, her stomach twisting itself into knots, reading and re-reading Jack's Facebook page—a terrible waste of her time. Time—or rather useful, productive time—was scarce that spring, scraped out of a few daytime hours, usually early in the morning when the chemicals cruelly forbade sleep. Also, she had no business in Jack's business. It was greedy and selfish and horrible of her to wonder where he'd spent his last weekend, although God knows she'd tried to pry it out of him over the course of a few casual-sounding emails.

"Want to go biking on the NCR trail this Saturday?" she'd written.

"Isn't that your niece's birthday party?" he'd written back.

It was.

"I'm getting sent to Virginia Wednesday. Debating whether to spend the night or drive home that night. I hate business travel, don't you? When was your last business trip?" Cecily had shown this to Jane, who pointed out that her segue needed some improvement.

"How far into Virginia?" Jack had written back. "If it's longer than three hours, I'd say take the free hotel room and spend the night."

"Just ask him," Jane had advised.

"It's none of—"

"Your business," Jane finished Cecily's sentence for her. "You know what you have to do," she said. "I think you're being ridiculous about your body image issues."

You would, Cecily groused to herself. Because you know absolutely nothing about having your body disassembled, part by painful, ugly part. It was an unfair sentiment. Jane had helped Cecily and their household above and beyond all expectation in the past few months. Remembering her gratitude for this, Cecily kept her comments to herself and instead started another mix CD for Suzie.

Jack flung open the door when Cecily knocked, and laughed when he saw the tiny sprouts of orange hair peeking out from under her orange baseball cap, next to her orange shirt. He had asked her to be certain to show some team spirit, and Cecily didn't do anything halfway.

He hugged her, then felt her stiffen and push lightly back.

"What?" Jack asked, with a hint of a smile still tugging at the corners of his mouth.

"Nothing," Cecily said, smiling forcibly. I'm not going to bring it up, she mentally drilled herself. It's none of my business. "Ready to go?"

"You're smiling with your neck muscles. It's kind of creepy. What's wrong?"

"Nothing! Come on! We're late!" Cecily pulled her phone out of her purse and checked the time. They had plenty of time to walk the six blocks to Camden Yards.

"You're so stubborn. It's so exasperating," Jack turned around and locked the door, then dropped his keys. He leaned down to pick them up, and his wallet dropped out of the side pocket of his orange-red plaid Bermuda shorts, his credit cards scattering.

Cecily leaned down to help pick them up. "Oh, wow!" she laughed as she picked up his driver's license. Jack lunged to wrestle the card out of her hand. "No!" he laughed. "I do so weigh 185."

"Where? On Mercury?" Cecily laughed, losing her balance from Jack's wrangling. Her knee landed on a folded piece of paper. She picked it up and unfolded it.

Jack snatched it out of her hand, but she had seen.

"It's your plane ticket to San Francisco from last weekend," she stated. "To visit Diana. I knew it. Why are you hiding this from me? Who's this Diana person? And why do you think I'd care that you're visiting her?" The milk carton had overturned, and the questions poured out in great glugs. She stopped herself abruptly. "I don't care, by the way. It's none of my business. We're friends, right? It's just, you don't have to hide things from me. We're friends."

Jack hastily reassembled his wallet and stood up. "Yes, we are" he half-muttered, almost to himself, not looking down at Cecily as she got to her feet.

He walked toward the stairs, still not looking at Cecily, who felt like she was scampering to catch up.

He stopped suddenly at the top of the stairs, causing Cecily to walk into his back, such were the delayed reflexes that had made her a terrible soccer goalie. "OK, you're right," he said. "I need to talk to you about Diana. Let's do this."

"OK, good," Cecily smiled, but her stomach dropped. Here it comes, all out in the open. Cecily inhaled deeply, and braced herself against the railing in the stairwell.

"I didn't want to tell you this until it became formal. Or maybe I didn't have the guts, because we've been hanging out," Jack re-organized his wallet and avoided Cecily's eyes.

"Really, Jack it's fine. It's a non-issue. I honestly didn't have any delusions, that—" Cecily felt the urge to throw up. She silently cursed the failures of her digestive system, then, inexplicably, erupted crying. "We were, that we are, there's that, we're friends. And I'm so happy we're friends. I'm so happy."

Cecily covered her face, sobbing. She knew she had become incoherent and insane in five short seconds, but she felt such physical relief from releasing the tears that even her stomach felt better. She wiped her nose with the back of her hand, and looked up at Jack, stunned with herself.

Jack, also looking stunned, stammered out, "You don't look super ... happy. Can I just explain what's going on?"

Cecily still leaked tears, but felt more in command of her senses. "Of course! It's just that I'm stupid. It's not your fault. I don't blame you. I'm the one who became ... dependent ... on you." Cecily's modicum of control slipped again. She took a deep breath and hiccupped. Great, she thought. Hiccups.

"Dependent? What are you talking about?" Jack took a package of tissues out of his pocket and handed one to Cecily. He carries tissues, she thought. That's so cute.

Jack ranted now. "I couldn't make you dependent on me if I wrote a command for it in Linux. I can barely get you to let me cook dinner. Or even acknowledge my existence. I call you. I text you. I feel like I stalk you. I put in 99 percent of the effort in this relationship, and I'm not complaining. I'm not—"

"I know. And I love you," Cecily hiccupped. Dang it! "For it. I love you FOR it." Cecily paused, then hiccupped loudly again. Jack laughed. Cecily froze, bracing for the sonic boom of humiliation. "As a friend," she added, uselessly.

Without seeming to move, Jack's face was suddenly five inches from Cecily's. "You … love me? For it?"

"Yes," Cecily said, hiccupping, annoyed by it.

Jack smiled wider, then placed both hands to the sides of Cecily's damp cheeks. He leaned in and touched his lips to hers. Cecily held her breath. His lips were so soft against hers, so warm. She kissed him back, her heart pounding, her breath held, her brain swirling slow and thick like soft ice cream. Oh no, this again, she thought.

Jack pressed her against the warm brick of the stairwell wall, his hand moving through the back of her too-short hair, his other arm pulling her so close into his body she could feel his blood pulsing through his body.

Cecily pushed back on him, swinging her head from side to side to extricate herself. "Wait, whoa. Weren't we, talking about—"

Jack, having broken through the kiss barrier again relished his freedom from the dreaded friend zone, again, and didn't plan to let Cecily's questions stop him, again. He kissed her to stop her from talking. "Nothing," he said between kisses, moving his lips to her neck, her ears, her eyelids, "We were talking about nothing."

Jack murmured into her hair, "Your hiccups are gone." He kissed her mouth.

"But, wait," Cecily pushed him back. "What about Diana?"

"OK, OK. I used to work with her at Foster GenTech in New York. Now she's in California at Google," he began.

"So, she's a former co-worker. Whom you visited last weekend, according to Facebook."

Jack laughed. "Cecily, no! She offered me a job at Google. In Silicon Valley."

315

"A job?" Cecily blinked. "From a 22-year-old?"

"A what?" Jack rubbed his forehead the way Cecily did when trying to dispel a developing tension headache.

"Oh," Cecily said. "So. To be completely clear about this: You're not ... dating her."

Jack laughed again. "You're too much today! I had no idea you read my Facebook page. Diana's in her late fifties, for one. She's a vice president. And two, I'm interested in you." Jack leaned in, and traced her neck with his lips again. "I don't know if I've made that obvious enough. Is this obvious enough now?"

Cecily looked around quickly, thinking it was probably obvious to his neighbors. But they were alone in the stairwell with only the sounds of traffic wafting up with the heat off the asphalt far below them. She smirked a little at their public display, then remembering, pushed him away again. "So. Wait. Silicon Valley? And the picture. What about that picture? She's not in her late fifties!"

"What picture?" Jack asked.

"Facebook. Her profile picture. Yes, I looked. She was posting a lot on your page. I checked her out," Cecily looked down at her feet.

But Jack only looked happier. "You were jealous?"

Cecily glared at him and said, "If you enjoy this too much, I'm going to deny it."

Jack laughed. "That picture is her daughter."

"Her daughter? Oh. This is embarrassing," Cecily covered her face in her hands to hide her blush.

"A lot of people have pictures of their kids as their profile pictures. Like your sister. Like—"

"OK, fine. So she's not 21. She offered you a job. I want to hear about the job," Cecily tried to steer the conversation back to where she suspected it should have started.

"It's an information systems analyst position, but it's irrelevant. I'm not going," Jack kissed her again, pressing her against the wall and sliding his hands from her face to her hair to the bottom hem of her tank top, where Cecily caught them.

"Are you crazy?" Cecily fought to keep the argument going. "Yes, you are." She kissed him again. "Taking that job, I mean. You're not-not taking it because we're kissing?" She wanted to clear that up first, although she'd concluded she didn't want to stop kissing him.

"I'm not," Jack whispered. "Shut up, you," he added.

"Yes, you are," Cecily argued.

Jack swept his arm under her legs, and picked her up with an ease that surprised Cecily. She knew darn well he didn't weigh 185. "I can't go now," he said. "This, here? Game changer. That job? Irrelevant." He carried Cecily back to his apartment door, his lips back at her neck.

Cecily maneuvered her head around so she could look him in the eye. "Jack, I'm not willing to let you throw away your career just because ..." She couldn't name it yet, the burgeoning coupledom that had been threatening to erupt for months now.

"I'm not throwing away my career. And I'm not willing to let you throw us away, not anymore," Jack said, fumbling in his pocket for his keys and nearly dropping Cecily.

"I'm not throwing us away," Cecily argued.

Jack got the key in the lock and kicked the door open. "Please don't," he said, turning sideways to step inside.

Sideswiped by the new information, the argument over the new information, and the kissing amidst the argument and the information, Cecily suddenly plugged her mind back into her surroundings, and noticed she was being carried inside. "What about the game?" she asked.

"Screw the game," Jack said, and kicked the door shut with his foot.

****

Cecily drifted slowly to the surface of consciousness, first becoming aware of the familiar smell of the sheets, the smell of Jack's laundry detergent, then becoming aware of Jack's arm around her. She mentally inventoried her pain. This morning, the absence of pain was notable, as it had been for a few days now. It always surprised her to wake up whole, intact and pain-free. The beginning of survivorship, she thought. I like it. Then she became aware of her nakedness, and Jack spooning her, and she briefly panicked before she remembered she still wore her bra. Her hat was gone though. She could cope with that. The new hair was short, spiky and bent strangely. But it was hair and it would do. The scars that crisscrossed her chest now looked like a toddler's red-magic-marker art project. She wasn't ready to show this part of her to anyone yet, and Jack had yet to press the issue, thank goodness.

"Good morning, beautiful," Jack wrapped himself tightly around her from behind and kissed her shoulder.

"What day is it?" Cecily asked, eyes still closed.

"Sunday," Jack answered, running his hand down her side and resting it on the rise of her hip.

"Oh no," Cecily said. "I was supposed to run with Jane this morning ... she's probably driving up and down I-95 looking for my car in a ditch. Where did we throw my phone?"

"Out the window," Jack said. "Or maybe in the dishwasher. We were in the kitchen."

"Oh, yeah," Cecily said, remembering. "Wow."

"Yeah, wow," Jack pulled her shoulder toward him and rolled her all the way on top of him, pinning her with his arms. "Let's do that again," he kissed her, rolling them both so he was now on top of her. The sheets had become unanchored at some point and rolled them into a thin, blue, cotton burrito.

For once, Cecily didn't argue. But she knew that today they had to untangle their limbs and reacquaint themselves with the fresh air of the world. Then, they'd work all week, and he would have to decide about the job in California. Whatever decisions were made here, in the presence of a semi-naked girl, on a mattress that appeared to have moved five feet across Jack's floor, it didn't change their circumstances or real life. She had to finish cancer treatment; he had to take the next step forward in his career. She wouldn't let him throw away his plans over her, not when she hadn't reacquired all her body parts yet. She was still sort of bald. The idea of any relationship that required her to take off her bra and wigs and scarves and accoutrements of disguise and discomfort with her body was simply out of the question.

But this morning she could let it slide, for a few more minutes anyway. She let him kiss her neck, his favorite spot to kiss and now hers, and ran her fingers lazily down his bare chest, so pale it practically glowed white in the dimness, the room darkened by a wall of heavy blackout curtains. She'd been surprised by his passion, his intensity, his raw, honest need, and by her response to him. Having always viewed him from arm's length or from the corner of her eye, she'd never taken the time to notice the almond shape of his brown eyes, the softness of his two-day growth of dark stubble. He was so beautiful, intense, and now pressing against her with growing persistence.

Cecily laughed. "Didn't you just wake up 15 seconds ago?"

It would happen like this, she figured: she and Jack would see each other on weekends. He'd take the train down to DC Friday night and leave Monday morning. They'd have four, five weekends like this? Then Cecily would dutifully report for service at the start of the next phase of reconstruction and she would again have to press the pause button on life.

She thought of Suzie's comment from a few weeks ago: [cancer] Life [cancer] is no life. But that *was* her actual life, she argued with the imaginary Suzie in her head. But maybe she's right. Am I overthinking this? No. The situation warrants worry, she concluded.

"We're so stupid," Cecily sighed. "Again."

"No," Jack sat up and faced the wall. "You're not doing that again." Exasperated, he ran his hands through his hair and turned around to face her. "I only even considered this job because you seemed to be moving on. I liked working with Diana, and I like California. The weather's nice. But, this? Us? It's real. I know you hate it when people give your cancer credit—"

Cecily shot him a warning look.

"But you have to know the events in your life affect more people than you. You posted it so casually. You were so blasé. I was stunned. I read your post and just like that, everything changed. It's like somebody hit 'reset' and 'reprioritize.' I said to myself, I can't have this passive outlook. I've always had feelings for you, for so long, and your post just shocked me into action. I thought, it's now or never. It's always been now or never, but I never realized it. Suddenly, there were no more excuses for being shy. I was shy. I'm still shy. But there's no excuse for it. Your cancer, yes, your cancer, told me: go get her." He lay back down on his side and faced her. He regarded her eyes, her sparse eyelashes, her freckles, her small, slightly upturned nose. He kissed it. "The new, aggressive me," he smiled.

Cecily closed her eyes to accept the kiss and smiled. "So that's why you swooped into action? I was beginning to wonder if you had a thing for sick, helpless girls."

"Yeah, I can see that, with the appendicitis," Jack laughed. "That was crazy."

"Man, that hospital social worker was right about me having a lot of things go wrong for my age. What am I going to be like when I'm my parents' age?" *If I reach my parents' age*, she thought, then mentally slapped down the thought.

"This is weird. You being cautious. My girlfriend is—" he paused. "Am I allowed to call you my girlfriend?"

"Ugh! Jack! Haven't you been listening? You don't want to get involved with me. I'm like a human Chernobyl." Cecily pulled the sheet up over her head.

"Yeah, so? I don't give a shit about your radiation levels," he said, ducking under the sheet to join her. "Talk about role reversal. I was always less likely to *carpe diem*, more likely to *sum testudo*. And now it's the opposite."

The Truth About Suzie

"Seize the testicles?" Cecily asked.

"*Testudo* is turtle, Cecily. Be a turtle. Hide."

"I have not gotten timid or testicular or turtle-like!" Cecily laughed and threw open the sheet. "Wouldn't it make sense that, in a crisis, I'd just become a more exaggerated version of me? Like being practical and thinking ahead. That's all I'm doing. I'm not scared!" Cecily rolled over so her head rested on his chest. "What would you do? If some cute boy started flirting with you, and your life was getting tossed in a salad spinner?"

Jack laid his head back on his pillow and ran his fingers along down her neck, shoulders, and side, resting on the side of her bra. "I don't know. Life is too short to waste on second-guessing yourself. I know what I want. I don't want the job. I want you."

Cecily smiled. "You can call me your girlfriend," she relented.

"I already do," Jack said.

Posted May 7, 2011 at 6:02 a.m.
Cecily Murphy

Woke up in "Get Through This" mode, then remembered it's not required anymore. Time for "Got Through This" mode: a lot of smiling. Time to rebuild, restore. I seem to have lost a few body parts along the way. Time to find those again. Chemo effects still here, but they're short-timers. Go ahead, I tell my fingers, swell to your heart's content. You'll be normal again by June.

Sent: May 7, 2011 at 7:40 a.m.
From: Michele Geraci
To: Cecily Murphy

Wow, someone's in a better mindset this Monday morning. Hmm. I wonder why?

Sent: May 7, 2011 at 7:42 a.m.
From: Cecily Murphy
To: Michele Geraci

Shut up. I know Jane told you!

Sent: May 7, 2011 at 7:48 a.m.
From: Michele Geraci
To: Cecily Murphy

Jane tells me lots of things. I ran into her a half hour ago in the Longworth cafeteria. Were your ears ringing? She said you were a no-show this weekend but you texted, and you're still worried about stupid things. I agreed, and told her you don't worry enough about things that actually could happen. For instance, did you know: going a long time without sex, then having a lot of it all at once causes urinary tract infections? Hit the pharmacy on the way home, Cec.

Sent: May 7, 2011 at 7:50 a.m.
From: Cecily Murphy
To: Michele Geraci

OMFG. Permission to discuss my sex life in the Senate cafeteria: denied.

Sent: May 7, 2011 at 7:51 a.m.
From: Cecily Murphy
To: Suzie London

Hey West Coast! I know it's unlikely, even with your hours, but are you awake? My friends are driving me nuts!

Sent: May 17, 2011 at 6:07 a.m.
From: Cecily Murphy
To: Suzie London

You awake? Guess not. The last chemo must be getting to you, finally, cause you're never logged on anymore.

I picked up Eileigh at preschool yesterday with no head covering! I'm developing Taffy's dogitude like you told me. But Eileigh was not pleased: "I can't believe you came to pick me up BALD." I was like, "Yeah, well, it's 102 degrees out, and that's too hot to pretend I have hair." Eileigh turns to her friend and says: "Told you I had a bald aunt!" Ha!

I had my surgery consult today. Surgery will be in late June, early July, probably ... depending on how fast I recover from chemo. A summer surgery—lovely time to get sliced and diced, don't you think? I told the doctor I was hoping to be done with the chemo side effects by now. She snorted before saying, "Ah, no." I said, "I'm only getting them one at a time now, like they're all coming out for one last curtain call. When does the side effect tap dance end?" Then I said, "If you say 'everyone's different' I'll scream.'" She considered saying it, saw that I really would scream, then said, "OK. Six months to a year."

An answer! And pretty much what you told me anyway. I just wanted the doctors to admit it, for some reason. Admit this is a big chunk of life. I should have also grilled her on what they really do to me in the operating room after I fall asleep. You were so right about all the curious, strange pains everywhere. Are they playing netball with us? Positioning us like an antenna to get cell reception? Pounding the backs of our calves with crab mallets? WTH? Write me when you're awake. I have boy drama of the fun variety to tell you about. :)

Sent: May 20, 2011 at 5:52 a.m.
From: Cecily Murphy
To: Suzie London

Hey West Coast! Miss you. Been a while since you've logged on at 3 a.m. Hope you're doing OK.

Sent: May 22, 2011 at 8:14 p.m.
From: Cecily Murphy
To: Suzie London

Suzie London. You write me back right now and tell me this isn't true. None of this Dr. Dick crap is true. Suzie, I'm serious. Right now, drop what you're doing and write me back, or call me, or text me. Or mail me. I don't care. I'm serious.

Sent: May 22, 2011 at 9:34 p.m.
From: Cecily Murphy
To: Suzie London

Come on. Come on, Suzie. Write me back. SUZIE.

Sent: May 22, 2011 at 9:44 p.m.
From: Cecily Murphy
To: Suzie London

Suzie!!!

Please, I have a mix tape for you. Please, Suzie.

Sent: May 22, 2011 at 9:46 p.m.
From: Cecily Murphy
To: Suzie London

PLEASE.

Chapter 30

June 2, 2011, 1:00 a.m.

"The ladies at the cancer center want to have a service for her. I can't do it by myself. I don't know anyone who knew her. I need your help. Or her phone." Cecily told Jace after the show at the Thunder Cat pool hall. Jack and Jace were getting hustled by the regulars, and Cecily watched from a bar stool, tired but content to be there, contemplating the Belgian ale Jace had bought her. Her neck was stiff from staring up at him for two hours, but after she heard Jace sing, she felt like she knew him, more so than when they'd spoken. Jace dropped his pretensions when he took hold of a microphone, to endearing result. He felt his way through his songs, but maneuvered his way through his life. He now held court over the pool table and their audience of three attentive UCLA co-eds.

Jace walked over to Cecily's bar stool and took a sip of his beer. "I can give you her phone, but I wouldn't go about it that way. There were a lot of people in her life, and some of them weren't the best influences. I'm talking about her drinking buddies. Her dealers. You wouldn't want to introduce her little cancer group to that side of Suz. Trust me on this. I've been paying off her debts to these people for months, since before she even left. My penance: financial janitorial service. They aren't the kind you'd want near your grandmum's handbag."

"But she had other friends too, right?"

"Everywhere," Jace said. "Flung far and near. Some flung harder than others."

"I'll leave it up to you, who you think should come. We don't have a lot of time. We leave tomorrow night on the red-eye. Today, actually. We have to leave for the airport by 11:30 p.m. I'm calling Anna, telling her we're going to have a moment to say goodbye to Suzie at the beach. The ladies there, they need that."

"That would be nice. Maybe a classier send-off than what her family did on *Dr. Dick*."

Cecily's stomach dropped. "What did they do on *Dr. Dick*? After, I mean?"

"Brad let Dr. Dick do some ceremony at the bedside. There was a priest: one of those reborn, screamy sorts. Brad's church. Scared the living shit out of Peter. The father was there, Suzie's father. She hadn't seen him since she was 11. It was vile. Suz flat out refused to meet him when the producers managed to unearth him and drag him out of the sewers of Oregon. He kept turning to the camera and holding up his business card, promoting his roofing business in Portland. Brad had a private church ceremony for just their family, too, in Maryland."

"Did you go? Were you invited?"

"No. Yes. I was invited. I declined to attend."

"Why?" If her line of inquiry was bothering him, Jace didn't show it. He took another sip of his beer, and watched Jack aim his cue ball on the pool table.

"I'm not fond of the in-laws, and the feeling is mutual I'm afraid. Your boyfriend's an excellent pool player. I think he's hustling the hustlers."

"He can be stealthy like that."

"That would explain the looks disparity."

"The what?"

"You're too bloody adorable for him."

Cecily burst out laughing. "Hardly!" she dismissed him with a wave of her hand. God, Jace was a horrible flirt. She kind of loved it. "You people are so vain here. So hung up on looks."

"No, it's true. He's the kind of guy who has to charm in other ways. Like me. It's why I learned to play guitar. Or so I was once told." Jace hoisted himself off the barstool, leather pants squeaking, and walked back over to the pool table to take his turn. He flashed his white teeth at the UCLA co-eds and picked up his cue.

Chapter 31

June 2, 2011, 8:00 p.m.

    Cecily personally invited roughly one-third of the group gathered on the beach at Santa Monica. Not a bad turnout, she concluded, and realized she'd worried. Regina, the barista, stood examining her nails. David Rothner and some of his apparent workmates from the Tiki Tata lounge stumbled through the still-warm sand in their high heels. The tallest of their crew had Howard Stern's hair and countenance, and the best dress in Cecily's opinion: a strapless blue maxi dress that brought out his eyes and matched his sandals. The two others were dressed too formally for the venue. A small, silver-haired Paula Deen look-alike actually wore panty hose.
    Behind them stood seven comparatively short retired ladies in matching pink head scarves blowing in the evening ocean breeze. Their identical pink t-shirts were emblazoned with the words: "Big or Small We Save Them All" printed on them in red ink. Perhaps Suzie had done a few breast cancer walks with them, Cecily guessed. Behind them, the Ferris wheel on the Santa Monica pier turned slowly.
    Jace and a friend he identified as "Snake" threw firewood they'd unloaded from Snake's pickup truck on a makeshift (and highly illegal) fire pit.
    "You worry too much, chap," Jace had tried to reassure Jack when he helpfully pointed out the fire's illegality, clearly visible on the sign posted on the lifeguard stand 10 yards up the beach from

where they stood. "The beach patrol will examine their trousers for 20 minutes tonight."

"You paid off the beach patrol?" Jack asked incredulously.

"You've never?" Jace returned. He handed Jack a pile of wood. "Be a lamb and take this over."

As the wood piled higher, more guests milled up through the sand, some looking like they'd shown up by happenstance. Cecily recognized none of them. A photographer with a lens that could have cost more than Cecily's car strolled up to the fire, leaning her head against her male companion's shoulder. She held her fingers on the camera around her neck but made no move to lift it. Lisa, Cecily guessed. Possible Lisa nodded hello to Regina, and hugged one of the scarf-wearing women before settling in next to them. She nodded at Rothner across the circle, and they exchanged a look containing an entire conversation they'd had many times before. Her eyes moved across the circle and met Cecily's. Cecily panicked a little at first, caught staring, but didn't avert her gaze. The photographer brushed her flyaway blonde bangs out of her eyes and smiled at Cecily, showing large white teeth. Ah, the photographer recognized her, Cecily understood. Cecily nodded at her to show that she recognized her as well. It had to be Lisa. Lisa's eyes continued around the circle, inspecting Jack, then stopping short at a tall, thin, blonde woman wearing a tiny sundress with a leather jacket and Doc Martens. Lisa's eyes dropped to her camera.

Before Cecily could try to identify the blonde standing to her right, Jace put his hand on Cecily's shoulder, and, almost using it as a podium, raised his voice into the ocean air. The soft murmurings of the guests quieted, and the sounds of the pier and the ocean filled the breeze. The sky faded into a pale, translucent pink behind him.

Jace cleared his throat and said, "I'd like to welcome all of you here to the Santa Monica beach bonfire celebrating the life of Susan Christina London. Also, I'd like to welcome our Skype guests, Suzie's family."

Jack held up the laptop. "Can you see?" he asked Brad, Wendie and Peter. They nodded. To Cecily, he whispered, "Hope my battery lasts."

"I want to go around the circle and talk about the Suzie London we knew. She presented herself to the world in facets. Shards and angles. No single person knew the whole story of her, and that's how she wanted it. If she were here, she would argue that was her right. Lord, that woman could argue."

A murmur of chuckles welled up though the crowd.

Jace paused, and dropped his face into his hand. Cecily couldn't tell if he was laughing or crying. After a moment, he continued.

"Some of us were only privy to her faults. Some of us were privy to her beauty. Others were privy to her kindness. But we all loved her at some point in some way, and I don't think anyone was fooled by any of her acts. Suzie London was bad at lying and she was a terrible, terrible actress."

The drag queens raised their painted-on eyebrows at this. Rothner pursed his lipsticked lips and murmured, "Mmm, mmm."

Jace rolled his eyes at them. "I mean that as a compliment."

Cecily jumped in to defend him. "It's like saying someone's a terrible politician, because they're bad at lying." Rothner nodded, trying to look appeased, but he wasn't.

"Exactly," Jace continued, then raised his voice again to continue his speech. "She was an artist of life. Life was her art. I'd like to go around the circle and introduce ourselves. Share how you knew Suzie and who Suzie was for you. Then pick up the branch in front of you and throw it in the fire."

"You go, Cecily," he said, motioning to his right. "I might add brevity is a virtue here, as we only have 20 minutes before the fuzz shuts down our little bonfire."

Cecily shook her head. "No. You start and go clockwise." She didn't care about clockwise. She was too afraid to speak in front of all these strangers

"OK," Jace said, and took a breath that lifted his chest under his leather jacket. "I met Suzie right here. At a party. I knew immediately she was my kind, my bloods, my crips, my tribe. I'm not good at public speaking, believe it or not, but I'm pretty comfortable singing. If you all bear with me, I can play a song for you."

He looked around the circle for approval. The group paused, exchanged looks, then clapped, unsure at first, until the elderly ladies started cheering, whistling and catcalling. One of them, whom Cecily recognized as Karla, yelled out, "You sing it, hotcakes!" Beulah elbowed her in the ribs.

Jace, who had perhaps anticipated a positive reaction, picked up the guitar that conveniently lay behind him in its case in the sand.

"It's called 'Come On' and it's not on any of my albums. I used to play it for her. It was about our first week, when we were obsessed. We never got un-obsessed. Dis-possessed? What's the word? Cease and desist? No, that came later. Here 'tis."

He picked up his guitar. Cecily inhaled, expecting a lyrical ballad and expecting to cry.

Instead, Jace swiped the guitar hard with his fingers, emitting a discordant twang, then loudly sang-screamed the words.

> *"Tired of work, sick of friction*
> *Right now I just need your fiction*
> *Easy to love easy to hate*
> *Get on my bike, we'll stay out late*
> *Come on baby come on*
> *Come on baby come on*
>
> *Tonight let's go and drink to dreams*
> *Don't care 'bout rent or dead-end jobs*
> *Tell me a tale with heart and soul*
> *An' I'll rip your dress off at the seams*
> *Come on baby come on*

Come on baby come on

Don't pull the plug
You're more than a drug
You're more than a mood you're more
Come on baby come on
Come on baby come on"

The drag queens couldn't refrain from hopping up and down on their heels, still others danced, and the blonde girl in the minidress twirled, letting the breeze lift the hem of her dress. The pink-scarved ladies clapped along and stomped their feet.

"Not what I expected," Cecily murmured to Jack, bouncing her head along with the music.

"You thought maybe a power ballad?" Jack whispered back. Cecily laughed.

The crowd erupted in screams and applause.

"MORE!" Karla screamed, earning another elbow to the ribs.

"Thank you. No," Jace said, trying for humility. "Let's go around the circle."

Just as Cecily thought Jace had a modest bone in his body after all, Jace blew Karla a kiss across the bonfire and called out, "It might go on the new album. It drops in October."

Wow, Suzie, she thought. That one is a piece of work. You were right to keep that one at arm's length, whatever his charms.

Two people Cecily didn't know gave brief accounts of their acquaintances with Suzie—one of them claimed to be Suzie's accomplice when she broke into a car containing a locked-in and overheated dog they took to a vet. The other, a man with a large afro, muttered about government spies and technology before tossing his branch into the fire and making a cross with his hand.

Rothner spoke next. He took out a Bible and read several passages, then led the group in a hymn that Jack knew but Cecily did not. Cecily hummed along, trying to at least stay present.

The other drag queens sang as well. The Howard Stern look-alike sang some sort of mashup of "Amazing Grace" and "Sweet Dreams" by the Eurythmics, and almost pulled it off in Cecily's opinion. But Jack and Jace cringed next to her.

Jace whispered to Jack, "Annie Lennox is a goddess. Somewhere in London, a chill just went down her spine."

Jack nodded in agreement.

Jace kept time for the group. They'd passed the 20-minute mark by the time the women in pink spoke, but nobody cut them off. At 30 minutes, the battery in Jack's computer died, and he gently laid it down on top of Jace's guitar case. The column of smoke changed directions. The breeze coming off the ocean reversed, and a much warmer wind blew out from the mainland.

At 40 minutes, Cecily was tired of standing. The ladies in pink had lowered themselves into the sand after they'd spoken, and Cecily planned to join them when the blonde next to Jack stepped forward, and she stopped mid-sit.

"My name is Gretchen Garrett."

Cecily froze. "I've been looking for you," she whispered.

Gretchen spoke softly, directing her words to the fire. "I knew Suzie a long time. Since we were kids. I was a bad friend to her. I hooked up with—" she paused, "a dude Suzie dated."

Rothner closed his eyes, shook his head and half-sang, half-said, "Mmmm, mmmm, mmm. Girl."

His two companions shook their heads, and joined Rothner in making tsking noises. The tall one inspected her nails, mouth downturned. Cecily thought she heard a whispered, "whore" coming from the drag queens' area.

Gretchen's eyes blazed in the light of the fire, and she flung her stick—a skinny twig—in the direction of the drag queens. It landed in the sand a good five feet short of its intended target, but the drag queens screamed anyway.

"HE'S THE WHORE," Gretchen bellowed, her voice dropping several octaves and her face steely. Cecily and Jack exchanged terrified glances.

"It's an insurrection, sponsored by Mary Kay," Jace quipped, but he saw the crowd, so enchanted by his guitar minutes earlier, had now turned on him. "I slept with her once. I was knockered."

"You both whores," Rothner called out, to a chorus of "Mmm, hmm," and "Tell it, Countess!"

Gretchen, a quiet talker, was not a quiet seether. She literally snarled and pointed her finger back at the drag queens. "You stay the fuck out of this, Rothner. You're the one who put her on TV. You're one to talk."

Cecily stepped forward and looked over at the pink-clad cancer center ladies. "I'm sorry," she mouthed. But the ladies sat, mouths agape, heads turning as though at a tennis match.

Cecily grabbed Jack's stick and banged it together with hers. Jack inhaled deeply and yelled, "SILENCE!" He looked surprised when the crowd complied. Satisfied, he told the group, "Cecily would like to say something."

Cecily's face froze, save for her eyeballs, which fearfully scanned the crowd. *Here I thought Jimmy was wasting his time with his diplomacy classes, Quelling a Riot 101 and whatever*, she thought. She waved away the smoke that now billowed toward her.

"Look, people. Whatever happened in the past is past. Before she died, Suzie was looking for Gretchen, to apologize to her, to tell her it was all water under the bridge. She asked me to find you, Gretchen."

Gretchen's eyes filled with tears as she turned to face Cecily. Once again, Cecily noticed how frail she looked, her eyes and cheeks sunken in around her pronounced, pale cheekbones, her legs knobby and fragile, balancing in their Doc Martens like skinny new trees in burlap sacks. "Really?" she asked. "She was looking for me?"

Cecily nodded to her. To the group, she said, "Can we let this woman make peace with Suzie London?"

"I don't want to say it out loud. Can I borrow your stick? I lost mine," Gretchen said.

"That's one way of putting it," Jack muttered under his breath.

Gretchen approached the bonfire quietly. She stood for a long moment with her chin on her breastbone—her blonde, wispy hair flying around her with her sundress flapping in the breeze. She lowered Cecily's stick into the fire, turned and left the circle.

Jack cleared his throat, took a piece of paper out of his pocket, and, checking his watch, read his speech, speaking quickly.

"I never met Suzie London. I knew her on a screen. All I know about her, I read or heard or watched. But, from all we've seen and done here in California, it sounds like you knew her this way too. The generosity she lacked in sharing information about herself, she made up for in generosity of spirit. Whether her random acts of kindness canceled out any demons she may have had is not for me to judge. All I know is that she was uncommonly kind to a woman I love, and I'd like to take this opportunity to thank her for lifting Cecily up and carrying her through a difficult time. She may have been right. Her truth was her own, and she owed the world no explanation. Elbert Hubbard once said, 'Never explain—your friends do not need it, and your enemies will not believe you anyway.'

Um, that's all. Goodbye, Suzie London and thank you."

Every member of the circle clapped after Jack's speech, Cecily the loudest, smiling the largest. Cecily followed, bolstered by Jack's kind words, yet aware they were burning wood on borrowed time. They also had a plane to catch. Their luggage waited for them behind the concierge desk at the hotel, a 15-minute cab ride from where they stood. Still, they had a few minutes, and Cecily needed them.

"I'm not good at public speaking either. I'm better when I'm just writing to her. I don't know what I'm going to do from now on, not writing to her. I'm just going to read you something I wrote to her Facebook page last night. I know that sounds crazy, writing to a ghost of a Facebook page. I was thinking, she's not going to get this. I'm just writing into the void. But it turns out I wasn't. I was writing to Jace. Jace read it, and Jace helped me to gather everybody tonight. So, I'd like to thank Jason Frost."

Jace still looked standoffish from the Gretchen brouhaha. He tossed another stick into the fire. "Not their damn business," he muttered.

"But it is their business. Suzie's life wasn't perfect. You weren't perfect to her. She wasn't perfect to you. I wasn't so great to her either when I was a kid. But she knew it was water under the bridge before she left us."

She took a deep breath and began, "I wrote this last night. After Jace scared me by writing back."

"Dear Suzie,

I understand some things now. Not everything, but some things.

I understand that all during my chemotherapy, you were not in chemotherapy. I've pieced it together. I was so slow to see. Maybe it was the drugs that made me slow. (Probably it wasn't the drugs.) Your oncologist gave you the news: your port wasn't the problem. Your cancer had spread to your lymph nodes in your neck. It was everywhere now. You were again trapped by your inheritance. You always have been. So have I. But you understood far more than I that we have choices in our circumstances. Even when none of them seem fair. In the most stifling, restrictive, airless corridor, you chose your poison. Literally. You said, I'm going to die on my own terms. Alcohol or cancer? You chose alcohol.

And you decided to keep this news from me, from most people in your life. This, I'm working to understand. I understand you didn't want pity from your family, from anyone. I get that. But I wouldn't have pitied you. Maybe you thought I'd judge you. I want you to know I wouldn't. You saved me, Suzie. When I had my mastectomy, when I lost my hair, through everything: you saved me.

I guess I could call this trip successful. I had a professor who used to say the best results were the ones that opened the door to more questions. If you have all the answers, he said, you're not asking the right questions. I'm so glad you opened the door between our lives. I will always be grateful and in your debt.

Good night, West Coast. Love you. Miss you.

****

"I'm a little disappointed David Crosby didn't perform," Karla said. "But other than that, it was a lovely service."

Cecily smiled at her. She hugged the ladies from the cancer center one by one, saying her goodbyes.

"That wasn't David Crosby, Karla!" Beulah scolded her.

"I don't know. Suzie always talked about him. I think—"

"Hey!" Jack called out. He walked up to Cecily after helping Jace and Snake douse the fire. "We've got to get going. But did you know, while you were talking, a firefly hovered right over your left shoulder? For, I don't know, maybe 30 seconds. I tried to catch it. It looked like you looked right at it, and then it was gone."

"I doubt it was a firefly," Anna said. "Fireflies aren't indigenous to southern California. I haven't seen one in years."

A summer life, Cecily thought. The ladies, carrying their sandals, had started walking toward the parking lot and their cars. Anna had offered them a ride to their hotel.

"I think it was a firefly," she smiled at Jack and Anna, then turned and walked up the beach.

Posted June 2, 2011 at 11:10 p.m.
Cecily Murphy

Is leaving on the red-eye. Suzie London, rest peacefully, sweet friend. Watch for Jason Frost's next album: "Circle of Fire." I'm on the beach with him, right now, in Santa Monica. I believe Suzie London made an appearance in spirit. She was right, you know, about a lot of things. And everything is beautiful in Santa Monica.

Sent: July 15, 2011 at 11:02 p.m.
From: Cecily Murphy
To: Suzie London

Dear Suzie,

Wednesday is my last ... last ... last cancer-related surgery. Can you believe it? I'll lose my port and get my long-awaited implants. Nervous, but excited. No more evil bricks! No more wondering if I'm injuring people by hugging them! I'm sure I'm going to steal more hospital socks when I wake up from it. Imagine: we could open a hospital sock museum on Route 66. We'll call it the Suzie and Cecily ... I don't know. You were the one with the fun ideas. Anyway, just wanted you to know. I really, truly miss you.

Love, Cecily

(P.S. Jace, if you're reading this, thanks for letting me write to Suzie here. Hope you're doing OK.)

Sent: July 30, 2011 at 9:18 p.m.
From: Cecily Murphy
To: Suzie London

Dear Suzie,

You were right about that surgery being a hard one. Don't know what I'd do without Jack's tireless feeding and care. I'm sure he didn't predict "helping me after surgery" would translate to "chasing me around the house when my head got stuck in my t-shirt for the fifth time because even though I know I can't lift my arms, I thought maybe this time I could."

Tonight Jack left to pick up dinner while I was asleep and supposedly out of harm's way. Of course, five minutes after he left, I woke up hungry, thirsty, having to pee, needing my pain pill, etc., but I couldn't get up! I spent 45 minutes building a leverage contraption out of pillows. Jack found me on floor talking to a pillow I named "Wilson" like in that Tom Hanks movie. We agreed, henceforth, it would be best to leave me with a phone. :) Miss you.

Cecily

(P.S. Jace, if you're reading this, my sister saw you on a billboard in DC!)

**Sent: August 31, 2011 at 11:51 p.m.
From: Cecily Murphy
To: Suzie London**

Dear Suzie,

Thought of you today when the nurse at the surgeon's office laughed at me. I guess I was wearing an atypically low neckline to my appointment. "No more baggy shirts, huh?" she said. "Now you've figured out what you're supposed to do with them!"

I brought Jack to our annual family beach vacation last week. I worried my family would act weird or show off because it's my first time bringing a date. Sure enough, we walk in to the beach house and Jimmy is reading to Eileigh: Democracy in America. Alexis de Toqueville. (Kids love it.) Cait and I were completely ripping on him for pretentiousness, but he said: at least I'm not filling Eileigh's head with fairy tales about princesses who fight off witches. And Cait said: that's our story. That's for the women in our family only. (I didn't correct her then. It's not just for the women ... Jimmy needs to be tested too, but anyway ...) But I started to understand why maybe she was a little jealous of you, and how maybe I could have been more understanding during chemo/surgery, etc. I thought of you and Brad and me and Cait. It's her story too, and I kept pushing her aside. She was there, ready to jump in, and I didn't let her. I told her all this, and she told me I was crazy, and hugged me and asked if I loved her anyway, despite the fact that she wasn't the perfect sister. And I told her she was the perfect sister, but not a perfect person and nobody was and maybe she needed to chill on the judgmental stuff, and we hugged and cried and Jimmy rolled his eyes and Eileigh piled on top of us. Jack, for some reason, was not even scared off by this ridiculousness. Anyway, I think we're all emotional because Cait's getting the blood test soon. My cousin Rebecca got it this summer, and she tested positive for the gene. That makes 2 out of 4 women in my generation, and 2 haven't been tested yet. Miss you. Missed you a lot today.

Cecily

(P.S. Jace, I'm hoping you didn't read this one, but if you did, I hope you got my email thanking you for the tickets and backstage passes. We can't wait to see you in October! I saw your single is #10 on iTunes! You know you're making it big when my niece is singing your song. She is the most pop culturally aware person in the family!)

Sent: October 2, 2011 at 10:12 p.m.
From: Cecily Murphy
To: Suzie London

Dear Suzie,

Saw Dr. Sharp Pointy Objects today. He dispensed travel advice to distract me during my sharp and pointy checkup. I wish you were here to warn me about that one. Anyway, Jack and I are going to Italy in the spring. Dr. SPO advised strongly against renting a car in Rome and eating wild boar. Sounds like something you would do: both of them!

I don't know why it took me this long, but I sent your wigs back with gratitude to Rothner. He'll donate them to support drag bingo, a fundraiser for AIDS charities. Now, instead of rotting in a suitcase in the attic, remembered only with nausea, they'll have a fabulous continued life on stage. From Rothner, to you, to me, to who knows where ... Have fun, hot pink wig. As Lady Gaga says, "Don't be a drag, just be a queen."

My hair situation is still kind of crazy. I got a new hairdresser, Rhonda. She came recommended by three friends. She's not much older than me, and had the same cancer as me, the same chemo as me, and consequently has the same hair as me. "It's straight in front, curly in the back," she explained. I said, "You're telling me I have a texture mullet?" "Yes," she said gently. Then she fixed it so it's cute like hers. She reminds me a lot of you; we're going to get our nails done together (we both have newfound appreciation for fingernails. This is very new for me!) I thought of you the whole time.

XO, Cecily

(P.S. Jace: can't wait for your show ... just a few weeks and you'll be here in DC!)

Sent: October 17, 2011 at 6:31 a.m.
From: Cecily Murphy
To: Suzie London

Dear Suzie,

Today is my first "is-it-really-gone-did-it-come-back" scan with Dr. SPO. Kind of wish it wasn't happening so very close to the exact anniversary of my diagnosis. So, yes, a little nervous, but nothing a few pieces of candy corn can't fix. So good, yet so gross. Gah. Wish you were here.

XO, C

Sent: October 17, 2011 at 11:27 a.m.
From: Cecily Murphy
To: Suzie London

Dear Suzie,

All clear! Dr. SPO still wildly proud of his work. "This looks fantastic, if I do say so myself." I don't think he's ever missed an opportunity to say so himself! Went out for celebratory mocha with Jack. Now going to see Muppets, then do some Italy trip planning. It's an awesome day after all.

XO, C

Sent: October 25, 2011 at 11:59 p.m.
From: Cecily Murphy
To: Suzie London

Dear Suzie,

Last week was one year since my diagnosis, but I didn't celebrate. (Technically, that's not true: every minute, hour, day, week, and month I'm given to live, I celebrate.)

You know what I'm going to celebrate annually instead of diagnosis day? Today. Because it was this day, one year ago, you reached out into the dark, and a friend lost was found again. So I declare today Small and Large Acts of Bravery Day, in honor of you. Because you're not here, I'll make up the rules. They're pretty easy: 1) Take a chance. I did that yesterday, by accepting a research position at NIH in the genetics lab: exciting stuff. And 2) Tell someone you love them and why. So, in the spirit of the holiday, I'll tell you that wherever and whatever you are now, you're still loved here. So, so loved. You kept me fighting and laughing. You never told me your battle had taken a turn, but I see it now, it was all written out for me, your goodbye. I wish I was there to hold your hand as your convertible headed into the Grand Canyon. Goodbye, my Thelma, my Louise, my feisty friend.

About the Author

Erica Rimlinger began her writing career as a journalist in Washington, DC. Now a freelance writer, she writes for regional magazines and teaches group fitness classes. She has conquered breast cancer (twice!) and continued teaching Zumba during treatment, sporting an array of multi-colored wigs. She lives in Baltimore with her husband, Kevin, and son, Max.

What Next?

Thank you for reading my book. I've put a lot into it, and I appreciate you investing your time and money in a debut author.

If you enjoyed this book, please help make it a success by spreading the word. Write a review on Amazon or Goodreads. Let people know through social media, or have a conversation with a friend over a cup of coffee or a glass of wine.

Stay Connected!

Visit my website at http://ericarimlinger.com where you can sign up for email updates that include information about new work, events, contests, and other news.

Follow me on Facebook, Twitter, Pinterest, Goodreads, or Google+.

Send comments, feedback, or questions directly to me at: http://ericarimlinger.com/contact.

Made in the USA
Lexington, KY
30 October 2014